A
Witch's Guide
to Fake Dating
a Demon

A WITCH'S GUIDE TO FAKE DATING A DEMON

SARAH HAWLEY

BERKLEY ROMANCE

NEW YORK

BERKLEY ROMANCE
Published by Berkley
An imprint of Penguin Random House LLC
penguinrandomhouse.com

Library of Congress Cataloging-in-Publication Data

Names: Hawley, Sarah, author.
Title: A witch's guide to fake dating a demon / Sarah Hawley.
Description: First edition. | New York: Berkley Romance, 2023.
Identifiers: LCCN 2022043481 (print) | LCCN 2022043482 (ebook) |
ISBN 9780593547922 (trade paperback) | ISBN 9780593547939 (ebook)
Subjects: LCGFT: Paranormal fiction. | Romance fiction. |
Novels. Classification: LCC PS3608.A8937 W58 2023 (print) |
LCC PS3608.A8937 (ebook) | DDC 813/.6—dc23/eng/20221006
LC record available at https://lccn.loc.gov/2022043481
LC ebook record available at https://lccn.loc.gov/2022043482

First Edition: March 2023

Printed in the United States of America
7th Printing

Book design by Daniel Brount

To my parents: thank you for fostering my curiosity and creativity and for cheering me on no matter what odd things I decide to write. (Please only read the redacted version I've provided you.)

A WITCH'S GUIDE TO FAKE DATING A DEMON

ONE

"OH, NO." MARIEL SPARK STARED AT THE STARTLED CHICKEN that had materialized on her kitchen counter. "That wasn't what I meant to do."

At the kitchen table, Calladia Cunnington nearly choked on her tea. "Well, that's surprising. At least they both have wings."

Mariel gave her friend a *look*. She'd recited a summoning spell for an air sprite, not poultry. "Literally the only thing they have in common."

"Points for creativity?" Despite the joke, Calladia's wince was sympathetic. As a witch and Mariel's longtime friend, she knew how upsetting it was for Mariel to mess up a spell yet again.

"It's a basic summoning spell, not a Jackson Pollock painting." Mariel blew a stray curl out of her face, frowning at the surprise avian guest currently preening its ruffled feathers next to her toaster. Her spells often backfired, but this was a new level of fucked-up-ness.

"Well, I think it's cute," their other friend Themmie—short for Themmaline—Tibayan said from where she sat cross-legged in midair. The pixie's iridescent wings fluttered as she took pictures of the bird with her smartphone.

"Sure, but what do I do with it?" The chicken was now scratching at the chalked pentagram beneath it. What would soothe an alarmed bird that had been teleported into a witch's kitchen?

"Can you send it back where it came from?" Calladia asked, tightening her blond ponytail. She looked disgustingly peppy for a Friday morning, her blue tank top damp with sweat from a recent gym visit.

Mariel bit her lip, trying not to snap. Calladia was the best person in the world, even if she set unreasonable fitness standards, but she'd never struggled with magic the way Mariel did. "Maybe. If I had any idea where it came from."

She wasn't sure how she'd summoned a chicken to begin with. Granted, her mind had wandered to her grocery list while chalking the spell, but it had been a brief distraction, hardly worth noting. And why a live chicken, rather than chicken cutlets or brussels sprouts or a gallon of milk?

Themmie cooed at the chicken as she took more photos. "Cluck for the camera, cutie. Strike that pose!" As a social media influencer, the Filipino American pixie documented everything, and her look changed constantly. This week, her straight black hair had been bespelled green and pink, and a nose ring winked in the sunlight cascading through the kitchen window.

Calladia rolled her eyes. "What is this, *America's Next Top Chicken?*"

America's Next Top Witch was a popular national TV show among both magic and nonmagic humans. The *America's Next Top Model* spinoff focused more on lingerie than spellcraft, but the models still cast illusions or shape-shifted during photo shoots. Mariel had enjoyed the show up until she'd realized as a teenager that she was way, *way* behind even those reality TV disasters in terms of magical competency.

"On the bright side," Themmie said, "you probably rescued it from the cruel world of cage farming." Environmental activism was never far from Themmie's mind, and her face lit up. "We can build it a coop."

"I'm not keeping it," Mariel said. Even though it did look adorable as it goggled at her air fryer.

"Try reversing the symbols," Calladia suggested. "That should send it back."

Normally her friends didn't sit in on her spellcraft practice sessions, but in this case, Mariel was glad they'd come. They didn't judge her for mucking up magic the way her family did.

Mariel took a deep breath, then marked the counter with chalk again. A pentagram, then the reversed summoning marks in each arm of the inverted star. Her handwriting wobbled with the attempt. Hecate, why was writing backward so hard? At least this was a fairly simple summoning and wouldn't require any of the big witchy guns like salt, sage, or newt sperm. The more complex the spell, the more opportunities to fuck it up.

For the billionth time, Mariel wished magic was as easy as baking or gardening. But while Mariel had perfected a killer cranberry tart and raised beautiful flowers, she couldn't manage even a simple cleaning spell without making a horrible mistake. Embarrassing for any witch, but doubly so for the prophesied Spark heir. Before Mariel's birth, the wind, earth, and stars had all signified that she was going to be the strongest witch in generations of the famed magic family.

Joke's on them, Mariel thought as she marked another uneven rune into the pentagram. *I suck.*

The chicken flapped awkwardly, then plummeted to the floor

in a rustle of feathers. It started clucking, pecking perilously close to her ankles.

Mariel closed her eyes and thought about her spell. Magic incantations weren't spoken in Latin, much to her chagrin, since at least Latin had a logical structure. Magic had a language all its own—one that was frustratingly complex. It was full of roots pulled from dozens of languages, as well as some that seemed made up wholesale, and the rules of grammar and conjugation were chaotic at best. Sometimes she was tempted to light the dictionary on fire.

"Uh, Chanticleer just took a dump on your floor," Themmie said.

"Chanticleer was a rooster," Mariel said, eyes still closed.

"Excuse me, Chaucer enthusiast. And, ew, that chicken apparently eats a *lot* of fiber."

Great. Mariel scrunched up her nose and dug for the words that would send the chicken back home before it sullied her kitchen further. "*Adolesen di pullo!*" she proclaimed.

The chicken exploded.

◆   ◆   ◆

"*AUFRASEN*," CALLADIA SAID GENTLY WHILE MARIEL SCRUBBED the floor. "The correct word was *aufrasen*."

"Too late." Tears pricked Mariel's eyes, and her stomach churned with nausea. She was generally okay with blood, but she'd just exploded a very cute chicken, and it felt different. Not to mention the gristly, bony . . . bits . . . that were sprayed all over her countertops. Her magic was apparently more like a Jackson Pollock painting than she'd thought. Mariel had a batch of muffins to make for Ms. Rostow down the street, but she wasn't sure she'd be able to stomach it.

Themmie, too, looked nauseated. She was hovering near the

ceiling, as far from the carnage as possible. "At least it died quickly."

And at least Themmie had stopped documenting the scene. Her followers probably wouldn't enjoy a chicken snuff film.

Mariel sat back on her heels and wiped her brow. Her skin came back streaked with blood, and she groaned, realizing chicken chunks were probably all over her, too. "I suck."

"You don't suck," Calladia said, coming to Mariel's defense as she always did. "Learning how to summon takes time. And you're amazing at nature magic."

Sure, it took time, but the two witches were the same age, and while Calladia had been successfully summoning for over a decade, Mariel was twenty-eight with the skills of a fifteen-year-old. Except when it came to plants, but—"You know my mom doesn't think much of nature magic," Mariel said morosely. Understatement of the century.

"Your mom's taste is questionable in general. Who cares, so long as it makes you happy?"

"I care. Mom says she'll only pay for grad school once I improve in teleportation and transmogrification."

Her mother, Diantha Spark, was one of the best teleporters in the world and couldn't understand why Mariel struggled with that skill, especially considering the prophecy. While Diantha had insisted on paying for college and a house for Mariel (in fact, it had been a battle to convince her that Mariel only needed a small bungalow, rather than a mansion with a bowling alley), she'd balked at the idea of grad school. And not because it was too expensive—a dragon with a hoarding problem and a black Amex couldn't dream of making a dent in the funds the Sparks had been building for centuries. No, Diantha simply hadn't wanted to fund "boring magic." It had taken Mariel a long time to convince her that an SoD—sorcery doctorate—in Magical Herbology was a good idea, since her mother didn't think plant magic was flashy enough. Eventually, they'd struck a compromise: if Mariel could show improvement in her nonnature-based spellcraft, her mother would release some of the vast Spark funds to pay tuition.

Calladia made a rude noise. "She's swimming in gold. She should support you without strings attached."

"Yeah, well, tell that to Sallie Mae." Mariel sighed. "At any rate, blowing things up isn't going to help my case."

"Maybe the issue is that you're summoning boring things," Themmie suggested from on high. "Who cares about some air sprite? You should conjure up a boyfriend."

Mariel rolled her eyes. "Just because I'm not dating doesn't mean I want to."

Themmie shrugged. "Then conjure a fuck buddy. Seriously, you're way too uptight about this whole Spark family legacy thing." Themmie was still in college, but even with her eyes glued to a phone all day, she'd managed to accumulate far more worldly experience than Mariel or Calladia had, with partners across the gender and species spectrums.

"Getting laid won't make me better at summoning."

"No, but it's a great stress relief."

Calladia crouched next to Mariel and reached out a hand as if to pat her shoulder. She hesitated, then pulled the hand back, and yep, there were definitely chicken bits all over Mariel. "I know you're worried about living up to the prophecy. But you'll master the skills on your timeline, not your mother's."

Mariel sighed. "I hope so."

✦ ✦ ✦

ALTHOUGH CALLADIA HAD OFFERED TO CLEAN THE KITCHEN with a spell, scrubbing it by hand felt like penance. Calladia and Themmie left her to it, promising to meet up soon. The moment they were out of the house, Mariel let a few tears escape for the dearly departed. "Sorry," she whispered to the gross mess in her garbage can. Being both a chicken and spectacularly dead, it didn't respond, but who knew? Maybe there was a separate spectral plane for dead poultry and the chicken's soul was staring across the veil right now, clucking the bird equivalent of *What the fuck.*

One long, very gross shower later, Mariel felt a bit better. She filled a watering pot and headed into her backyard, where a small greenhouse sat amid beds of herbs. The glass house was her favorite place in the world.

Gardening was one area in which Mariel excelled, both magically and nonmagically. She'd won Best in Class for Dianthus and Alstroemeria at the previous year's Pacific Northwest Floral Championships—Supernatural Division, which was one of the tentpole events of the annual Glimmer Falls Autumn Festival. In just a few weeks, Mariel would be gunning for Best in Show with a display of magically enhanced blooms.

Thousands of tourists of all species descended on Glimmer Falls for the Autumn Festival, and it was one of Mariel's favorite times of year. Autumn's fiery shades swept over the majestic Cascade Mountains, and the town nestled into the foothills sparkled with magic shows.

Glimmer Falls would have been like any other twenty-first-century American town—mostly human, with a lively and visible subculture of witches and other supernaturals—except for a rare confluence of ley lines that infused the land with magic. As a result, the town drew a vast array of magical humans and other creatures. There were nonmagical humans, too, of course, since society had been integrated for all of recorded history, but while witches and warlocks comprised fifteen percent of the human population worldwide, in Glimmer Falls it was more like seventy percent . . . and that was before considering the centaurs, pixies, sirens, werewolves, and other species who called it home. Glimmer Falls was exciting, unpredictable, and wonderfully weird, and Mariel loved her hometown with all her heart.

Her shoulders relaxed as soon as she inhaled the warm, fragrant air inside the greenhouse. "Hi, babies," she told the plants. She started watering them, testing the soil in each bed with her finger to ensure nothing was still damp. As she passed, the blossoms tilted towards her as if she were the sun.

"Good girl," she murmured to her fire lily as it caressed her fingers with its long red petals. She could feel the plant's contentment, a soft happiness at having its needs fulfilled.

Garden magic lacked the drama of transmogrification or teleportation, but it was the one magical skill Mariel had taken to instantly. Even as a child, plants had leaned towards her, and her first pet had been a rosebush. As Mariel walked up and down the rows of plants, she infused each one with a brush of magic, feeding the roots with life. Thanks to her skill, her plants blossomed year-round, unaffected by the outside weather. October was already digging its chill fingers into Glimmer Falls, but inside the greenhouse, time seemed to stand still.

Her phone buzzed in her pocket, and Mariel groaned. Time for her mother's daily check-in. The plants recoiled in sympathy. Mariel answered the phone, already dreading the interrogation to come. "Hi, Mom."

"How is your spellcraft going?" Diantha Spark's strident voice burst through the speaker, and Mariel pulled the phone away from her ear. "Did you summon an air sprite correctly?"

"I summoned," Mariel said, omitting several key facts.

"Oh, good. Useless things, always flittering about, but they're helpful when you need a stiff breeze to blow up some bitch's skirt. Speaking of bitches, did I tell you I ran into Cynthia Cunnington the other day?" Cynthia was Calladia's mother, as well as Diantha's frenemy and magical rival. "She wanted me to know all about her daughter's transmogrification practice. Are you still hanging around that girl?"

"Yes, Mom." Mariel pinched the bridge of her nose. She and Calladia—rhymed with Cascadia—had been best friends since elementary school. It was an odd pairing on the surface—rough-and-tumble Calladia had been suspended more than once for fighting, while dreamy Mariel had spent her recesses playing with weeds on the playground—but they fit together. Add the stress of a matching pair of overbearing mothers, and there had been no separating them.

"Well, keep an eye on her," Diantha said. "Keep your enemies close, but not close enough to exchange fluids, that's what I always say."

Mariel made a face. "Calladia isn't my enemy."

"Everyone's your enemy when you're the best. I know you don't know how that feels yet, but there weren't any prophecies delivered at Calladia's birth, so I'm certain you'll show her up soon. You're the daughter of the best teleporter in three hundred years, after all."

"Two hundred and eighty," Mariel said, taking secret glee from repeating her mother's least favorite fact. "Griselda Spark was better."

Diantha made a rude noise. "The historical record is full of inaccuracies."

If her mom started griping about family history, there would be no escaping the call anytime soon. "I'd love to chat," Mariel said, sandwiching the phone between her ear and shoulder as she caressed the leaves of her jade vine, "but I'm in the middle of gardening."

"You and your plants. It's a marvel you have the focus for that, but not for fulfilling your destiny. The stars didn't say anything about daisies, you know."

Mariel rolled her eyes. "I like gardening. I got two awards for it last year, if you'll recall."

"Ribbons," Diantha said scornfully. "Do you know what they give Best National Spellcaster? A golden trophy studded with precious jewels."

"Yes, I'm aware." There was a display case of trophies in the entry hall of her parents' house, a constant reminder of the family legacy she was failing to live up to. Moving out of that house for college had been a massive relief, not least because she no longer had to look at those stupid trophies every time she came or went.

"You'll get one this year, I'm sure of it. You're just a late bloomer. Your father says sometimes genius works like that. A witch seems like a useless idiot for years, and then something clicks. Have you tried Ritalin? I heard it does wonders for improving focus."

"I don't have ADHD, Mom."

"Yes, I know, but abusing drugs can be surprisingly useful. I once went on the longest cleaning spree after snorting coke with your father in college . . ."

Mariel let her mother yammer on, knowing there was no stopping it unless she outright hung up. Diantha Spark was a force of nature, known for her strident opinions, alarming uses of teleportation, and questionable boundaries. She was both beloved and feared in Glimmer Falls.

Talking to her mother, much like gardening and baking, required patience and precision. Mariel bided her time, waiting for the perfect moment to escape.

"—and you know she lords it over me, the salty bitch. Best pie, never mind that I teleported chocolate from Belgium and wasted two hours of my time trying to show her up."

Mariel rolled her eyes. She'd been hearing about Cynthia Cunnington's levitating rhubarb pie ever since last year's Autumn Festival. Funny how her mom had derided baking until her "friend"—aka magical nemesis—had decided to try her hand at enchanting a pie.

"Baking is beneath me," Diantha said, "but she said that nasty thing and I had to destroy her somehow, and your father wouldn't let me port her into a volcano. Do you think she bribed the festival judge?"

"No."

"You have such a trusting nature. You should work on that. Anyway, this year I'm going all out. A chocolate truffle pie with truffles imported from France, topped with authentic gold leaf and ensorcelled to shoot fireworks." She cackled. "Let her try to beat that!"

Mariel seized the moment. "Speaking of teleporting truffles, I hate to cut this conversation short, but I need to bake some muffins."

"Ugh. I bake out of spite; I would never willingly subject myself to it otherwise." Diantha sighed. "All right, dear. Make sure to teleport the ingredients from abroad."

"Will do."

"Only the best for the Sparks, that's what I always say."

"Yep."

"You'll live up to the family reputation soon, I'm sure of it." Diantha made smacking kiss sounds into the phone. "Goodbye, Mariel dear, make your ancestors proud today."

"Bye, Mom." Mariel hung up, then sagged against the glass wall. "I'm exhausted," she told her tulips. "It's ten a.m., and I'm exhausted just from listening to her."

The tulips nodded in sympathy.

"'Make your ancestors proud today,'" Mariel mimicked. It was her mother's standard sign-off. "Josiah Spark was a garden witch, and no one makes fun of him for it." Because he'd been dead for three centuries, probably. Diantha Spark, for all her flaws, held the past in high regard. Legacy was everything to her.

"Maybe she'll be proud of me if I get hit by a bus." Mariel sighed as the jade vine brushed her cheek. "I don't mean it. I'm just tired of never being good enough, you know?"

Her plants didn't know though. They, unlike Mariel, were perfect. She'd made them that way, yet she had no talent to do the same thing to herself.

"Whatever," Mariel muttered, standing straight again. "I have muffins to make. And unlike Mom's pies, they'll actually be good."

Ten minutes later, Mariel had a bright orange apron tied around her waist and a mixing bowl in front of her. She reached for the flour, then hesitated. While she liked keeping baking separate from magic—it was nice to have a hobby totally unconnected to the Spark legacy—she had told her mother she'd import the ingredients.

She huffed and reached for the chalk. This time she drew the pentagram on the floor, not wanting to take up precious counter space. What was the rune for food again? She drew a wobbly line with three crosshatches in the top spot, then filled the rest of the pentagram with summoning signs and more specifics about what she wanted. Then she closed her eyes, reaching for her magic.

Magic is half intention, her mom had taught her. *You have to want something to make it happen.*

What Mariel *wanted* was to feel like less of a failure. She wanted flowers and muffins and the contentment of being exactly enough for someone.

She racked her brain, trying to come up with the spell. *Conspersa* was Latin for flour, but that wasn't right. *Harina* wasn't right either. This was one of those weird magic words that didn't take its root from any known language. *Ozro*, maybe? Or something like that for the noun.

After lengthy consideration, she finally had the spell sorted out. "*Ozroth din convosen*," she said, infusing the words with a wish to get this right, for once. She'd sell her soul for the chance to live up to her stupid legacy. She was sick of being the failed Spark.

A crack of lightning split the air, and Mariel jumped, eyes flying open. A pillar of smoke rose from the pentagram, spiraling towards the ceiling. Then it faded, revealing . . . a man?

Mariel shrieked and jumped back. She held out her hands as the man stared at her. He must be so frightened! "I'm so sorry, sir. It was an accident. I meant to summon some flour, and I must have gotten the spell wrong, though I don't know how I bungled it that badly. But you haven't exploded, so that's good news!" She winced. She babbled when she was nervous. "I probably shouldn't have said that."

The man's forehead furrowed. Mariel blinked, taking in the details of his appearance. He was tall and muscular, with golden skin and jet-black hair. His black jeans and T-shirt matched the intricate tattoo wreathing his left bicep. Had she subconsciously channeled Themmie's fuck buddy suggestion? But then he cocked his head, and wait, were those *horns* flowing in elegant onyx lines along the sides of his head?

Appreciation turned to dread. *I would sell my soul . . .* "Oh, no," she said, realizing the true extent of her fuckup. "This isn't good."

TWO

O ZROTH THE RUTHLESS HAD ONCE BEEN THE BEST AT HIS
job. He'd collected human souls for centuries, driving such
hard bargains that even millennia-old demons had whistled in
appreciation. The demon plane was filled with evidence of his
work, the golden soul orbs drifting through the air, filling the
plane with magic and life. He had been feared and respected, and
he'd liked it.

Now one tiny slipup later, he'd lost it all. Ozroth the Ruthless
was a laughingstock. The only demon to accidentally *gain* a soul,
rather than take one. He could feel that soul in his chest now, an
uncomfortable, ominous warmth. He kept himself under tight
control, but there was always the threat that the soul might act
up. That he might—horrible thought—*feel* too much.

He stared at the witch who had summoned him to Glimmer
Falls. It was rare that anyone requested him specifically for a
bargain. Most desperate witches and warlocks cast a wide net
with their spells, assuming any demon would do—an idea Ozroth
sneered at. Some bargains were more intricate than others, and

some demons were denser than others. Why use a blunt instrument for precision work?

Ozroth had built a fearsome reputation from his vengeance bargains in particular. The last time someone had summoned him by name, it was because the warlock had heard about his bargain with a sheriff whose wife had been killed by mobsters. The five assassins had all died in bizarre natural disasters, with no one to point a finger at.

This woman didn't look the type to strike a revenge pact. Her expression was alarmed, rather than desperate, furious, or cunning. Her generous curves were wrapped in an orange apron, her curly brown hair was tangled and spotted with leaves, and her cheek was smudged with dirt. She was shockingly pretty.

"I'm so sorry, sir," she said, launching into a babbling explanation that made little sense. She was summoning . . . flour? She was happy he hadn't exploded? And what kind of witch called a demon "sir"? Ozroth cocked his head, growing more intrigued by the second.

Then her eyes drifted up to his head, and fear washed over her face. "Oh, no," she said. "This isn't good."

That was more in line with the reactions Ozroth was used to. He stepped out of the pentagram and spread his hands. "It is I," he intoned—experience had taught him witches preferred their demons on the dramatic side—"Ozroth the Ruthless. Tell me what you would bargain your soul for."

She frantically crossed her hands in front of her in the universal sign for *no*. "That's not what I want. No bargaining. Nope, not me. Um, go away?"

Well, this was confusing. "You can't tell me to go away," he said, baffled by the very idea. "You summoned me by name." And to Glimmer Falls, no less, which was renowned across the planes for being a hot spot of magic. Every time a generic bargain summons emanated from that town or one of the dozen or so other magical hot spots on Earth, demons nearly knocked each other over in their urgency to teleport to Earth and hopefully gain a powerful soul. In this case, the witch had requested Ozroth specifically, when most witches didn't even know they could choose a preferred bargainer.

"No, I summoned flour by name," she corrected. "You showed up."

"That's not how it works." He crossed his arms, and her eyes darted to his tattoo. He had been marked by his mentor as a child, the runes spelling out his responsibility as a soul bargainer. "Now tell me what you would trade your soul for, mortal."

"Nothing."

He shrugged. "A poor choice, but if you want to give it to me—"

"No!" she yelped. "My soul is not up for grabs. Go back to Hell or—or wherever you came from."

He squinted at her. "What are they teaching in universities these days?" he asked, too appalled to maintain the dramatic demon act any longer. Humans and magical beings had been living side by side for all of recorded time, and even schools that didn't teach magic ought to offer basic Interspecies Relations courses. "There's no such thing as Hell. I live in the demon plane."

"Well, go back there, then!" She planted her hands on her hips, looking madder by the moment. That was unusual, too. No one talked back to a demon, much less Ozroth the Ruthless.

"I can't," he said through gritted teeth. Must he endure the disrespect of mortals, too? "As I explained earlier, you summoned me by name. I'm bound here until you complete the pact."

"Oh, Hecate," she said, stamping her foot. "Why can't anything ever be easy?" She opened her cabinet, pulling out a bundle of sage, a saltshaker, and various small bottles.

He studied her intently as she arranged the items on her

countertop. There was something odd about her—well, there were a lot of odd things about her, but something was making his skin prickle. A nearby movement caught his attention, and he watched as a houseplant on the windowsill reached out a tendril as if to stroke her.

He couldn't sense the magic of any other creatures, including demons, but witch magic glowed like a beacon. Still, he normally didn't *feel* it like this—not without focusing. He closed his eyes and concentrated on that prickling energy, opening all his senses to it.

Power. Pure, raw power. The hair on his arms rose, and he shivered in appreciation. The witch was brimming with it—golden, brilliant magic such as he hadn't seen in centuries. While witchery traveled down family lines, it was rare for someone to inherit not just the innate talent for spellcraft but the raw power to achieve substantial works. Her soul would be a brilliant source of energy for the twilit demon plane.

His eyes snapped open. "You," he said, "are very interesting."

His pulse sped as excitement built. No one believed him capable of striking difficult deals anymore. To claim a soul this powerful . . .

You're useless to me like this, his mentor, Astaroth of the Nine, had spat when Ozroth had first returned with an inconvenient mortal soul lodged in his chest. *I need you cold and efficient.*

Honor and duty were important concepts to demons, and the honor of collecting souls to benefit the demon realm—whether through straightforward bargains or more complicated ones requiring trickery, threats, or violence—was the greatest of all. With the witch's soul in hand, Ozroth would prove his worth and regain the honor he'd lost.

"I am *not* interesting," the witch said, shaking her head as she drew a wobbly pentagram on the countertop with chalk, then circled it with salt. One of the leaves in her hair came loose and fluttered towards the floor, changing its trajectory partway down so it could cling to her shin instead. "I am very boring. I like to garden and bake, and I am not even a little bit interesting, and I would really appreciate it if you forgave this little . . . misstep and went back to Hell. The demon plane." She waved a hand. "Wherever."

Ozroth definitely wouldn't be leaving, even if he could. This short, curvy, odd witch was exactly the leverage he needed to regain his fearsome reputation. Accidentally bargained or not, her soul could light up the demon plane all on its own. "No."

She made a low sound that was almost a growl as she dotted pungent oil in the arms of the pentagram. Then she lit the gas stove and ignited the sage in the flames. "Begone, pest," she said, waving the smoking sage in his general direction. "In the name of Hecate, I expel you from this realm! *Relinquosen e' daemon!*"

Ozroth sneezed.

The witch waited a few seconds, staring at him as if hoping he would vanish. Then she shook salt in a new pattern over the pentagram. "*Destruoum te ollasen!*"

The teapot on her stove shattered, and Ozroth shielded his eyes as ceramic shards pelted him like shrapnel. The pieces clattered to the floor in a musical cacophony.

The witch looked at the remnants of her teapot, face painted with tragedy. "I really liked that teapot," she whispered. Then she glared at Ozroth. "This is your fault."

Ozroth picked ceramic pieces out of his hair, grimacing at the cheerful yellow flowers painted on the porcelain. "I don't see how."

"Ugh!" She threw up her hands and stomped away, then started rummaging through a bookshelf in the hall outside the kitchen.

He crossed his arms and leaned back against her counter, beginning to enjoy himself. Not that soul bargainers ought to enjoy things, he reminded the unwanted soul in his chest, which was apparently determined to have feelings about everything. Still, an accidental summoning was at least intriguing.

She muttered to herself as she tossed books over her shoulder. They were mostly cookbooks, along with a few self-help books: *Never Good Enough?* and *The Magic of Dating: A Practical Guide for Lonely Witches*. Finally, she straightened with an "Aha!," a thick, leather-bound tome in her hand. She carried it into the kitchen, dropping it onto the table with a *whump*. *The Omnibus Encyclopedia of Magical Creatures* was scrolled across the cover in gilt script. She pointed at Ozroth. "I'm going to figure out how to get out of this."

He watched as she turned the pages, muttering to herself. It was a futile exercise, but he had to appreciate her determination. He'd had people try to get out of bargains before—*after* they'd received whatever boon he'd granted in exchange, of course—but not like this. She hadn't even asked him for anything. "Are you sure there's nothing I can give you?" he asked. "Money, love, revenge against your enemies?"

She rolled her eyes. "You are such a cliché."

His jaw dropped. "Excuse me?"

She ignored him, continuing to skim through the book. She paused on a page with an illustration of a being with horns. Ozroth stepped closer to read over her shoulder. The image had clearly been drawn by someone who had never met a demon. The legs were backward-jointed, and the horns stuck straight up, rather than following the curve of the head and pointing back. The fangs were heavily exaggerated, too. His canines were long, but not *that* long, and he'd never slobbered like that in his life. Was this really how mortals saw his species?

He skimmed the entry. *Demon: A humanoid species that resides in a separate physical plane. They can offer a witch or warlock any boon, but at a high price. In exchange for giving a witch their heart's desire, the demon eats their soul.*

He snorted. "We don't eat souls. Who wrote this garbage?"

She looked up at him with wide hazel eyes. "What do you do with the souls you take, then?" Her brow furrowed. "I'm not even sure what a soul is, to be honest."

"It's the spark inside. The place where magic comes from." The pulsing, beating, *feeling* part that made humans powerful yet fragile . . . and impossible to predict. All humans possessed that chaotic, passionate core, but only witches and warlocks produced magic from it . . . or had the ability to trade it away.

"You take away people's magic?" She looked horrified.

Magic came tangled with emotion, too—after completing a deal, humans became cold and entirely cerebral—but she didn't need to know that. "It's their choice," Ozroth said. "In return, they get everything they've ever wanted"—assuming he couldn't find a way to twist the words of the deal to his advantage. Humans had a tendency to wish for batshit, logistically intensive things, and it was a mark of pride in the demon community whenever anyone circumvented a particularly wild deal.

Others might find it odd for a species so fixated on honor to praise cunning and deceit, but when deceit kept a community alive, what shame was there in it?

"You still haven't told me what you do with the souls," she said.

To be honest, no one had ever asked him that. Historically, people had been too caught up in the "trading my soul" angst to worry about what happened to said soul. "The souls provide our realm with energy and light."

She blinked. "That was not what I was expecting."

"What were you expecting?" he asked, thinking about the drawing with the fangs and weird legs and copious saliva droplets.

She waved a small hand. "Dark rituals, eternal torture, blood orgies . . . the usual."

It was his turn to be taken aback. "That's your *usual?*"

"Not me." She grimaced. "The blood orgies are more my mother's thing."

Ozroth was too distracted by the energy pouring off her to care about her mother. To his demon senses, her magic glowed like a small sun in her chest. The witch *burned* with possibility.

Realizing he was staring at her—at her soul, really—he shook himself. "The eternal torture thing is mythological nonsense," he said. "Some witch with half a foot in the human world bollocked it up, and now everyone thinks demons steal souls, drink blood, and tear into people's delicate bits in the afterlife."

"So there's no punishment in the afterlife?"

He scoffed. "I'm still alive, last time I checked."

"Good point. So, what, do human souls power your electrical grid?"

"It's hard to explain." The demon plane had no visible sun, just a thick layer of clouds that limited the sky to shades of gray, purple, and black. The floating golden orbs of mortal souls provided illumination, but it was more than that. Demons couldn't produce their own magical energy—other than the soul bargaining or other types of magic a rare few inherited—so they had to take it from others. Without that magic, the demonic realm would slowly darken, its inhabitants losing life and energy with it. Eventually, everything would crumble into dust.

She shook her head, leaf-strewn curls bouncing. "This whole thing is stupid."

"Excuse me," he snapped, temper flaring. "Do you know who I am?" He was the architect of countless important bargains, including the assassination of no less than twelve world leaders. Sure, his reputation was currently in tatters on the demon plane, but there were entire chapters of necronomica dedicated to him.

"An inconvenience," she shot back. "I'm already the most incompetent witch ever to exist. I don't need to accidentally summon a demon on top of that."

"Incompetent?" He shook his head. "I can feel your magic, witch."

"Yeah, so did the stars and the wind and the earth, and look at us now." She sighed and thunked her forehead against the table. "So what happens now? You hang around until I give you my soul?"

This was a unique experience. Normally witches were gagging to give him their souls, desperate for whatever prizes he could offer in return. "Well . . . yes."

She picked up her head and glared at him. "Never going to happen."

He shrugged. "I'm immortal. I have time."

She parted her lips—probably to say some other rude thing—but the moment was interrupted by a doorbell ringing. "Mariel, dear!" a female voice called, the sound muffled. "Come give your mother a kiss!"

The witch's name was Mariel. Pretty.

Ozroth watched with interest as the color drained from Mariel's cheeks, making her freckles stand out. "She can't know I summoned you," she whispered, panic written across her face.

Ozroth sensed an opening. "If you give me your soul, I won't tell her."

"Yeah, no thanks." Mariel stood and darted to the hallway closet, returning with a pink knitted cap, which she tugged over his head before he could stop her. He shivered as the fabric stretched over his sensitive horns. "Wear this, and don't you dare move. I'll be back in a few."

She hurried down the hallway as the doorbell rang again. Ozroth ran a hand over the hat, which was no doubt intended to hide his horns. What was *wrong* with this witch? His horns were considered very handsome on the demon plane, and no one dared come near them without his approval. This witch had just trampled over one of the most sacred boundaries of demonkind, much like she trampled over basic politeness.

But Ozroth needed Mariel to warm up to the idea of a soul pact, so he kept the cap on, despite the way it made his horns itch.

He followed Mariel, watching as she finger-combed her messy hair and scrubbed at the dirt on her cheek. She took a deep breath, then opened the door. "Hi, Mom! It's really not a good time—"

The words were cut off when a middle-aged woman in a white pantsuit forced her way in. She was thin and wiry, with Mariel's curly brown hair and the sharp-featured face of a predator. Her lips were painted blood red, and a pair of designer sunglasses rested on top of her head. "Darling," she cooed, kissing the air on either side of Mariel's face with loud smacking sounds. "I know we just talked, but I was in the area, and I couldn't wait to see how your summoning went."

Mariel edged in front of her mother, standing between her and the kitchen, where Ozroth watched from the doorway. "I can't chat right now."

"Oh, hush," the woman said. "Where's your spell? Has your handwriting gotten any better? I cannot tell you how much I regret sending you to public school for second grade."

"Mom, no—"

It was no use though. The small woman slid around Mariel like oil. She took two steps towards the kitchen, then stopped at the sight of Ozroth. Her eyes widened. "Who is that?" she demanded, pointing a long, manicured nail at him.

He grinned, exposing his sharp canines. "As a matter of fact, I'm—"

"My boyfriend!" Mariel shouted before Ozroth could finish the sentence.

Silence fell in the wake of that announcement.

Ozroth gaped at Mariel. He was *what*?

And then Mariel's mother burst into tears.

THREE

"Finally," Diantha Spark wailed. "I'd nearly given up on grandbabies."

Mariel shared an alarmed look with the demon, though she suspected they were alarmed about different things. Ozroth the Ruthless, otherwise known as Ozroth the Massive Inconvenience. His gold eyes—a color she'd never seen on a human—were wide, and for once in their short acquaintance, he seemed speechless. The pink beanie stretched awkwardly over his horns, but she was counting on Diantha being too distracted to notice.

"Yes, we're very happy," Mariel said, hurrying towards the demon. She wrapped her hand around his arm, though her skin crawled at the contact with his too-warm skin. She lifted up on her toes as if she was going to kiss his cheek. "If you don't play along," she whispered, "I will explode you."

Mariel didn't think she was capable of blowing up anyone—animal, demon, or otherwise—on purpose, but he didn't know that. She glared at him as ferociously as she could, and the demon swallowed, then nodded.

Mariel switched her attention back to her mother. "So as I said, I'm busy right now and can't—"

"Tell me everything," Diantha said, rushing forward. She grabbed Ozroth's free hand, and Mariel winced. "How did you meet my baby girl? Do you have a stable job? What's your magical ability level? I know she's incompetent, but she's trying, bless her."

"Mom!"

"We met recently," Ozroth said, voice smooth as silk. He had the most interesting accent—like British mixed with Australian and spiced with something archaic. Though he couldn't have enjoyed being grabbed, his smile was warm and wide as he focused his attention on Diantha. "Mariel is a lovely woman, and that's all to your credit, Mrs. . . ."

He trailed off, but luckily, Diantha was too excited to question it. "Oh, please call me Diantha! She's never dated before, you know. Such an odd duck! But the prophecy—" She shivered, and a blissful smile broke out over her red lips. "Well, once it comes to pass, you're going to be a very lucky man, indeed." She patted his hand. "Just try to endure until then, all right?"

Mariel's cheeks burned. It was embarrassing enough to have accidentally summoned a demon. Her mother meeting said demon and then shaming Mariel in front of him was an extra level of humiliation. The exploded chicken was shaping up to be the high point of the day.

"I'm already lucky," the demon said, extricating his hand from Diantha's. He grabbed Mariel's fingers, then brought her hand to his lips. His mouth, like his fingers, was hot, and his eyes burned with mischief as he kissed the back of her hand.

Mariel scoffed. Of course he was capable of being charming. How else was he supposed to seduce souls out of the unwary? But Mariel was no naïf to be tricked by soft lips and sweet compliments—her mother's knowledge of Mariel's dating history was thankfully limited through a mixture of elaborate subterfuge and blind luck—and she knew what festered behind those pretty gold eyes. Demons were deceptive monsters, which meant she couldn't trust a word that came out of his mouth.

"Now tell me about you," Ozroth said, switching his attention to Diantha. "I can already tell you're a fascinating woman."

✦ ✦ ✦

AN HOUR LATER, MARIEL WAS ON HER SECOND MUG OF CHAMO-mile tea, wondering how long a man—or demon, rather—could manage to look interested in a conversation. They'd migrated to the living room, where Ozroth sat on a couch with her mother while Mariel perched in a floral-patterned armchair. Diantha had regaled Ozroth the Ruthless with her entire life story and then some, yet he still leaned forward and smiled, even though she hadn't even asked him his name.

"And you won the trophy for the tenth time," Ozroth said in a low, purr-like voice. "What an amazing accomplishment."

Diantha preened, fluffing her hair. "Not that amazing, considering my skill."

Ozroth nodded. "You're powerful. I can feel it."

That drew the attention of both witches. "You can feel magical power?" Diantha asked, sitting up straight.

He was still grinning like a fricking toothpaste ad. His canines were sharp and slightly overlong, and Mariel wondered if he ever bit his prey. "My own talents as a warlock are minimal," he said, "but my one skill is sensing magic. Mariel is exceptionally powerful." He nodded at Diantha. "Good genes."

Mariel bit her tongue. He should add lying and blowing smoke up people's asses to his list of skills.

Diantha shot a damning look at Mariel. "Unfortunately, she hasn't learned to harness that power."

Mariel flinched. "Yes, thank you. You've only told him a million times how terrible I am."

Diantha pouted. "I'm only trying to help. A bit of pressure can be useful."

A "bit of pressure" had made a wreck of Mariel's life. She wasn't in therapy for nothing.

"Your daughter," Ozroth said, "has the brightest magical aura I've ever encountered. She's destined for great things." His gaze slid to Mariel, and a smirk tilted his detestable lips. The "great things" he was envisioning probably involved her sacrificing her immortal soul to power his Wi-Fi.

"Speaking of destiny," Mariel said, seizing the moment and standing up, "I need to do some research. I'm so sorry to leave, but I really think this will help me improve my spellcraft."

Diantha nodded. "Go study, dear. Your boyfriend can entertain me."

Was Mariel imagining things, or had Ozroth winced? "Actually," he said, rising from the couch, "I need to go . . . feed my cat." He nodded. "Yes, my cat is very hungry."

"I didn't know you had a cat," Mariel said in a saccharine tone. "Are you sure you can't stay?"

"Yes, do stay," Diantha said, pouting her bloodred lips.

"I do have a cat," Ozroth confirmed. "And no, I have to go." He looped an arm around Mariel's waist, and Mariel nearly choked on her own spit. "I'm sure you have very important places to be, too."

"Oh, yes!" Diantha stood, fanning herself with one manicured hand. "There's never enough time in the day, is there?"

It took twenty more minutes to get her mom out of the house. When she was gone, Mariel sagged against the closed front door. Ozroth ripped the pink beanie off and threw it on the floor, then ran a hand through his dark hair, fluffing it back to its earlier perfection. It was long enough to conceal parts of the onyx horns that curved along his head.

"That was . . . a lot," he said.

Mariel groaned. "Welcome to my life."

"Is she always like that?"

Mariel grimaced. "She's gotten more intense over the years. Back when I was a kid and she thought I would be the best witch in a thousand years, she was all compliments. It was only when I started to fail that she got so . . ." She paused, trying to think of an appropriate descriptor for her mother. Obsessive? Rude? Terrifying? "Overbearing."

He cocked his head again, eyes tracing over her. His gaze was eerily intense, like he was looking under her skin. Maybe he was—Mariel knew jack shit about demons. "You are powerful," he said. "It's plain to see."

Mariel was tired of hearing about her supposed power. Plants loved her, but all she'd managed to do otherwise was blow things up and summon inappropriate objects, and she didn't want to think about the accidental enchantments. Love spells weren't so fun when Mariel had accidentally gotten distracted by the state of her cucumbers while trying to help a friend with her crush.

"Try telling my magic that," she said bitterly, pushing past the demon to return to her kitchen. The book sat open on the table, taunting her with knowledge out of her reach. *They can offer a witch or warlock any boon, but at a high price.* Yeah, but how did she get rid of a demon?

She stepped on a shard of teapot and winced as it dug into her heel. Yet another casualty of Mariel's lack of talent.

The brush of leaves against her cheek made her sigh. She turned her head towards her spider plant, which stroked her with its long fronds. "Can you get rid of a demon?" she asked it softly. "Maybe the apple tree can help." The image of Ozroth trapped in a tangle of roots before being sucked underground was an appealing one, but unfortunately, Mariel didn't think she could be that cruel. Even to a demon.

"So you have trouble with your magic." Ozroth leaned against the refrigerator, and Mariel was distracted by how large he was. He was tall and broad, and when he crossed his arms, his biceps strained against his black T-shirt. Apparently working out was a *thing* in Hell.

The demon plane, she corrected herself. Although that made her think of an airplane full of brooding demons all bitching about the lack of legroom.

He snapped his fingers, and Mariel jerked back to awareness. "What?" she asked, cheeks heating as she realized she'd zoned out while staring at his chest.

"You're having trouble with your magic," Ozroth said. "I can help with that."

She scoffed. "Let me guess, for the price of my soul? I'd get control of my magic, and then you'd immediately take it away."

He scowled. "I shouldn't have told you it worked like that."

"Yeah, well, you did." She grabbed a broom from the closet, then started sweeping up the remains of her teapot. What a mess she'd gotten herself into.

A large hand closed around the broom handle, and Mariel flinched. "Allow me," the demon said.

She relinquished the broom, backing away. She didn't like how hot the air was around him or the way her skin prickled at his nearness. "I am not buying your housekeeping services," she said as she bumped into the table. "Just to be clear."

He made a huffing sound as he started sweeping. Was he laughing at her? "You know," he said conversationally as he gathered the teapot shards into a pile, "I can help you with your magic anyway. Without the soul."

"Why would you do that?"

He shrugged. "It'll entertain me while you figure out what favor you want."

He was really convinced she was going to make a deal with him. Mariel might not have inherited anything else from Diantha Spark, but she only bent so far when challenged. When Mariel dug her heels in, she dug in *hard*. "Never going to happen. There's nothing I want enough to give my soul to you." Legacy aside, keeping her soul—and thus her magic—meant keeping her garden alive. It meant the warm, cozy thrum of power in her chest. It meant the chance to someday make her family proud.

Ozroth smirked. "We'll see."

FOUR

MARIEL WAS GIVING HIM THE SILENT TREATMENT. After her last rejection of his offer, she'd refused to acknowledge him in any way. Instead, she'd marched around the house, cleaning and reorganizing things with furious intent. Considering all the clutter, it apparently wasn't a common occurrence. Ozroth's own den back home was minimalist and tidy; he couldn't imagine living in this sort of chaos.

He winced as he swiped a fingertip over her bookshelf and came up with dust. "How do you live like this?"

She made an angry noise but otherwise ignored him.

"I can see the root of the problem," Ozroth said as he followed her into the hallway, where she grabbed fresh linens from the closet. "Magic requires specificity, precision, and order. If you get a single motion, rune, or incantation syllable wrong, the entire spell falls apart. And that's before you take into account the caster's thoughts and intentions."

"Can't see what that has to do with my bookshelf," she muttered under her breath.

"If you're disorganized in one part of your life, you're disorganized in another." He followed her into the bedroom, recoiling at the sight of clothes piled high in the corner. "Are those clean or dirty?"

She ignored him while she stripped the bed. The sheets were yellow, and a puff of floral scent burst into the air as she flung them aside. Ozroth inhaled deeply, wondering if everything she touched smelled like that. He wandered over to the pile of clothes, picked up a shirt, and sniffed.

"Hey!" Apparently he'd alarmed her into speaking directly to him again. "What are you doing with my clothes?"

"Finding out if they're clean or dirty." These smelled clean, with a faint undertone of detergent. "What's the point in washing your clothes if you don't hang them up?" he grumbled as he folded a T-shirt. "They'll get wrinkled, and you'll have to wash them all over again."

"I don't care if they're wrinkled."

"Well, I do." Ozroth started going through drawers, trying to figure out her organizational system. There wasn't one, as far as he could tell. The fabrics clung together, and he winced at a blue zap of static electricity from a drawer pull. Did she even use dryer sheets? "Where do shirts go?"

"*Clauseyez il pectum!*" The drawer slammed shut so fast he almost lost his fingers. She glared at him, one hand on her hip and one pointing at her drawer. "You do *not* get to go through my things." Then her eyes widened. "I shut the drawer."

His brows drew together. "So?" Small magic like that was so simple, a witch didn't need the power boost provided by physical rituals like chalking or weaving thread.

For the first time in their brief and odd acquaintance, a smile lifted the corners of her mouth. It was a nice mouth, he realized, with a precise dip at the top and a full bottom lip. It fit with the soft beauty of her other features. "It didn't explode."

"You normally can't even manage a spell that simple?" Ozroth asked disbelievingly.

Her face fell. "Dick," she muttered before turning her attention back to the bed.

A stab of guilt went through Ozroth's chest. He winced, rubbing over his heart. *Absolutely not*, he told the soul that throbbed with sympathy for the girl. *Quit acting up.* Being an excellent soul bargainer required emotional coldness and clarity of vision: things Ozroth hadn't struggled with before the bargain gone wrong. Now, it was a daily struggle not to become embroiled in emotional reactions more suited to the brief lives of mortals.

He shoved the sympathy down and focused on more practical matters. The stronger the witch's soul when he took it, the more good it would do his reputation. "What went differently that time?" he asked as he carried an armful of garishly colorful dresses towards the closet. Thankfully, she at least owned hangers. "Why did it work?"

"Hecate knows." When she turned to see him hanging up her dresses, she grimaced. "Why are you putting away my clothes?"

"Someone needs to. I'm about to break out in hives." Mariel's chaos made him itchy, and he'd only been here a few hours.

"Do demons get hives?" she asked.

"This one will if you leave clothes piled on the floor."

She walked over, ripped a purple dress out of his hands, and threw it on the floor. "There," she said, crossing her arms. "If you don't like it, don't stay."

Undeterred, Ozroth picked up the dress and carried on organizing. "You can't stop me. Unless you want to strike a bargain?"

"Ugh!" She threw up her hands, then grabbed the clean powder-blue sheets. "You are impossible."

They worked in silence for a few minutes, and the tension slowly drained out of Ozroth. He liked things in their proper places. Without order, there was no meaning. No purpose. Astaroth had taught him that early on, when Ozroth had been an insecure demon child desperate to prove his worth. Material possessions should be as minimal as possible and meticulously organized. By taking control of the world around him, he also took control of himself.

Considering the state of the witch's room, it was no wonder she struggled with magic. "Seriously though," he said, "what was different about this time you used magic?"

Her movements slowed as she considered the question. "I don't know. I didn't think about it."

"Do you normally think about it?"

She huffed. "Obviously. Everyone's always yammering on about the importance of intent, and the language of magic is disgustingly complicated."

Ozroth considered the words. "So you acted on instinct, and it worked better than when you do things more deliberately."

She glared at him. "I was also mad at you. Normally I don't have a pain-in-the-ass demon messing with my things."

He wondered if he'd ever get used to her disrespect. "You know no one talks to demons like this, right?"

"Well, I do." She returned her attention to tucking the sheet in.

Horror filled him at the sight. "Have you ever heard of hospital corners?"

"Yes," she said, continuing to stuff the sheet under the mattress in haphazard clumps. Her head snapped up, and he was coming to recognize the expression she wore when she was about to ask a random question. "Wait, do demons have hospitals? Aren't you immortal?"

This was too much. "Move," he snapped, getting into her space.

"Hey!" She smacked his arm when he nudged her aside. "Stop touching my shit!"

He ignored her in favor of redoing the fold. Soon, the sheet was fitted tightly, the corners perfectly creased. He stepped back, brushing his hands with satisfaction.

When he turned, he found her gaping at him. "What?" he asked.

"A demon just made my bed." Mariel's nose wrinkled. "That's . . . bizarre."

"For the small price of your soul, I'll clean your whole house." It wouldn't be the most pathetic soul bargain ever struck, though it would be close.

"Tempting," she said, "but no."

She headed outside, and Ozroth followed, never letting her get more than a few feet away. If she planned to try to outlast him, he planned to be as annoying as possible. By the way she kept grumbling and glowering at him, it was working.

He followed her into a small greenhouse, then stopped in the entrance. Life burst in every corner, and the air was heavy with the rich floral scent he'd smelled on her sheets. "This is surprisingly organized," he said, noting the way she'd arranged the plants in neat lines.

In response, she flipped him off.

He watched as she wandered through the plants, whispering to them and stroking them. They stroked her back, twining in her hair and patting her shoulders as if comforting her.

A sharp pain in the back of his hand made him jump. He glared at the offender—a rosebush that was drawing its sharp thorns back. "Using your garden magic for ill?" he called over his shoulder.

She huffed. "They're only protecting me."

"You do realize the intention comes from you, right? They aren't acting on their own."

He wondered how many of her glares he would accumulate

before their bargain was out. Each one sent a simmer through him, a flash of amusement mixed with outrage at her gall. "Don't talk about my plants like that," she snapped. A lily brushed its petals against her hand. "They do what they like."

Another obnoxious, unwelcome pang of feeling struck him. She was clearly trying to self-soothe with the plants and had apparently convinced herself they were her *friends*. In reality, they cared as little for her as a stone would. She was the engine powering their movements.

"I'll stop talking about your plants if you—"

"Nope," she said, turning away.

The day progressed like that, with Ozroth trying to wear Mariel down and Mariel cycling between ignoring him and being outright rude. It became a strange game—how many things could he offer in exchange for her soul?

A rare orchid. A kitchen renovation. A sports car to replace her bicycle.

She rejected them all. As Ozroth followed her around, his mind churned over the question of what Mariel Spark wanted more than anything else in the world.

Normally it was a cliché answer: money, love, sex, revenge, or power. Sometimes witches and warlocks had more personal needs, like a resurrected loved one or the curing of a terminal illness. He had a feeling Mariel was more likely to be enticed by the latter category than the former.

"Has anyone you love died recently?" he asked.

She'd been poring over spell books at the kitchen table, and at the words, her head popped up. "What kind of question is that?"

"I can resurrect them." It took a lot of effort, and reanimated corpses smelled awful at first, but if that was what it took to win Mariel's soul for the demon plane, he'd do it gladly.

A disgusted look crossed her face. "That's a terrible offer."

"Is it?"

"I certainly wouldn't want to be brought back to life. And what about decomposition?"

All right, no reanimating dead relatives. "Would you like a basket of kittens?" he asked, trying another tack. "Think what good company they'd be."

She shook her head, making her curls bounce. "Just . . . shut up for a bit, will you?"

It was his turn to glare at her. "You are the rudest human I've ever encountered."

"That's too bad," she said, shoulder checking him as she left the kitchen. "You deserve way worse than this."

◆ ◆ ◆

THAT EVENING, OZROTH WATCHED AS MARIEL PRACTICED SUM-moning. She stood in the kitchen, which seemed to be her favorite room of the house, scowling at the pentagram she'd chalked onto the countertop. The kitchen, like the greenhouse, was far more orderly than the rest of the house, and Ozroth suspected Mariel only put effort in for things she cared about deeply. Why her magic wouldn't be in that category was a mystery he planned to solve.

"The lines aren't straight," he said, eyeing her pentagram.

"Very helpful," she muttered. Then she sighed and wiped the lines clean. "How does anyone do this?"

"Practice."

She grabbed a yardstick from the pantry, then placed it on the counter and chalked along it. "I'm a joke of a witch. Can't even draw a straight line."

He didn't answer, instead leaning against the fridge with his arms crossed as he waited to see what she would do or say next.

"Mom says the stars told her I have the potential to be a ruler."

She laughed bitterly. "She must have misheard. I have the poten-tial to *use* a ruler." She punctuated the words with a whack of the yardstick against the counter.

It was clear Diantha Spark had done damage to Mariel's self-confidence. Maybe this was the key to her soul. Ozroth couldn't use his power to make her better at magic—that would contradict the necessary requirement of *taking* her magic—but maybe he could seize one of those insecurities and dig until he found her breaking point. "Do you think she loves you?" he asked.

Her entire body jerked. "Of course she does." She blinked rap-idly. "Right?" The last word was whispered so quietly, he knew it wasn't meant for him.

"Hmm," was all he said. He winced as an ache started in his chest. His soul was determined to have a conscience, despite the fact that Ozroth had done far worse to force a bargain in the past, from kidnapping loved ones to light torture. He ignored the emo-tion and focused on watching the witch work.

Mariel muttered to herself as she continued sketching the pentagram. He caught only stray words, *demon* and *prick* among them.

It was true—Ozroth was a prick. Keeping the demon plane—and his people—alive meant using any and every tactic to exploit vulnerabilities. Threats, coercion, blackmail, seduction . . .

He considered the last one, eyes tracing over her form. She was beautiful, there was no doubt about that. Curvaceous, too, with wide hips and thick thighs made for gripping. Did she have anyone to pleasure her? Diantha Spark had seemed to think not, so maybe that was another avenue he could exploit.

"Is anyone fucking you?" he asked.

The chalk snapped in half. Mariel turned, pointing the jagged piece at him. "That is none of your business."

He could read the answer in the way her eyes met his, then

darted away. "Would you like to be fucked?" It would be a new angle for Ozroth the Ruthless, who had built a reputation on more aggressive deals, but he didn't mind the concept. In fact, he thought, as he eyed those hips, it was more than a little appealing.

"You have terrible manners," she said, turning back to her pentagram. Her cheeks were pink.

"So you do want to be fucked."

"What I want," she said, scribbling aggressively, "is for you to shut up and let me work on my spellcraft!"

"I'll shut up if you—"

"No!" She closed her eyes and pinched the bridge of her nose. "Honestly, it's like having a toddler."

That was the most offensive thing she'd said yet. "I am more than two hundred years old," he said, sounding pissy even to himself. "Hardly a toddler."

She ignored him, chalking runes faster. Then she closed her eyes and took a deep breath. "*Volupto e ayorsin!*"

There was a flash of light . . .

And a giant purple dildo manifested on the counter.

They both stared at it for a long, silent moment. Ozroth eyed the veins, the glitter, the sheer *size* of the thing, and decided Mariel was, if not realistic, at least ambitious. Even he was no match for that monstrosity.

"Oh, no." The words came out of Mariel's mouth at an unnaturally high pitch. She hurriedly started erasing and reversing the symbols. "No, no, no."

Ozroth's lips twitched. "That answers the question of whether or not you want to be fucked."

Chalk scraped over the counter. "We are *not* discussing this." Mariel closed her eyes. "*Aufrasen e volupto!*"

The dildo vanished in a puff of smoke.

Mariel stared at the empty spot on the counter. "It worked," she said, sounding shocked. "That never works."

"Never?"

She shook her head.

"So what went differently this time?" Ozroth pressed. Dildo aside, he was fascinated by the witch's vast magic and seeming inability to manage it.

"I really, really wanted that thing out of here," she muttered.

"Intent," Ozroth said. "And focus. You only cared about one thing—demanifesting the dildo." He tapped his fingers on his bicep, considering the puzzle of the witch. She had so much raw power—perhaps the problem was that she had no ability to use it precisely. "You need to bring structure to your magic. Once your mind and rituals are more organized, you'll be better at this."

"I don't want your magic advice." She pressed the heels of her palms into her eyes. "I don't want anything from you."

For some reason, the words stung. Ozroth rubbed his chest, wondering what his unwelcome soul had taken offense to now.

He hadn't understood at the time of that fateful deal exactly what he was getting into. He'd been making deals for hundreds of years, after all, and he'd never come out the worse for one. So even if the dying warlock's request a few months ago had been odd, he'd thought nothing of the strange wording.

My soul for a painless passing, and may it pass then to where there is pain. Solum te aufrasil.

Typical cryptic warlock bullshit. Ozroth the Ruthless had been cold as ice since he'd begun his training under Astaroth centuries ago; what did it matter what good the old fool thought he was doing with his soul? There was pain in every plane of existence. This soul would light the demon realm like all the rest.

Except it hadn't.

After the old warlock had breathed his final, painless breath, the soul had risen out of the corpse, a golden orb visible only to demon eyes. And then, to Ozroth's shock, it had sunk into his own chest, filling him with warmth and an entire encyclopedia's worth of feelings he had no idea what to do with.

A demon with a human soul. There had never been such a thing in recorded history.

Mariel was rummaging in the refrigerator now, pulling out meat and vegetables. She poured olive oil into a cast-iron skillet and turned on the burner before beginning to chop onions and peel garlic. The onion made a hissing sound as it hit the hot oil.

Soon the kitchen smelled like spice and garlic, and Ozroth's stomach grumbled. He frowned down at his abdomen. Demons ate less frequently than humans and solely for sustenance. For some reason, the warlock's soul had enhanced his sense of taste and smell, too. Rather than eating once every two weeks to maintain his strength, now Ozroth couldn't go more than a day without food. Similarly, he needed nightly sleep, too, which was proving to be a massive waste of time.

The meal took shape—pasta with a rich, meaty tomato sauce. As Mariel stirred, Ozroth stared, mouth watering at the thought of what that sauce would taste like. Maybe he could steal a bite when she was done . . .

"Where are you staying?" Mariel asked.

He snapped out of his intense focus on the food. "What?"

"Where are you spending the night?"

His brow furrowed. "I told you, I can't leave until we strike a bargain."

"Yeah, but I thought—isn't there a hotel you can go to or something?"

Truthfully, Ozroth could probably find one close enough to be within the parameters of their new bond—he didn't have to be in the same room, just within a few miles' radius—but that required effort, and it would mean less time spent figuring out what Mariel's deepest desire was. The longer it took him to strike this bargain, the worse he would look in Astaroth's eyes. "No," he said.

"Great," she said with zero enthusiasm, resuming stirring. "An unwanted demonic houseguest."

"You're the one who summoned me," he said, offended by the dismissal.

"And believe me, it was the worst mistake of my life."

Ozroth's chest was tight, and his stomach was starting to feel sour, so he turned and stalked out of the kitchen. Lucifer, why did so many human emotions feel like physical illness? It was a wonder humans didn't visit the doctor on an hourly basis. Then again, Glimmer Falls was located in America, and news of the horrors of the American medical system had reached even the demon plane. "Admirable," Astaroth had once said. "We could stand to learn a few things about ruthless manipulation and one-sided bargains from American healthcare insurers."

Ozroth sat on the couch in the darkened living room, looking out the window at the occasional headlights that passed by. It was foolish to feel offended. Foolish to give one witch's words the power to hurt him. But his soul apparently liked hurting, because the ache in his chest didn't let up.

Had anyone ever wanted him around?

He'd never considered the question before. Bargains were transactions: he was chosen by desperate witches because of what he could do, not who he was. He socialized the normal amount for a bargainer in the demon plane—which was to say, barely at all—but the friendships there were more like alliances.

Or maybe that was just how he had seen them.

Demons weren't entirely emotionless, of course; their range was just more limited than humans'. If he had to describe the experience, it would be like eating meat and potatoes all your life, then suddenly being exposed to a buffet filled with cuisine from around the world. New flavors, new feelings, new shades of experience.

Maybe the transformation had been especially startling because Astaroth had liked Ozroth cold, like all legendary soul collectors. For the elite few who kept their realm alive, feelings were a weakness to be rooted out through strict training and punishment. Other demons could express emotions or form relationships, but Ozroth had been trained since childhood not to acknowledge or allow any such vulnerability. Sentiment was too easily exploited by enemies—a fact bargainers knew better than anyone, since that exploitation was their bread and butter.

The creak of a floorboard drew his attention away from the window. Mariel stood in the doorway, silhouetted by warm kitchen light. She held a steaming bowl in her hand. "Dinner?" she said hesitantly.

He was confused. "Yes, you are having dinner."

She sighed and set the bowl on the floor. "Fine, eat out here if you want."

He stared at the bowl after she returned to the kitchen. The food was for him? Why?

The smell was too good to resist. He walked over to pick up the bowl, lifting it to his face to inhale deeply. A growl of contentment vibrated out of his throat at the sharp, spicy scent. He twirled noodles on the fork and took a bite, suppressing a moan at how good it was.

He joined her at the kitchen table, eating in silence. As much as he tried to savor the dish, it was impossible to eat slowly. It tasted incredible, and it was the first time in memory anyone had made him food.

"Wow," she said, watching him plow through the pasta. "You must be really hungry."

He paused, then slurped up the spaghetti dangling from his mouth. "Why did you do it?" he asked.

"Do what?"

"Cook for me."

She toyed with her fork, not meeting his eyes. "Because you're my guest."

"An unwanted one," he shot back. "The worst mistake of your life." The words still rankled, although the pasta was going a long way towards soothing his temper.

"You're still my guest," she repeated. "Now shut up and eat your food."

Ozroth did, feeling confused and grateful and some other shimmering, undefinable thing he didn't know how to put words to. Eventually, he stopped trying. There was still a soul to claim, but for now, there was spaghetti.

FIVE

T HE DEMON WAS WEIRD.

Mariel contemplated the weirdness of the demon as she repotted a philodendron. Inadvertent demonic bargain or not, she hadn't wanted to shirk her part-time job at Ben's Plant Emporium. While she was still hoping for Spark family funds for grad school, she was saving every penny she could.

Since Ozroth apparently needed to be attached to her at the hip, he was stalking her from an aisle away (*There will be no bargain ever if you keep stepping on me*, she'd snapped after he'd run into her for the bazillionth time when she'd stopped to water a plant), but she was all too aware of his presence nearby.

His hot, horrible, *weird* presence.

Ozroth the Ruthless had proven himself to be, so far, Ozroth the Very Annoying, Ozroth the Unwanted Magic Tutor, and Ozroth the Ravenous Dinner Eater. When he'd eaten her spaghetti last night, he'd looked alarmed and amazed, like no one had ever fed him before. He hadn't said thanks, but he'd done the dishes, then stared at her wide-eyed before practically running to sleep on the couch.

Mariel wasn't sure how the demon realm worked, but the little she'd heard about demonic deals hadn't prepared her for this. She'd expected fire, evil laughter, and an eternity in Hell. Now even the existence of Hell was in question. The demon was cocky, easily offended, and annoying, but he hadn't laughed maniacally even once, and when Mariel had called summoning him the worst mistake of her life, he'd looked . . . hurt?

But seriously, what was she supposed to do? Give her soul—and her magic—away to make him leave? Absolutely not.

"Patient for you, Mariel," her boss, Ben Rosewood, called out, snapping Mariel out of her reverie. She stood, wiping her brow with a dirt-streaked hand.

Working at the Emporium made her happy, but she worried about the plants who went home with customers. Many of them were fragile, requiring attentive care, and the unlucky ones ended up with owners who struggled to make them thrive. It was why she'd set up Mariel's Plant ER in a corner of the shop so she could magic struggling houseplants better.

Ben looked up from his notebook as Mariel approached the front counter. Why he insisted on paper records in the era of the internet was a mystery, but Mariel chalked pentagrams, so she could hardly judge. The werewolf was notoriously serious, but he looked a bit silly in Mariel's opinion, with gold-rimmed glasses perched on his aquiline nose and his massive chest testing the limits of an argyle sweater vest. His brown hair was as shaggy as his pelt would be on the full moon.

"What's the damage?" Mariel asked.

"Looks pretty dead to me."

Mariel turned at the familiar voice and grinned to see Calladia. She was clearly fresh from the gym, her long blond hair tied up in a damp bun and her cheeks rosy from exercise. A desiccated houseplant was tucked under her arm. Calladia didn't own any houseplants besides a cactus, so this must be a rescue.

Calladia set the plant on the counter. "I'm not sure even you can fix this one, but I figured it was worth a shot."

Mariel concentrated on the plant: a pothos whose heart-shaped leaves had browned and withered. "How do you even kill a pothos?" she muttered. "They're, like, the easiest plant to raise." She set a finger on one leaf and closed her eyes, reaching out with her magic. Thankfully, she sensed kernels of life hidden in the stems, waiting to be coaxed out. "It isn't terminal."

"Just a flesh wound?" Calladia asked dryly.

"Can I get some water?" Mariel asked, and Ben appeared at once with a pitcher. "Thanks." She wetted the soil a bit at a time, cooing praise to the pothos. "Good baby. You're going to be fine. I can't wait to see your handsome leaves!"

Ben snorted and shook his head. "Weird plant lady."

She wrinkled her nose. "Grumpy werewolf bastard."

The words were spoken with fondness. In the years she'd spent working at the Emporium, her boss's dour nature had become a joke between them. And under his surly-yet-nerdy exterior, Ben really was a good guy.

Her other coworker, a gorgeous naiad named Rani, passed by carrying a potted palm. She'd just taken her morning hydration break: her brown skin was damp and gleaming, and the rainbow scales along her hairline were still vivid. "Wow, how did someone manage to fuck up a pothos?" Rani asked as she headed for the back.

"Right?" Mariel fed magic into the plant, and a green flush gradually crept over the brown. The leaves plumped, and soon the plant was thriving again. "I'm taking you home with me," she told the pothos. "No more neglectful owners." The pothos brushed a leaf against her hand in gratitude.

"I can't believe how easy that is for you," Calladia said. "You didn't even need to say a spell! Every time I try messing with plants, I end up with pollen on my face and a bunch of angry bees in pursuit."

Casting without a spoken spell was difficult but not impossible if a witch was naturally inclined towards a gift or had practiced it extensively. Mariel would need the language of magic for bigger workings, but her nature magic was instinctive, and it was easy to give a bit of her energy to plants to help them thrive. "Thank you for bringing it to me," she said. "Where'd you find it?"

"A garbage can on Mom's street." Calladia winced. "After we had a very uncomfortable talk about the resort."

"Oof. How'd that go?"

Like Diantha, Calladia's mother was enthusiastic about investing in a resort and spa that was slated to be built in the woods outside town. As the mayor of Glimmer Falls, Cynthia Cunnington had been the instigator of the deal with the property developers, and neither Calladia nor Mariel had forgiven her for it. They were both vehemently opposed to the construction, which would disrupt the local ecosystem.

Calladia made a rude noise. "Put me in a barrel full of nails and roll me over a cliff, and I guarantee it'll be more enjoyable than trying to make Mom see reason." Her eyes widened. "Oh, I forgot to tell you! Themmie arranged a protest today at City Hall. The construction company is supposed to break ground this week."

"Digging already?" The idea made Mariel's stomach churn. "We haven't even had a town hall about this yet."

Glimmer Falls town halls were . . . something. Because so many magic families lived there, you never knew who might summon lightning or teleport something unwanted into the meeting. At one particularly memorable event, Diantha Spark had decided to add a little oomph to her petition for the town to take care of a feral raccoon colony. When twenty spitting-mad raccoons were dropped into the meeting, Diantha quickly won the popular vote to relocate them.

"I'm working to move the town hall up," Calladia said. "There are too many questions about the land sale."

The land in question was on a forested hill to the east of town. It was dotted with hot springs, and steaming waterfalls trailed down the rocky parts of the slope. Fire-breathing salamanders and glimmering, translucent fish lived in the pools, and other exotic creatures made their homes in the earth and trees. It was a rare ecosystem sprung from the magic woven into the earth.

That parcel of land was owned by someone long dead whose name was illegible on the deed, and a variety of impostors had risen up over the years, claiming the signature belonged to a relative. Those petitions had always been dismissed—until Cynthia Cunnington had been voted in as mayor, claimed the deed had finally been interpreted to leave the land to the city, and immediately granted rights to a prominent nonmagical real estate developer. From there, the plans to open the resort had moved at a breakneck pace.

"When's the protest?" Mariel asked. "I'm off work in thirty."

"An hour." Calladia's brown eyes moved over Mariel's shoulder, then widened. "Holy hottie," she whispered. "Don't look, but a sexy man is standing next to the marigolds." Her brow crinkled. "He's sort of . . . glaring at you?"

Mariel groaned. She knew exactly who that was. "Ignore him," she said, moving into the fertilizer aisle.

"Um, that's shady as fuck," Calladia said, tossing glances over her shoulder. "Do you know him?"

"Yes."

"Is he a creep? I can fight him."

Calladia's dating history had left her with a hair trigger when it came to shitty men, and she loved fighting, especially when defending a friend, but Mariel wasn't sure she wanted to sic Calladia on the demon just yet. She looked over her shoulder, frowning at Ozroth, who was lingering suspiciously near a white-flowered phlox she'd magicked to bloom out of season. The broad-brimmed black hat she'd bought him at a thrift store that morning covered his horns but made him look like an extra in *Westworld*. *Go away*, she mouthed at him.

In response, he spread his hands as if to say, *What else am I supposed to do?*

"Mariel." Calladia gripped her shoulder. "Is he stalking you or something?"

"Yes and no . . ."

"That's it." Calladia pulled a hank of thread from her pocket and started weaving a design between her fingers. "I'm taking him out."

Magic normally required three things: intent, precise language, and focus. For complex workings, a physical focus like chalked runes or woven string was often used to keep a witch's attention fixed on the spell. Mariel was learning the chalk technique right now, but Calladia was an incredible thread witch. If she said she was going to take someone out, they were in real danger.

"No, wait," Mariel said, grabbing Calladia's wrist before she tied a knot that chopped off the demon's dick or something. "It's my fault. He has no choice about following me around."

Calladia's eyebrows shot up. "Is that what he told you?"

"It's complicated—"

"Well, you'd better uncomplicate it before I end up in jail for brawling again."

Mariel did not want to explain what was going on, but Calladia was a world-class snoop and could always sniff out a lie. Eventually, she'd need to come clean. "Not here," Mariel whispered. "Somewhere we can shield. Your truck?" Mariel didn't own a vehicle, preferring to bike everywhere.

They headed into the strip mall parking lot, and Calladia beckoned Mariel to hop into the passenger seat of her ancient red truck. Once inside, Calladia knitted a spell for a shield of silence. "*Silente a veiliguz.*"

All sound from outside the truck cab ceased. The spell would ensure no one could hear anything from inside the truck either. Ozroth had followed them; he leaned against the shopping cart corral for the small apothecary next door to Ben's, arms crossed and face creased in a ferocious frown.

"Now," Calladia said. "Tell me why a hot, evil-looking cowboy is stalking you."

Mariel took a deep breath, then told Calladia about the muffins, the summoned ingredients, and her quest for the correct spell. "So I messed up the word for flour," she said, cringing internally, "and instead accidentally summoned, uh, a demon."

"What?!" Calladia screeched.

"His name is Ozroth the Ruthless, and—"

"You summoned *Ozroth the Ruthless*?" Calladia looked like she was going to pass out. "Hasn't he eaten, like, a billion souls or something?"

"They don't eat them. I guess it has something to do with their power grid?"

Calladia shook her head. "Girl, you are in so much trouble. How are you going to get rid of him?"

"Well, that's the thing." Mariel's fingers twisted in her mint-green skirt. "Apparently I summoned him for a soul pact, and he can't leave until I give him my soul."

Calladia's mouth opened and closed a few times. "That's . . . huh."

"Yeah."

"Wow."

"Yup."

Calladia contemplated the demon standing a few yards away. "I thought he'd have fangs," she said. "And red skin and a tail."

"Apparently not." In a way, Mariel wished he did. If he looked like a true monster, maybe it would be easier to contemplate extreme measures like exploding him. Of course, being immortal, he might knit himself back together anyway—she had no idea how those logistics worked. But Ozroth was a tall, brooding, absolute snack of a man, cowboy hat and all.

"Is he horrible?"

"He's . . . strange." He looked absurd, scowling next to a line of red shopping carts. A man tried to return his cart, saw Ozroth, then abandoned the cart in the middle of the parking lot. "He's supposedly hundreds of years old and some amazing badass, but he keeps trying to make the most ludicrous deals with me. And he genuinely tried to help me with my magic for no reason, and I think I offended him last night when I told him he was an unwelcome houseguest?"

"Houseguest?" Calladia's head snapped around. "Don't tell me . . ."

"Yep," Mariel said, popping the *p*. "The terms of the deal require him to stay near me until we complete a contract."

Calladia looked scandalized and fascinated. "So is he sleeping in your bed?"

"No!" Mariel crossed her hands vehemently. "Absolutely not. Ew. He's sleeping on the couch." Sort of. Ozroth was so large, he barely fit. Mariel had come out of her bedroom that morning to discover him sprawled on his back, one leg draped over the armrest, the other planted on the floor. His arms had been akimbo, too, and he'd looked in danger of toppling off the furniture.

He'd looked so harmless—and uncomfortable—that Mariel had made a guilt-fueled early-morning trip to the store to buy giant-sized clothing and a hat capable of hiding those horns. It wasn't his fault he was in her house, after all, and Mariel had been raised by Glimmer Falls's consummate hostess. While Diantha Spark's dinner parties were colorful, no one could fault her when it came to providing the best of everything.

"Wow." Calladia stared at the demon. "So let me get this straight: you're now roommates with a demon you accidentally summoned, and the demon can't leave until you've made a bargain to give up your soul?"

Mariel thunked her head against the headrest a few times. "That about sums it up."

"Well, shit."

✦ ✦ ✦

"TWO, FOUR, SIX, EIGHT, WHAT DO WE APPRECIATE? THE WOODS! Hey hey, the woods!"

Mariel shouted the lines along with the other protestors. There were only nine of them marching outside City Hall, but the protest was drawing attention. Passersby slowed down or stopped to watch.

Mariel hefted her sign higher. PROTECT THE FOREST! PROTECT THE MAGIC! was written on it in purple paint. "Stop the spa!" she shouted. "Keep our forest magical!"

A teenager shook his head as he walked by. "Weirdos."

"Apathy isn't cool!" Calladia called after him.

Mariel stifled a laugh. "He's, like, sixteen. I think he gets a pass."

Calladia sighed. "I just wish the people who actually need to hear this protest were here."

"Like our moms?" Mariel asked dryly.

Next to them, Themmie passed out pamphlets detailing why the resort would be disastrous for the local environment. Her pink-and-green hair was in pigtails, and she'd painted tiny black salamanders on the apples of her brown cheeks. "There are animals in those woods," she told a man she had cornered. "The resort will destroy their habitat."

"Huh," he said, gripping the pamphlet, eyes darting as if he was searching for an escape.

Themmie wrinkled her nose. "Would you like a selfie?" She had her phone out before he could respond. "Ooh, that's a cute one! Thanks for supporting the cause!"

Mariel looked at Calladia and subtly rolled her eyes. But honestly, without Themmie's help, this protest wouldn't gain any traction. Once she posted on her Pixtagram, support would come rolling in—or so Mariel hoped.

The man finally escaped, and Themmie focused her attention elsewhere. "Hi!" she chirped, prancing towards her new target. "Do you support nature?"

Mariel groaned as she saw who Themmie had approached: Ozroth, who was leaning against a telephone pole, arms crossed over his chest and hat tipped low like he didn't want anyone to know he was associated with the protest. Mariel had tried to get him to hold a sign, but he'd refused, saying, *There's a concept in the demon plane I'm not sure you've heard of. It's called dignity.*

And yeah, that had stung a bit, but Mariel cared more about the well-being of Glimmer Falls and its surrounding ecosystem than the mood swings of a fussy old demon, so she'd ignored him and started marching.

"No," Ozroth said, glowering down at the pixie. The top of Themmie's head only came up to his breastbone.

Themmie frowned. "That's not very nice."

Ozroth shrugged.

"The fire salamander is extremely endangered," Themmie said, undeterred. "It only lives here and at one other confluence of ley lines in France. And the resort is going to turn those springs into *hot tubs*."

"Sounds like an interesting ambience," Ozroth said. "Are the salamanders a bonus feature?"

Mariel cut in. "No," she snapped. "The salamanders will die or be 'relocated,' probably to some horrible zoo where they'll also die. They need the magic in the earth and water."

Ozroth switched his attention to her. "You care about these salamanders."

"Obviously."

His mouth curved up on one side, and Mariel was *not* going to focus on how soft his lips looked. "If only you knew someone who could help save them."

It felt like the breath had been knocked out of her. "That's not fair," she whispered.

"Life isn't fair," he shot back.

Themmie looked between them, forehead scrunched in confusion. "Um, do you guys know each other?"

"Yes." Ozroth smirked. "She's my girlfriend."

Mariel was going to punch him, she really was.

Themmie gaped at Mariel. "You have a boyfriend? Since when? Why didn't you tell us about him yesterday?"

Mariel winced. Damn the meddling demon. She'd confessed the summoning mishap to Calladia, but Calladia had seen pretty much every magical mistake Mariel had made over the years, so the embarrassment was somewhat blunted. She'd been friends with Themmie for a few years, but the pixie hadn't witnessed the true extent of Mariel's failures as a witch. And sure, Themmie was endlessly supportive, but the shred of pride Mariel had left stung, and she didn't want to admit the truth yet. Not until she had a way to fix this.

"I didn't want to tell anyone until it was official," Mariel said, narrowing her eyes at Ozroth. "Don't you think this is jumping the gun, *dear*?"

He shrugged, smug and unbothered.

Themmie looked between them, clearly picking up on the weird vibes. "Okay, we obviously need some follow-up after the protest, but for now, let me get him an extra sign—"

"No," Ozroth interrupted. "No signs."

Themmie's surprise quickly shifted to outrage, and she flicked Ozroth on the upper arm. "You do not get to date Mariel and not march with her, Mister Jump-the-Gun Surprise Boyfriend." Her wings fluttered rapidly with irritation. "Hey, Calladia," she called. "Bring me a sign."

"Which one?" Calladia asked.

Themmie's eyes narrowed with vindictive glee. "The hot pink one."

Ozroth stiffened as Calladia jogged over with a pink sign covered in glittery writing. I ♡ FIRE SALAMANDERS was written on it. "Absolutely not."

Themmie grabbed the sign, then shoved it at him. "Time to step up, mister. Prove you're more than a pretty face."

Mariel's shoulders shook with suppressed laughter. Hecate, she loved her friends.

Ozroth gaped at the pixie, apparently stunned speechless. Themmie shoved the sign at him again, then started thwacking his chest with it.

Calladia looked between them. "What's going on?"

"Mariel's boyfriend doesn't support the cause," Themmie snapped.

Calladia coughed. "Her . . . boyfriend?" She cast a wide-eyed glance at Mariel, who cringed.

"It's a long story," Mariel said.

"He won't be her boyfriend for long if he doesn't march with us," Themmie said. "I'll break up with him for you, Mariel."

Oh, Themmie, if only you could. But pixies were low magical creatures whose skills were limited to flying and some snappy cleaning magic. Perfect for flipping a house, less perfect for banishing a demon. "It's all right," Mariel said. "He doesn't have to march."

Calladia folded her arms. "I'm with Themmie," she said, pinning Ozroth with a damning glare. "Your . . . boyfriend . . . had better step up if he wants to stay in your good graces."

Ozroth's throat worked as the three women stared him down. "Fine," he said at last, grabbing the sign.

Themmie cheered, then lifted her phone. "Selfie for the cause!" she crowed, snapping a pic of the four of them standing together.

And oh, the look of baffled outrage on Ozroth's face was worth all of this. *Selfie?* he mouthed at Mariel as Themmie flitted away.

She shrugged. "Gotta get with the times, old man." Then she raised her voice. "Two, four, six, eight, what do we appreciate?"

Ozroth didn't say anything, so Mariel elbowed him in the ribs.

"Ow," he said. When she just stared at him, he expelled a heavy breath. "The woods," he mumbled.

Mariel grinned. "That's better. Hey hey, the woods!"

SIX

ZROTH KNEW THERE WAS NO SUCH THING AS HELL, BUT at the moment, he was starting to question that.

He sat crammed into the corner of a booth at a grimy, noisy dive bar, staring into his tumbler of scotch. Mariel sat to his left, while Themmie and Calladia sat across from them. Themmie had gotten over her earlier pique and was all smiles, though the way Calladia was staring daggers made Ozroth think she was well aware of his demon status.

If only he hadn't taken that ridiculous sign. Then he wouldn't have had to march with them, cringing and mumbling his way through their asinine chants. And then he wouldn't have found himself swept up in the screeching post-protest cries of "Happy hour!" Even if he'd wanted to leave, he couldn't have shaken off Themmie, who had attached herself to his arm and dragged him towards the bar with surprising strength. "Reforming Mariel's boyfriend" had become her pet cause, and she was approaching it with the intensity of a general heading a military campaign.

Weren't pixies supposed to be meek and sweet? But like the

two witches, who ought to know that demons were intimidating and dangerous and not to be fucked with, she'd apparently missed the memo.

Themmie slapped her hand on the table, making Ozroth jump. He looked up to find all three women staring at him. "What?" he asked.

Themmie rolled her dark brown eyes. "I *said*, you never even introduced yourself. You're dating my friend, we're two drinks in, and I have no idea what your name is."

He should never have parroted the lie Mariel had told her mother about them dating. It had seemed like a good way to needle her at the time, but it had led to this nightmare.

Well, if the pixie had read any magic history tomes, she might recognize the name. Let Mariel talk her way out of *that*. "My name is—"

"Oz!" Mariel declared loudly. She tucked her hand into his elbow. "It's Oz."

Ozroth's attention was torn between the offensive nickname she'd given him and her hand on his arm. Two margaritas were apparently enough to loosen Mariel up, because she'd gotten louder and more rambling as the evening had gone on. Now she was touching him?

"Oz," Calladia repeated, crossing her muscular arms. And yes, she definitely knew exactly who he was. If looks could immolate, Ozroth would be a pillar of fire right now. "What a creative name."

"Shhhh," Mariel said, not at all subtly. She made the motion to zip her lips.

"Oz is such a cute name!" Themmie squealed. She lifted her daiquiri in a toast. "To the redemption of Oz, world's worst boy-friend." Thankfully, no one else drank to that. Themmie belched, then hit her breastbone with the top of her fist. "If my followers could see me now."

"They'd still love you," Mariel said earnestly, swaying until her shoulder pressed against Ozroth's. He held perfectly still, unsure what the right strategy was. In all of demon history, no one he knew had ended up in a situation like this.

Then again, no one had ended up with a soul either. A soul that was tingling and being warm and—*ugh*—feeling things about the shoulder contact. And his brain was following right behind, wondering when someone had last touched him with kindness—or, at least, drunkenness. The touch felt better than it had any right to.

"You're right," Themmie said, pointing at Mariel. "Let's test it out." She fluffed her vibrant hair, then positioned her phone in front of her and gave a toothy grin. "Heyyyyy," she said. "How are my Pixtagram peeps tonight? I'm coming to you live from my favorite dive bar in the whole world, Le Chapeau Magique."

Ozroth turned his head to murmur in Mariel's ear. "Is this really necessary?"

"Hmm?" She blinked sleepily at him. "Oh, Themmie? You just have to get used to it."

"I absolutely do not. *You* need to pick a bargain."

She sat up straight, then punched his shoulder lightly. "You are a pain in the ass, you know that?"

"Yeah, well, there's a very simple way to make me leave." His eyes traced over her freckles, then dropped to her mouth.

"Sorry it's loud in here," Themmie said, startling Ozroth out of his intense focus on the curve of Mariel's lips. "My friends are talking. They're, like, a supercute couple though. Aesthetically, at least." She burped. "Let me show you!"

"Wait," Mariel said at the same time Ozroth said, "Absolutely not."

It was no use though. Themmie beamed, pointing the phone at them. "Wave at the camera, sweethearts!"

Mariel waved half-heartedly, but Ozroth scowled. "Put that thing away," he snapped.

Themmie snorted. "Fine, no one wants to see your grumpy face anyway." She walked away, resuming her monologue to the camera.

Ozroth shredded his cocktail napkin. "Pixtagram," he muttered. "Never heard of such an asinine thing."

"Yeah, you're old and out of touch," Mariel said. "We know."

"This is humiliating. Over two hundred years of terrorizing mankind, and I end up on some social media . . . thing."

"It could be good." Mariel crinkled her nose, and he was distracted by her charming spray of freckles. "You could build your brand. Ozroth the Social Media Guru."

"No, thank you."

She pouted. "Oh, come on. It has potential. Ozroth the Ruthless is so eighteenth century." Then she jumped in her chair. "Ow!" She glared across the table at Calladia. "That was unnecessary."

Calladia's eyebrows were about to disappear into her hairline. "Was it? Because it looks to me like you're flirting."

"No!" Mariel said, frantically waving her hands the way she had when he'd asked what she wanted to trade her soul for. "No flirting. Zero flirting. Gross."

Ozroth's stomach did some weird dipping thing that didn't feel good. He drained the rest of the scotch. "I'm leaving."

"Why?" Mariel asked in a sugary tone. "Got to feed your cat?"

"He has a cat?" Calladia asked. "What, like a Hell-cat?"

"Hell isn't real," Mariel said. "There's like, a plane . . ." She trailed off and giggled. "Oh boy, I can see you with your knees jammed against your chest, glaring at the flight attendants."

"What?" Ozroth and Calladia asked in unison. They shared a baffled look before Calladia apparently remembered she hated him. She actually bared her teeth.

"My margarita is empty," Mariel said sadly, looking into the bottom of her glass. Then she perked up. "Should we get another round?"

"No," Ozroth said vehemently. The last thing he wanted to do was spend another hour at girls' night. "Let's go home." He wrapped his hand around Mariel's arm to help her stand.

"It isn't your home," Calladia snapped.

"Your opinion is noted and has been deemed irrelevant," Ozroth shot back.

"What a fucking prick." She reached out for Mariel's hand. "Do you want to crash at mine? You can sleep in my bed and he can sleep in the yard or something."

"It'll be cold," Mariel said mournfully. "What kind of hostess would that make me?"

"A hostess?" Calladia scoffed. "Mariel, you're basically being held captive by this soul bargain. You aren't a hostess."

"You know she summoned me, right?" Ozroth asked. "If anything, she's holding *me* hostage."

"Bullshit. You're trying to get her to give up her soul—"

"Which I have no choice about, and you know it—"

"Just so you can, like, have electricity or something—"

"It's more complicated than that—"

"You are insufferable! Why can't you fuck off already?"

The bar quieted at Calladia's loud words. Themmie looked over with alarm. "Uh oh, my friends are fighting," she said. "Gotta go!"

Ozroth would be damned before he suffered through another three-on-one interrogation or unwanted selfie. Plus, he had a feeling Calladia was about five seconds away from punching him, and brawling with mortals in a seedy dive bar would be degrading.

His tattoo started prickling, and he winced. It was simultane-

ously great and awful timing. "I have to take a call," he said, si-
dling around Mariel. He rushed towards the bathroom as the
prickling turned into stabbing pain. The tattoo was the price of
mentorship—the moment he'd entered Astaroth's castle, he'd been
marked so Astaroth would always be able to contact him.

He locked himself in the bathroom, grimacing at the stained
walls, then turned off the lights. He took a deep breath and cleared
his throat. "I await you, Master."

The pain stopped as a figure manifested in front of him. It
was an astral projection—his master's body was back in the demon plane—but Ozroth swore he could feel an echo of the fiery
heat that emanated from Astaroth.

Astaroth was medium height and lean, with high cheekbones,
pale skin, and white-blond hair that contrasted sharply with his
black horns. He wore an impeccable black suit with a golden
pocket watch, and his black cane was topped with a crystal skull.
Unlike Ozroth, Astaroth lived part-time on Earth and enjoyed
the mortal fashion scene, claiming that his bargaining was improved by having a personal brand with a distinct aesthetic.

Ozroth felt a mixture of fear and awe, as he always did when
confronted by his master, though the fear had only gotten worse
since the soul had arrived. Astaroth had broken down the weak
boy Ozroth had once been and reshaped him into a powerful demon, but the sight of his mentor still made Ozroth's stomach
twist. He cast his eyes down, not wanting the demon to see any
trace of emotion in his expression.

"Ozroth." Astaroth's voice was as hard and sophisticated as
the rest of him, with a crisp British accent he'd acquired over
many years spent making bargains on Earth. He claimed England as his exclusive territory. "It's been a day since you were
summoned. Why haven't you sealed a bargain yet?"

Ozroth shifted. "It's an unusual case."

Astaroth raised one pale brow. "How so?"

There was no way this conversation would turn out well. The only thing to do was get through it as quickly as possible. "She summoned me by accident. She doesn't want to make a deal."

There were a few moments of excruciating silence . . . and then Astaroth scoffed. "So you have an incompetent witch. Find her breaking point and be done with it."

"I'm working on it."

Astaroth's light blue eyes were like ice. "This is a simple task. Are you unworthy of it?"

"No!" Panic rose in Ozroth's chest at the thought that Astaroth might find him lacking. Astaroth had trained him in everything from doublespeak to ripping out fingernails, and guilt at disappointing him had been one of Ozroth's first emotions after gaining the soul. But the witch was strange and difficult, and he needed time to find the fundamental cracks in her psyche.

Inspiration struck—a way to please Astaroth while buying more time. "She's powerful," he said. "More so than any other witch or warlock I've met. The harder the fight, the better the reward."

"Hmm." Astaroth narrowed his eyes. "If she's powerful, why did she summon you by accident?"

"She doesn't know how to use her power yet. She lacks discipline."

"That'll be good for you." Astaroth cocked his head. "What does she love? What are her weaknesses?"

Ozroth thought about pretty, odd, chaotic Mariel. He'd never met anyone like her, and some terrible, weak part of him didn't want Astaroth to know any of her secrets. Once Astaroth learned a secret, he used it mercilessly.

Ozroth knew what his own weakness was: the soul. A real demon would answer without hesitating. "She loves nature," he said, shoving down his too-human guilt. He'd exploited far worse secrets than this in past deals. "She has a greenhouse full of plants that she personifies. There's a resort going up near her town, and she's been protesting to protect the local ecosystem."

"Boring." Astaroth checked the time on his pocket watch, which he insisted on using even though he always had a smartphone in his pocket. "Give me the real meat."

Ozroth took a deep breath, ignoring the sick feeling in his stomach. "Her mother is cruel to her. She's spent her whole life trying to be a better witch, and her family belittles her for her failures. She fears they don't love her."

"Dig into that," Astaroth said. "Make her hurt. Promise you can make her family value her, then take her soul in exchange." His smile was sharp. "After the deal, she won't care anyway."

The idea made Ozroth feel ill, but he nodded anyway. This was the way of things. The need to be ruthless while protecting their species was exactly why Astaroth had taught Ozroth to be cold and unfeeling. "I'll do it," he vowed.

"Good." Astaroth tapped his cane against his boot. "There's more than your reputation riding on this. There's a bet in leadership about you."

A chill raced down Ozroth's spine. "What sort of bet?"

"Whether or not you'll ever be a proper demon again." Astaroth eyed his fingernails as he delivered the damning news. "I bet on you succeeding in your next soul bargain, despite my reservations, so you need to succeed." *Or else* was unspoken.

Ozroth swallowed hard. The high council consisted of nine archdemons who were among the oldest and most experienced of their kind. If they were betting on his abilities, Ozroth would be in serious trouble if he failed—the kind of trouble that severed a head from a body, which was the only way to kill an immortal. "I'll deliver. I swear it."

"You will," Astaroth said, then disappeared.

Ozroth sagged, and the tips of his horns hit the gross bathroom wall. The lightning shock of pain was nothing compared to the horrible, sickly soul emotions that made him feel feverish and frozen all at once.

"Fuck."

◆ ◆ ◆

OZROTH STORMED THROUGH THE BAR. "WE'RE LEAVING," HE said as he approached the table.

"Huh?" Mariel's head popped up from where she'd pillowed it on her arms. She looked at him through bleary eyes. "Where are we going?"

A mostly empty third margarita sat in front of her. *Damn* the witch and pixie for getting her another drink when she was clearly going to be ill. Ozroth glared at Calladia. "Wasn't she drunk enough?"

The blond witch shot out of her seat, apparently eager for the fight. "It's a fucking girls' night," she said, cracking her knuckles. "If you weren't here, there wouldn't be a problem."

"If I weren't here, she'd still be too drunk to function."

"I can function," Mariel protested. "I'm just tired."

"And what are you tired from?" Calladia asked. "Is it the demon on your couch, making you so worried you can't sleep?"

Themmie gasped, then burst out of the booth, wings fluttering as she launched towards the ceiling. "A demon?" she screeched.

"Yeah, a demon." Calladia glared at Ozroth. "One of the worst ones, too."

"Excuse me?" How could this witch dismiss him and his species without knowing anything about them? *You used to like inspiring mortal fear*, his brain pointed out, but logic had taken a back seat.

Themmie flittered back down to the ground. "But if there's a demon on her couch," she slurred, "surely Oz can take care of that? He looks like he can fight."

Once again Ozroth and Calladia shared a look of disbelief at Themmie's ignorance, which quickly returned to a scowling competition.

"I'm tired," Mariel announced, standing abruptly and then bracing herself against the wall. "I want to go home."

"Finally," Ozroth muttered.

Calladia wrapped her arm around the drunk witch. "You're staying at mine," she said firmly. "And that's that."

"Wait," Ozroth said. "I—"

Calladia turned a venomous glare on him. "I don't give a shit what you want."

"But—"

"She's right," Themmie said, wings buzzing again. "Mariel is drunk and needs to sleep somewhere safe."

"You don't think I'm safe?" Ozroth asked, although he was very cognizant that he wasn't.

Themmie wrinkled her nose. "Uh, remember the demon on her couch? And besides, you're a dude. So no."

Ozroth had seen enough of human history to know that was unfortunately true. But still, he felt an uncomfortable urge to carry Mariel home, make her drink water, then tuck her into bed. The soul bargaining would start the next day, of course, more ruthless than before.

Astaroth's advice from a long time past sounded in his head. *Try to get the warlocks drunk. You won't believe the deals they'll make.*

Ozroth . . . couldn't do that. "Fine," he snarled. "Take her home with you. Do you have a spare couch?"

"No," Calladia said.

"I do!" Themmie chirped. "Though you'll be sharing it with three cats. And I have mace in my nightstand, just so you know. And a dagger."

"Appealing as that sounds," Ozroth said, "I think I'll be fine."

Calladia's upper lip lifted in a sneer. "I hope not."

◆   ◆   ◆

AN HOUR LATER, OZROTH LAY ON CALLADIA'S BACK LAWN, wrapped in blankets. The blankets were Mariel's idea—even drunk and in someone else's house, she'd felt the need to be a good hostess. And although Calladia had stared at Ozroth like she hoped he would die a horrible, painful death, she'd agreed.

That said, Ozroth could sense the wards around the house. Calladia had gone above and beyond bolstering her security. If he dared enter, he was pretty sure his testicles would explode.

This was one demon skill—sensing power and the general meaning of a spell. But the language of magic was complicated, and a huge portion of spellcraft was internal, tied to emotion and intent, so only witches and warlocks knew exactly how to create those spells.

Demonic bargaining magic was different. There was no verbal component, and the magic was so rare, no one entirely knew how it worked. If Ozroth had to describe it, he'd say it was like sorting through a thousand invisible threads, each connected to a possible future. With intent, he could choose which threads were followed: an early death for one person, a series of misfortunes for another. He could craft new threads, too, like when granting a mortal beauty or wealth. After centuries of practice, the process was fast and nearly thoughtless.

Mortal magic always required thought, and he could sense the anger in Calladia's wards. She was powerful. Not as powerful as Mariel, but enough that Ozroth spent a few moments contemplating if he could somehow bargain for her soul instead. Of course, that would mean interacting with the harpy again, so he discarded the idea.

He had to admit he was begrudgingly impressed with the tall, athletic witch. She had set herself as Mariel's protector, and not even his dark reputation was enough to make her budge.

Mariel clearly needed protection. From her mother, her own chaotic magic . . . and now Ozroth himself.

His chest ached at the thought.

Above, the stars shone like diamonds fixed to black velvet, so many of them that even an immortal like Ozroth would never be able to count them. There were no stars in the demon realm, just a dark sky, gray mist, and the drifting lights of human souls. His home was starkly beautiful, but there was something compelling about the vibrant, messy human world. Colors were brighter, scents were richer, and there was so much to look at that Ozroth often felt overwhelmed. He couldn't remember feeling this way the other times he'd visited the human plane. Another consequence of his new soul, then.

He shivered. The temperature had plummeted, and moisture beaded on the grass. He wondered if Mariel was warm in the cheerful yellow bungalow. He wondered if she was sleeping.

What are you tired from? Is it the demon on your couch, making you so worried you can't sleep?

He hated thinking that his presence in her home had cost Mariel sleep. Was he a figure from her nightmares?

Whatever witches thought about demons, they weren't monsters. Or if they were, Ozroth didn't understand what made a monster. Demons were part of a magical ecosystem, that was all. There was no torture, no eternal fire. Just an exchange—human magic and emotion for rare prizes only demon powers could provide.

The laws of summoning magic had apparently never accounted for a situation like this though. No one summoned a demon accidentally. And because the stakes were so high, there was no way out for either party. The demon provided the service. The human provided the soul.

Ozroth covered his eyes with his forearm, blotting out the stars. Ozroth might not think himself a monster, but Mariel certainly did.

What happened when the monster had no choice?

SEVEN

ARIEL WOKE WITH HER FACE MASHED INTO A FAMILIAR yellow pillow. She and Calladia had slept over at each other's houses countless times. They lived close enough that they could have walked home after a night out, but it was more fun to stay with each other.

She sat up and yawned, rubbing her eyes. Last night's drinking had left a slight headache, but nothing a batch of coffee and some breakfast wouldn't fix. Calladia had forced Mariel to eat and drink water last night, which had staved off the worst of the hangover.

For a moment, life felt the way it always had. Just Mariel and Calladia, having a sleepover for the umpteenth time since they'd been two odd kids in desperate need of friendship. Calladia would already be up—she always got up for her morning workout, no matter how drunk she'd gotten the night before—and once Mariel staggered out, they'd make breakfast together. A typical lazy Sunday morning.

Mariel's eyes drifted to the window, and she stiffened. Ozroth was pacing on the lawn outside, a tall, dark figure that reminded her of every bad thing that had happened in the last few days. His black cowboy hat was discarded on the grass, and his hands were jammed in his dark hair above his horns. He looked like he was muttering to himself.

Mariel started to feel ill again, and it wasn't the hangover. What was she supposed to do? She was bound so closely to a demon, he'd had to sleep on the ground to be near her. It was awful and suffocating, and she still felt guilty that he'd been uncomfortable.

There was a knock on the door, and Calladia burst in, carrying coffee and a plate full of bacon and eggs. "Good, you're up." Calladia looked disgustingly peppy in her pink exercise spandex with her damp hair in a bun. "I thought eleven a.m. was a bit much, even for you." She set the plate on the nightstand, then crossed her arms. "Eat some goddamn bacon, and then we are going to talk."

"Yes, ma'am," Mariel said, saluting. She dove in, shoveling eggs into her mouth before biting into Calladia's perfectly cooked bacon. "Mmm," she said, closing her eyes in bliss. "This is way better than what I feed you."

"Are you kidding me?" Calladia asked. "You feed me homemade cinnamon rolls. Those are a million times harder to make."

Mariel shrugged; her mouth was so full she couldn't respond. She washed the bacon down with coffee, wincing as it burned her mouth.

Calladia paced to the window, then looked out. Mariel knew what she would see: a moody demon wearing a track in her back lawn. "Do you think an exorcism would work?" Calladia asked.

Mariel almost choked on the bacon. "What, are you a Catholic priest now?"

"No, but I bet I'd be more effective."

Mariel set the rest of the bacon strip on the plate. "Oz told me the whole Christian concept of demons and Hell is bullshit."

"And you trust a demon?"

"You were an atheist, like, yesterday. You suddenly believe in eternal damnation?"

Calladia sighed. "No, I don't. Demons are just a different species who live in a different plane. But I don't like him. And I don't like what he wants from you."

"My soul." Mariel toyed with the piece of bacon. "He told me it's where my magic comes from."

"So he'd take your magic, too?" When Mariel nodded, Calladia let out an irritated growl. "There's got to be a way around this."

Mariel looked out the window again. Oz was leaning against a tree now, arms crossed. His eyes wandered over the house, then came to rest on her window and stayed there. "He isn't that bad," Mariel said, staring at Oz in return. "He's annoying more than anything." Annoying, weird . . . and hot.

"And overbearing," Calladia said. "And rude as hell."

Mariel rolled her eyes. "You were just as rude to him."

"Yeah, well, he wants my best friend's magic and soul. So sue me."

Mariel set the plate down on the nightstand, the porcelain clinking against wood. "It's my fault. If I wasn't such a terrible witch—"

"You aren't a terrible witch," Calladia interrupted. "You made a mistake. There's no reason it should have consequences this steep." She nibbled her lip. "I hate to say it, but—"

"No." Mariel already knew where Calladia was going.

"She has more experience—"

"Uh-uh." Mariel shook her head vehemently. "I'd rather lose

my soul than suffer through the humiliation of telling Mom. She'll shame me for decades if she finds out."

"We could tell my mom instead?"

"Who would immediately tell my mom, followed by the entire town." Cynthia Cunnington, like Diantha Spark, hated having her own family's dirty laundry aired, but she loved gossiping about her rivals and their children. She would be overjoyed to share a humiliating story about the Sparks.

Calladia winced. "Well . . . yeah."

Mariel cradled the coffee to her chest, soaking in the warmth. "There have to be other resources."

"Spell books, historical records, other witches?"

"I was thinking Google."

Calladia laughed. "Well, it can't hurt."

◆　◆　◆

MANY, MANY GOOGLE SEARCHES LATER, MARIEL WAS NO BET-ter informed about how to make a demon go away. She was, however, well versed in the sensitivity of demon horns, the impressive size of demon cock, and every way in which a witch could request a sexual encounter from the demon plane (a transaction that apparently didn't require a soul bargain, lucky bitches). Granted, the porn demons were clearly heavily made-up humans designed to look like the drawings in Mariel's magical creatures book, but surely even porn held a seed of truth?

"Is the internet almost entirely pornography?" Mariel asked after the umpteenth failed search.

Calladia snickered. "You didn't know that already?"

They were seated on rolling chairs in Calladia's home office. Ozroth was still pacing outside, although he took frequent breaks from brooding to glare at the window.

"I am very familiar with porn," Mariel said, offended at the implication that she was a wide-eyed innocent. "I just don't understand why we haven't found any legitimate facts about demons."

Part of her wondered about the impressive demon cock though. Was that legit? Or was it the stuff of myth, like the backward-jointed knees? She hadn't really paid attention to Ozroth's crotch—okay, not *that* much attention (surely a few surreptitious, guilty glances didn't count)—but he did seem to have an impressive bulge.

"I hate to break it to you," Calladia said, "but you should probably go to the library."

Mariel grimaced. The Glimmer Falls Library was an incredible resource, but the head librarian was one of her mother's friends. Which meant any book Mariel checked out would be reported on. "Can't you do it for me?" she asked, widening her eyes beseechingly.

Calladia crossed her arms. "Girl, I love you, but it's your soul. If you can't risk being uncomfortable for that, you might as well give it to the demon."

Mariel sighed, shoulders slumping. "You're right. I'll go home and freshen up, then hit the stacks." If she showed up at the library in wrinkled, day-old clothes, her mother would never let her hear the end of it.

Calladia gave her a hug. "We'll find a way out of this. I promise."

Mariel blinked hard to stop the tears that wanted to form. "I hope so."

"And if not . . ." Calladia shrugged. "I have a chain saw, a shovel, and a big backyard."

Mariel slapped her friend's arm. "No murder!"

"I make no promises," Calladia muttered, glaring out the window.

When Mariel exited the house, Ozroth straightened from his

position against the tree. "About time," he said acidly. He was a mess—shirt wrinkled, hair mussed, and eyes shadowed with exhaustion.

"Sorry," Mariel said, feeling guilty for leaving him outside. Then she imagined what Calladia would say and straightened her shoulders. Why should she feel guilty? It wasn't like she'd had a choice. "You know what? No, I'm not sorry." She marched over to him, then poked a finger into his chest. His pectoral was deliciously firm under her finger. "You picked a fight with my friend last night, you're rude and overbearing, and you're acting like it's my fault you had to sleep on the grass."

He narrowed his eyes. "It was your fault."

"Because you're stuck with me?" She shook her head. "If you hadn't been such a dick to Calladia, maybe she'd have let you sleep inside."

He scoffed. "Doubtful."

Yes, it was doubtful, but Mariel was tired of him acting like a sullen child. "Look, we're in this together. Instead of being a massive grump, you could actually work with me to try to find a loophole that lets us out of this deal."

"There are no loopholes."

"How do you know?"

He looked at her disbelievingly. "Because there's no record of one in all of demon history?"

"Yeah, and you hadn't heard of an accidental summoning either, had you?"

His mouth opened and closed. "No," he finally said.

Mariel felt a surge of triumph. She'd finally gotten one over on the demon. "Then stop being so smug and condescending and help me," she said, heading for the street. "And by the way," she called over her shoulder, "you have grass in your hair."

Ozroth shook his head like a dog, making grass pieces fly

everywhere. Then he jogged to catch up with her, jamming his black hat back on his head.

They walked in silence for a few minutes. Mariel glanced his way on occasion, unable to resist her curiosity. He exuded heat, a warm glow against her skin that made her think of winter nights spent in front of the fireplace. His profile was strong, with a sharp jawline and a slightly overlarge nose.

"Are all demons hot?" she asked before she could think better of it. Her mouth worked like that sometimes—okay, more than sometimes—firing off thoughts before her mind caught up. Her cheeks immediately grew warm, but there was nothing to do but brazen it out.

Ozroth looked at her askance. "Like . . . our body temperature?"

". . . Sure." Let him interpret it that way. He didn't need to know Mariel had a thing for big noses.

"Our core temperature is hotter than humans', yes."

At least they'd veered away from Mariel's inappropriate expression of sexual attraction, but his answer brought up more questions. "Do you still get fevers when you're sick? Do demons even get sick?" She imagined Ozroth spotted with chicken pox or sneezing into a handkerchief—a black one, of course, to match his dismal aesthetic.

"Your mind," he muttered.

Mariel wrinkled her nose. "What about it?"

"You hop from topic to topic so fast it's hard to keep up."

"Calladia says that, too," Mariel admitted. "She says 'Squirrel!' whenever I go on a tangent."

"Squirrel?"

"Haven't seen the movie *Up*, have you?" At his disbelieving look, she rolled her eyes. "That's a no, then."

"The majority of human entertainment is puerile and vapid, serving no purpose but to distract humans from their brief lives."

"Wow." She snorted at his prissy tone, then used her hand to mimic a phone call. "Nine-one-one, I'd like to report a theft. Debbie Downer wants her shtick back."

Ozroth squinted at her. ". . . What?"

"Never mind."

Mariel was feeling more chipper from teasing the demon. *Teasing the Demon*—that sounded like one of the pornos her Googling had produced. She had a vision of Ozroth tied up and scowling in her bed, which was . . . um.

Mariel forced her mind away from that dangerous path and focused on the scenery. Many of the residential streets in Glimmer Falls were paved in red brick, including this one. Tree branches intertwined in an arch overhead, and Mariel smiled when a yellow leaf fluttered down to rest on her shoulder. The fire of autumn was everywhere, and soon the branches would be bare, twigs laced together like delicate filigree. All part of nature's steady cycle.

Mariel liked the predictable chaos of the natural world. Glimmer Falls's ecosystem was complex, but some things could always be relied on. The leaves changed, the air grew crisp, and for the few weeks of the Autumn Festival, the whole town would smell like pumpkins and spice while magic lit up every street corner.

They crossed the south end of Main Street. The heart of downtown was a fifteen-minute walk north: City Hall, countless coffee shops, eateries, and stores . . . and the Glimmer Falls Library, where she had an upcoming date with some demonic research.

"Are there libraries in the demon plane?" Mariel asked.

"Of course," Ozroth said. "Why?"

"Maybe there are books that might help our situation." If anyone had the key to escaping an accidental summoning, it would be a demon historian. She imagined a vast, dramatic library full of flickering torches and arcane tomes bound in questionably sourced leather. Then again, torches probably weren't the best choice with so much paper. Maybe the library was lit by soul-generated electricity. "Soul-er power," she muttered under her breath, then giggled at her own joke.

Ozroth eyed her askance. "I trained for decades before my first soul bargain. I've read every book there is on the topic."

That seemed unlikely. Sure, he was apparently centuries old, but there were a *lot* of books in the universe. "Even the ones written by humans?"

He scoffed. "You saw that drawing in your encyclopedia. Do you really think human books are a reliable resource when it comes to demons?"

"So you're a snob. Great to have that confirmed again."

Ozroth looked so put out that Mariel couldn't help but grin. He was so easy to rattle. If she had to be tied to him 24/7, she might as well get some fun out of it.

They turned onto her street, and Mariel froze. "Oh, no." The red convertible parked outside her house was as familiar as the sinking sensation in her stomach.

"What is it?"

"My mother's here." And so, she realized, were a lot of other people. Her front lawn was full of witches, warlocks, and a few ordinary humans eating, drinking, and chatting. Apparently Diantha Spark had decided to host a party, though why it had to be on Mariel's front lawn, she had no idea.

Her great-great-great-great-times-a-lot-grandfather, Alzapraz, hovered awkwardly near the edge of the party, eating cheese off a toothpick and looking like he'd rather be anywhere else. His attire was always dramatically odd, and today was no different: he wore red velvet robes and bunny ears. His white beard hung to his waist, and his beady black eyes were barely visible beneath bristling white eyebrows.

Most spellcasters were generalists, but Alzapraz was the rare warlock who had perfected one element of sorcery: extending his life span. Unfortunately, he hadn't learned how to extend his physical health to match it, and he looked as ancient as he was, with a stooped back, age-spotted skin, and more wrinkles than a pug. He'd been complaining about his aching joints for centuries.

The old warlock noticed Mariel and hobbled over. "You still have functional joints," he said in a creaky voice. "Why aren't you running?"

Mariel wasn't the only one who dreaded Spark family events. She leaned over to give the ancient warlock a hug, careful not to squeeze too hard. "How'd Mom loop you into showing up for . . . whatever this is?"

She liked Alzapraz, crankiness and all. He looked harmless, but she'd heard stories about his wild early centuries, full of criminal mischief and bacchanalian excesses.

Alzapraz scowled. "She said you were ready for your lesson in the language of magic."

Mariel pinched her brow. While better than her mother, Alzapraz was also baffled about her inability to turn Spark genes into successful spellcraft, so she generally avoided seeking his help. GhoulTube online tutorials weren't doing enough to further her memorization of the language of magic though, and she'd had a weak moment after blowing up her last iPhone at family dinner. "Maybe another time."

The last thing she wanted was to discuss magic with any of her family members, but if her mother was here, there would be no avoiding it. Her stomach felt hollow at the thought. That prophecy was always hanging over her head like an anvil, ready to squash her cartoonishly flat.

Alzapraz looked Ozroth up and down. The wrinkles on his forehead deepened. "Huh."

A whistle split the air. "Yoo-hoo, darling!" Diantha called from the front yard, waving excitedly. "Come here!"

There would be no escaping now. "Shit." Mariel forced herself into motion, dread curdling in her gut.

Diantha met them on the sidewalk. She was dressed in a lilac pantsuit and red stilettos, and she was holding a glass of champagne. "Mariel, dear, where have you been? I thought you would miss your own party."

"Why am I having a party?" Mariel asked with what she considered remarkable calmness, given the situation. All she wanted to do was shower and change, then go to the library. Now she'd be stuck entertaining her mother's friends while facing unwelcome questions about her training.

Diantha laughed, then pinched Mariel's cheek. "To celebrate your new relationship, silly. I thought the day would never come!"

"Oh, no," Ozroth said, looking at the gathering with an expression of growing alarm.

"Everyone!" Diantha tapped one long nail against her champagne glass. Conversation dwindled as the assembled guests looked over. "I'd love to introduce . . ." She trailed off, then looked at Ozroth, apparently realizing she'd never asked his name.

"Oz," Mariel said.

"Oz!" Diantha raised her glass in a toast. "Mariel's new boyfriend!"

EIGHT

Faced with upwards of forty mortals staring at him like a zoo animal, Ozroth chastised himself for his life choices. The fake relationship hadn't seemed like a big deal at first—sure, let Mariel's annoying mother and her annoying friend Themmie think they were dating—but it had escalated into something completely out of control.

"To Oz!" Diantha cried, raising her glass high.

The party cheered. Mariel looked like she wanted to sink into the ground and disappear—a sentiment he identified with strongly.

Mariel's grassy front yard had been transformed. The guests stood around round tables with silver tablecloths, and waiters moved through the crowd bearing trays of champagne and hors d'oeuvres. In front of the living room window, a table with a chocolate fountain had been set up. Illusions of birds and butterflies flitted overhead, leaving trails of glittering magic behind. Mariel grabbed a champagne glass and downed half of it in one swallow as the guests descended on them.

"Congratulations!" a rotund man with a florid face said, slapping Ozroth's shoulder. "It isn't every man who gets to date a Spark."

Ozroth grunted in response.

"How did you two meet?" a witch asked, and Ozroth's brain stalled out. Lucifer, how was he supposed to answer?

"Bumbelina," Mariel said, thinking faster than him. "A lucky swipe."

Ozroth had no idea what she was talking about. "Bumbelina?" he asked under his breath once the witch had moved away, but there was no time for her to answer before someone else was greeting them. He met a councilwoman, a policeman, members of Diantha's magical dueling club, and more, until the faces and names blurred together. The way the guests fawned over Diantha while complimenting Ozroth and Mariel made him grimace. Clearly Diantha was an influential figure in Glimmer Falls, though why so many people found her charming escaped him.

Diantha drifted away eventually, thankfully, and most of the crowd moved with her like those little fish that attached themselves to sharks. Mariel blew out a breath. "Wow. My mother has really outdone herself this time."

"Is this sort of occurrence common?" Ozroth asked.

Mariel drained her glass, then set it down. "Anything dramatic is a common occurrence around her, especially if it's something I find personally mortifying."

He scowled at where Diantha had joined a group of well-dressed women. "She ought to consider your feelings."

Mariel laughed loudly. "Diantha Spark considering any feelings but her own? What a joke."

Now would be an ideal time to dig into her insecurities and make her more vulnerable, but Ozroth didn't like the bitterness in Mariel's eyes.

He could imagine Astaroth's mocking voice in his head. *Going soft?*

He wasn't soft. He was just biding his time.

"Oh, no." Mariel gripped his forearm. "My mother is bringing Cynthia Cunnington over."

He looked at where her small fingers pressed into his skin. It was hard to think when she was touching him. "Cunnington?"

"Calladia's mother. She's like the ice queen version of my mom."

Ozroth grimaced. "I don't think I can handle two of your mother."

"Then brace yourself."

Ozroth planted his boots in the grass like a soldier facing an oncoming foe. When Mariel grabbed a second glass of champagne from the passing waiter, he took a glass, too. Mariel raised her eyebrows, and he lifted his glass in response. "When on Earth," he muttered before taking a sip. The liquid burst in his mouth, a cacophony of tart sweetness that threatened to overwhelm his taste buds. He was keyed up, every sense on edge as the colors, sounds, and tastes of the mortal world enveloped him.

"Here we are!" Diantha strode towards them, wobbling as her heels punched holes in the grass. She was arm in arm with a tall, middle-aged woman in a blue pantsuit. The other woman's blond hair was pulled back in a chignon, and the pearls at her neck and ears were the perfect accessory for her haughty expression. "This is Oz, Mariel's boyfriend," Diantha said. "Remind me, Cynthia dear, is Calladia seeing anyone?"

"Not at the moment," Cynthia said in a throaty voice, arching a perfect eyebrow. "She's too busy mastering spellcraft."

Diantha let out a brittle laugh. "Well, I hope she doesn't drag her heels too much. I know she's always been . . . opinionated . . . but youth and beauty are fleeting."

Cynthia looked Diantha up and down. "So they are." She smirked, then raised her hand in front of Ozroth, flashing a diamond big enough to take out someone's eye. "Cynthia Cunnington, mayor of Glimmer Falls."

"Only because I didn't run for office," Diantha muttered.

He could see the resemblance to Calladia in Cynthia's height, buttery blond hair, and oval face, but that was about it. Her eyes were blue and cold, unlike Calladia's warm brown, and he couldn't envision this woman lifting weights or trying to start a bar brawl with a demon.

It was clear she expected him to kiss the back of her hand, but Ozroth didn't feel like getting that close. Instead, he gripped the tips of her fingers and shook, dropping her hand immediately.

Cynthia looked taken aback, but she recovered quickly. "So, how in the world did our little Mariel capture your heart?"

Her tone of polite disbelief raised Ozroth's hackles. He looked at Mariel with an expression meant to convey *What is wrong with these people?* She shrugged and gave a tiny smile. He forced his attention back to Cynthia. "We met on Bum . . ." Shit, what was the name of whatever thing Mariel had been talking about earlier?

"Bumbelina," she thankfully interjected.

"Yes, Bumbelina." He nodded. "A lucky swipe." Whatever the fuck that meant.

"Is that one of those dating apps?" Cynthia asked with clear distaste. "In my day, we met people in person before agreeing to date."

"Your day was quite some time ago, darling," Diantha said with sweet venom. "I'm glad Mariel's using every tool at her disposal to find love."

Mariel made a choking sound. "It's, ah, a little soon to toss that word around, Mom."

Oz could think of plenty of words that encapsulated how

Mariel felt about him. *Disdain* topped the list, followed closely by *annoyance*. Since demons were normally feared and disliked, that shouldn't have bothered him as much as it did.

Diantha's brow furrowed. "Why? Your father and I knew we were in love the first time we had sex and every object in the room levitated. That was three hours after meeting each other at the National Spellcaster Competition. I'd just won the trophy, and—"

"Yes, we are all very familiar with this story," Cynthia interjected. "Though some might argue it's tacky to reveal the details of one's sex life in public."

"Spoken like someone without a sex life." Diantha fluffed her curly hair, smiling at Cynthia. "How is dear old Bertrand these days? He's getting up there, but I hear there's a very nice doctor in town who specializes in all kinds of age-related . . . issues."

Cynthia's smile was sharp. "Sometimes I wonder how the two of us became such good friends, Diantha."

"Oh, darling," Diantha said, looping her arm through Cynthia's. "This is what best friends do! We tease because we care."

Ozroth shared a skeptical glance with Mariel. If these two were best friends, he was an air sprite. She rolled her eyes and shook her head.

He took another sip of champagne, nearly wincing at the intense flavor. It was one of those moments when everything seemed too bright and sharp—the drink in his mouth, the sun on his skin, the chatter of these obnoxious mortals. How did they stand being overwhelmed by sensation all the time? Nervous sweat rolled down his spine, and he shifted uncomfortably.

"So," Cynthia said. "What do you do, Oz?"

He froze with the glass halfway to his lips. "Pardon?"

"What's your job?"

Shit. His mind whirred as he tried to think of something plausible but not easy to verify. Sure, he could have told them he was a demon who collected souls for a living, but Mariel's wide eyes were begging him not to, and he wanted to preserve whatever ground he'd gained with her. Disdain was an improvement on hate, after all. "I . . ." He cleared his throat, wishing the buzzing in his head would fade so he could return to his cold, sharp self. "I'm . . ."

"A historian!" Mariel chirped. Her hand wound around his arm, her fingers pressing into his bicep. Oddly, it made Ozroth feel more stable in the midst of all the noise and color. "Oz is very intelligent."

"A historian." Cynthia's eyes dipped to his chest. "I can't recall ever seeing a historian so . . . physically fit."

The look was too polite to be a leer, but Ozroth still felt uncomfortable. "I work out sometimes."

He worked out more than *sometimes*, truth be told. Life grew dull between bargains, and now that his soul kept pushing unwanted feelings on him, he'd been exercising to drown them out.

"Are you a professor?" Cynthia asked. The two older witches were eyeing him like lionesses sizing up a gazelle, and he could tell that title would give him prestige in their eyes. He'd known many mortals like this: rich, privileged, and highly educated, who saw those traits as what separated the elite from the rabble. They reminded him of a famous witch actress he'd made a deal with, taking her soul in exchange for her daughter's admission into a top ten university.

"Yes," he said. "On sabbatical."

"Where do you teach?" Diantha's eyes shone with excitement. "Mariel's always wanted a bit of scholarly discipline." She licked her lips, eyeing him up and down. "And you look like you'd be excellent at discipline."

He choked on his mouthful of champagne.

"He teaches in New Zealand," Mariel said, ignoring the innuendo somehow. Years of practice, he supposed. "At the College of Antipodean Witchery."

Ozroth suppressed a snort. Where had she pulled that from?

"Oh?" Cynthia's eyebrows rose. "I've never heard of that institution. It must not be very prestigious."

"On the contrary," Ozroth said. "It's so prestigious, its existence is kept largely secret. Our selection process is rigorous, and students have to be invited to apply."

The lies were flowing more easily now that he'd found his footing. He glanced over at Mariel, who was clearly struggling not to smile. A dimple peeked in and out on her cheek, and he had the oddest impulse to put his lips to it, as if he could taste her joy.

He mentally slapped himself. Why was he indulging those sorts of thoughts about the target of his soul bargain? This could only end one way, and when it did, all the humor and fire he found attractive about Mariel would be gone.

The thought made him queasy.

Diantha was talking again, and he snapped back to the conversation. "—can't be that exclusive. How could you not have selected me? Or Mariel? Or any of our ancestors? The Sparks are the premier magical dynasty. We can trace our roots back to Stonehenge!"

"Pretty sure that's not how genealogy works," Mariel muttered under her breath.

"Or the Cunningtons," Cynthia said, looking equally affronted. "Also the premier magical dynasty."

"Pretty sure that's not how the word *premier* works," Ozroth whispered to Mariel. She giggled, then clapped a hand over her mouth. He felt a surge of pleasure at the response, like his chest had swelled to two times its size.

"At least Alzapraz should have heard of it." Diantha waved her hand. "Come here, Alzapraz dear!"

At the edge of the lawn, the tiny, ancient-looking warlock visibly recoiled. He started to scurry towards the sidewalk, but he could only move so fast, and Diantha soon caught him and dragged him back. She deposited the warlock in front of Ozroth. "Alzapraz is my great-great-great-great-great-great—"

"Please stop," Alzapraz said.

"—pain in my ass," Diantha finished. The two glared at each other. "Anyway, he's been around the block and then some, though probably not in the euphemistic sense, given . . . all that." She gestured at the warlock's long beard, velvet robes, and hunched back. "But he would surely know about the College of Antipodean Witchery."

"The what?" Alzapraz cupped a hand to his ear.

"The College of Antipodean Witchery," Diantha repeated loudly. "Apparently one of the most elite magic schools in the world, which Oz teaches at. Frankly, I have my doubts. How could any prestigious school omit the Sparks?"

Alzapraz looked at Ozroth, then Diantha, then Ozroth again. His eyes narrowed under those caterpillar brows before he turned back to Diantha. "Yes," he said in a quavering voice. "I've heard of that school. Got an invitation myself back in the day. But, you know, the time zones, especially when we had to travel by Viking longship . . ."

Mariel coughed into her fist.

Diantha looked taken aback. "But if you were invited, why wasn't I?"

Alzapraz shrugged. "If you have to ask, you already know the answer."

Mariel's cheeks were pink, and now there were two of those captivating dimples. When she looked up at Ozroth, her eyes were filled with hilarity.

Her smile was doing something funny to his insides. He felt

warm, and the corners of his lips kept wanting to turn up to match her expression. It was like he was on a seesaw, his new and unstable emotions wobbling between guilt, something that felt like swallowing sunshine, and the desire to lock himself in a dark, quiet place and never come out.

No wonder humans made such irrational deals. Their souls were kaleidoscopes of feelings and impulses, shifting at the slightest provocation.

"Mariel could still get an invitation." Diantha looked at Ozroth beseechingly. "She's just a late bloomer. Maybe it'll be exactly what she needs to fulfill her destiny."

"You keep talking about this destiny," Cynthia drawled. "Are you sure you didn't hallucinate it on a drug trip?"

Diantha gasped, looking outraged. "I will have you know I was very sober when the stars, earth, and wind delivered the prophecy. I was in my thirty-sixth hour of labor—bless you, Mariel, but you had a fat head—and the doctor was ready to cut me open when I begged the stars for a portent to get me through."

Mariel winced. "Do you have to tell this story? My birthday isn't for another seven months."

"She tells this story on your birthday?" Ozroth asked, appalled.

"Every year," Mariel said sadly.

Around them, people were listening in. Their expressions were a mix of fashionable boredom and fawning adulation—probably coinciding with who had the most social capital to gain.

"You only begged the stars because you were giving birth outside like a barn animal," Cynthia said.

Diantha sniffed. "I'll take an outdoor, natural birth to your C-section any day. I'm convinced the experience deepened the bond between Mariel and me."

Mariel's fingers twitched on Ozroth's bicep. "Nope," she muttered.

Diantha took a deep breath, and Ozroth felt a prickle of dread, sensing the arrival of a monologue. "I suppose I could have gone to the hospital," she said, "but I wanted Mariel's first moments to be connected to magic, and it's hard to access magic while machines are beeping and a doctor is elbow-deep in your vagina."

"Please stop talking about your vagina," Mariel said.

Diantha looked at her fondly. "Darling, I don't know how you turned out to be such a prude. We're all adults here, and at least half of us have vaginas. It's the same as talking about an elbow."

"Is it?" Cynthia asked skeptically.

Ozroth leaned down to whisper in Mariel's ear. "If you give me your soul, I'll make sure she never talks about her vagina ever again."

She rolled her eyes. "I was wondering when you'd get back to offering silly deals." Then she sighed. "That one's tempting though."

"It was a water birth under the open sky," Diantha said, ignoring her daughter's palpable distress. "I had three witch doulas at my side and a surgeon waiting nearby—at Roland's insistence . . . you know how he worries—and we'd cast a spell for success. The doulas surrounded the tub with a pentagram of candles, then bathed my vagina three times in lamb's blood. Then I ate the lamb's heart."

Ozroth grimaced. "It's not too late," he whispered to Mariel. "The offer still stands."

"Sorry, I can't hear you," she said. "I'm disassociating from my body."

"It was three a.m. when she finally started to crown." Diantha shook her head. "Mariel, dear, did you know I had to get ten stitches after? You just ripped me up. I didn't pee right for a decade."

"Yes," Mariel choked out. "You've told me multiple times exactly how I ruined your body."

"Well, I think it's only fair children should know how their mothers suffered for them." She blinked a few times, looking around. "Where did Alzapraz go? He knows not to leave when I'm in the middle of a story."

Ozroth hadn't noticed the diminutive warlock leaving either. Maybe he should find him and ask for tips on how to disappear. "I'm sure it was an emergency," he said, applying demon charm despite his personal discomfort. He had a feeling contradicting Diantha would only drag things out. "Your stories are so riveting."

"Oz is a diplomat." Cynthia signaled for the waiter, then took her time perusing the champagne. "Of course," she said, plucking a glass off the tray, "some people might prefer the term *liar*."

Diantha huffed. "Oh, please. Did you know I was the speech and debate champion in high school?"

"Yes," Cynthia and Mariel said in unison. They drank in unison, too.

"I just talked and talked, and my opponents could never get a word in." She beamed. "Anyway, on that fateful night, Mariel's head had started to emerge from between my bloody thighs. As agony ripped through me, I called on my magic and shouted to the stars. *Behold a new Spark!* I cried. *Give me a sign of her future.* And wouldn't you know, the sky lit up with a cascade of falling stars, the wind swirled in a mighty gust, and the earth itself trembled. And one word rang in my head: *Power.*"

There were a few moments of silence, and then the more obsequious-looking guests started applauding. "Incredible," one witch said. "The stars themselves!"

Ozroth contemplated the story. It could be bullshit, but Diantha had the conviction of a fanatic about Mariel's destiny, and that had to have come from somewhere. He'd heard of other witches and warlocks being born to mystical portents, so why not Mariel?

"Then she popped right out," Diantha said, shattering the moment. "Ripped me from stem to stern. You should have seen the fat, bloody little thing! Wailing her head off like she wanted to crawl right back inside." She beamed. "She's always been a mama's girl."

Mariel was staring into her glass of champagne as if it held answers to the mysteries of the universe. "I'm not here," she whispered. "This is a terrible dream, and I will wake up at any moment."

He grabbed her free hand, squeezing it in his. Her head jerked up, and she looked at him with surprise. "Darling," he said, "didn't you promise to show me your garden?"

Her forehead wrinkled, and then her eyes widened with realization. "Oh, yes! Thank you for remembering, sweetheart." Her hand tightened on his as she looked at Diantha. "Oz is very interested in my fire lilies. I really think I stand a chance at Best in Show at the Pacific Northwest Floral Championships this year."

"You and your plants." Diantha looked at their intertwined hands, and her expression softened. "All right, lovebirds. Go frolic in the garden." They were halfway to the house when Diantha called after them, "And don't use protection!"

When the door closed behind them, Mariel sank to the floor. She wrapped her arms around her bent legs, then buried her face in her knees. "I'm mortified. Every time I think she can't humiliate me more, she somehow tops her previous efforts."

Ozroth lowered himself to the floor next to her. It was blessedly quiet and cool in the house, and his muscles relaxed knowing the party was locked safely outside. "Why do you let her?"

Her head popped up, and she glared at him. "What, like I should just smile at her stories and pretend they don't humiliate me?"

"No," he said. "Why don't you tell her to stop?"

Mariel groaned. "I have. It never works."

There was a simple solution to that. "Then stop seeing her."

"She's my mother," Mariel said. "I can't just ignore her."

"Why not, if she makes you miserable?"

Mariel tipped her head back against the door. "Maybe demons don't understand families."

He scoffed. "You think I emerged fully formed from some fiery abyss? Of course demons have families."

"Really?" she asked, perking up. "What's yours like?"

Fuck. Ozroth really shouldn't have brought that up—he knew Mariel's fondness for questions. He stared down her entry hall, eyeing the rainbow-hued carpet runner and the framed paintings of flowers on her wall. How could he explain his upbringing to someone so young and full of optimism? "I don't have a family anymore," he finally said.

"Oh, I'm so sorry." She rested a hand on his arm, and he shivered at the contact. "You're an orphan?"

He shook his head. "No, I have a mother out there somewhere. I just don't know if I would recognize her, or if she would recognize me."

There was a long pause. He stared straight ahead, though his peripheral vision told him Mariel was studying him closely. "You can't leave it at that," she said. "Come on, you've gotten a peek at my fucked-up family dynamics."

He shifted uncomfortably. "Our survival as a species depends on souls, so being a bargainer is a prestigious position. Only a few demons can do it—you need innate magical talent to make impossible things happen. Finding demon children capable of that is a big deal."

"There are children who take souls?"

He'd never questioned the practice, but her horrified expression made him realize other people might feel differently about it. "They don't take souls as children," he explained, needing her to understand the enormous responsibility of what he did, "but they have to be trained. The magic is nuanced. And it takes a certain type of demon to make bargains without flinching. You have to stay calm and cold."

Be ice, Astaroth had told him more than once. *That way nothing can touch you.*

"So your family trained you?"

"My father was a bargainer," Ozroth said, coming to the answer the roundabout way. "A very successful one. My only memories of him are of him telling me the importance of what he did." Truthfully, there was little to glean from those scraps. No voice left to associate with Ozroth's father, no face, nothing but a blurry impression of meaning. "He died in 1793, when I was very young."

"That's awful," Mariel said, looking distressed. "I thought demons were immortal."

"Beheading will kill one," Ozroth said. "He hadn't been to the human plane in a few years, and he'd heard there was some unrest, so he took a vacation to France to catch up on anything he'd missed."

"In 1793?" Mariel winced. "Bad timing."

"Indeed. Especially since his strategy with mortals involved looking rich and sophisticated." That vacation had been cut very short, so to speak. "It was a humiliating way for a demon to die."

"I'm so sorry for your loss." Mariel's fingertips brushed his arm again. "I don't see why it's humiliating though."

He laughed humorlessly. "You spend centuries as a hero to your people, only to have your head lopped off by mortals because you chose the wrong tourist destination? If my father had died collecting souls, at least there would have been some honor in it."

That was something Astaroth regularly reminded him of. Ozroth had the weight of his father's legacy on his shoulders . . . but he also had his father's shame to overcome.

"I don't like that way of thinking," Mariel said, full lips turning down.

"You'd be a terrible demon, then," Ozroth said. "Honor is one of our most important values." Bargainers held the burden of their species' survival on their shoulders. To falter from that duty was to earn shame.

She snorted. "Oh, I know I'd be a terrible demon." She waited a few moments, then nudged him. "What happened with your mother?"

"The high council already had their eyes on me because of my father," Ozroth said. His throat felt closed off, like his body didn't want the words to escape. This had never been a comfortable memory, even before the soul had shattered his control. Now he couldn't help but dwell on the small slices of that old life he could remember. His mother's mahogany-colored horns and black hair. The warmth of his bed before a raging fire. The feeling that he *belonged* somewhere. "Bargainers have to be trained from a young age, and it seemed like a good time to send me away, since the family was experiencing a transition anyway."

"She sent you away?" Mariel sounded appalled. "How old were you?"

"Six." Honestly, he didn't know if his mother had sent him away gladly or out of a sense of duty. One day, he'd been crying in their warm, underground family den, missing his father, and the next, he'd been brought to a cold stone castle far outside of town. There had been no soft pillows in his new bedroom, no roaring fires, and after that first day, Ozroth had been taught never to cry again. "I was lucky. The demon who trained me was one of the high council, the nine most powerful demons. Astaroth raised me, taught me how to be a man."

She shivered. "I feel like I've heard that name."

"You probably have." Astaroth had been famous for centuries before Ozroth had been born. "He taught me how to manifest wishes, even the most impossible ones. He taught me about negotiation and manipulation. I am the demon I am today because of him."

And Astaroth had placed a bet on Ozroth's success. The thought sent his mood plummeting further. Hadn't he promised he'd be more ruthless today? But he was tired and overwhelmed by the constant stimulation of the human plane, and he wouldn't be capable of striking a hard bargain. *Soon*, he promised himself. As soon as he'd wrangled his capricious soul into submission.

Mariel shifted, crossing her legs under her. Her sundress pooled in her lap, and Ozroth was distracted by the improved view of her creamy thighs. "That sounds like a difficult childhood," she said.

He jerked his gaze away from her legs. "Demon society is different from human society. It was a duty and an honor."

"And your mother?" she asked softly.

"I don't know." He swallowed past the thickness in his throat. "I never saw her again."

Silence fell, broken only by the ticking of the clock on her wall. It had a whimsical face: half sun, half moon, with both sides smiling as the hands spun endlessly, counting down the time that humans had so little of and Ozroth had too much of. Next to the clock was a curio cabinet filled with odd figurines and delicate vases, none of which looked like they served any practical purpose.

Mariel's life was bursting with *things*. In his own den on the demon plane, he had little but books and workout equipment. Looking at Mariel's chaotic clutter, he wondered for the first time what items he might decorate his home with. What did he care about enough to surround himself with every day?

In over two hundred years, he'd accumulated less than this human had in twenty-eight. There was something hollow about the thought.

"That's a sad story," Mariel said. When he looked at her, her eyes were brimming with compassion. "You never got to have a family. Never got to be a kid."

"I can't miss what I don't know," he said. "And I got more than many others could dream of. Prestige, honor, a purpose . . . I can take pride in helping my people."

Her fingers interlaced with his, and he looked down in surprise. A day ago she'd hated him, and now she was holding his hand.

She probably still hated him. She was a good person; this was what good people did. They offered comfort even to their enemies. His pride demanded he reject her pity, but Ozroth couldn't seem to let go of her hand.

"Do you want to get out of here?" Her thumb rubbed over his knuckles. "I can show you the forest. Though I want a shower first."

It was an odd non sequitur, but the idea of being outside was appealing. His chest was too tight, and the murmur of voices beyond the front door was an itch in his brain. Allowing himself to get closer to Mariel was a double-edged sword—he might learn what she wanted more than her magic, but he also risked growing too attached to her. It was a risk he'd never had to consider before.

One more day couldn't hurt though. Right?

He nodded. "I'd like that."

NINE

MARIEL FELT BETTER ONCE SHE'D SHOWERED AND changed. That was the key to life as the failed Spark: the ability to shake things off. Her mother would never stop saying embarrassing things, and the seed of anxiety planted in Mariel's breast had been there forever, so she knew how to live around it.

Someday soon Mariel would figure out her magic and earn her mother's financial support for her SoD. Given the residual churn of her stomach, that day wouldn't be today. And besides, she'd rather focus on showing Oz the woods.

The air had a nip to it, so she wore an unzipped hoodie over her dress and thick wool socks under her hiking boots. She led Oz into the backyard, taking a moment to whisper to her plants. Then they hopped the fence, sneaking down her neighbor's side yard to get to the next street.

"Will your mother come looking for you?" Oz asked.

Mariel made a face. "Not when she has networking to do on my front lawn." She sighed. "The poor grass. I'll have to magic it better after they leave." At least her mother's high heels were a free aeration service, she supposed, and the grass was browning with autumn anyway.

He grunted in response. Mariel studied him as they walked, adding to the picture of him in her head. He looked big and dangerous, with his tattooed bicep and perpetual scowl, although the Wild West hat took away a little of his deadly glamour. The wrinkled shirt and grass-stained jeans didn't help either. "We'll get you some more clothes later today," she said. "Shoot, I should have offered you a shower, too. And a toothbrush. Do demons brush their teeth?"

"No, we prefer to let the blood and saliva drip from our fangs." When she shot a disbelieving look at him, he snorted. "Yes, we brush our teeth."

His sly humor was something she hadn't expected when he'd manifested in her kitchen. Oz was a cynic, but a funny one. A damaged one, too.

She couldn't believe the story he'd told her. Losing his father at a young age, then being ripped away from his mother to study the art of stealing souls . . . *You have to stay calm and cold*, he'd told her. Had Astaroth really taught that lesson to a six-year-old? With a nickname like Ozroth the Ruthless, she had a feeling he'd been taught that and worse over the years.

The odd thing was, he didn't seem calm and cold with her. He cracked jokes, and he hadn't made a real effort to force a bargain out of her after their first hours together. Rather than being ruthless, he seemed perplexed. It was clear he didn't know what to do in this situation either.

"You're staring," he said.

"Yeah," she admitted. Hard to deny that one.

"Why are you staring?"

"Why aren't you?" When he cast her a baffled look, she decided to tease him. "Don't you like my dress?" She spun, making the blue, daisy-spotted fabric flare around her. It was one of her cuter dresses, with a sweetheart neckline that showed just enough cleavage to make it inappropriate for work.

His eyes flicked up and down her body, fixating a moment too long on her cleavage. Then he turned his head away and cleared his throat. "It's a nice dress. I like those . . . flower things."

"Daisies. I grow a rare purple varietal in my greenhouse."

"Hmm," he said in response.

They were heading towards the edge of her neighborhood, which backed onto the slope leading up to Glimmer Falls's legendary hot springs. This lane terminated in a line of trees, where a dirt path would lead them deeper into the woods. She couldn't wait to get Oz out of town and into nature. This was where she went when she was upset, and while she could definitely use some comforting, she hoped the magic of nature would soothe him, too.

Why she wanted to soothe her unwanted demonic guest was a question she'd revisit another time.

The moment they passed under the autumn-bright forest canopy, Mariel breathed a sigh of relief. The air was crisper here, humming with magic. The trees bent towards her in greeting, and a climbing vine slipped loose to wind its way into her wet hair. She laughed as she extricated it from her curls. "You'll get tangled up in there, and then we'll be stuck here forever."

Oz was looking at her oddly. "You really think they're acting of their own free will."

She bristled at the implication that she was forcing them to do anything. "They like me," she said defensively.

"Hmm," he said again, turning to keep walking up the path.

Deciding to show him what happened when she did make a plant do something, she whispered, *"Ascensren ta worta"* under her breath. The language of magic was much easier to remember when plants were involved.

A root lifted out of the soil in front of Ozroth. He tripped, catching himself from falling by planting a hand on a tree trunk. He glared over his shoulder. "Was that necessary?"

"I don't know what you're talking about." She bit her cheek to stop from laughing as she caught up to him.

The forest contained a mix of evergreen and deciduous trees, including western hemlock, ponderosa pine, red alder, Douglas fir, big-leaf maples, and more. Rare flowers, ferns, and climbing vines wove between the trees, fed by the minerals of the hot springs and the magic laced through the earth.

Mariel loved the life in plants, but she could appreciate the beauty of the dying season. Like the phoenix, these plants would resurrect in the spring. The crunch of orange and yellow leaves underfoot, the chill in the air, and the rich scent of decay mixed into a beautiful autumn concoction, and Mariel sighed with happiness.

She ducked under a low branch, leaving the path and leading Oz into the underbrush. This deer path was so well hidden that no one but Mariel (and the deer and a few perytons) ever seemed to use it. It led to one of her favorite spots in the forest.

Oz shoved his way through the bushes clumsily, then cursed and batted at a vine that snagged his hat. "Stop that," he said, snatching the hat back.

"That one wasn't me." Plants always took on a life of their own around her. "Be nice to the plants, and they'll be nice to you."

He grumbled, then took his hat off and tucked it under his arm. Mariel eyed his horns, wondering what their purpose was. They looked pretty in the dappled sunlight, all glossy black and smooth. "Why do you have horns?" she asked.

"Why do you have so many questions?" he shot back. He lifted a hand, brushing a horn with his fingertip. "There's a nightbeast on the demon plane that attacks from behind. It's our only natural predator, so we developed horns as an adaptation. If it takes you down, you slam your head back and stab it. There's a protein in the outer coating that's toxic to them, so it drives them off."

"Oh." Mariel gently brushed aside a branch, asking it to please not snap back and hit Oz in the face. She only used the language of magic sometimes when dealing with plants—most of the time, a polite request or a spark of magic from her fingers would do the trick. The branch reluctantly obeyed, allowing the demon to pass. "I wasn't expecting such a scientific answer."

"What, you think demons live in the Middle Ages?" When he blundered into another branch, a leaf tipped dew into his hair, and he swore before slapping the hat back on.

Truthfully, she hadn't thought about it. But now that he mentioned it . . . "I guess I was envisioning something low-tech. Demon tribunals and ancient rituals and all that."

"We don't have Earth's level of technology, but we don't need to. Our lives are simple, and anything beyond what we have can be attained in the human world."

"Do you have refrigerators?" Mariel asked. "Microwaves?"

"Generally, no. Demons only need to eat occasionally, so we mostly get takeout." When she stared at him uncomprehendingly, he elaborated. "We go to Earth and order something there."

She laughed. "You don't cook your own food?"

"What's the point when you don't need to eat every day?"

That didn't sound right. "You ate dinner last night. And I caught you raiding my cereal after I got out of the shower."

He looked embarrassed. "I, uh, need more calories than most demons. Soul collecting is taxing."

"But you haven't actually collected my soul."

He squinted up into the trees. "What kind of bird is that?"

She filed the misdirection away for further analysis. It was one more thing that didn't line up with how Oz told her a demon ought to be.

She looked up, then gasped at the sight of a large red bird with a golden tail perched at the top of a Douglas fir. "Oh, a phoenix! I'm so glad we saw one. They're rare, and they self-immolate for the winter, so this might be the last one I see this year."

"Doesn't sound like a fun way to spend the winter," Oz said.

She shrugged. "If I could self-immolate and regenerate a few months later looking younger than ever, why not? Plus, it would be an excellent way to get out of my mother's dinner parties. *Sorry, Mom, I'm a pile of ashes for the next three months.*" Then she groaned. "Shoot, it's Sunday, isn't it? That means family dinner." Mariel's least favorite event of the week. Her chest tightened, and she rubbed her sternum to ease the ache.

A waist-high boulder blocked the path. Mariel got ready to scramble over, then squeaked when Oz's hands surrounded her waist. He lifted her, depositing her on top of the rock, then climbed over it himself. "Thank you," she said as she hopped down the other side. She could still feel the warmth where his fingers had pressed into her waist.

Why was he being so nice to her? Was this a weird way of trying to get inside her head?

"Why don't you skip dinner?" Oz asked, as if his display of courtesy—and strength—wasn't worth acknowledging. "If she's rude and you hate it, you aren't obligated to go."

"If I don't show up, she'll teleport something awful into my house." One time it had been invitation cards, which wouldn't have been so bad if her mother hadn't graduated from sending one at a time to five thousand in one drop. Mariel's house had overflowed with invitations of all kinds until she'd finally caved. She'd thought that was bad . . . until the next time she'd tried to skip, and a honey badger had appeared in her living room.

"Someone needs to rein her in," Oz muttered. "Why hasn't your father intervened?"

Mariel laughed at the preposterous idea. "My father learned a long time ago to be quiet and let her have her way. He loves her, but he's only a Spark by marriage, so she gets the final say in everything."

"Is that how marriage works in the human realm these days? When I first visited in the 1800s, men got the final say in everything."

Thank Hecate it wasn't the 1800s anymore. "I am of the firm belief that both parties' opinions are valid and should be respected," Mariel said.

The path gained elevation, and the foliage grew thicker. During the summer, this trail would be lined with lush greenery and wild blue roses the size of dinner plates, but with autumn underway, the trees had turned as fiery as phoenix feathers. Leaves fluttered down, some of them changing their path to grace her shoulders and hair.

Plants had always loved her, no matter what Oz thought. One of her earliest memories was of the pansies in her father's garden turning their faces towards her. She had always returned from play sessions with leaves and grass woven into her hair and stuck to her skin, much to her parents' dismay. It wasn't that Mariel had been particularly wild—the plants just liked being close to her.

The path seemed to terminate in a thick tangle of bushes. "We're here!" Mariel announced. She reached out to the bush, infusing her touch with a brush of magic as she whispered, "*Aviosen a malei.*" The bush parted, letting them through.

Beyond was a small oasis. A hot spring bubbled in the center of a clearing, its mineral-orange edges outlining cloudy turquoise water. Steam rose into the crisp air. The flowers in this clearing bloomed year-round, fed by the magic and the springs, and a kaleidoscope of color surrounded the pool.

Oz stood with his mouth agape.

"Well?" Mariel asked.

"This is . . . nice," he finally said.

"It's more than nice." Mariel nudged him with her shoulder. "Come on, tell me it isn't one of the most beautiful things you've ever seen."

He reached out to trail his fingers over a dark purple blossom. Wanting to reward him for his gentleness, Mariel sent a thread of magic its way, encouraging it to stroke his hand. His Adam's apple bobbed as the petals brushed his skin. "I'm not used to being enthusiastic about things," he said. "But yes. It's beautiful."

Over two centuries old, and he didn't know how to be excited about something? Mariel's heart ached for him. What would it be like to spend your entire life cold, to deny beauty and constrain feelings? She would have withered within a year on the demon plane.

Maybe not all of the demon plane was like that though. Maybe it was just the way he'd been trained.

"Come on," Mariel said, bending over to remove her hiking boots, then strip off her wool socks. The grass was soft under her toes, the magic and warmth keeping it lush even in the depths of winter. "Dip your feet in."

When she stood back up, she swore she caught him staring at her ass. He quickly looked away, and Mariel hid a smile as she padded to the edge of the pool. She sat on the mineral-streaked rock, then dipped her toes in, hissing at the pleasure-pain of hot water against cold feet. Oz came to stand next to her, boots still laced as he watched her slowly lower her feet into the water.

"Oh, come on." She patted the rock next to her. "Your demon dignity can survive taking your shoes off."

He grumbled, then bent over to undo the laces. He carefully folded his black socks, placed them and the hat on the ground, then rolled up the cuffs of his dark jeans, exposing hair-dusted calves. He awkwardly lowered himself to the rock, then submerged his lower legs in the water.

"Oh, wow," Mariel said. "Not even going to build up to it?" She was still getting her ankles acclimated, though the heat was already doing wonders for her residual tension from the party.

"Demon," he said by way of explanation. "We run hot."

I bet you do, she thought, eyeing his muscled calves and the stretch of his jeans over his thighs. She was a curvy girl, but she felt practically petite next to him. "Are all demons big?" she blurted.

". . . In what context?" he asked after an awkward pause.

Mariel's cheeks grew hot. Hecate, she hadn't meant it like that, but now it was too late. Her brain started racing down that track, wondering how big demon dicks were. Were they barbed? She'd read a romance novel like that once. Some fan fiction, too. What if demons knotted their mates? Was there biting involved in sex? How did the horns come into play?

Her mind was so busy chasing itself in thirsty circles that she didn't notice she had glazed over while staring at his crotch until he cleared his throat. She blinked a few times—and okay, yes, that was definitely a bulge, and . . . was it getting bigger?—before she snapped her eyes back up. "Big," she blurted. "You. Tall, I mean. And like . . . broad." She gestured at his shoulders. "Like, you could play in the NFL." Another stray thought assailed her. "Do they have a demon NFL?"

His mouth opened and closed a few times. "Your thought process," he said, shaking his head.

"What about it?" She knew she was prone to flights of fancy and sudden tangents, but what else was she supposed to do when there were so many interesting things to think about? Like demon dick, for instance.

"It's like watching a hellhound try to decide which of eight types of prey to murder," he said. "Darting all over the place."

"*Hell*hound?" she asked. "Shouldn't it be *the-demon-plane-hound*?"

He sighed. "The word *hell* existed in Old Demonish long before humans appropriated it. It means 'loyal.'"

"What do they look like?"

"Three heads, red eyes, fangs." He shrugged. "They're a common domestic pet."

She wanted to ask about Old Demonish and demon domestic pets, but he still hadn't answered her earlier questions, and she was going to lose track. "So are you all big? And what about sports?"

"No NFL," he said, tipping his head back to look at the sky. "We have many sports. Some you'd recognize, most you wouldn't. And yes, demons tend to be on the larger side compared to humans, but it varies."

"Are you the biggest?"

He slid her a sidelong glance, then smirked. "Depends what you're asking about."

The sly demon. First jokes, then innuendo—what would be next? She wanted so badly to ask if demon dicks had barbs, but asking people about their genitals definitely wasn't polite. She dunked the rest of her calves into the water all at once to distract herself, hissing as the hot water hit her skin. A few painful seconds later, she acclimated, and the heat started to feel amazing. She giggled as an inquisitive fish nibbled her toes.

Ozroth jerked, splashing water everywhere. "What was that?" he demanded, staring into the cloudy turquoise water.

"Toe nibbling?" she asked. When he nodded, she explained. "There are fish who live in these pools and eat dead skin. It's better than a pedicure."

He grimaced. "That's disgusting." He didn't take his feet out though. "We have hot water fish in the demon plane, but I didn't realize humans had them."

"This is one of the only places in the world where you can find them. Most hot springs are too hostile for life. But there's magic in everything here, from the trees to the water to the fish." She looked around, trying to spot other creatures. A robin preened on a nearby branch, and a blue butterfly flitted around one of the flowers. "I hope we see a fire salamander," she said. "They're even rarer than phoenixes."

"I can see why you like it here," he said. "It's colorful but not overwhelming. It's peaceful."

"For now." Her mouth twisted. "When they build the resort and spa, it'll all be ruined."

Oz frowned. "They're building right here?"

"Not exactly here," Mariel said, swirling her feet in the water. "There's a cluster of interconnected pools further up the slope. They're going to flatten the land around it, cut down the trees, and line the pools with tile. No more fish or fire salamanders then."

The building project had kept her up worrying many nights. Glimmer Falls had always been an oasis—a place where magic thrived and witches mingled with ordinary humans and mystical creatures in harmony. There was a balance to everything, from the people to the environment, and she'd been grateful to live in a place where the rapid expansion and concrete high-rises of the big cities had yet to intrude.

Then Cynthia Cunnington had been elected mayor, and her ambitions to make Glimmer Falls a tourist destination hadn't been clear until far too late. The magical community should have risen up in protest, but the Sparks and Cunningtons were pillars of the community, and rich witches like Cynthia and Diantha were too self-absorbed to realize the damage unrestrained capitalism would do to this haven. Poorer, less prestigious witches didn't have the clout to stand against them.

Mariel wished her mother and Cynthia could feel the land the way she did. Like many other witches though, their power was flashy. They didn't feel a connection to the natural world. The web of magic under Glimmer Falls was dense but delicate, and Mariel knew if the landscape was stripped, it would quickly start to unravel.

"I understand the protest now," Ozroth said. "Places with this much magic are rare." He sniffed a few times. "You can practically smell it in the air."

"You can smell magic?"

"I can sense it. And see it when I open my demon senses. Human magic is like a golden light." He looked at her, eyes trailing over her face, then lower. "It's how I know you're powerful. Your soul glows the brightest gold."

She made a face. "Powerful, but unable to use it."

"You used it today," he said. "When you tripped me. And later, when you made the bush let us through." His forehead furrowed. "Maybe a few other times, though I didn't hear you speak a spell."

"I don't always have to. Only when I want to force a specific outcome. Most of the time I just feed the plants magic and ask nicely."

"It's rare for a witch to be able to use magic without speaking the words. Does your family know you can do that?"

"I don't know," Mariel admitted. "They've never thought much of garden magic, so they don't ask many questions about it. But I was working with plants before I ever learned the language of magic, so maybe? At any rate, my mother can teleport some things without using the words, so it isn't exactly special."

He was studying her intently. "It is special. And I think calling it garden magic is limiting. It's the whole natural world you're attuned to."

Hearing her magic praised for once was a heady sensation, and Mariel squirmed in pleasure. "You say the nicest things."

He snorted. "It's the truth."

She twisted to face him, planting one hand on the rock so she could lean in. Her other hand cupped his cheek. His skin was fever-warm. "Oz," she said seriously. "You may be here to steal my soul, but you've been kinder about my magic in the last day than anyone aside from my friends has been in years."

"It's not stealing," he grumbled. "The whole point is that it's a trade." He shifted his head, pressing deeper into her palm, and Mariel gasped when his lips barely brushed her skin.

"Shut up and let me thank you," she said breathlessly. Energy was building between them—not the prickle of magic, but something more elemental. She'd drifted closer without realizing it, and she felt goosebumps as his breath puffed against her lips. His eyes were wide, the gold irises nearly swallowed by black pupils. His hand settled on her waist, and Mariel shivered.

This attraction wasn't one-sided. She knew it, as certain as she knew the magic wound into the roots.

"You shouldn't have to thank people for telling the truth," he rasped. His chest rose and fell rapidly. His eyes flicked to her lips and back up.

There were two voices in Mariel's head. One was Calladia's, screaming, *What the fuck are you doing?!* The other was urging her on. *Close the gap. Kiss the demon. Find out firsthand how big he is.*

She licked her lips and leaned in—

A small but ferocious roar was her only warning. She flinched to the side, and the stream of fire grazed her upper arm rather than landing straight on her back. "Son of a bitch!" she swore, leaping to her feet.

Oz shot up so fast, he almost toppled into the pool. He shoved her behind him, positioning himself between her and the threat. "What is it?" he demanded. "What's here?"

"Look down," she said, cupping the burn on her arm.

"What is *that*?" Oz asked.

She peered around him to see the attacker. A few feet in front of Oz, an orange salamander the size of a house cat stood in an attack stance, its feet braced wide. Its tail twitched, and it roared again. A plume of fire shot out of its mouth, enveloping Oz's bare feet.

"Oh, no!" Mariel cried. She tried to tug him back, but he held his ground. "Are you okay?" A direct hit like that would have left her blistered, but he hadn't even flinched.

"Demon," he said curtly. He glared at the salamander like he was about to rip out its innards. "And this is a fire salamander, I presume. You were protesting to save *this*?"

"They're extremely endangered." Mariel tugged on his arm again, appreciating the steely feel of his bicep. "And it wasn't his fault. We're in his territory, and he must have let out a few warning hisses when climbing out of the pool, but I didn't hear them." Because she'd been distracted by demon dick and demon chest and demon *mouth*.

He looked over his shoulder. "I'm inclined to stomp this thing flat for burning you, but something tells me you wouldn't like that."

"Do not stomp it flat!" Inside, though, she felt a weird thrill at the idea that he would murder something for hurting her. Calladia's voice was shrieking some sort of horrified advice in her head again, but Mariel ignored it in favor of wrapping her other arm around his waist, biting her lip when she encountered the hard ridges of a six-pack. Hecate, this was not what she should be doing with a demon who wanted her soul, but Mariel had poor impulse control at the best of times, and she hadn't gotten laid in years. "We need to back away slowly," she said. "If you turn and run, it'll chase you."

"Ridiculous," Oz muttered. He backed up though, and Mariel moved with him. It was an odd sort of dance, since she was pressed tight to his back, but she didn't feel like relinquishing his bicep or his abs. The salamander watched them go, round black eyes somehow conveying outrage.

Mariel stopped abruptly. "Ow!" she said when Oz trod on her toes.

"Sorry." Then he scowled over his shoulder, apparently remembering he was supposed to be grumpy and intimidating. "If you don't want to get stepped on, don't stop when I can't see you."

Mariel dodged around him to approach the salamander. She shook Oz off when his hand landed on her shoulder. "Something's wrong," she said. The burn on her arm throbbed, but she ignored the pain.

The salamander's eyes had a thin film over them, and the red mottling she would have expected on its skin was dull brown. It opened its mouth, but the roar was more of a huff this time, and only a slim flame came out. Dark red blood started trickling from its mouth.

"It's sick," Mariel said, feeling ill herself. She'd never seen a sick animal in these woods. Everything had its life span, but creatures here died of old age, not illness.

"So?" Oz asked. "Mariel, back up. It's going to burn you again."

She ignored him, crouching to inspect the animal more closely. "Nothing gets sick here."

She closed her eyes, opening her senses to the forest. Leaves rustled, trees built strength by swaying in the wind, and the rich tapestry of life was as dense and wild as ever. But then her mind brushed against a patch of land that felt . . . wrong. Instead of green and rich, it felt dark and empty.

She shot to her feet and started running, not bothering to grab her boots. Healing an animal was complicated magic she hadn't learned yet, so there was nothing she could do for the salamander, but maybe she could do something for the woods.

Oz shouted, but she ignored him, plunging into the bushes. They parted, sensing her need, but she heard Oz swear when they closed after her. He was following anyway—the snapping sounds and the throbbing outrage of the plants told her that—but Mariel couldn't stop. She needed to find out what was wrong with her forest. Her bare feet pounded over roots and fallen leaves as she sought out the sick, empty feeling.

She found the source of the darkness: a giant Douglas fir. Its trunk was black and rotted, with an indentation in the bark a foot wider and taller than Mariel. The grass at its roots was black, and the darkness spread in tendrils over the surrounding ground, following the root structure.

Mariel dropped to her knees, then pressed her hand against one dark slice through the grass. Under the earth, the root was festering. She fed magic to the suffering root . . . and nothing happened.

Mariel squeezed her eyes closed and focused. "*Cicararek en arboreum.*" Heal the forest.

With the language of magic framing the spell, she felt the black decay recede. Not enough though. She said it again, then again. The roots gradually healed, but something foul still nested within the trunk.

Oz finally caught up to her, panting and with leaves stuck to his hat. "Mariel, what in Lucifer's name are you doing?"

She ignored him, placing her hand on the trunk. "*Cicararek en arboreum.*" The rot shrank again. She felt abruptly light-headed and sank back on her heels. "The forest is sick," she said. Black spots swam in front of her eyes. "And my magic is only fixing small pieces."

Oz crouched beside her. "This isn't normal?"

"No, it's not," Mariel snapped. "I can heal any plant." Her head hurt, and she felt like passing out and vomiting all at once. The rot wasn't gone, but she wasn't sure if she could manage another spell. "My magic should have fixed it."

Oz's eyes flicked up and down the tree trunk. He poked a finger in the soil, then sniffed the air. "I don't sense witch magic."

"It can't be natural." Mariel wrapped her arms around the trunk, not caring that she was getting her cutest dress dirty. "*Cicararek en arboreum!*" She shouted the spell, envisioning magic seeping out of her skin and into the tree. She sent every ounce of her love for nature into the spell, wishing desperately for it to be enough.

The black rot vanished, but the dark spots in her vision expanded. Then there was nothing.

TEN

OZROTH WATCHED IN HORROR AS MARIEL SLUMPED TO THE ground. The tree trunk looked healthy, but Mariel's face was ashen.

He scooped her up, cradling her in his lap. "Wake up," he said, brushing leaf-tangled curls from her face. Her freckles stood out starkly against her skin, and her waxy pallor sent a jolt of fear through him. Was she sick? Humans were so fragile, their lives delicate as spiderweb. What if she died?

If she died, Ozroth would be free of the soul pact, but he didn't want to be. It wasn't just because he didn't want to fail Astaroth, he realized—he wasn't ready to say goodbye to Mariel yet.

That thought was almost as terrifying as the idea of her dying. He felt like he'd stepped into quicksand and was sinking deeper no matter how hard he fought.

"Come on," he said, lightly patting her cheek. She was still breathing, at least. He shifted her until he could press his ear to her chest. Her heartbeat thumped in a steady rhythm. That was a good sign.

How did people treat sick humans? Demons got minor illnesses, but never anything devastating, and Ozroth's encounters with humans, while varied, hadn't focused on much but the particulars of deals. Leeches weren't appropriate these days; he knew that much. Was he supposed to put a cold compress on her forehead? They were at a hot spring—would a warm compress work?

He lifted her into his arms, feeling a shiver of pleasure in spite of his fear. She was soft and curved, and he felt strong as he carried her back towards the hot spring. She was vulnerable, but he would protect her.

The plants parted for them easily, though a thorny vine nicked his shoulder as if chastising him for plowing through the thicket while pursuing Mariel. The plants' behavior was odd. Mariel was unconscious, so she couldn't be casting magic on them, yet they acted as if she were.

The fire salamander was thankfully gone by the time he set Mariel at the edge of the pool, pillowing her head on a tuffet of grass. He stripped off his shirt, then dipped the fabric in hot water before placing it over her forehead. Then he sat back on his heels, staring at her.

What now?

The only other technique of modern human medicine he was marginally familiar with was CPR, but he had no idea if it was applicable in this situation or precisely how to do it. Hesitantly, he placed his hand in the center of Mariel's chest and lightly pressed. It felt uncomfortably like he was groping her while she was unconscious, so he removed his hand. The chest pressing was probably for bad heartbeats, so maybe he didn't need to do it.

Her breathing did seem shallow, so he leaned over her, feeling like a creep as he stared at her plush pink lips. They were slightly parted, and he could feel the soft puff of her breath.

He wouldn't be kissing her, he told himself. He'd be blowing air into her lungs to help heal her. Why that would heal her, he didn't know, but he'd seen an episode of *Grey's Anatomy* once while overnighting in a human hotel, and that was something one of the doctors had done.

He opened his mouth and dipped his head down.

Her eyelashes fluttered open when he was a few inches away. She blinked, then made an alarmed squawking sound.

Ozroth flung himself backward, landing on his ass on the rock edge of the hot spring. He had too much momentum though, and he toppled into the pool. He made the mistake of sucking in a startled breath as hot water surrounded him. His feet hit rock, and he pushed himself upright, coughing and sputtering as his head broke the surface.

Mariel was sitting up now, looking at him with wide eyes. "Are you okay?"

He was too busy coughing up a lung to answer. Fuck, that burned.

She scooted closer, reaching out to him. "Are you choking on a fish? Do you need the Heimlich?"

He wasn't sure what the Heimlich was, but he probably didn't want it. He shook his head. "Breathed in," he gasped between hacking coughs.

Finally, the coughs diminished, though his throat and chest hurt. He dashed water from his eyes and pushed his sopping hair back from his forehead. "Are you all right?" he asked, wading towards the edge of the pool.

Mariel sat there, looking bemused. "I think so. What happened? All I remember is trying to heal the tree."

"You passed out." Ozroth coughed again. "I didn't know what to do, so I brought you back here and put a hot compress on your forehead."

"That was nice of you," she said, though she was eyeing him

suspiciously. "Why are you shirtless? And why were you three inches from my face when I woke up?"

He winced. "I thought . . . maybe CPR? And the shirt was the compress." It was currently sitting in a sad, wet heap on the grass.

Her eyebrows shot up. "You tried CPR on me? And I missed it?"

"I wouldn't say I tried it successfully," he said. "I didn't know what to do. I was thinking about it when you woke up."

Something slithered up the leg of his jeans, and he yelped and scrambled out of the pool. He ripped the jeans off without thinking, shoving them down his thighs, then shaking them out. A tiny white snake dropped back into the water with a plop. "What was that?" he demanded.

When he turned to Mariel though, she wasn't looking at the pool or the snake at all. Her eyes were round as saucers as they darted between his chest and his crotch.

Ozroth looked down at himself. Oh. The only thing he was wearing was a pair of black boxer briefs, and thanks to the drenching they'd gotten, they left little to the imagination. He turned away, not wanting to alarm her. "Sorry," he choked out. "There was a snake in my pants."

"I'll say," she muttered.

This was mortifying. His dick was, against all odds, taking interest in the proceedings. He laced his hands in front of his crotch, keeping his back to her. Maybe if he focused on the snake again, his erection would get the memo that this was not an appropriate moment. "What was that snake?" he asked. "It was white and about five inches long."

"An albino hot springs snake. Not venomous, but they do tend to be cuddly."

He grimaced. That snake had been on a mission to cuddle his testicles, considering how swiftly it had been moving. "Not a trait I appreciate in a snake."

She laughed. "Oh, snakes are lovely. You should try cuddling them more often."

He shook his head. "No, thank you." Luckily, his boner had started to recede, so he turned—still keeping a hand over his crotch—and grabbed his jeans off the grass. He struggled into them, wincing as wet fabric stuck to his skin.

When he finished, he realized Mariel was still staring at him avidly. He scowled. "Enjoying the show?"

Mariel averted her eyes. "Just zoned out." She looked healthier now, the color restored to her cheeks.

"So what happened?" Ozroth asked, collecting his shirt and tugging it over his head. Mariel made a sad little noise as he covered up. "You were healing the tree, and then you were unconscious."

"I overexerted myself. Gave too much power to the spell." She shook her head. "It's never happened before."

"Whatever that rot is must be strong." It seemed unnatural, but he hadn't sensed any magic. Then again, the only magic he could sense was human—even demon magic was imperceptible to other demons—so maybe another supernatural creature had been responsible. He helped Mariel to her feet. "Can you walk?"

She rolled her eyes. "I'm not fragile."

She was though. An infection, a stray knock to the head, unlucky genetics . . . any of it could kill her so easily. Otherwise healthy humans could die of an aneurysm in an instant. The species walked on the edge of a knife, yet humans had no conception of exactly how delicate their lives were.

It made him angry, though he couldn't have articulated why.

"Let's get you home," he said. "You should rest."

"I feel fine," she argued, but she swayed when she took a step towards the trees. He caught her elbow, supporting her.

"Bed," he ordered. "Now."

She shivered. "Yes, sir."

Ozroth liked that response a little too much. "Finally, some respect," he muttered.

Her dimple popped out. "Don't count on it continuing."

Strangely enough, Ozroth didn't mind.

They hiked back through the forest, moving slower than before. Ozroth kept his hand on Mariel's elbow in case she fell again. His wet clothes chafed his skin, cooling rapidly, and his footsteps grew clumsy.

Mariel noticed. "Are you okay?"

"Fine," he gritted through chattering teeth. "Demons aren't meant to be cold, that's all."

"Oh, no!" She looked distressed. "You're taking a hot shower the moment we get home."

That phrasing did a funny thing to his stomach. *The moment we get home.* Ozroth had never been part of a "we" before.

By the time they made it back to the street, Ozroth was experiencing full-body shudders while Mariel swayed on her feet. They clung to each other's arms, walking a drunken path back to Mariel's house. Thankfully, the party had dissipated, so they were able to enter through the front door.

"Bed," he ordered.

"Shower," she said just as firmly. She dragged him towards the bathroom with a surprising amount of strength. He watched as she turned the dials, holding her hand under the stream. Then she looked over her shoulder. "I guess you don't mind if it's scalding."

He shook his head, teeth chattering too hard to answer.

She cranked the dial all the way over and switched the stream to the shower setting. He thought she would leave then, but instead, she tugged at the hem of his soaked shirt. "Off."

She wanted to undress him? Ozroth's dick would have taken

interest in that if it hadn't been impersonating an icicle. He let her pull the fabric up, lifting his arms so she could strip it over his head.

They were both breathing harder when she'd finished. Goosebumps prickled over Ozroth's exposed skin. Mariel licked her lips, then reached for the button of his jeans.

Alarm bells rang in his mind. Something was happening here that went beyond demon deals or a fake relationship, but his mind was too muddled to make sense of it. He was freezing, she was sick, and one of them had to put a stop to this. Unfortunately, it looked like it had to be him.

He put his hand on her wrist. "Go rest," he said, more gently than before.

Her face fell. "Right," she said, turning her back on him. "Try not to drown."

After she was gone, Ozroth took the longest shower of his life. The first half was taken up by warming his core temperature back to normal while castigating himself for the entire catalog of his failures. He wasn't any closer to making a soul deal, and worse, he was growing uncomfortably close to the target of his bargain—so close that he found himself wondering what would have happened if he'd let Mariel unbutton his jeans.

That thought inspired the second half of his shower. Once his dick had gotten back up to proper temperature, there'd been no reasoning with it. He'd finally had to take himself in hand, bracing himself against the tile as he indulged in lewd fantasies. Mariel naked in the shower, water slicking her generous curves. Mariel on her knees, looking up at him with wide hazel eyes. Ozroth's mouth between her thighs as she moaned and writhed.

He'd never been an overly sexual being, although Astaroth had encouraged him to gain experience in case he needed to use seduction to strike a bargain. Ozroth had never liked the idea of sex with the targets of his soul bargains though, so all of his trysts had been with other demons, and there'd never been much to those encounters other than mutual release. Ultimately, he'd lost interest, and it had been decades since he'd had a partner.

Now he felt those urges stronger than ever. They burned through him, making him gasp and arch his hips. How much of it was the soul, and how much of it was Mariel? Mariel with her big, beautiful eyes and her dimples and her fucking masterpiece of a body. Mariel with the bright laughter, who teased him, then held his hand.

The climax hit hard and fast, and he muffled his shout with his free hand.

When it was over, his body tingled with endorphins, but guilt and self-recrimination swamped him. He was fantasizing about the woman he was going to turn into an emotionless, magicless husk. He was a joke of a demon, so pathetic he'd started to get feelings for a mortal. Astaroth would be ashamed of him if he knew. No, more than ashamed. Outraged and disgusted.

As Ozroth scrubbed the shower wall clean, he felt disgusted with himself, too. What was he doing? This could only end one way.

It was a onetime weakness, he told himself. A single wank to get it out of his system. After he left the shower, he would be back to his old self and ready to start scheming.

His clothes still lay in a sodden heap on the floor, so he tossed them in the hamper before wrapping the towel around his waist and leaving the bathroom.

Mariel's bedroom door was open. He hesitated, wondering if she was mad at him. Then he mentally slapped himself. Who cared if she was mad at him? He was Ozroth the Ruthless, for Lucifer's sake. People were always mad at him.

He should probably make sure she hadn't fainted again. He needed her conscious for a soul bargain, after all.

He peeked his head in. Mariel was curled up in bed with the covers pulled to her chin. Her cheeks were pink, and her breathing was low and even. Sleeping, then. Her hair lay in a tangle on her pillowcase, leaves and twigs still woven into the brown curls.

Ozroth's heart squeezed in an alarming way, and warmth filled his chest. He backed away quickly, then hurried down the hall, putting as much space as he could between him and the soft, sleeping woman.

"Cold and rational," he muttered to himself. "Be ruthless."

But the warmth lingered, and his stomach had joined the conspiracy, and he suddenly understood why humans talked about feeling butterflies. His entire body was a riot of sensation, and his heart and head were full of a strange, giddy desperation.

"Fuck," he said, collapsing on the couch.

He was in so much trouble.

ELEVEN

THAT AFTERNOON, MARIEL OPENED THE FRONT DOOR TO
find Calladia on the doorstep. The blond witch scowled as
she held out a paper bag. "Here," she said. "But I did it for you,
not him."

Mariel smiled. "Thanks, babe." She beckoned Calladia in, putting her finger to her mouth. "He's sleeping," she whispered.

Calladia looked as they walked past the entrance to the living
room, and then her head snapped towards Mariel. "He's shirtless," she said flatly.

"I told you," Mariel said as she guided Calladia down the
hallway to the kitchen. "He fell in the hot spring."

"And you couldn't give him one of your oversized hoodies to
cover up with?"

Truthfully, Mariel probably had something that would fit
him—she loved big, cozy sweatshirts. But when she'd seen him
stretched out on her couch, white towel knotted low on his hips
and miles of muscles on display, she'd experienced a moment of

weakness. His skin was smooth and golden, free of hair except for the hint of happy trail peeking above the towel.

She tried to look innocent. "I guess it slipped my mind."

Calladia snorted. "Sure. The sacred V didn't influence your thinking at all."

"The sacred V" was what they had termed that seemingly mythical cut of muscles arrowing towards a man's groin. Often seen in magazine ads but never in real life . . . until Oz had shown up. The bands of muscle were so pronounced, it made her want to nibble them. "The V had very little to do with it," Mariel said primly. "The pecs though . . ."

Calladia slapped her arm. "Cut it out. He's here to steal your soul, not love you up."

Mariel put a kettle on to boil, fighting the ball of disappointment that settled in her stomach. She pulled out Calladia's favorite tea: orange and ginger. "If my soul is in jeopardy, at least let me get some solid leering out of it."

"Your soul isn't in jeopardy," Calladia said as Mariel joined her at the table. "You're not going to make a deal."

"I know. But then what? Does he just . . . hang around for the rest of my life?" The prospect didn't sound as awful as it should. "He has a job to get back to. Friends and a life." Although he hadn't mentioned any friends, just that terrible mentor of his. Still, it wasn't fair to expect him to follow her around forever.

Calladia raised her brows incredulously. "You would seriously trade your soul so he can hang out with his friends again?"

"No. I just feel terrible about the whole situation."

She really did. Oz was trapped here because of her. She'd been the one to request a deal, and now he was left trailing at her heels, forced to tolerate Diantha Spark, trouser snakes, and dousing in hot springs.

And speaking of that trouser snake . . . Wow. His boxer briefs had clung indecently when he'd gotten out of the pool, giving her a good look at what the demon was packing. It would be a lot to take, but Mariel was willing to give it the old college try.

"You shouldn't feel bad. He's a jerk." Calladia tightened her high ponytail. Given the pristine look of her hair and blue workout top, she hadn't returned to the gym yet but would be heading there shortly for her personal training gig.

The kettle whistled. "He really isn't," Mariel said as she busied herself pouring two mugs of tea. "He's gruff, and you two definitely started off on the wrong foot, but he's actually kind of . . . sweet."

She thought of the way he'd complimented her magic and the concerns he'd expressed about how her family treated her. The way he'd panicked when she'd fainted, apparently agonizing over whether or not to give her CPR. The way he'd tentatively touched the petals of a flower in that clearing, looking amazed when the flower had stroked him back.

Then she thought about how he'd stopped her from taking his pants off, and her cheeks burned with mortification. She wasn't sure what she'd been thinking—she hadn't really been thinking, truthfully, just acting on horny impulse. Being rejected stung, but there was something sweet in that, too. He'd wanted her to rest.

"Earth to Mariel. Come in, Mariel."

Mariel snapped back to attention. She'd glazed over while stirring the tea, remembering how close her fingers had gotten to discovering everything about demon dick. She brought the mugs to the table. "Sorry. Got distracted."

"Thinking about his pecs again?" Calladia asked acidly.

"No." More like the bulge in his jeans. "Anyway, he's not that bad. Definitely not ruthless. And he's been really kind about my magic."

Calladia looked sympathetic. "Darling, I hate to say it, but your family's been so rude about your magic that I think you'd take anything other than an outright insult as kindness."

Mariel hid her flinch behind her upraised mug. "Harsh but true." The tea scalded her tongue when she drank, and she spat it back out with a yelp.

Calladia was already drinking hers. She'd never struggled with coffee or tea being too hot—a similarity she shared with Oz. He'd probably enjoy drinking lava.

"Do you suppose there's lava in the demon plane?" Mariel asked.

"Squirrel!"

"It's a legitimate question," Mariel protested. "There are hellhounds, after all."

"*Hell*hounds?" Calladia asked disbelievingly.

Mariel rolled her eyes. "I know. Apparently *hell* means 'loyal' in Old Demonish."

"There's no such thing as Hell," Calladia mocked in a comically low voice. "Except when I, Ozroth the Ruthless, say there is." She switched back to her normal voice. "So is he teaching a class on Intro to Demons or what?"

Mariel shrugged as she stirred her tea. She could try a spell to lower the temperature, but knowing her luck, she'd probably turn it into actual lava, since she'd been thinking about it. "We talk a lot. Or at least, I talk a lot, and he answers all my questions."

"He must be very patient," Calladia said.

Mariel stuck out her tongue. "Jerk."

"I'm just saying, even a Magic Eight Ball would fling itself off a cliff if it had to answer all your questions."

"How would it even get to the cliff? It doesn't have legs."

Calladia pointed at her. "See? More questions."

Mariel felt more relaxed than she had in days. This felt good. Just her and Calladia, making fun of each other the way they always had. She sagged back in her chair, holding the mug against her chest. "How have you been these last few days?" she asked. "I feel like my demon drama is kind of upstaging everything."

"As it should." Calladia set the mug down and leaned in. "I got the town hall moved up, much to my mother's annoyance. It's tomorrow night at six p.m."

"That's going to be awkward." Cynthia and Calladia often butted heads, but rarely so publicly.

"I don't give a fuck. She's the one prioritizing pedicures over her community's well-being." Calladia punched her open palm menacingly. "I hope the contractor is there, too, so I can perform a construction project on his face."

"I'd like to see that." The conversation reminded Mariel of what she'd seen earlier, and her stomach grew sour. "Something else is wrong in the forest. I found a sick fire salamander."

She explained the sequence of events, leaving out the moment when she'd been so distracted by the thought of kissing Oz that she'd missed the warning hisses. The burn was now bandaged, but the dull throb of it reminded her how foolish she'd been. "I healed that tree," Mariel said at the end of her story, "but what if there are others?"

Calladia's forehead was pinched with concern. "I can't believe it took that much magic to heal it. You're like a nuclear reactor for plant magic."

"Right?" Mariel shivered. "And it didn't feel like normal tree rot. It felt more like magic, but not any kind I've encountered before."

"I wonder if there's a warlock on the construction team. Maybe they're trying to justify chopping the trees down?"

"Maybe." The thought made Mariel sick. "It would need to be a strong warlock though. And Oz said it didn't feel like human magic."

"And you believe him? Demons are notorious liars." Calladia stiffened, eyes widening. "Mariel, what if Oz did it?"

"What?" She rejected the possibility instantly. "Of course he didn't do it. He was worried when I spent so much magic trying to fix it."

"Demon," Calladia said. "Liar. What are you missing about this concept?"

Oz didn't seem like a liar though—fake backstory for her mother aside. Practiced liars were smooth, and Oz was anything but. "You just don't like him," Mariel said, setting her mug down on the table so hard liquid sloshed over the edge.

"Of course I don't like him. He's trying to steal my friend's soul."

"It isn't stealing—"

"Arguing semantics doesn't make it any better." Calladia's voice rose. "Mariel, I love you, but you are being obtuse about this. His entire existence revolves around making soul bargains, but you expect me to think he's really a sweet, upstanding guy?" She scoffed. "Come on. If I were trying to trick you into giving up your soul, the first thing I'd do would be to threaten the thing you love most. You've made it clear how much you love those woods."

Mariel recoiled. "Don't say things like that."

"Why? Because it might mean the hot demon on your couch is actually your enemy?" Calladia jammed her fingers into her hair, not seeming to care that she was messing up her ponytail. "Your mom's brainwashed you to put up with anything, and now you're trying to turn this horrible situation into some kind of fairy tale—"

"Stop it!" Mariel shot to her feet. Her eyes stung. "You don't get to talk about my family like that."

Calladia stood, too. "Should I stop telling you the truth just because you don't like hearing it? That's not what friends do."

Mariel couldn't bear thinking about Oz destroying the woods behind her back while being charming to her face. What would that make the near-kiss? "You don't know what you're talking about."

"Why is it so hard to believe that *Ozroth the Ruthless* is doing everything he can to take your soul?" Calladia demanded.

The tears spilled over. "Because it would mean everything he's said to me is a lie."

Calladia's frustrated look told Mariel she didn't understand. "So what?"

How could she explain the pain of thinking that every compliment, every lingering look, every moment of strange camaraderie was an act? That he would have gladly kissed her, then seized her magic without a moment's regret? "No one has ever valued me," Mariel said bitterly. She lifted a hand to cut off Calladia's protest. "You do, but that doesn't make the rest of it easier to take."

"You think the demon values you?"

Strangely, Mariel had actually begun to believe that. "I don't know," she whispered brokenly.

Calladia's angry expression melted into pity. "Oh, honey." She stepped around the table to wrap Mariel in a hug. "I'm sorry I upset you. You are valuable. You don't need a demon to tell you that."

"Mariel?" The low, sleep-fuzzed voice came from the doorway. Oz stood there in his towel, black hair mussed around his horns and eyes bleary from his nap. "I heard crying. Are you all right?"

Mariel cried harder. How could anyone act that well?

Two centuries of experience, she reminded herself. He'd lived over eight times longer than her.

Ozroth stepped forward, then stopped when Calladia looked over her shoulder, and Mariel wondered how murderous her friend's expression was.

"She's fine," Calladia snapped. "The best thing you can do is leave her alone."

He flinched. Those weary, sad eyes met Mariel's again. "Is that what you want?"

Mariel nodded. The lump in her throat felt like it would choke her.

"All right." He drove a hand through his hair, tugging like he wanted to rip it out. "I'll leave you alone. But if you're hurt, will you tell me? Please?"

Mariel nodded again, then buried her face in Calladia's shoulder.

The kitchen was quiet for a while, the stillness broken only by Mariel's muffled sobs and Calladia's soothing whispers. Eventually, she regained control of herself. "Sorry," she said, sniffling. "I don't know why I'm so emotional about this."

"It's a big, scary thing." Calladia handed Mariel a tissue so she could blow her nose. "You're in danger of losing your magic, but the guy threatening to do it is hot and being nice to you." She opened the screen door to the backyard, gesturing for Mariel to follow. "Come on. Plant therapy time."

The trees surrounding Mariel's property had turned orange and crimson with the season. Autumn sunlight cast spindly shadows over the browning grass and bounced off the glass walls of the greenhouse. The outside world was dying, but it was comforting knowing the plants inside her greenhouse would thrive no matter what. They were the one constant in a life she sometimes felt she had no control over.

As soon as Mariel entered the greenhouse, she was surrounded by inquisitive plant tendrils. A bloodred rose brushed her wet cheek with its petals, and Mariel smiled despite herself.

"I can see what you mean about the demon though." Calladia looked troubled as she stared back at the house, her fingers absently stroking the jade vine. "He's really convincing."

Mariel nodded. "I get what you're saying, but every time I talk to him it seems so genuine."

"Plus you have a crush on him."

Mariel recoiled at the accusation. "I do not." *Liar, liar, pants on fire.*

Calladia rolled her eyes. "Mariel, it's obvious. You eye him like he's a piece of chocolate cake, and you're spending more energy defending him than you are trying to figure out how to get out of this deal."

Shit. Mariel had said she'd go to the library, hadn't she? "I'll do more research, I promise. But we got waylaid by my mother on the way home, and then Oz was upset, and I thought the forest would be good for him . . ."

"Oz was upset," Calladia repeated. "You're prioritizing his needs over yours. What does he even have to be upset about?"

"Besides being stuck on Earth with an incompetent witch? He told me about his shitty childhood."

Calladia sighed. "Let me guess. You think that big, broody exterior is hiding a wounded heart, and all he needs is love and understanding."

This felt like a trap. ". . . Maybe."

Calladia grabbed her hand and led her deeper into the greenhouse. She stopped in front of a short tree with a climbing vine wound around the trunk. "Toxic men have this very clever trick," she said with the bitterness of experience. "They excuse their bad behavior by telling you their vulnerabilities. Because it's hard to get emotional confessions out of men, we feel flattered that they confide in us, and because we're natural caretakers, we want to help them. So we forgive and excuse away behavior because it's a symptom of our loved one's emotional damage." She gestured at the vine. "So they wind themselves around us, getting their hooks into our bark, and we flatter ourselves that they would collapse without us. And they slowly take us over."

"Oz isn't Sam," Mariel said softly. Calladia's awful ex-boyfriend had left her inclined to think the worst of men.

Calladia scowled. "Maybe not, but aren't they all the same? Once they find a weakness, they exploit it."

Mariel gripped Calladia's hands. "He isn't belittling me. And he isn't behaving badly, except for being grumpy. He hasn't even been pushing for me to trade my soul recently."

"That doesn't mean he won't." Fear shone in Calladia's brown eyes. Her scars went deep, and Mariel knew trauma was making the argument for her. Calladia pretended she was too dedicated to fitness and studying witchcraft to date, but that was an excuse plastered over the real reason. She was afraid.

"I promise you," Mariel said through a thick throat, "if Oz insults me or starts treating me badly, I will tell you. If he does anything to hurt me, I will tell you."

Calladia swallowed hard, then nodded. "And if he does . . . can I beat him up?"

Mariel smiled. "Yes, you can beat him up."

"Good." Calladia sighed, shoulders slumping. "Sorry to lecture. I'm in mama bear mode."

"Understandable." Mariel scrubbed at a salt trail on her cheek. "I'll hit the library after work tomorrow. If we can undo this, everything will be fine." She shook her head. "I'm not even sure Ozroth wants my soul, to be honest."

Mariel could see Calladia wanted to argue, but her friend clamped her mouth shut. "Maybe," was all she said.

It was as good of a concession as Mariel would get out of Calladia. They'd been fighting—and making up—for years. And while their spats could be stormy, they always came from a place of love and ended quickly.

The light coming through the greenhouse glass had taken on

the rich golden hue of late afternoon. "Ugh," Mariel said. "I need to get ready for Sunday dinner." She cast a longing glance at the beginnings of her display for the Pacific Northwest Floral Championships, which she'd much rather spend her time working on.

"Do you think you can skip, considering your 'new boyfriend'?" Calladia gave the term air quotes. "Like, surely you deserve some connubial bliss."

"I wish." Mariel grimaced. "Mom would just unleash an army of crabs in my bedroom or something."

"Does Oz have to go?"

Mariel hadn't considered that yet. She knew the answer though. "Absolutely. My mother would teleport me into that guano cave from *Planet Earth* if I didn't bring him to dinner."

Calladia's smile was evil. "Seat him closest to her. And make sure Diantha knows that he loves being asked intrusive questions."

Mariel chuckled. "Easy there, Dr. Evil. No need to be a sadist."

They exited the greenhouse side by side, and Calladia headed to the wooden side gate. She paused with her hand on the latch. "I love you, you know?"

Mariel smiled. "I love you, too. Now go destroy a rowing machine."

Calladia saluted, then left.

Mariel sagged against the gate. She felt emotionally wrung out, and she still had a three-hour-plus family dinner to get through.

A curtain twitched, and she looked in time to see Oz peeking at her. He quickly retreated, and the curtain fell back into place.

"Ozroth the Ruthless, indeed," she muttered. Still, the question remained—a dark possibility that wouldn't leave her mind now that Calladia had brought it up.

How good of a liar was Oz?

TWELVE

OZROTH SCOWLED AT THE MIRROR. "NO."

Bad enough that he was trapped on Earth, pathetically pining over the witch he ought to be terrorizing or manipulating into a soul bargain. Bad enough that he'd been dismissed like he was nothing when she'd clearly been upset and in need of help. But this? This was an indignity too far.

"Yes," Mariel said. "It's the only option." She stood behind and to the side of him, and the reflection showed a dimple peeking out over the hand she'd pressed to her mouth. She was laughing at him.

For good reason.

The shirt seemed to stare at him in the mirror, too, a tie-dyed monstrosity that featured a repeating motif of parrots and palm trees. Somehow, it was too big for his broad frame, hanging loose at the waist. Ozroth wondered how many thrift stores Calladia had visited looking for the perfect outfit to humiliate him. "She did this on purpose," he said accusingly.

Mariel finally cracked and started laughing. "Absolutely."

Apparently he would get no sympathy from that quarter. At

least the boxers fit, though he could have done without the heart print. The socks were . . . something . . . but his jeans were long enough to cover up the kitten pattern. The jeans matched the size he'd been wearing when he'd arrived, and he wondered if Mariel had peered at the tags while he'd been sleeping. His original clothes were currently in the washing machine, spinning far too slowly for his liking.

"We can wait until the washer finishes," he said.

"And have you wear sopping-wet clothing again?" Mariel shook her head. "I refuse to let my demon freeze to death."

He scowled harder at the way his heart leapt. *My demon.* If he'd been her demon, she would have let him comfort her when she'd been crying. He could have massacred whatever was causing her grief.

"You look like you want to drop that shirt in a volcano," Mariel said. "It isn't that bad." At his stormy look, she clarified. "Well, maybe it is that bad, but it's only one night."

"One night with your family."

"So? You've seen how Alzapraz dresses."

And yes, this wasn't as bad as bunny ears, but that wasn't the point. "It's the principle of the thing. Any boyfriend of yours should try to look nice when meeting your family. Even a fake boyfriend."

She looked at him like she'd discovered a brand-new species of plant. "Oz, that is downright sweet."

"It isn't sweet," he grumbled, dragging her comb through his hair. "It's the honorable thing to do." He winced when he tugged on a tangle so hard the comb knocked into one of his horns, causing a lightning flash of pain.

"You demons and your honor. I swear you're secretly Klingons."

"What's a Klingon?"

"Never mind." When he ripped through another tangle,

Mariel snatched the comb out of his hand. "You can't comb like that or you're going to damage your hair."

"It grows back."

"But it's so pretty." She trailed her fingers over the waving strands. "It would be a shame to damage it."

He was momentarily stunned into silence at any part of him being deemed "pretty." Mariel took the opportunity to start working the comb through his hair, starting at the ends. He hunched to make it easier on her. Maybe he should have refused the help, but he'd never had his hair brushed before—not that he could remember—and it felt shockingly good.

He watched in the mirror as she worked methodically. There was a furrow in her brow, like she wanted to do this perfectly. He rarely got the chance to stare at her for uninterrupted periods of time, so he took advantage of her focus and let his eyes wander over her. She was so beautiful, with her heart-shaped face and dreamy hazel eyes. She'd braided her hair, but a few curls had escaped to curve against her forehead, and a red flower had been tucked into the braid. She looked soft and sweet, and he wondered what her freckle-dotted skin would taste like. Roses and vanilla, maybe. Sunshine with a hint of cinnamon.

She worked carefully around his horns. "Are they sensitive?" she asked, trailing a finger over one the way she would stroke a friendly plant.

Shivery pleasure shot from his horn to his groin, and he made an inarticulate sound.

"Sorry!" She snatched her hand back. "Did that hurt?"

"No," he croaked. Imagining how she tasted had started his erection, but with that touch, he was now testing the capacity of his new jeans.

"Then what was that . . . oh." Her eyes fixed low on his body in the mirror.

"Sorry." He tried to angle his body so she wouldn't see his erection. "They're sensitive. In . . . in that way."

"Oh!" Mariel giggled, looking flushed. "Even when you're stabbing that nightbeast on the demon plane?"

"Not then. It's, ah, situation-specific." Hitting anything with his horns hurt, but soft touches were something else entirely.

He tried to twist his pelvis further away from her view, but she grabbed his arm, stilling the movement. "It's okay," she said. "It's just biology. I guess it would be the equivalent of you sticking your hand up my dress, right?"

He groaned and closed his eyes, not wanting to think about what was up her skirt. She was wearing another innocently sexy dress. This one was checkered red and white, with faux lacing up the front and a pretty red bow perched between her breasts. It wasn't the most revealing dress, but it emphasized her lush hourglass figure.

The skirt wasn't tight. He could put his hand on her thigh and slide it up . . .

"Is there lava on the demon plane?" Mariel asked.

He opened his eyes, startled out of his reverie. "Pardon?" He could usually follow her tangents, but he was lost on this one.

Mariel was combing his hair again, running her fingers through the locks to arrange them. "I was thinking about dropping that shirt in a volcano, and the question came up earlier when I was talking with Calladia. Lava seems like a cliché, but so do hellhounds, so who knows?"

Did she not realize what she'd done to him by touching his horn, then casually mentioning reaching up her dress? She was chattering away like normal, looking totally at ease. Then her eyes flickered to his crotch and back again, and he realized she was trying to move past the awkward moment.

He cleared his throat and tried to corral his thoughts. "Yes. Lava. We have a few volcanoes."

"Do you swim in them?"

He chuckled. "We run hot, but not molten-rock hot."

"That does sound excessive." She bit her lip and smiled, and he felt light-headed. What was happening to him?

Oh, who was he kidding? He knew exactly what was happening, even if he'd never experienced it before. Human books were full of this stuff, and although he read mostly historical nonfiction and textbooks about murder, he'd dabbled in other literature. There were several terms for the woozy, giddy, horrific emotion that had seized his internal organs in an iron grip, and if he'd never understood the concept before, he did now. That fucking soul in his chest was absolutely gagging to lay itself on the altar of love.

Not that he was in love; that was a step too far. But the altar of infatuation wasn't as poetic. Neither was the altar of illicit shower masturbation.

Whatever he called the disease, he'd never guessed the onset of symptoms would be so rapid. He'd met her two days ago, and he was already a complete mess. Then again, the soul was human, and humans had shortened life spans—it made sense they'd do everything as quickly as possible.

"All done," Mariel said with a final swipe at his hair. She parted it carefully, arranging the strands over his horns with gentle precision. Then she frowned. "Shoot, I forgot about that awful hat."

"All that work for nothing." When she glared at him, he relented. "Thank you. For not damaging my hair."

Her smile warmed his insides better than flaming demon grog, and he realized he was on the verge of addiction.

"You're welcome," she said. "Now come on. We have a dinner party to go to."

THIRTEEN

MARIEL AND OZ TURNED ONTO THE STREET LEADING UP to the Spark family home. The moon rose fat and white over the top of the hill, casting its light on elegant houses. Compared to these mansions, Mariel's bungalow might as well have been a shack, but she loved having a space that was all her own.

"What are your life goals?" Oz asked.

Mariel blinked. "Trying to suss out my weaknesses, demon?"

He made a face. "I'm curious."

"I want to get my doctorate in Magical Herbology. I'd love to be a teacher." She grimaced. "My mother would prefer I get an SoD in another discipline, but I had a C average during my undergrad studying General Magical Arts."

"Is C . . . good?" Oz asked. "Demon universities don't have a ranking system."

"C means average, though if you listen to my mother, it's complete and utter failure." She looked at him. "If you don't have a ranking system, how does school work?"

His brow furrowed. "What do you mean?"

"How do you know who's done well?"

"Our schools teach young demons until they understand the material. They all do well."

Her laugh sounded unhinged. "So it isn't a hypercompetitive meritocracy that doesn't account for individual learning styles? Next you'll tell me there are no student loans in the demon plane."

"Why would students take out loans?" Oz looked baffled.

Mariel was equally baffled. "To pay tuition? How do you afford to pay teacher salaries and maintain buildings if you aren't charging the students?"

"It hardly seems fair to make young people pay for the education they need. And demon society operates on the barter system for the most part, but if anyone is struggling and can't trade time or resources, the entire community pitches in."

Huh. Trust literal demons to be kinder to their children than the American education system.

They passed a Halloween display that included several electric-lit pumpkins and a cutout of a red, fanged demon with a pitchfork. Mariel hid a smile at Oz's heavy sigh.

"Why do teachers teach if they don't get a salary?" she asked.

"We live forever. Demons are free to follow one interest, then another. If they find value in educating the youth, why shouldn't they spend their time like that? Obviously bargainers can't switch career paths, but many others do."

"I like that demons help others because they want to, not because they need money." She kicked a pebble, sending it skittering into a bush. The bush squawked, and a bird with six wings and way too many eyes burst into the air. "Sorry!" Mariel called as it flew away.

"You have so many different creatures here," Oz said.

"The magic draws them." Mariel pointed out more wonders as

they walked. A three-legged crow pecked at a dying lawn, and everywhere it hopped, the grass turned gold. Ribbons covered the gnarled branches of a tree, each signifying a wish or charm. A griffin perched on a gabled roof, tail lashing as it stared into the distance.

"It's so alive," Oz said.

Mariel spun, making her dress flare out. "I love it here. I can't imagine leaving." When she stopped, she saw Oz's eyes flick up quickly from her thighs.

"You're the most alive thing of all. You see so much joy in the world." A gloomy expression fell over his features at the words.

The night was too beautiful for whatever dark thoughts Oz was entertaining. "Don't look so morose," Mariel said. "Come on, try to make a goofy bargain with me."

Oz grimaced, but when Mariel stared at him expectantly, he conceded. "Fine. If you give me your soul, I'll give you your very own griffin to ride."

Mariel hummed. "Flying would be fun, but they're smelly up close."

"If you give me your soul, I'll make sure your hiking boots are always good as new."

Mariel peered down at her scuffed boots. "New boots have to be worn in. I'd get blisters."

They were approaching the top of the hill. On the left was a gray stone mansion with a gabled roof and an autumn wreath on the door—the Cunnington house. On the right was an odd, jumbled construction that was a hodgepodge of different architectural styles. Even though Mariel didn't particularly want to go inside, she smiled at the sight of the eccentric building. The marble central portion was neoclassical, with pillars fronting the facade. One wing was limestone, carved with elaborate Gothic sensibilities, while the other wing had a Tudor look, with its white plastered walls and black-painted beams. A turret rose from each wing, and a purple flag rippled at the top of the centermost one.

"Welcome to nearly two centuries of questionable architectural choices!" Mariel announced.

Oz looked appalled. "This is your mother's house?"

"The Spark family home," Mariel confirmed. "The central portion was built by one of Glimmer Falls's founders, Galahad Spark, in 1842. Various relatives have, ah, improved on it since then."

"If you give me your soul, I'll raze the monstrosity to the ground."

Mariel giggled. "I actually like it. I know it's tacky, but it has character."

"It certainly has something."

"The Cunningtons live opposite," Mariel said. "Casper Cunnington, Glimmer Falls's other cofounder, had a much more subdued style."

Mariel looked across the street in time to see a curtain fall back into place. Cynthia Cunnington, probably, eager to spy on her "friend." Why those two women chose to spend so much time together when they clearly hated each other, Mariel would never understand.

A stained glass window covered the top third of the front door, and a crest hung below: a griffin and a peryton rampant, with a sun and crossed wands in the middle. The ribbon on top of the shield read NOS IMPERARE SUPREMA. We rule supreme.

"No one can accuse your family of humility," Oz said.

"Tell me about it." Mariel grabbed the brass knocker—clenched in the teeth of a dragon—and pounded three times. "That crest dates back to medieval times when Gorvenal Spark was Europe's preeminent court wizard."

The door swung open, revealing Diantha. She wore a purple

gown, black opera gloves, and a necklace of black opals. "Darlings!" she cried. "Welcome."

Oz held out a bottle of wine from Mariel's stash. Diantha took
the bottle, eyed the label, then tossed it over her shoulder. Oz
flinched, but Mariel just sighed.

"*Vintno a returnsen.*" The wine vanished and reappeared in
her mother's hand. "Just a party trick. Come in, lovebirds!"

They stepped inside, and both Oz's leather jacket and Mariel's
sweater flew off and hung themselves on hooks. The entry hall
was paneled in blond wood with an Oriental carpet runner, and
portraits of odd-looking witches and warlocks lined the walls.
One-eyed Lizetta Spark beamed from her portrait, a parrot
perched on her head. In the next one, a warlock posed dramatically with his shirt undone and hair blowing in the wind: Phineas
Spark, who could have cornered the romance novel cover market
if he'd been born a century later.

"These meals are the best part of the week," Diantha said.
"Nothing like family to keep your spirits up, that's what I always say."

Next to Mariel, Oz looked askance at a portrait of a grim-
looking warlock with a machete and a face tattoo.

"That's Great-Great-Uncle Trenton," Mariel whispered. "We
don't talk about him."

"Your mother doesn't talk about something?" he asked sotto
voce. "How shocking."

"If you had a murderous relative who spent his last years in
prison researching resurrection magic, you wouldn't talk about
him much either."

"Here we are!" Diantha guided them into the large dining
room. It was decorated like a hunting lodge, with exposed roof
beams, flickering candles, and heads of rare beasts mounted on
the walls. "They're fake," Diantha said when she caught Oz look-

ing with horror at an endangered white dragon's head. "But they're fun." She waved a hand in front of the dragon's snout, and it turned its head and blew a puff of smoke out of its nostrils. "My youngest brother, Wallace, likes animatronics. He moved to Pasadena last year, which was a terrible choice, if you ask me, which he didn't."

"Though she told him anyway," Mariel whispered. "Many times." She missed Wally and his husband, Hector, but she called them frequently, and they were thriving in California.

"Wallace specializes in creating impossible animatronics that combine machines and magic." Diantha snapped her fingers, and a basilisk head hissed. "They're all the rage in theme parks these days, so at least he's rich."

The long dining table could have housed twenty people, though only four were seated. Mariel's father sat at the head of the table reading a newspaper, his gray hair neatly combed in its usual side part and square spectacles perched on the tip of his nose. To his left sat Alzapraz in pink robes and a pointed blue hat, staring morosely into his wine. Across from Alzapraz was Lancelot, Mariel's cousin, an emo-looking teenage boy with purple nail polish, black hair, and a band T-shirt for My Alchemical Bromance.

Mariel stopped short at the sight of the guest next to Lancelot. "Themmie?"

The pink-and-green-haired pixie launched out of her chair and fluttered over on rainbow-hued wings. "Mariel!" Themmie cried as she hugged her. "I'm so happy you're here. Your father has been keeping us entertained by reading news about the stock market out loud."

"Fools," Mariel's father muttered. "Wasting time on speculation when they could hire a decent prognosticator. It's corporate anti-magic bias at its finest."

Mariel hugged Themmie back, though she was confused. "What are you doing at family dinner?"

"Your mom told me I could come anytime, and my professor gave us an assignment to complete an ethnographic study on an event in our local community." Themmie winked. "We're learning about shifter-pack dynamics, and my final project will focus on hyena shifters, so I figured this would be good practice."

Mariel was taken aback by the comment. Sure, Themmie knew her family was difficult, but *hyenas*?

"Hi, Oz!" Themmie hugged him, to his obvious consternation. "Are you being a good boyfriend?"

"He saw a fire salamander today," Mariel said, shoving back her offense at the hyena comment. Themmie had clearly been joking, and Mariel had thin skin when it came to her family. "And he carried me to safety when I fainted in the forest."

"Oh, that's so romantic! Did he wake you with a kiss?"

"More like an aborted CPR attempt."

"You fainted? Why?" Mariel's mother hurried over to feel her forehead. "You don't feel feverish."

Thankfully, Oz intervened before Mariel had to talk about the dead spot in the forest. "She was practicing spellcraft and used too much magic."

Mariel cast him a grateful glance.

Her mother patted her cheek. "I've been there, dear. All part of the learning process." She smiled at Oz. "I've never seen her so dedicated to the craft! It's amazing how motivating good dick can be. Isn't that right, darling?" she called over her shoulder.

Mariel's father didn't look up from his reading. "Whatever you say, dear."

Themmie pulled out a notebook and started scribbling. "This is great," she said. "Did you know the mother hyena is the dominant one?"

Mariel buried her face in her hands.

Diantha was already bustling over to the table. "Roland, put that paper away. Oz, Mariel, go sit next to Alzapraz. Lancelot, must you look so gloomy? We're having steak!"

Oz took the seat next to Alzapraz, and Mariel sat to his left. There was a pink rose in a vase next to the candelabra centerpiece. Mariel generally didn't like cutting flowers, but when she reached out, this one seemed content to show off its vibrant petals.

Alzapraz stared at Oz for an uncomfortably long time, white eyebrows twitching like hairy caterpillars. "You should invest in a more fashionable hat," he finally said in his wheezy voice. "The twenty-first century doesn't have enough imagination."

Mariel nudged Oz and gestured at the teenager across the way. "Lancelot is my cousin. His father, Quincy, is Mom's younger brother, and his mother, Lupe, is from a prominent magical family in New Mexico." Lancelot waved awkwardly, and Mariel smiled. She liked the seventeen-year-old. He'd been a quiet, sensitive child, and it was a delight to see him growing into an artistic, thoughtful young man. "I like your nail polish," she said.

He finger-combed the swoop of black hair that nearly covered his eyes, looking embarrassed. "Thanks."

"Where are dear Quincy and Lupe?" Diantha asked. "It's not like them to skip." She took a seat at the far end of the table opposite her husband, then muttered something. The table abruptly shortened, bringing her seat careening towards them fast enough to make Mariel flinch. Soon the table was normal-sized.

"Mom has a stomach bug," Lancelot said. "So does Dad." As Diantha launched into a list of magical remedies for stomach flu, Lancelot looked at Mariel with sad eyes. "I get to have it next week."

"The old ritual sacrifice technique." They'd seen it plenty with Wally and Hector before they'd moved away. It was amazing how often one of them had been "sick."

"You know, hot springs can do wonders for the health," Diantha said, oblivious to the side conversation. "Quincy and Lupe simply must get a spa membership once the resort is built."

Mariel stiffened. "Mom, we've talked about this. The resort will damage the forest—"

"Oh, nonsense. We have so few luxuries in Glimmer Falls, and my skin is dying for a pampering."

"You already get a manicure once a week."

"Yes, but this spa is going to have all sorts of amenities. Mud baths, massage, facials, microneedling, hair demanifestation . . ." Diantha sighed dreamily. "And I'm an investor, so I'll earn money off its success."

"You have plenty of money already," Mariel said. "It isn't worth destroying the local ecosystem." A hot ball of anger was growing in her gut. She relaxed her grip on the stem of her wineglass so she wouldn't inadvertently snap it.

Diantha made a rude noise. "Please. It's just a few trees." She tipped her glass towards Mariel. "You know, if you spent half the time you spend in those woods studying spellcraft, you'd be a proper witch."

Mariel flinched. That quickly, anger morphed back into anxiety. Dinner had barely started, and her mother was already haranguing her about magic. Mariel knew from bitter experience that on nights like this, it would only get worse. Bad enough in normal times, but tonight there were witnesses.

Oz was looking at her with an expression too close to pity for her liking. "Are you all right?"

Mariel forced a smile. "Fine." She just had to put her head down and get through this.

Roland Spark cleared his throat. "So," he said, looking at Oz over his spectacles. "You're the boyfriend."

"I am." Oz looked nervous.

"You met on one of those apps."

"We did. A lucky swipe." From the hesitant way he said it, Mariel could tell he still had no idea what that meant.

Her father studied Oz for a few more seconds, then nodded. "Treat her well, or I'll turn your intestines into a pile of rats."

"Dad!" Hecate, there was a reason she never told her parents about her love life.

"Oz, what are you wearing?" Diantha abruptly asked.

He looked down at the Hawaiian shirt. "It's laundry day."

"Not that." She waved it off. "You should see the getups Alzapraz has shown up in. On one memorable occasion, he wore nothing but bedazzled pasties and a banana hammock."

Mariel winced. She remembered that incident vividly.

"And yet she still didn't kick me out," Alzapraz said mournfully.

"I'm talking about the hat," Diantha said. "Why are you wearing a hat indoors? Alzapraz has a defined aesthetic, so we allow it, but normally it's rude to wear hats at the dinner table."

"Yes," Alzapraz parroted, taking another swig of wine. "Why *are* you wearing a hat indoors?"

Mariel looked at Oz, wondering how he was going to get out of this one.

"I have . . . a condition," Oz said after a pause.

"What kind of condition?" Diantha waved her glass. "I can give you medical advice."

"It's hereditary. And, unfortunately, my grandfather's line was cursed with the inability to talk about any details."

Clever demon. Mariel hid a smile. Alzapraz snorted, then chugged more wine.

"I suppose we can allow it." Diantha frowned. "I hope your condition isn't too unsightly though. We want the best genes for the Spark line."

Mariel hated when her mom harangued her about procreating. "It's awful," she said. "Your grandchildren will look like lizard people."

Diantha looked horrified, but when Mariel's solemn expression finally cracked, her face relaxed. "Don't be cruel to your dear mother," she said. "I refuse to allow any Sparks to be lizard people." She switched her attention to Oz. "But really, how bad is your affliction on a scale of one to ten?"

"Curse," Oz said. "Can't speak."

Diantha grimaced. "Of course the first eligible bachelor who likes Mariel comes with a catch." Her glare promised death. "If you make my grandchildren faulty, I will teleport you to the Moon."

Mariel gaped at her mother. *Faulty?*

"Those grandchildren are hypothetical," Oz said in a voice like steel, "but I would never tolerate someone treating my children badly. And I would never accept anyone calling them faulty."

An uncomfortable silence fell over the table. Mariel's heart skipped as she looked at Oz's stern profile. Ruthless, her ass. For a moment, she imagined him with a toddler on his shoulders, puttering around the house. No child of his would ever have a messy room, but he would keep them safe, and she'd bet they would always feel good enough.

An ache started behind Mariel's breastbone.

"Well." Diantha twirled her empty wineglass. "He's good father material, I suppose. Roland?"

Mariel's father grabbed the wine bottle from the sideboard, then crossed to Diantha to refill her glass. "Diantha, love, I can't wait to taste what you've prepared. Where does tonight's meal come from?"

Her face brightened. "Oh, yes, I should bring dinner in!" She spoke a spell, and a full meal materialized on the table. "Today's steak comes from a Michelin-starred restaurant in Los Angeles, the salad is from Greece, the bread is from France, and the cabernet is from a private vineyard in Malta."

"Pretty sure that's stealing," Lancelot muttered, picking at his nail polish and glowering at his glass of water.

"It isn't stealing. It's using my natural gifts to ensure the well-being and happiness of my family." Diantha raised her glass. "To the Sparks! *Nos imperare suprema.*"

Mariel repeated the toast along with her family, then caught Themmie's baffled expression. She gave a half shrug, which Themmie returned. "*Nos imperare suprema,*" the pixie said before ripping off a hunk of bread.

The steak was perfectly cooked, with a pink center. Mariel took a bite, sighing with pleasure as the flavor settled over her tongue.

"This is really good." Oz was staring at his steak with a look akin to wonder.

"It's very filling," Alzapraz said. His head barely came up to Oz's shoulder, though his hat made up the difference. He was having trouble manipulating the fork and knife over the high edge of the table, and his fork let out a horrendous screech as he dragged it over the plate. "You probably won't need to eat again for a few weeks."

Mariel squinted at Alzapraz. What was he talking about?

The fork screeched again, louder this time, and everyone winced.

"Do you need a booster seat, dear Alzapraz?" Diantha asked in a poison-sweet voice.

Alzapraz set his silverware down and glared at her. "I could launch you into orbit if I felt like it."

She shrugged. "I'd teleport back down."

"I could turn you into a frog."

"I could put you in a nursing home."

Silence fell after that threat, punctuated only by the scrape of silverware and the scribbling of Themmie's pen. She looked up from her notebook, met Mariel's eyes, and mouthed, *What the fuck?*

Hecate, this was embarrassing. She was used to the antagonistic chaos of Spark Sunday dinners—or at least resigned to it—but Themmie had probably never interacted with a family that wasn't stable and loving.

Mariel's parents did love her, she told herself. They just expressed it oddly.

She rubbed her breastbone, trying to dispel the longing ache that lingered there. Wishing for a different life was pointless. This was the one she had, and she should be grateful for it.

She ate with diligent determination, trying to finish as quickly as possible so they could leave before her mother started another conversation about spellcraft. It was a popular topic at family dinner, but Mariel's nerves were already shot from introducing Oz and Themmie to this shit show. She'd rather hear her birth story for the hundredth time than go anywhere near the topic of her magical misfires.

Just as Mariel began to think she'd get away mostly scot-free, Diantha spoke again. "Mariel, tell us about your spellcraft. What have you been practicing?"

Her stomach dropped, and she focused intently on her plate. The truth obviously wouldn't do. "All sorts of things."

"Details, darling."

Well, it had been worth a shot. Mariel cleared her throat. "Um, some teleportation. Transmogrification. Things like that." If she kept it vague, maybe her mom would move on.

"Excellent!" Diantha clapped, and a griffin head on the wall roared. Oz jumped. "Show us some of what you've learned."

"I'd rather eat." Mariel cut into her steak forcefully, even though her appetite was dwindling.

Diantha pouted. "Oh, come on. Something small. Bring the salt over to your plate."

The saltshaker sat at her father's elbow. He sat back in his chair, watching the proceedings.

Mariel winced. "Do I have to?" Her stomach was full of butterflies, but not the good kind. These ones were drunk and wielding razor blades.

"I insist." Diantha's nails drummed on the table. "If you want the family to fund your gardening degree, you need to prove you're willing to put in the work to become the witch the stars said you would be."

"It's not a gardening degree," Mariel muttered, though anxiety dug its claws into her at the mention of the SoD in Magical Herbology. She wanted to go to grad school without debt, but her mom got the final say on that.

Mariel's stomach cramped; there would definitely be no more steak for her tonight.

Lancelot made a sympathetic face, while Themmie looked curious. The pixie knew about Mariel's frustrations with her magical failures, but she'd never witnessed much of it firsthand—exploded chicken aside.

Whatever happened couldn't be worse than that, at least.

Oz whispered in her ear. "We can leave."

She shook her head. "Trust me, we can't," she said bitterly.

"Lovebirds!" Diantha clapped her hands again, eliciting another squawking roar. "You can canoodle later. It's essential that Mariel progress in her magic. Isn't that right, Roland?"

"Absolutely, my love."

Mariel had long since stopped looking for an ally in that corner. Her father always took his wife's side, no matter what.

Sweat beaded her palms. She rubbed them on her skirt, then took a deep breath and straightened her shoulders. It was a small spell. Everything would be fine.

"*Zouta en liikulisen*," she said, voice shaking.

The saltshaker launched into the air, embedding itself in the ceiling. Lancelot guffawed, then quickly stopped when Oz glared at him.

Diantha looked up at the saltshaker. "Dramatic, but not what I was hoping for. Can you summon it from there?"

Mariel clenched her fists so hard her nails dug into her palms. It wasn't too late to fix this. She closed her eyes, hunting for the correct word. *Come on, stars, give me a hint.* If they insisted on setting unrealistic expectations, they could at least help a bitch out. "*Zouta en lekuzessen.*"

"Oh, no," Alzapraz said. It was the only warning before the saltshaker started vibrating with increasing intensity. It finally shattered, raining salt and shards of glass over the table. Oz grabbed Mariel, sheltering her against his chest as glass pattered against his hat.

"Mariel!" Diantha sounded furious. "What have you done?"

"Oversalted the steak," Alzapraz said mildly, picking glass out of his wine. "To each their own, I suppose."

Mariel couldn't stop shaking. She was a failure of a witch, a disappointment to her family, the stars . . . and herself. Incompetent, useless, never good enough for anyone. Tears welled, and she buried her face in Oz's shirt. Why couldn't she be the perfect daughter her mother wanted? Or at least a mediocre daughter? Despair burned like acid in her chest. She wanted to disappear, but if she couldn't even move a saltshaker, there was no way she could manage teleportation.

Oz stroked her hair soothingly. "It's all right," he murmured. "I've got you."

He didn't though, did he? It was easy to fall into the habit of relying on him, but he was another symptom of her failure.

Maybe she should trade her soul. Get rid of her magic once and for all, failing her mother so utterly that she would give up on Mariel entirely.

Mariel felt a soft wave of concern from the rose in the center of the table. She took a deep, shuddering breath. Could she really give up her connection to nature?

No. Still, Mariel didn't know how to face a lifetime as the failed Spark.

When she lifted her head, Oz's shirt was damp. "Sorry," she said, wiping her eyes. "I just wanted to eat."

Diantha was on her feet, surveying the table with outrage. "Well, none of us can eat now, thanks to you. There's glass everywhere."

"You could teleport it out," Lancelot said.

Diantha glared at him. "Not the point."

Roland's sigh was long-suffering. He leaned in, lacing his hands before him on the tablecloth. "Mariel," he said solemnly, "you know we love you. But can you please try harder? This is very disappointing."

His quiet disapproval stung almost as badly as her mother's outrage. Mariel hunched over as if she could make herself as small as she felt inside.

Oz abruptly stood. "If you don't want glass in your food, don't demand your guests perform tricks for you."

The lights flickered overhead as energy swelled, but Mariel didn't know which witch or warlock it was coming from. Maybe it was coming from her own disordered emotions.

Diantha waved a dismissive hand. "Oz, I'm sure you mean well, but in this house, we have a responsibility to produce exceptional witches. Mariel is embarrassing the family, and if she can't manage a simple summoning spell, she could hurt people."

Hurt people. Hecate, she hadn't thought of that. What if the exploded chicken was just the start?

"I bet she could manage a spell if you weren't haranguing her about it," Oz said. "I've seen her use magic effortlessly."

"Watch your tone," Mariel's father said with a scowl. "That's my wife you're talking to."

"And that's your daughter crying because everyone treats her like a badly trained show pony," Oz snapped back.

Mariel flinched at the harsh words.

"I like this guy." Alzapraz took a swig of wine, glass and all.

Mariel tugged on Oz's shirt, cheeks burning. "Please sit down." It was mortifying having him defend her. Why should he, anyway? There was no denying she was a failure.

"It doesn't have to be like this," Oz said, though he did sit. "Magic isn't a party trick to be performed on command. It's a complex web of intention and ritual that requires focus and commitment."

Great, now even Oz was explaining magic to her.

"Exactly." Diantha pointed at Mariel. "She lacks focus."

"Not where I was going with that," Oz growled. "It has to be something she wants to do."

"Why wouldn't she want to do it?" Roland asked. His brows were drawn in a look of annoyance. "It's the family legacy."

"She can want to do magic on her own terms," Oz said. "Not if you're forcing her."

Themmie looked appalled, but she was still writing. Mariel glared at the notepad, which now held all the sordid details of the disaster. Her gut churned with a toxic mix of anger and mortification, and she felt hot and cold in waves. She wanted to scream, *I'm right here. Stop talking about me like I'm not.*

Diantha scoffed. "I was forced to perform all sorts of tricks for my tutors, and I turned out fabulous."

"Questionable," Lancelot muttered.

"Mariel's magic is powerful," Oz said, "but your approach clearly isn't working. You need to consider who she is, not who you wish she was."

And oh, that cut like a knife. Because who Mariel was would never be what her mother wished for.

Her emotions boiled over, and she stood so abruptly she knocked over her wineglass. "Can you all please stop discussing me like I'm not here?" she shouted.

Everyone stared at her. The wine soaked into the white tablecloth like spilled blood.

Her mouth opened and closed a few times, but no words came out.

Mariel turned and ran.

FOURTEEN

THE SLAM OF THE FRONT DOOR FOLLOWED MARIEL'S DE-
parture.

"Well, I never," Diantha said. "So rude! And she's going to
miss the chocolate cake I summoned from Belgium."

Ozroth was on his feet instantly. He ignored Diantha's protests as he ran after Mariel.

Themmie caught up with him as he snagged his coat and
Mariel's sweater, then wrenched open the door. "I don't want to
be there anymore," Themmie said, looking distressed as she hovered beside him. "I thought Mariel was exaggerating about
her mom."

"She wasn't," Ozroth growled. "In fact, she's been far too kind."

Terrible demon parents existed, but since demon offspring
were rare, entire neighborhoods raised those children. The species thrived or failed together. Ozroth hadn't experienced that
community help as a child, but that was because he had been
raised for duty.

Mariel had apparently been raised to feel terrible about herself.

He wanted to strangle something. This was the kind of mood that would translate well to crafting a revenge bargain. He would gladly rip out someone's intestines if it fixed the pain on Mariel's face.

Themmie flew beside him as he stormed down the street. Mariel was already halfway down the hill. "Wait!" he called.

"Fuck all of you!" she shouted back. She tripped and fell, letting out a pained cry.

He sprinted towards her huddled form. "Let me see your ankle," he ordered.

She recoiled from his outstretched hand. "Leave me alone."

Why was she angry at him? "Are you hurt?"

In response, she turned her face away.

Themmie knelt next to Mariel. "Come on, babe. Talk to us." She stroked Mariel's braid, and Ozroth saw with a pang that the flower was crushed. "That was fucked up, but if you're hurt, we need to help you."

"Why don't you livestream my humiliation?" Mariel asked nastily. "That's what you were here for, right? To document my fucked-up family? You can tell your followers all about it."

Themmie looked hurt. "That's not fair. My professor told us to find a community event."

"And you thought of the thing most like a pack of hyenas, right?" Mariel laughed bitterly. "Let me know what hyenas do to the weakest members of the pack, will you?"

"You aren't weak," Ozroth said.

Mariel glared at him. "Oz, I would really like you to stop talking. It wasn't your place to speak up for me."

"Then whose place was it, Mariel?" he snapped, anger spilling out messily. "You didn't defend yourself." That was part of what had been so unbelievable—that Mariel had just sat there and taken it.

"You don't know what it's like. What you saw in there? That was nothing."

"What I saw in there was appalling."

"And next time, it'll be worse because you made a spectacle of both of us. Now my mother will rattle on about how I need a thicker skin."

"*I* made a spectacle?" He was getting really fucking pissed. The streetlamp overhead flickered, then burst with a loud *pop*. "Your mother is a spectacle."

"And you've known me for three days," Mariel snapped. "So kindly shut up about my family."

Themmie reached out to stroke Mariel's hair again, but she jerked away. "Come on, Mariel," Themmie said. "We're trying to help."

"You could have helped by not turning my family into a science project."

Themmie's wings fluttered in an agitated staccato. "It's not that deep. I was supposed to take notes about an event, and the hyena thing was a joke. Mostly."

Mariel glared at the pixie. "Yes, a hilarious one. Make sure you tweet about it."

Themmie shot off the ground. "Look, what happened in there sucked, but you don't need to be a bitch to the people on your side." She looked at Ozroth. "I'm out." With that, Themmie took off, wings carrying her over the roof of the nearest house.

Ozroth had never seen Mariel like this. Her face was red with anger, but her eyes were pools of tragedy. She sniffled and wiped her nose. "There," she said, "that's one more person who thinks I don't measure up."

Ozroth could understand her anger at her family, but this strain of self-pity wasn't productive. "She'll get over it. And besides, you did that to yourself."

"Gee, thanks. World's most supportive boyfriend."

"I'm not your boyfriend," he snapped. The air felt charged and heavy, like they were on the cusp of a lightning storm.

"No," she shot back. "You're the demon who wants to steal my soul. I'm sure your motivations are very noble. At what point are you going to milk my humiliation to get a deal out of me?"

The accusation stung. The soul bargain hadn't been even a remote part of his thought process when he'd confronted her family. He'd just wanted to protect her.

It was clear she didn't want his protection though. "You're right," he said. "I'm a horrible monster with no compassion. Fine. Here's my proposed deal: if you give me your soul, I'll give you a fucking backbone."

With that, he walked away.

◆   ◆   ◆

OZROTH'S TATTOO STARTED TINGLING WHEN HE WAS HALFWAY to Mariel's house. "Not now," he growled. It was no use though. The tattoo started burning, and Ozroth stopped beneath a half-skeletal maple tree. He punched the trunk, then felt remorse when dead leaves showered to the ground. What plants were comforting Mariel right now?

"What?" he demanded when Astaroth shimmered into view.

Astaroth's pale eyebrows shot up. "Is that any way to greet your mentor?"

The demon was dressed as neatly as always in a steel-gray suit with a black vest and tie. His tiepin was an upside-down cross, which Mariel definitely would have found cliché. Firelight flickered over Astaroth's white-blond hair, which meant he was most likely in council quarters. The archdemons enjoyed dramatic firelight.

"Sorry," Ozroth gritted out. "It's a bad time."

"Given your track record of late, I wonder whether you have any good times." Astaroth's hand flexed on the skull head of his cane. "You haven't updated me on the progress of the deal."

"I'm working on it."

"Not very hard, apparently." Astaroth looked Ozroth up and down, and horror painted his face. "What is that monstrosity you're wearing?"

"A shirt."

"It's bloody disgusting." Astaroth grimaced. "I know Glimmer Falls isn't London, but surely there are clothing options that don't scream *middle-aged father who's lost the will to live*."

"Did you summon me to talk about my wardrobe?" Ozroth asked. "Or is there a point to this conversation?"

Astaroth's gaze was piercing. The archdemon wasn't particularly large—Ozroth had a few inches and plenty of muscle on him—but there was an ancient cunning behind those ice-blue eyes. "You've developed quite a mouth since entering the human realm," Astaroth said. "Are the mortals affecting your manners, or are you losing control of your impulses?"

"I am not losing control," Ozroth said, even though that was exactly what was happening. "I just don't appreciate being micromanaged."

"Trust me. If I were micromanaging you, you'd know." Astaroth tapped his cane against his boot. "Well?"

Ozroth knew what the demon wanted to hear. Unfortunately, he couldn't say it. "She still doesn't want to make a deal."

"Seriously? How difficult can the witch be?"

"You have no idea." Pretty, obstinate, *maddening* Mariel.

"Maybe I should pay her a visit." Astaroth gripped the head of his cane, then pulled a thin silver sword from the sheath. He eyed it critically, turning the blade this way and that. "She may respond better to my techniques."

"No!" Panic filled Ozroth at the thought of Astaroth wielding that deadly blade against Mariel. There were rumors about how Astaroth had seized power. Demon society had been more feudal when he'd risen to the top, and what he'd lacked in size, he'd made up for in brutality. "I'll take care of it."

"You'd better." Astaroth sheathed his blade. "I don't push you out of cruelty. That soul in your chest is a liability, and we need to find out how much it's going to affect your performance."

"And you want to win the bet." It still rankled that Astaroth had placed odds on his success.

Astaroth inclined his head. "Think of it as extra motivation. You have until the end of the mortal month."

He vanished.

Ozroth slumped against the tree, staring blindly out at the sleeping town. Some fey creature trilled overhead, and river sprites sang their lonely melodics in the distance.

He'd been raised with one purpose: protecting the demon realm by striking hard bargains. If he failed in this task, failed the demon who had raised and mentored him, then what had all those years of loneliness and toil been for?

But inside Ozroth, a fire burned, warming the dark places in his psyche that had been neglected for so long. If he could have ripped his soul out to light the demon plane, he would have, but demons could only harvest the souls of mortals.

If he took Mariel's soul, what would happen to this oasis of magic? Would the trees and plants still thrive? Would anyone care enough to stop construction on the resort?

More importantly, what would happen to Mariel? She was young in human terms, if painfully short-lived to a demon. She would spend the remaining decades of her life as a cold shell: feeling nothing, wanting nothing, hoping for nothing.

She'd become what he had been for centuries.

FIFTEEN

Mariel trudged home an hour after her meltdown, feeling like shit. Her eyes were puffy from crying, and her stomach was tied in knots. Her emotions were a jumbled mess of embarrassment, grief, anger . . . and regret.

I'm sorry, she'd texted Themmie. Themmie hadn't responded.

Oz didn't have a phone, and Mariel wasn't sure what she would text him if he did.

You're a jackass for telling me to get a backbone, but you also stood up for me, but also I didn't ask you to, so I'm still pissed?

You're right, I don't have a backbone, but you're not allowed to say that?

It makes me mad when you act like you care because I know you're only here to steal my magic and my soul, but I'm catching feelings for you and it hurts?

Truthfully, tonight had messed her up badly. She was used to her mother belittling her. Every Sunday night, she came home feeling two feet tall. But she'd never had anyone outside her family witness her humiliation, and she was mortified that both

Themmie and Oz had seen it. When Oz had blown up at her parents, she'd wanted to sink into the floor. She was an incompetent witch as it was, and now she'd be the witch who couldn't fight her own battles. When Oz had started discussing Mariel's magic with her parents, it had been too much to take. Why did everyone think they knew exactly what she needed to get better at magic?

But Oz had looked so hurt after she'd shouted at him. Like he actually . . . cared.

If he did, where did that leave them?

"Hecate, this is a mess," she told an aspen as she passed. Its leaves rustled in response.

When she got home, she braced herself for the sight of Oz, but he wasn't on the couch or in the kitchen. Worry filled her. What if he was wandering the streets and a rogue manticore snapped him up? What if he was shivering in some alleyway? It was a cold night—it wouldn't be long before the first frost.

A tall silhouette in the moonlit greenhouse caught her eye. She hurried outside and yanked open the glass door. Moist heat spilled out—she kept a few heaters running round the clock. "Oz?" she asked, voice rough from crying.

He didn't answer for a few moments. "I'm here," he finally said.

She made her way towards him, eyes adjusting to the dark. He stood in front of her fire lily, watching the flame that flickered inside, dim as the lit end of a cigarette. "We have these in the demon plane," he said. "I recognized the cinnamon smell."

"Really? I bought the seeds online." Mariel stopped next to him, looking at his face rather than the lily. He seemed older, wearier somehow, though his immortality had frozen him looking thirty at most. He was suspended in time, like an insect trapped in amber.

Insects in amber never changed though. And if he'd once been Ozroth the Ruthless, that wasn't the person she'd come to know. Maybe Oz was a good liar, but Mariel had a mind, a heart, and sharp instincts, and she couldn't believe him capable of deceiving her so well and so cruelly.

"In the demon plane," Oz said, "they only bloom on the darkest, coldest night in the middle of winter. On that night, the mothers tell their children stories of the early age, when everything was cold and black as obsidian." He sounded distant, like he was lost in a fairy tale. "It was a primordial plane then, full of raw chaos and nothing to tame it. Then the first demon arrived, bringing light with him. Slowly but surely, our species blossomed out of the dark like fire lilies."

"That's beautiful," Mariel said.

"My mother took me to see the lilies burn. I'd forgotten until I saw this one. But she took my hand and led me outside on the longest, blackest night of the year and said that as long as there was light, there was hope."

There was anything but hope on his face though, and Mariel had the disquieting sense something more than their spat was bothering him.

"Let me show you something." Oz turned to the nearest rosebush and pressed his thumb against a thorn, and Mariel made a noise of protest as blood welled. He returned to the fire lily, then tipped his hand. The drop of blood trembled, then slid down his skin and fell into the center of the flower. Immediately, the flame strengthened, and sparks of gold burst from within like miniature fireworks.

Mariel gasped. "I didn't know it could do that."

"Demons feed our world with everything in us. Our work, our pain, our bodies . . . Without our care and the light we bring, the plants cannot thrive. Without them, the insects don't feed, which means the frogs and lizards don't, and the effect cascades until everyone goes hungry."

Outside the greenhouse, wind whipped the tops of the trees. Spatters of rain smacked against the glass. Mariel imagined a field of fire lilies, tiny sparks holding back the dark. "I'm sorry," she said. "You were only trying to help."

He stirred from his reverie and looked at her with a grim expression. "No, I'm sorry." There was a heaviness to the words, like he was apologizing for more sins than she knew.

"It's hard having people I care about see me at my lowest," she said. "I want to be strong, but I'm not. So I lashed out."

The fire lily cast a red glow on the side of Oz's face, bringing out his craggy angles. The square jaw, the big nose, the cliffs of his cheekbones. He was beautiful, she realized. Not perfect, but beautiful, like a rugged, untamed landscape.

"You are strong," he said. "You've put up with so much shit for years, but you keep fighting. You still feel hope. You still smile." He said it like smiling was a victory rather than an everyday thing, and maybe for him it was. Oz sighed. "I'm sorry Themmie saw you like that. I know you care about her."

He thought she was only upset about being vulnerable in front of Themmie?

Mariel felt the sick giddiness of standing at the edge of a long drop. It was like when her family had visited New Mexico to meet Lupe's family in Taos before Lupe's marriage to Uncle Quincy. They'd walked out onto the Rio Grande Gorge Bridge, six hundred fifty feet over the river, and nine-year-old Mariel's stomach had wanted to trade places with her brain when she'd peered over the side.

Some impulses were irresistible though, and Mariel had never been good at resisting impulses anyway. Fuck the drop. "Not just Themmie," she said, stepping closer to Oz.

His brow furrowed, then cleared. "Lancelot. Truly, your family has some of the most ludicrous names—"

Because he still wasn't getting it, and because Mariel wasn't sure she could produce articulate words to explain herself, she did the only reasonable thing. She stood on her tiptoes and kissed the demon.

When their lips met, Oz made a startled sound. He pulled back, staring at her with wild eyes, then cursed and hauled her into his arms. His mouth crashed over hers, hot and rough. Mariel melted into him, lacing her arms around his neck. He was hot everywhere, his body and lips feverish.

This was what she'd been needing. He infuriated her, grounded her, challenged her, and encouraged her, and there was a magnetic pull between them she couldn't explain. As Mariel kissed him, she pulled him closer, wrapping a leg around his like a climbing vine. In response, Oz gripped her ass in two massive hands and lifted her off the ground like she weighed nothing. Mariel locked her ankles behind his back as he carried her towards the house, mouths fused the whole time. Her back hit the siding, and she gasped as Oz moved to suck her neck.

"Mariel," he whispered against her skin. Her name was followed by a nip to her earlobe. "Fuck. How can I want this so much?"

"I want it, too." Her voice came out breathy.

Oz pressed his hips harder into her, and Mariel moaned. Her skirt had slid up, revealing her bare thighs to the cool night, but she barely noticed the chill. His lips traced fire over her neck before returning to her mouth for more deep, drugging kisses. He was hard beneath his jeans, and she rocked against him as much as she could while pinned against the wall.

Mariel whimpered when he hit the perfect spot, sending a bolt of pleasure through her. "Yes," she gasped, clawing at his shoulders.

He cursed, then squeezed her ass tighter, grinding against her in a hard, urgent rhythm. Hecate, he was strong. His biceps were like steel when she ran her hands over them. What would it feel like to have his massive body on top of her, his breath hot in her ear as he thrust inside her?

The thought made Mariel wetter. She hadn't had sex in years, and never with someone who turned her on this much. She kissed him desperately, sliding her tongue over his, then nipping at his lower lip. Fallen autumn leaves swirled in a fury as her pleasure grew, and blue lightning danced across the night sky.

"Oz, please," she begged against his lips. "Take me to bed."

He groaned. "You're tormenting me, Mariel."

"You're the demon," she teased. "Aren't you the professional tormentor?"

Oz abruptly stilled. A second later, Mariel was dumped back on her feet. She sagged against the wall, trying to catch her breath as Oz backed away. His expression was agonized as he jammed his hands into his hair, tugging on the dark locks. "Shit."

"What's wrong?" She'd only meant to tease him, but he looked truly wounded. When he turned his back on her, hurt arrowed through her heart. "Oz, please talk to me."

He shook his head. "This was a mistake." His voice was raw and ragged. "It can never happen again." Then he yanked open the side gate and disappeared into the night.

Mariel was left alone and throbbing with unfulfilled need. She shivered as cold air wrapped around her. What the demon plane had just happened?

SIXTEEN

THE BELL TINKLED AS THE ALL-NIGHT DINER'S DOOR opened. Mariel looked up from her plate of comfort fries and was surprised to see both Themmie and Calladia. She'd only texted Calladia.

Calladia was dressed like normal, but Themmie wore a unicorn onesie with a back flap for her wings to stick out of. Her bunny slippers were cute, but her scowl was anything but. "Let it be known I'm here reluctantly," Themmie announced as she slid into the booth opposite Mariel. Like most establishments in town, there was a gap between the seat and the back so flying folk could settle their wings comfortably.

"I'm sorry," Mariel said. "I texted you."

Themmie sniffed. "It wasn't a very specific apology."

"I'm sorry I snapped at you," Mariel said, swallowing her pride. "And sorry that I said that mean stuff about social media. I was feeling humiliated, so I lashed out." She slid the fries across the table, looking at Themmie contritely. "Am I forgiven?"

Themmie picked up a fry and bit into it. "Now you are," she

said. "And if it makes you feel better, I decided to write about a different event for class. So come on, what emergency requires therapy at one a.m.?"

Mariel's text to Calladia had been admittedly vague, typed in a panic as she'd jogged down the street trying to find Oz: *I maybe did something bad? Or good? But I'm freaking out and also you are going to be so mad at me.*

Calladia had texted back almost immediately. *The Centaur Cafe, twenty minutes.*

There was only one other patron at this hour: a professor-looking type in a fedora who was reading a magical tome. Maybe Mariel should ask him if it contained any advice about romancing demons.

Calladia sat to Themmie's left, arms crossed. "Yeah, tell me why I'm about to be mad at you."

Mariel hadn't thought this through. She'd been panicked, horny, and confused, and all she'd known was that she needed to rant to someone. Now, with both Themmie and Calladia staring at her, she wondered how she was going to confess what she'd done.

Calladia arched a blond brow. "Well?"

"ImadeoutwithOz," Mariel said, far too fast and high-pitched.

Themmie wrinkled her nose. "What?"

Mariel took a deep breath. "I made out with Oz." She cringed in anticipation of Calladia's rebuke.

"You didn't!" Calladia exclaimed, sitting bolt upright. "Mariel, you horny disaster."

Themmie still looked confused. "Why is that a big deal? He's her boyfriend."

Mariel winced. Right. Themmie was still unclear about the particulars of her "relationship." "It's . . . complicated."

Themmie rolled her eyes. "If you don't tell me what in Tinker Bell's name is going on, I'm leaving. I have to stream in the morning."

"Yeah," Calladia said, smirking at Mariel. "Why don't you tell Themmie exactly what's happening with Oz? I'm sure she'll be *fascinated* to know."

Mariel glared at Calladia. This could have been avoided if Calladia hadn't invited the pixie. Then again, Mariel hadn't mentioned the issue was about Oz, and the three of them had held many other late-night counseling sessions over the years since they'd met Themmie in Glimmer Falls's Environmental Protection Club.

Themmie snagged another fry, dipping it in Mariel's ketchup. "This ought to be good."

"So about Oz," Mariel said. "I know I said he's my boyfriend, but . . . he's not."

Themmie wrinkled her nose. "So what is he? A friend with benefits?"

"Not that either." Although after tonight, she had no idea what they were. "Basically, my mother saw us together, and I panicked."

"Spit it out," Calladia said. "The news isn't going to improve with time."

She was right. Mariel decided to plunge right in. "You remember the demon I mentioned? The one on my couch?"

"Yeah, you, like, have a squatter? I thought Oz was going to beat him up." Themmie's eyes widened, and Mariel saw the moment the pixie realized. "Wait, no."

"Yes. Oz is a demon."

Themmie shot out of her seat, the same way she had when this had first been brought up at Le Chapeau Magique. The movement knocked the unicorn hood back, revealing her sleep-tousled hair. Her wings blurred, and she lifted several feet off the ground. "I hugged him!" she whisper-shrieked. "We had dinner together! What the fuck, Mariel?"

"Sit down," Calladia said. "It gets worse."

Themmie settled back into the seat, eyes wide.

Mariel shoved three fries into her mouth. If only salt and grease could cure all of life's ills. "I was baking," she said around the food, "and I tried to summon flour. But I kind of messed up the spell and summoned a demon instead."

"Sweet Flora, Fauna, and Merryweather," Themmie said. "I know the language of magic is incomprehensible to the rest of us, but surely the words for *flour* and *demon* aren't that similar."

"When you fuck up, they are," Mariel muttered.

"So Oz appeared in your kitchen? Like *poof, here's a hot demon*?"

"Yeah." Mariel grimaced. "And he can't go back to the demon plane until I give him my soul in exchange for some impossible favor."

Themmie gaped at her.

Mariel fidgeted uncomfortably. "Look, can we move on to the part where I made out with him? I need advice."

"What even is a soul?" Themmie asked. "I thought it was a religious metaphor."

"Apparently it's our magic. Demons don't produce their own." Mariel frowned. "Except some have bargaining magic, but I guess it doesn't count."

"Other humans don't have magic. Do they have souls?"

"Maybe it's an issue of verbiage. Like how *hell* means 'loyal' in Old Demonish. Maybe *soul* means 'witch magic,' and English bungled it up."

Calladia smacked a hand on the table. "Can we stop speculating about etymology and focus on the issue at hand? You hooked up with a demon."

Themmie leaned in, brown eyes gleaming with interest. "You absolute freak. Was it good?"

"Ugh." Mariel buried her head in her arms. "So good," she muttered. "I almost came."

"Whoa, whoa, whoa," Calladia said. "I thought you were just making out."

Mariel looked up sheepishly. "I mean, yes, but there was grinding involved . . ."

Themmie signaled the waiter for a strawberry milkshake. "Tell us everything."

Mariel summed up the situation while Themmie listened raptly, sucking noisily on her milkshake.

"He's so strong," Mariel said, swirling a fry in ketchup and looking dreamily into the distance. "He probably could have carried me for days without breaking a sweat."

"Ugh, that's so hot," Themmie said.

Calladia whacked Mariel's head with a rolled-up napkin. "Go to horny jail." She hit Themmie next. "You, too. You should not be encouraging this."

"Why not?" Themmie asked. "Mariel hasn't been laid in . . . how long?"

"Five years," Mariel supplied immediately. She'd had a few short relationships in college and immediately after, but she was working on a demon plane of a dry spell.

"Oof." Themmie grimaced. "Have you asked the gyno to check for cobwebs?" Mariel threw a fry at her, and Themmie laughed. "Anyway," the pixie said, shoving the assault fry in her mouth, "if he's going to be around forever, Mariel might as well get on good terms with him." She waggled her eyebrows. "How big is his dick?"

"Big," Mariel said. "I mean, I didn't get a hand around it or anything, but he's a big guy. And I saw his dick print when he got dunked in the hot spring."

Calladia plugged her ears. "La la la, I can't hear you."

"You know, the demon thing freaked me out," Themmie said, "but he seems decent. Now, that is. He was kind of a jerk at first."

"I think he is decent," Mariel said. "It's not like he wanted to get summoned. He's not even trying that hard to get my soul."

Themmie winked. "Sounds like he's trying to get something else."

"But that's the thing. He freaked out and said we couldn't do this again." She didn't even know where he was, though he had to be somewhere in her general vicinity. Was he sitting on a bench in the park? Sleeping in an alleyway? Oz was a big, tough demon, but it was cold and the hour was late, and she worried about him.

Calladia toyed with her ponytail. "Is he withholding sex until you make a bargain? If so, he must think a lot of his penis."

"I doubt it." Mariel worried her lip between her teeth. "He ran after I said something."

"What?"

Mariel grabbed Calladia's rolled-up napkin and shredded it, watching the pieces fall like ragged snow into her lap. "He said I was tormenting him. And then I said that since he's a demon, he's the professional tormentor. And just like that, it was over." She pictured his devastated expression, and her stomach twisted. "He looked really upset."

Calladia considered, lips pursed. "Sounds like he didn't like being called a tormentor. That's weird though. He's literally named Ozroth the Ruthless."

Themmie snorted. "Men and their egos and their ridiculous bro nicknames. I've seen the way he looks at you, Mariel. That demon is soft as a kitten." She noisily sucked up the last drop of milkshake, then signaled the waiter for another. Pixies were notorious sugar fiends, their metabolisms seemingly on par with hummingbirds.

Mariel wasn't sure Oz could be called soft as a kitten, but there was obviously *some* attraction between them. "So I hurt his feelings by calling him a tormentor? That's not fair. He called me the same thing."

"Have you considered he may feel guilty about being here?"

Calladia squinted at Themmie. "What do you mean? Collecting souls is his job."

Themmie grabbed the new milkshake, thanked the waiter, then started chugging that one, too. "I'm just saying," she said, a drip of strawberry shake trailing down her chin, "aren't soul bargains usually consensual? This one was an accident, but he can't get out of it even if he wants to. Plus, he feels attracted to you, which is tough when he's obligated to take your magic." She shrugged. "Wouldn't you feel like shit if you were him?"

Silence fell, punctuated only by Themmie's slurping sounds. Even Calladia looked stricken by the thought. "I hadn't considered that," the blond witch finally said.

Mariel felt even guiltier. "It's my fault," she said, wishing her glass of water were a glass of vodka. "I summoned him. He had no choice."

"It was an accident," Themmie said. "And it's only been a few days, right? You'll figure something out."

"Maybe." But if Oz had never heard of a situation like this in hundreds of years, how was Mariel supposed to get them out of it?

"And if you don't, why not get romantic with him?" Themmie sighed, looking wistful. "Maybe he's your soul mate, and you're meant to be together forever. Maybe you never would have met if it wasn't for the bargain."

"Hard to have a soul mate when only one person has a soul," Calladia grumbled.

It was ridiculous, Disney-style nonsense, but Mariel still felt a pang of longing. She'd basically entrapped Oz into staying with her, but the romantic part of her wished what Themmie was saying was true—that Mariel and Oz had such a connection, they'd never need or want to be parted. She'd never felt particularly lovable, and the idea of a strong, handsome guy who adored her and never wanted to leave her side was intoxicating.

Oz wanted to leave her side though. And, logistically speaking, one or the other of them would eventually get tired of forced proximity. Even Mariel's romantic heart could acknowledge that.

And even if this was some wild, fabled love that defied reason . . . it would still end in tragedy.

"Oz is immortal," Mariel said. "Do you really want him following me around a memory care facility in seventy years when I have no idea who he is?"

"Oh." Themmie's face fell. "I forgot that bit."

More silence followed. Mariel rested her head in her pillowed arms again. The table smelled like stale barbecue sauce.

"You don't have to figure everything out right now," Calladia said gently. "It's two a.m., and none of us are thinking straight. You can hit the library tomorrow."

"I have work and then the town hall."

Calladia tsked. "You have at least three hours between work and the town hall. You can keep alternating between helplessness and horniness, but I, personally, would like to find a solution to your problem."

Mariel popped her head up to glare at her friend. "You suck."

"Guilty as charged." Calladia reached across the table to stroke the side of Mariel's head. "Come on. It's late, and you're exhausted."

Mariel sighed. "Fine." Then she looked between her two friends, feeling unaccountably like crying. "Thank you. For being here and listening to me."

"Thank *you*," Themmie said vehemently. "This is delicious gossip." Mariel slapped her arm, and Themmie laughed. "But really, call me whenever. This shit is wild."

They parted ways to walk (or fly, in Themmie's case) to their respective houses. As Mariel trudged home, she kept her eyes peeled for signs of Oz. She wasn't sure how close he had to stay, and she hoped he wasn't curled up under some bush, freezing to death.

She finally found Oz sitting on the curb outside her house. His horns gleamed in the soft light of the ivy-bound streetlamp. He didn't look up as she approached.

Mariel sat next to him and cleared her throat. "You aren't a tormentor. I think you're a lovely person."

He grimaced. "Categorically untrue, and you barely know me."

"I know you're kind and supportive. And I know you don't want to make a bargain any more than I do."

"Yes, I do," he was quick to say. "Making bargains is my sole purpose in life." He didn't look convincing though. If he frowned any harder, his death stare might bore a hole into the asphalt.

"I don't think you have to be defined by your job."

"You do when you're a bargainer." He ran a hand through his hair, tugging on it. She was learning his tells; he fussed with his hair when he was upset. "If I fail, it affects more than just me. The demon plane relies on the magic I bring."

"But you don't want to take my magic because you know I don't want to lose it. I put you in an impossible situation when I summoned you."

He grimaced. "A proper demon wouldn't care how a bargain came about."

"Then I'm glad you're not a proper demon."

"Tell that to Astaroth. I'm sure he'll be overjoyed."

Mariel would gladly tell Astaroth many things, none of them polite. She was about to say so when Oz shivered. "Come on," she said, nudging him with her shoulder. "It's late, and you're cold."

"I'm not cold," he said stubbornly, though he shivered again.

"What will sitting outside all night accomplish? Will it make you feel better?"

". . . No."

"Then come on." She stood and held out her hand, biting her lip at Oz's sulky look. "You're one step away from self-flagellation, and that's way too medieval for a classy demon like you."

He huffed as he pushed to his feet, fingers grazing hers in acknowledgment of the offer of help. "You're very annoying sometimes," he said as they headed towards the house.

"I'm delighted to hear it," she said as she unlocked the door. "I was getting tired of being perfect all the time."

When Oz tried to turn into the living room, Mariel gripped his arm. "That couch can't be comfortable."

He grunted. "It's fine."

What a liar. Mariel tugged on his arm until he followed her down the hallway. "You're going to sleep in a proper bed tonight under a pile of blankets."

"Where will you sleep?"

Her heart raced. Maybe this was a terrible idea, considering what had happened, but she didn't want him to be cold and uncomfortable. She was being charitable, right? "Next to you."

"Mariel . . ." He said her name like a warning. "I told you we couldn't do that again."

It was the first acknowledgment of their hookup, and the rejection stung just as much the second time around. But Calladia had been right—nothing would be solved tonight. "Just to sleep," she said. "I'm exhausted, and tomorrow's going to be a long day."

Despite his grumbling, she badgered him into brushing his teeth with the toothbrush Calladia had brought earlier, then stripping to his—heart-patterned?—boxers. He sat at the edge of her bed, looking awkward. She squinted at his feet. "Are those kitten socks?"

He immediately swung his legs onto the bed and slid his feet under the covers. "You can thank Calladia for that. And the underwear."

Mariel definitely would. She took a moment to admire the sight of Oz tucking himself in. His muscles rippled as he tugged the blanket to his shoulders, and his horns looked sleek and sharp against the blue satin pillowcase. He took up most of the space, and Mariel felt weirdly triumphant at having such a big, virile demon in her bed.

She left to brush her teeth and change into an oversized black T-shirt that fell almost to her knees. She'd gotten it at a concert for their local grunge band The Pixies (No Not Those Ones), and it was her favorite to sleep in. When she padded barefoot back to her room, she smiled to see that Oz had grabbed more blankets from the linen closet. He was a large lump under the covers, black hair and the tips of his horns barely peeking out.

She slid into bed next to him and turned off the light. It was deliciously warm under the covers. Who needed a heated blanket when you could sleep next to a demon?

Mariel yawned, exhaustion hitting her like a truck. She could tell from Oz's breathing that he was awake, but she was slipping quickly towards slumber. "'Night, Oz," she mumbled. "Try not to stay up brooding for too long."

The covers rustled as he shifted. "Annoying," he muttered, though the word lacked any real vitriol.

Mariel smiled as she drifted into sleep.

SEVENTEEN

OZROTH WOKE GRADUALLY, DREAMS BLURRING BEFORE
fading away. He was warm and comfortable, wrapped in
something soft and fluffy. He curled himself tighter around his
pillow.

The pillow let out a soft, feminine murmur, and his eyes shot
open.

Mariel lay with her back to him, brown hair splayed over the
pillow they were sharing. Ozroth's arm was banded around her
stomach, and he realized with a mix of delight and dismay that
her ass was nestled against his morning erection.

She made another kittenish sound and squirmed, turning her
face deeper into the pillow. Ozroth hissed as her ass rubbed his
dick. He should have shot out of bed, removing himself from the
source of temptation, but his body refused to obey. She was so soft
in his arms, her skin cool compared to his heat, and he wanted
nothing more than to hold her and keep her warm forever.

Her hips shifted again, and alarm bells blared in his mind. He
was seconds from thrusting against her, and it would be wrong to

do that to a sleeping woman. He slid his hand off her stomach, intending to stop touching her, but his fingertips grazed bare skin, and he froze. Her sleeping shirt had rucked up during the night and was twisted around her waist. He trailed his fingers gently over her hip, cursing under his breath when he brushed the edge of her cotton underwear.

Truly, how much self-control was a demon expected to have when faced with unbearable temptation?

Mariel's breath hitched, and she squirmed again. Her hips rocked under his hand once, then again, her ass dragging slowly over his cock. Not asleep, then, and not willing to stop this either.

Ozroth should have gotten up. He should have denied both of them. But it was easy to pretend, here in this dim bedroom with morning light spilling from a crack in the curtains, that this was how things were between them. He inhaled the scent of her hair, fingers squeezing her hip as he guided her against him.

It was a slow, sensual grind. Ozroth moved his other hand from beneath the pillow, sliding it under her so he could cup one of her breasts. She made a soft noise and arched her back, pressing into his palm. Her breast filled his hand perfectly, and the point of her nipple stood up under the cotton shirt.

This woman was a paradise of curves. He slid the hand on her hip under her shirt, caressing the soft swell of her lower belly. His fingers teased at the waistband of her underwear, and Mariel moved against him more urgently. Her eyes were still closed, dark lashes feathered against her cheek, but she was breathing unevenly.

This was how a demon came undone. Ozroth panted into her hair, grinding against her. His pinky traced lower, brushing over her mons, and she jerked in his arms. Was she wet?

"Oz," she breathed. Her hand came to his wrist, guiding him to reach beneath her underwear. His fingers brushed coarse curls, and his heart was racing so fast, he thought he might pass out. He vowed to make her come so hard, she never forgot the feel of his fingers inside her.

BEEP BEEP BEEP BEEP BEEP

Ozroth jumped like a startled cat at the loud, shrill sound. He tumbled off the edge of the bed, cracking his horns against the nightstand. Pain shot through him, and he curled up on his side with a groan.

"Oh, Hecate!" Mariel cried out. He heard her scrambling over the covers, then the sound of her fumbling at something on the nightstand. "Stupid fucking alarm." The noise finally stopped. "Are you okay?"

He looked up to see her peering over the edge of the bed, forehead furrowed in concern. "Unh," he said, unable to articulate the mix of arousal, terror, and pain he was currently feeling.

Mariel clambered out of bed and knelt next to him. "Are your horns all right?" Her fingers hovered over one, and he was glad she didn't touch it, since his dick was confused enough.

"Fine." He sounded very not-fine, even to his own ears.

"Can I get you anything? Ice? Ibuprofen?"

"Just . . . give me a moment." Ozroth closed his eyes, breathing deeply. His erection was flagging, thanks to the loud noise and sudden pain, and with the haze of arousal gone, he could think more clearly.

What had he been thinking, humping Mariel like a hormonal human? Hadn't he told her not even twelve hours before that this could never happen again? Yet here he was, indulging his lust, even though he would eventually be her undoing.

He smacked his forehead against his knees once, then again.

"Hey." Mariel's hand rested on his shoulder. "Are you okay?"

"Fine." This one sounded even less convincing.

"Talk to me."

She always wanted to talk, as if that would fix anything. Oz-roth wanted to snap at her, but his souring mood wasn't her fault, so he restrained himself. "Let's move on, all right?"

There were a few moments of silence. Then he heard rustling as Mariel moved away. "Fine." She sounded pissed, which she probably had every right to be, but Ozroth didn't have the energy to follow up. It was only seven thirty a.m., and he was already overwhelmed by the day.

He stayed in the bedroom while she showered, only using the bathroom once she went to the kitchen. He felt like a coward tip-toeing around and hoping she wouldn't confront him about the dry humping, but what else was he supposed to do?

"I'm going to work," Mariel called out. "I don't care what you do." The front door slammed behind her.

When Ozroth entered the kitchen, he felt a pang in his chest at the sight of an untouched bowl of cereal with a carton of milk set beside it. Pissed or not, Mariel was feeding him.

His stomach grumbled, and he glared down at his gut. "How do humans get anything done with all this eating and sleeping?" he groused. Guilt built as he sat down to eat. He was a mess, un-able to act like a proper demon. The emotions that had come with gaining a soul had been easier to manage in the demon plane, but since coming to Earth, it had become impossible to control them. Illogical impulses assailed him—like *grinding against the woman whose soul he was supposed to collect*—and he veered wildly be-tween lust, anger, and guilt. As if his own internal landscape wasn't chaotic enough, the outside world felt so raw, colorful, and loud that it was difficult to cope. Even the cinnamon flavor of the cereal he was spooning into his mouth made him want to cry.

"Having a soul is terrible," he muttered.

There was a tugging sensation under his breastbone, like someone had looped thread around his ribs and was pulling on the end. Mariel had gotten far enough away that the bargain magic required him to follow. He finished the cereal, then left the house, following the mystical pull.

Glimmer Falls was a pretty town, full of colorful houses with sharply angled roofs. After fifteen minutes of walking, Ozroth reached downtown, where a golden clock stood at the entrance to a small park surrounded by shops and restaurants. The clock had a multitude of hands pointing at different numbers and runes. Some symbols he recognized—it was early afternoon in the demon plane, for instance—but others were a mystery. One hand circled relentlessly, speeding up and slowing down at irregular intervals. When thin blue streaks of electric energy started dancing around the clock face, Ozroth hurried away.

The people wandering the streets were no less colorful. He passed an elderly witch with green hair and a rat on her shoulder, then a street entertainer casting a fireworks show. Rainbow wings flashed at the other end of the park as a male pixie alighted outside an ice-cream parlor. What other types of people would Ozroth see here? Werewolves? Centaurs? Selkies?

The fountain in the center of the park was a marble sculpture of two warlocks with their hands raised. Water cascaded from their fingertips and collected in the basin. CASPER CUNNINGTON AND GALAHAD SPARK, a plaque read. FOUNDERS OF GLIMMER FALLS. 1842. Ozroth eyed Galahad Spark's deep-set eyes and elaborate mustache. There was nothing of Mariel in his narrow face, but then again, there didn't seem to be much of her in the rest of the family either.

Something burst out of the water, and Ozroth swore and leapt back. A woman was treading water—how deep *was* this fountain?—and staring at him. Her black hair was woven with seaweed, and her brown skin glistened with rainbow scales around her hairline and neck. A naiad, then, a type of nymph that transitioned easily between land and water. Her gills were barely visible now that she'd shifted to breathing air. "You're new," she said.

Ozroth put his hand up to make sure his hat was still on. "Recently moved."

She glided towards the edge of the fountain. "You're hot. Are you single?" When she pulled herself up, Ozroth was alarmed to realize she was nude.

He turned his back. What would Mariel think if she saw him conversing with a naked naiad? "No. Is swimming nude in fountains normal behavior around here?"

She laughed. "There's no such thing as normal behavior in Glimmer Falls."

"I'm starting to get that."

He heard rustling. "It's safe," the naiad called out.

When he turned, she was dressed in jeans and a baggy *Save the Coelacanths* T-shirt. She wrung out her hair, then clipped it on top of her head. "I'm on my hydration break," she said. "The river's too far of a walk from work."

"Right." Why did mortals insist on making idle conversation with strangers? "I'm leaving now," he said after an uncomfortable pause.

"Hi, Leaving Now," the naiad said. "I'm Rani."

He stared at her blankly.

Rani rolled her eyes. "No dad jokes for you, huh?" Now that she was out of the water, the colorful scales along her hairline were fading. "Fine, I'll leave you alone." She walked off, whistling.

"This place is strange," Ozroth said. Most cities around the world had a supernatural contingent, but Glimmer Falls had cornered the market on magical oddities.

"Strange!" The echoing squawk came from a nearby tree, and

Ozroth saw a puff of red feathers among the autumn leaves and the gold gleam of scales winding around the trunk.

He had no idea what that creature was and no desire to find out. The magic was tugging at his ribs again, and he didn't want to engage with anyone but Mariel, human or otherwise.

A banner reading GLIMMER FALLS AUTUMN FESTIVAL hung over Main Street. Had the festival already started? Time seemed to be passing too slowly and too quickly all at once. Ozroth stopped to look at a newspaper box. *October 24.*

Astaroth's words rang in his head. *You have until the end of the mortal month.* His stomach plummeted. One week to win Mariel's soul. It wasn't enough time.

Ozroth knew he was lying to himself though. He'd used threats, manipulation, and violence to force deals out of warlocks who had dragged their heels or tried to change the terms at the last minute. There were all sorts of ways to motivate a human to make the ultimate sacrifice, so long as you knew what they cared about—or feared—most.

Making her afraid was out of the question, but Ozroth knew what Mariel cared about. Her friends and nature, certainly. But the deep wish, the one that cut into her heart, was the longing to be good enough. To be loved just as she was.

As Ozroth watched a child painting a pumpkin outside an arts and crafts store, he thought about the deals he could make with Mariel.

I can make you the most famous witch in the world.

I can make your mother proud of you.

I can make someone love you.

Ozroth's heart hurt. Anything he brought Mariel would ultimately be a lie. The universe would branch, as it had many times before, people shifting into new trajectories with no one but Ozroth to know how else their lives might have gone. It had never bothered him before, but the thought of forcing anyone to love Mariel made him sick. She deserved to be loved all on her own.

And what would happen to the people forced to love her after her emotions faded? They would be trapped loving a shell, hopelessly devoted to the pale echo of who Mariel had once been. Most of the witches and warlocks he'd dealt with in the past had already been cold and calculating, but Mariel was the opposite of that: loving, vibrant, and deserving of so much more than a purely cerebral existence.

Collateral damage, Astaroth had told Ozroth when he'd balked at a love bargain a century past. *The warlock chose this path; you are merely the instrument for his ambitions. A weapon is not to blame for the actions of the person wielding it.*

Ozroth was tired of being a weapon or the means to someone else's ends. He wanted to be the one making decisions. And if he had the choice . . . he very well might choose to stay chained to Mariel forever.

Leaves skidded past his boots on a gust of wind. Ozroth wondered if they were headed towards her, too.

This stasis was intolerable, but Ozroth couldn't bear to see it end. Still, Astaroth was right: choice wasn't an option for a bargainer.

But he wasn't sure his soul—or his heart—could bear what needed to be done.

EIGHTEEN

MARIEL SCOWLED AS SHE WATERED AN IRIS. THE PLANT shrank, and she patted its leaves in apology. "It's not you," she explained. "It's Oz."

The temerity of that demon! Humping her into the mattress, then hiding like a coward.

"What?" Ben looked up from his ledger. He looked like a nerdy lumberjack in a plaid shirt and worn jeans.

"I told the plant I wasn't mad at it. It was worried."

"If you say so," he said skeptically, nudging gold-frame glasses up his nose.

Mariel moved down the line of flowers, watering and petting them. As she did, some of the tightness in her chest eased. She fell into the familiar, meditative rhythm of work, letting the motions carry her worried thoughts away.

"What do you mean there's no VIP service?" The familiar voice shattered Mariel's concentration. She set the watering can aside and hurried towards the front.

Ben was standing with his hands on his hips and his toe tapping. Facing him down was Cynthia Cunnington, looking as Waspy as ever in a pink dress belted at the waist, augmented by pearls, a white designer handbag, and oversized sunglasses perched on her blond updo.

"I own this store," Ben said, gesturing towards the BEN'S PLANT EMPORIUM sign hanging over the register, which Mariel had hand-painted as a present. "That's as VIP as it gets."

Cynthia sniffed and looked him up and down. "Then get me diamond begonias."

"I already told you, we're sold out."

Diamond begonias were a rare, glittering varietal that had a libido-enhancing effect when eaten. During the months they were in season, they were snapped up almost as soon as they were put on shelves.

"You don't understand. I need them *today*."

"Sounds like you procrastinated baking your festival pie," Mariel called out. It was the Autumn Festival's opening day, and the baking competition would play out that afternoon—something her mother's frantic text messages had made abundantly clear. Mariel hadn't answered those texts yet, some foolish part of her hoping her mother would at least acknowledge, if not apologize for, the dinner party disaster.

"Mariel," Cynthia said. "So happy to see you here." Her tone made it clear she was anything but.

"We have other edible flowers like pansies and marigolds," Ben said. "If you'll come this way . . ."

Cynthia cut him off with a sharp movement of her hand. "I don't want other flowers." She turned to Mariel. "This man is useless. Surely you can get me diamond begonias?"

Mariel crossed her arms, glaring at Cynthia. "Ben owns this shop. If he says we don't have them, we don't have them."

Cynthia sniffed. "I'm the *mayor*." She said it like a magic word that would open a secret begonia stash.

"Trust me, we know," Ben said dryly.

Cynthia turned her back on him. "I hate talking to manual laborers. Mariel?"

Ben looked baffled and offended, and Mariel's temper spiked. What did Cynthia expect her to do, conjure some out of nowhere? Since plants were involved, there was a possibility Mariel would get it right, but she wasn't going to try. "No," she said.

"What?"

"I said no." Mariel pointed at the door. "Now get out."

Cynthia gasped. "Excuse me?"

"Say whatever you want to me, but do *not* be rude to my friends."

"Do you know what I can do to this store?" Cynthia asked. "I could shut it down today."

Ben made a distressed sound.

Mariel lifted her chin so she could look down—or up—her nose at the taller witch. "We have CCTV with audio, which means your threats and nasty comments could go viral." She fingered the phone in her dress pocket. "In fact, my friend is an influencer. Should I text her?"

The words felt exhilarating but also nauseating. She'd never snapped at Cynthia Cunnington this way. Cynthia was like Diantha: her power unforgiving, her influence unquestionable. Mariel clenched her hands in her pockets to stop their trembling.

The shop bell tinkled, and Mariel felt a mix of anger and relief at the sight of a tall, brooding figure in a cowboy hat. Apparently Oz was done cowering.

Cynthia didn't acknowledge the newcomer. "Every day I thank the stars that I have Calladia as a daughter instead of you," she said in a low, hard voice.

Mariel flinched.

"Watch it," Ben growled.

"You're a laughingstock," Cynthia continued. "*The most powerful witch in centuries*, please." She chuckled. "Everyone jokes about it when Diantha isn't around."

Mariel's stomach twisted at the cruel words, but she kept her spine straight. She was tired of letting people walk all over her.

A large hand came to rest on Cynthia's shoulder, and she jumped. "Time to go," Oz said curtly, steering her towards the door.

"Don't manhandle me!" Cynthia shook him off. "Don't you know who I am?"

"Yes. Unfortunately."

Cynthia grabbed her pearls and started working the beads in her fingers, whispering under her breath.

Alarm spiked through Mariel. "Oz, watch out—"

A shock wave thumped into Mariel's chest as Oz was launched backward. Blue electricity forked overhead as he crashed into shelves holding succulents. The shelves collapsed on top of him, sending plants flying as terra-cotta pots shattered. Mariel cried out at the sudden pain of bruised leaves.

She rushed over to Oz, who was staggering back to his feet. "Are you okay?" Her nose burned with the acrid scent of ozone.

He grunted. "I'll be fine."

Mariel patted him, searching for injuries. He didn't seem to be bleeding, but when she touched his shoulder, he winced. He grabbed her wrists, stilling her. "I mean it," he said, his expression surprisingly soft. "I'm tougher than I look."

He must be a fucking tank, then, because Oz looked plenty tough already. Mariel spun on Cynthia. Hot rage bloomed in her chest, and the air grew thick with incipient magic. Plants thrashed in their pots, and a climbing vine reached a tendril towards Cynthia's neck. Cynthia's eyes widened as Mariel approached.

"You will never try to hurt him again," Mariel said through gritted teeth. "And you will never step foot in this store again either. Do you understand me?" The pump of fury in her veins was intoxicating, and Mariel clenched her fists, imagining striking the older witch.

Cynthia's mouth worked. "Well, I never—"

"*Bocca en fechersen!*" The words burst from Mariel without conscious thought. Cynthia's mouth snapped shut, and she made a muffled noise of alarm behind her sealed lips.

Power buzzed in Mariel's veins, and exhilaration filled her at realizing the spell had worked. No chalk needed, just pure rage. "Get out."

Cynthia gestured at her sealed lips, eyes wide.

Mariel shrugged. "Find someone else to lift the spell. I'm a laughingstock, right?"

She turned her back and started setting the store to rights. A muffled scream was followed by the tinkling of the bell as the door slammed open. When Mariel looked over her shoulder, Cynthia was gone.

Mariel leaned against the nearest shelf, sucking in a deep breath. The prickle of magic in the air diminished.

"Wow." Ben rubbed his bearded chin. "That was something."

"Sorry. I got mad."

"I'll say." The werewolf ruffled her hair, smiling lopsidedly. "Remind me not to piss you off, little one."

Suddenly, Oz inserted himself between them. He crossed his arms, eyes narrowed. "Who are you?"

Mariel rolled her eyes. "Ben's my boss." She tried to nudge Oz out of the way, but he didn't budge. Testosterone practically rolled off him.

Ben looked unimpressed. "Who are *you*?"

"I'm her boyfriend," Oz snapped.

"Since when?"

"Friday."

The werewolf laughed. "And you're already stomping around like a possessive caveman?" Luckily, Ben was an easygoing type, and he shook his head and stepped back, defusing the tension. "Keep an eye on that one," he told Mariel. "Overprotective boyfriends get old fast."

Mariel snorted. "Lots of things get old fast, I'm learning." Like the emotional yo-yo of fake dating a demon who couldn't seem to decide whether he wanted to kiss her or rip out her eternal soul. At the thought, some of her residual anger sparked.

Oz still looked tense. He frowned down at her. "Are you all right?"

"I'm not the one who got launched across the room."

"But the things she said . . ."

"I don't want to think about that." All she wanted to think about was her successful spell and putting the shop back together. She crouched before the mess of spilled dirt, shattered terra-cotta, and distressed plants and flexed her fingers. She murmured a spell, and magic flowed out of her easily as she healed snapped leaves and coaxed exposed plants to pull the spilled earth back around their roots. While she healed the plants, Ben swept up shards of shattered pots.

The bell tinkled, and she looked up to see her coworker, Rani, standing in the doorway. The naiad's long black hair was damp from one of her daily swims. She blinked at the scene. "It looks like a bomb went off in here."

"Cynthia Cunnington, more like," Mariel said.

Rani made a face. "Ew. I thought she was too highbrow for a place like this." At Ben's scowl, Rani shrugged. "Being lowbrow isn't a bad thing." Her gaze wandered, then found Oz. She yelped. "The hot newcomer!"

"What?" Mariel asked. "You know Oz?"

"He saw me hydrating," Rani said cheerfully.

An ugly seed of jealousy planted itself in Mariel's chest. Her head whipped around, and she glared at Oz. "Is that so?"

He held his hands out placatingly. "I was looking at the fountain. I wasn't expecting anyone to be in it."

Mariel huffed. "You should assume there's someone in every fountain."

"Hold up." Rani looked back and forth between them. "Are you dating?"

Mariel shifted uncomfortably. "Yes."

Rani's jaw dropped. "You weren't dating anyone last week."

Maybe it wasn't an accusation, but to Mariel's guilty conscience, it sounded like one. "It was very fast." She scowled at Oz, who was gazing at the door, clearly wanting to escape. Could he at least *pretend* he wanted to be near her? "He just swept me off my feet."

"Hopefully in a less violent manner than Cynthia Cunnington just swept him off his," Ben said mildly.

Oz glared at him. "I could have stopped her."

The werewolf raised his eyebrows. "Really? Why didn't you?"

"I chose not to." Oz shoved his hands into his jeans pockets, one boot tapping angrily.

Ben turned away from Oz, subtly flicking his eyes towards the ceiling. "Good luck," he muttered to Mariel.

"What?" Oz asked.

Ben resumed repotting plants. "Nothing. Just wishing Mariel the best as she navigates the world of toxic masculinity."

Oz stiffened. "Excuse me?"

Ben waved a hand, still focused on the wreckage. "You're excused."

Oz's chest puffed up. "Now look here, that's my woman—"

"Stop." Mariel grabbed Oz's forearm. "Did you seriously just say I'm your woman? I didn't realize you could time travel back to a less enlightened age, but if you can, please go back to this morning and the ass you made of yourself." She'd had enough of the way he pulled her close one moment, then pushed her away another.

He gaped at her. "An ass? How?"

Rani and Ben were watching intently, and Mariel's cheeks flushed. She didn't want to back down from the fight though. "You dismiss me when it's just us, then get pissed and call me your woman a few hours later." She drilled a finger into Oz's chest. "I don't belong to you."

"I didn't say you did."

"Then what was that *my woman* shit?"

He made a frustrated noise. "I didn't mean it like that."

"Then how did you mean it?"

His eyes darted. "I . . . uh . . ."

Mariel threw her hands up. "Have men heard of emotional communication?"

His forehead furrowed. "What?"

"Obviously not." Mariel pinched her nose, struggling for calm. "Look. You're being a massive grump, and you can't seem to decide how you feel about me, so I am asking you to please go somewhere else and leave me and my friends in peace for a few hours."

Oz's face fell. "Fine," he said, turning on his heel. "I'll remove my objectionable self from your presence."

The door slammed behind him.

Rani looked between Mariel and the door. "I've never heard you raise your voice before."

"Yeah, well, he brings out the worst in me." Mariel started scooping up plants again. "Sorry, Ben. He's not that bad once you get to know him."

The werewolf snorted. "What a ringing endorsement."

She grimaced. "I guess you could say we're going through a rocky patch." What would Dear Sphinxie of the *Glimmer Falls Gazette* say about a fake relationship / soul bargain gone awry?

"After three days?" Ben asked skeptically.

"I don't think he brought out the worst in you," Rani said. "He needed to be put in his place. You did it." The naiad shrugged. "I say that's pretty badass."

Mariel had never been called badass before. She liked it. "Anyway, this will give us both time to cool off." She checked her watch and realized she only had thirty minutes left in her shift. "Do you mind if I leave a few minutes early?" she asked Ben. "Once this is cleaned up, of course."

Ben waved her away. "Go on. There's not much left to do."

"You're the best." Mariel kissed his cheek. "See you later!"

Time to hit the stacks.

NINETEEN

MARIEL LOCKED HER BIKE IN FRONT OF THE GLIMMER Falls Library. It was an eccentric building, with a brick tower containing magical texts and a glass pyramid housing ordinary books.

Mariel headed into the tower. The curving walls were lined with books, and a ladder ran on grooved tracks up and down the spiral. The ladder whooshed past as she climbed, having been summoned by someone farther up the ramp.

She stopped at the section dedicated to magical creatures. "*Escalen a veniresen.*" To her delight, the golden ladder zoomed into view, stopping in front of her. She climbed carefully, perusing the shelves. Wyverns, Succubi, Dragons . . . Demons.

The first on the shelf was *Intro to Demonology*. The leather felt old and unloved, with cracks like a dry creek bed. One problem for a small town with a massive magical library was that there weren't enough people to care for the books. Even a witch with an affinity for literature would be at it for years, since the collection extended deep underground. Some levels were forbidden to anyone without the security credentials to access tomes of black magic, and it was rumored a few levels only appeared once a century to a chosen witch or warlock.

Small sitting areas had been carved into the thick walls, cozy niches lit by stained glass windows. Mariel carried a stack of books to a desk and, with rainbow light cascading over the pages, began reading.

Chapter 1: Demon Cosmology
In the beginning, the void waited for the spark of life.
*   So begins the Origatorium.*

Her arms prickled. "Ooh, peak drama."

According to the fundamental text of demon lore, Lucifer the Bright was banished from Earth by an evil warlock for aiding a mortal in achieving a painless death. He was sent to a pitch-black void. But the human's soul accompanied the demon, and upon seeing how it glowed, Lucifer called on his brethren to make their home on that dark plane, free from mortal persecution.

Mariel flipped pages, looking for something less mythological.

Chapter 6: Soul Bargainers
Soul bargaining is the most important duty a demon can have. Very few are born with the talent to collect souls, and without their efforts, it is believed the demon plane will return to darkness and all the beings within it will die.

Yikes. She'd known the souls provided some sort of power in the demon realm, but would demons seriously die without them?

If so, that put Oz's obsession with duty in perspective—though it didn't explain why he wasn't trying very hard to win her soul.

This is the curse of demonkind—they rely on the magic of witches and warlocks to live, but they are unable to produce it themselves. Thus, to be a bargainer is a position deserving of the highest respect. They must be trained as shrewd, cutthroat negotiators, as any emotional or intellectual weakness could result in a bargain gone awry. Once a demon has been summoned to fulfill a deal, they must carry out that deal, which means terms occasionally need to be negotiated for hours or days at a time to ensure both parties are satisfied.

Her stomach sank. Why was that a rule? And what would it take to break it?

There was a subheading: *Examples of famous deals.* Opposite the text was a sketch of a demon. It was reasonably accurate, with a humanoid frame and smaller horns, but the horns pointed up rather than back, and the fangs were . . . excessive.

In the tenth century CE, Olga of Kiev called upon a demon for aid after a neighboring tribe, the Drevlians, tortured and murdered her husband. Together with soul bargainer Blednica, she crafted a violent revenge. They laid siege to the city where her husband had been slain. After a year, Olga promised mercy if every house in the city sent three pigeons and three sparrows in tribute. Blednica produced sulphur, which Olga then bound to the birds with pieces of cloth. Blednica set the sulphur on fire, and when the birds flew back to their roosts, the city—and all its residents—burned to the ground.

Mariel's eyebrows rose. That was pretty freaking metal. She skimmed a few more entries, finding historical figures who had bartered for money, power, and vengeance.

A famous example of trickery related to a deal involves Astaroth of the Nine, seen as one of the best bargainers of all time due to his silver tongue and delight in subverting human expectations. When US president Richard Nixon asked to be reelected and to have his name go down in history books, Nixon got more than he'd bargained for.

She glowered at Astaroth's name. It was shocking to realize demons had affected so many events in human history. Then again, a human had requested each bargain.

Mariel skipped ahead and stopped with her finger on a promising page.

Chapter 10: Demon Physiology

"Please have a section on dick," Mariel begged.

Demons are immortal, though they can be killed by beheading, and, as mentioned earlier, by the loss of all magic in their home plane (a hypothetical, but one backed up by centuries of research, including the malaise suffered by the species when bargainers tried targeting egalitarian societies rather than meritocracies).

Demons are taller than humans by a few inches on average and have hotter core temperatures. Their horns serve to deter predators.

"They're also an erogenous zone." Mariel flipped to the inside cover, then sighed at the author bio. "Of course it's a dude. Zero imagination."

> *Demons eat every two to three weeks. They sleep once or twice a week, but no more.*

Clearly this book had been written by someone who didn't know what they were talking about, so Mariel shut it and reached for the next one.

> *Demons are limited in their emotions. The bargainer is the perfect example of cold, cruel purpose, offering nothing but malicious trickery to his victim.*

Mariel tossed the book aside. "Next."

> *Demons are violent, malevolent creatures who glory in human suffering and feast on the morally impure every three weeks. Their rabies-infested fangs—*

"Next!"

> *Callidus daemonium seek sustenance every two to three weeks. They sleep approximately once a week. As life is extended, so, too, is the time between necessary functions.*

Okay, this was weird. This book had been authored by a professor of demonology, yet Oz was nothing like what was described.

The next volume was slim, its crimson cover stamped with gold writing. *Soul Bargainers of Note.* The publication year was 1953.

The demons were listed alphabetically, and Mariel skimmed until she hit the Os.

Ozroth the Ruthless

A protégé of Astaroth of the Nine, Ozroth is a notoriously effective bargainer. His first bargain was aiding Napoleon in his escape from Elba—and twisting the wording so he would ensure Napoleon would seize France, but not necessarily keep it. When mobster Al Capone traded his soul to avoid being prosecuted for a bevy of crimes, Ozroth neglected to include tax evasion in the deal. His cleverness is only matched by his viciousness, and revenge bargains and assassinations are his specialty.

Mariel frowned. That didn't sound like the Oz she knew at all.

Someone cleared their throat, and Mariel looked up. A vaguely familiar, tweed-wearing man had entered the alcove while she was absorbed in research. He was lean, with pale blond hair, horn-rimmed glasses, and a fedora. His cheekbones were knife sharp. "Excuse me," he said with a British accent. "I couldn't help but notice you're researching demons."

"I am," she said warily. The stranger was handsome in a runway model kind of way, but men who approached women out of the blue didn't necessarily have friendly intentions. Besides, this man was way more Calladia's type—Mariel always joked that Calladia went for men she could snap like a twig.

"I'm writing a book about human psychology and the difference between wants, needs, and undeniable impulses."

"O . . . kay?"

He adjusted his glasses. "Well, it seems to me that demonic bargains are the perfect way to determine how humans view essential versus nonessential desires. There's quite a sliding scale when it comes to what people value most. What would motivate you to trade your soul, for instance?"

Mariel wanted to laugh, or maybe cry. If only this guy knew the pickle she'd gotten herself into. "I would never trade my soul."

"Hmm." He pursed his lips, looking thoughtful. "I suppose for me it would have to be something big. Saving the planet, maybe."

"Okay, if we're talking planetary extinction, sure. Since the alternative would be death."

"Or saving an endangered species." The man nodded. "I think I could be convinced for that."

That hit too close to home, considering her worries about the fire salamanders, so Mariel changed the subject. "Are you visiting for the Autumn Festival?"

"Oh!" He snapped out of his scholarly reverie. "I'm sorry, I'm being terribly rude. Rambling at a stranger for no reason." He held out his hand. "I'm James Higgins, and I'm a journalist here to report on the festival, but I'm also doing my own original research, as you can see."

His hand was warm. Mariel shook it, wondering with a pang where Oz was. He'd gotten pissy enough about Ben; he'd probably go ballistic if he saw her talking with yet another handsome stranger. "Mariel," she said, half wishing Oz *would* show up so they could shout at each other some more. "Pleased to meet you."

James smiled. "The pleasure's all mine. If you could recommend a book about bargains, I would be most grateful."

Mariel handed him *Soul Bargainers of Note*, since she didn't feel like reading about Oz's dark past anymore. James thanked her and settled at his desk.

Mariel sighed and grabbed another book.

An hour and a mountain of books later, Mariel sat back with a groan. She'd learned plenty of trivia about demons: their core temperature is 101.3°F on average, they have strong communal bonds, and the nine archdemons are engaged in a continual battle for supremacy. None of it told her how to get out of a deal.

"Fascinating creatures," James said.

Mariel had forgotten the journalist's presence. "What?"

"Demons." James gestured at a book. "We know so much yet so little about them. Did you know, for instance, that there are cases of them falling in love with humans?"

Mariel sat up straighter. "Really?"

James nodded. "Some humans ask for immortality in exchange for their souls so they can spend eternity with their demon lovers."

Mariel didn't know what to say to that. "Huh."

"Interesting stuff." James gathered his things, smiling at her. "I think I'd be tempted. To never have to be alone again . . . what a gift, indeed."

He walked away, leaving Mariel alone with her books. She stared at the leather covers, mind churning over possibilities she'd never considered.

Would she trade her soul to save an endangered species? What if she could stop wars or fix world hunger?

Would she do it for love?

The thing that scared Mariel was . . . she didn't know.

✦   ✦   ✦

WITH AN HOUR AND A HALF LEFT BEFORE THE TOWN HALL, Mariel biked to the woods. The trail she took led to one of the most magnificent hot springs.

Dying leaves rustled in the breeze, and stray raindrops pattered off the crimson petals of phoenix flowers. Birds chattered overhead, and a distant wyvern's call echoed off the hills.

She hadn't spent nearly enough time in the woods since Oz's arrival. Every step deeper into the wilderness lifted some of her stress.

The trail flattened and wound around a rock outcropping. The hot spring would be beyond the curve. Unlike Mariel's secret oasis, this was a popular pool, and she'd bet there would be a few humans and naiads enjoying an afternoon soak.

Mariel turned the corner—and gasped.

There was no one in the steaming pool. Instead, construction equipment sat near it, yellow, dirty, and hulking. The birdsong had been replaced by the noisy hum of machinery. As Mariel watched, an excavator dug into the ground, churning up earth and rock.

"It's too soon," she whispered. They weren't supposed to break ground until after the town hall.

"Stop!" she shouted, but the machines drowned her out. A backhoe scooped up soil near the roots of a tree, and birds burst from the branches, squawking.

Pain stabbed Mariel's chest, and she collapsed to her knees. A loud cracking sound was followed by a massive thud, and her eyes flooded at the sight of a formerly proud tree now lying flat on the ground. They were ripping up the forest, and her magic throbbed with the reflected grief and pain of the natural world.

Plants died naturally all the time. Those deaths didn't hurt Mariel. But this . . . this was cruel.

She dug her hands into the soil, whispering a spell as she sent magic coursing through the wounded earth. Snapped stems and tattered leaves sewed back together. There was nothing to be done for the tree, but she comforted the stump anyway. "You'll grow back," she whispered.

As her range expanded, her magic brushed against something ugly, dark . . . and familiar. Beyond the cruel metal teeth of the construction equipment, something else was eating into the forest.

Mariel couldn't stop the construction on her own, but she could fight this other enemy. She got to her feet, wiping away tears, and headed deeper into the woods. She stepped carefully, gently touching the branches that reached towards her. There was a blind, urgent need in the way they sought her out, and she did what she could to soothe them and heal their small injuries.

The noise faded the farther she got away from the pool, but it lingered in the background, a grinding hum that set her teeth on edge. Her head throbbed, and she felt sick to her stomach.

A few minutes later, she found it.

A stream trickled down a rocky slope; alongside it, black rot spread from a tree at the crest of the hill. As Mariel watched, horrified, a branching finger of darkness stretched towards the water. When it touched the bank, the stream started running black. A fish leapt out of the water, then flopped on the ground, its scales darkening until it fell still.

Mariel ran towards the tree, stumbling over the uneven ground. The rot was spreading more rapidly now, the stream carrying it to previously uninfected areas. Mariel knelt and pressed her hands against the tree, shivering at the malevolent energy that pulsed beneath her fingertips. She called on her magic, sending every bit of love and determination she possessed into the trunk. "*Cicararek en arboreum.*" She repeated the spell again and again.

The rot started contracting, but it was moving too slowly. She was sweating and dizzy, but if she stopped now, whatever the malevolent magic was would continue.

She remembered the words of the man in the library: *saving an endangered species.* An icy chill went down her spine. Seeing her beloved woods in pain hurt on a primal level. Her plant magic was her sole success in a lifetime of failure, and the forest was her greatest comfort, the only place she truly felt free and safe. She couldn't bear watching it be destroyed.

But would she give her soul to save it? And if she didn't . . . what did that say about her?

Mariel closed her eyes and saw the web of magic dancing behind her eyelids, streaks of green and gold where ley lines met natural wells of power. This black patch was like a hole in a beautiful tapestry.

She imagined pulling the edges of that hole together, coaxing the magic in the soil to rise and join her own power. She might not be able to fix this on her own, but if she'd learned anything from nature, it was that every part of the ecosystem mattered. From the roots to the canopy, from the worms to the birds, nature was a symphony that relied on the contributions of each piece.

Mariel was part of that symphony, too. She fed magic into the soil and called on its magic to rise in return. Roots twined over her fingers, pinning her hands to the ground. When she opened her eyes, she gasped at the sight of a thousand tiny shoots pushing through the blackened earth. As Mariel gave the forest everything she had, the forest reciprocated, and the magic built and built. The rot receded, and soon the slope was awash with greenery. When the final black spot disappeared, Mariel breathed a sigh of relief. "Thank you," she whispered.

The roots caressed her hands, then sank back into the earth. Mariel stayed on her knees, watching the fragile shoots unfurl. They wouldn't last long once winter descended, but it was a comforting reminder that there was always life in the soil, waiting to burst out.

She stood, then braced herself against the tree as her head spun. It wasn't as bad as when she'd tried to heal the first black patch on her own, but she still felt depleted.

There was a buzz in her ears: the grating sound of construction that shouldn't be happening without the town's approval. It was a grim reminder that more than one thing was wrong with the forest.

Mariel hiked back towards the pool, determined to snap a few photos as proof that the construction was proceeding illegally. If Cynthia Cunnington and her cronies thought they could build the resort with no consequences, they were about to learn otherwise.

TWENTY

OZROTH PACED AT THE EDGE OF THE FOREST. HE KNEW Mariel was up in those hills, and the soul bargain had chained him this close, but he didn't want to intrude on her privacy. She'd hated seeing him at her work, after all, and he couldn't imagine she'd like seeing him here either.

He was ruining her life. Even without the soul bargain hanging over their heads, he made her miserable, and yet he couldn't stop the incessant longing to be with her.

My woman. He cringed at the memory of the words. He'd been two seconds away from beating his chest while shouting "Mine!" Now that the surge of masculine . . . whatever that was . . . had dissipated, he felt embarrassed.

Mariel had been right to chastise him. He'd seen her smiling at that giant, hairy man—a werewolf, he'd bet—and a surge of jealousy had swamped his rational thought process. He'd acted on instinct.

How did humans manage these horrible impulses and feelings? The fact there weren't *more* homicides on Earth was shocking.

Ozroth's frustration at himself needed an outlet. His shoulder throbbed from being blasted into a wall, but he deserved worse pain than that. He drove his hands through his hair, pulling hard at the roots, then rammed one of his horns into a tree trunk.

"Ow!" He recoiled. That tree was harder than it looked.

"It's ironbark."

He jumped, then spun to find Mariel standing at the base of the trail, arms crossed. "What?"

She sighed, then walked over and reached up as if to touch his throbbing horn. She seemingly thought better of it and dropped her hand to her side, and Ozroth felt a stab of disappointment. "Ironbark," she repeated. "There's a witch in town who likes to experiment with new construction materials. Ironbark wood is laced with metal."

"Oh." Ozroth shifted from foot to foot, embarrassed that she'd seen him headbutting a tree. "I'm sorry."

Her eyes narrowed. "For what?"

Lucifer, what wasn't he sorry for? For being summoned, for scheming to steal her soul, for being a shit demon, for drowning in unstable emotions . . . "I behaved badly."

"You did." Her face was still closed off.

He'd need to do better than that to get her to forgive him. Not that she should forgive him. Lucifer, this was a mess.

Ozroth was contemptible and unstable, but Mariel was a good person who deserved the best all the planes had to offer. At the very least, she deserved to know how he felt, even if it wouldn't help the situation. So Ozroth took a deep breath and attempted . . . emotional communication.

"I'm not used to feeling things," he admitted. "It's overwhelming. Everything about this plane is overwhelming, honestly. The sounds and colors and tastes are bad enough. But then there's you, and you're so much more . . ."

"Bad?" she asked, brows raised. "Heck of an apology you're working on."

"No!" He closed his eyes, trying to marshal the words to explain what she was. "Bright," he settled on. "You're vibrant and interesting and so fucking pretty it kills me, and if we weren't in this horrible situation, I would . . ."

"What?" she asked when he trailed off. She settled a hand on his forearm, and Ozroth shivered at the contact. "What would you do, Oz?"

Her voice was as pretty as the rest of her, musical and expressive like a tumbling brook. He hadn't been prone to overwrought similes before the soul either. And never, never had he been prey to an impulse like this one, which could only complicate things more.

But Ozroth had already gone too far down this path. There was no hiding the truth. "I would court you," he admitted quietly.

"Court me?" Realization washed over her expression. "You mean date me?"

Date didn't seem like a sufficient word. That brought to mind mortals sitting side by side in a darkened movie theater, holding disgusting, buttery hands. "In the demon plane, courtship is different than it is here."

Mariel's expression grew soft, and Ozroth's stomach did an uncomfortable flipping thing. He was sweating, even though the air was chilly. Normally it took close proximity to a lava vent to make him sweat, but here he was, perspiring in front of the beautiful woman who held his heart in her small fist.

"What's courtship like in the demon plane?" Mariel asked. The hand on his forearm slid down until her fingers twined with his, and he experienced a concerning heart palpitation. If the French called orgasm *le petit mort*, then falling in love must be *le grand mort*. He'd probably end up in the hospital by day's end.

Love. It was such a human word—small but imbued with disproportionate meaning.

Terrifying.

"When someone finds the demon they want to woo, they start with small gifts." Ozroth looked around for flowers, but there were none this far from the hot springs, so he bent down, still clinging to her hand as he reached for a branch of autumn berries. He stopped himself right before snapping the branch off the bush—*that* would be a terrible gift for a plant witch—and instead scooped up a jagged stone with quartz inclusions glittering from its gray surface.

"Here." He straightened and gave it to her.

She looked puzzled. "A rock?"

He gestured around them. "I don't exactly have a lot of options. And pieces of the natural world are common courtship gifts, symbolizing our connection with the land." He would have preferred giving her a rare lava opal, but this would have to do.

Her pink lips curved, and the dimples made an appearance. "That's sweet."

Ozroth realized he'd been holding his breath. He exhaled shakily. "We also perform tasks for the potential mate. Cooking, cleaning, procuring supplies. That way we prove our resourcefulness."

"Gifts and acts of service." Mariel giggled. "I didn't know demons knew the five love languages."

"Pardon?" He'd thought mortal courtship was straightforward—a few dates leading up to sex, followed by cohabitation, then marriage or an otherwise binding partnership to prevent the desired mate from escaping. Did humans really learn new languages while wooing?

She must have seen the panic on his face, because she shook her head. "It's a joke. Don't worry about it."

"Oh." Ozroth wasn't sure why she was making jokes when he

was about to die from the stress of emotional communication, but at least she wasn't shouting at him.

"You cleaned my house the day you showed up," Mariel said. "Were you courting me then?"

Lucifer, had he been courting her? He was fairly sure he'd just been trying to trick her into giving up her soul, but he'd never cleaned the house of one of his targets before, so clearly *something* had been amiss. "I . . . I don't know."

She bit her lip, which conjured a vision of him biting it instead. If he had her naked and spread out on his bed, he'd spend hours tasting every inch of her. At the thought of his love bites marking the smooth slope of her breast, his jeans grew uncomfortably tight.

"What else do demons do when courting?" Mariel asked.

He refocused on the topic at hand. "Well, over the next few years—"

"Years?" she screeched.

"Immortal," he reminded her. "No need to rush into things."

"Right." Her face fell. "Sometimes I forget."

She looked so downcast that Ozroth felt a pinch of alarm. "What's wrong?" he asked, squeezing her hand.

"Even if you were courting me, you live forever. I don't."

The words hit Ozroth like a punch. He was used to seeing the human world flicker by while his life stayed largely the same, but he hadn't allowed himself to imagine Mariel dying. He'd focused on the immediate future and the conflict between his duty to the demon plane and his obsessive desire for Mariel.

Far too soon though, Mariel would grow old. Her freckled skin would wrinkle; her brown hair would turn white. Her joints would swell, arthritis making it harder to work in the garden. Still, he could imagine her smiling through the decades, joy stamped permanently in the deepening lines of her face.

And then she would die, and the world would grow dimmer.

"Yes," he said, voice rough. The weight of endless years pressed down on him. After she was gone, what would he have left? Was duty enough to keep him going century after century?

Mariel tugged her hand out of his. "This is a fantasy," she said bluntly. "You said you'd court me *if* we weren't in this situation. But we are in this situation, and even if we weren't, there's no future for us."

The brutal truth was nothing Ozroth didn't already know. Still, it felt like something vital had been ripped out of his chest.

Thunder crackled overhead; the clouds had lowered while they were speaking, and now blue lightning ripped across the gray sky, as jagged as Ozroth's emotions. Rain started pattering against his hat.

"Oh, Oz," Mariel whispered. "What are we going to do?"

In the distance, a bell tolled. Mariel pulled her phone out of her pocket. "Shoot. We're going to be late for the town hall."

Ozroth didn't give a shit about the town hall, but Mariel was already backing away.

"I have to go," she said, not meeting his eyes as she unlocked her bicycle. "I'm sorry, but this is the last chance to stop the construction."

The spa project. Right. He forced himself to nod. "I'll follow you there."

"You can stay outside if you like. Go get an ice cream or something." Her brow crinkled. "Is there ice cream in the demon plane?"

There was that incessant, charming curiosity. "No ice cream. And I'll sit with you. If you like, that is." He'd done enough trampling over Mariel's boundaries.

Her eyes were soft again when she looked at him. "I'd like that."

TWENTY-ONE

C ITY HALL'S CONFERENCE ROOM WAS PACKED.
Ozroth hurried down a side aisle, feeling uncomfortable
as dozens of eyes followed him. Cynthia Cunnington sat on a
raised platform at the front of the room, gleaming in a white suit
accented with diamonds.

The conversation had already begun. "You're slimy and corrupt!" a warlock in a top hat shouted. "Running for office for all
of us, then selling the town out to line your pockets."

Mariel and Calladia were seated together near the end of a
row, and Ozroth took the empty chair on the aisle. The room
looked more like a mix between a church and a brothel than a
government facility. The walls were covered in red velvet brocade, and stained glass windows marched along one wall. Elaborate candelabras provided lighting, and in addition to the rows
of folding chairs, crimson chaise longues lined the perimeter of
the room.

Cynthia leaned into the microphone on the table in front of
her. "That language is not appropriate."

"You can take what's appropriate and shove it up your ass!"

Murmurs spread through the room, along with a few exclamations containing the words *Cunnington* and *respect*. The mix of people was eclectic—there were robed witches and warlocks, a contingent of elderly nonmagical women with purple dresses and red hats, a group of centaurs, and even a drunk pixie wearing nothing but a G-string and fire salamander–shaped pasties. Mariel's werewolf boss scowled from the other side of the room, while Themmie hovered above the crowd, sitting cross-legged in midair as she filmed the proceedings on her smartphone.

"When I ran for office, I promised to protect the interests of Glimmer Falls," Cynthia said. "That means ensuring we keep up with the times."

"Keep up with the times?'" Rani stood, her *Save the Coelacanths* T-shirt replaced by one that said *Fire Salamander Rights!* Seaweed was braided into her black hair. "You mean keep up with the capitalist hellscape of the big cities?"

"The resort will bring needed business. With those funds, we can tackle key infrastructure projects—"

"Nonsense," Rani said. "We bring in plenty of business, and if you would actually work with my nonprofit, the Glimmer Falls Resiliency Project, you would learn there are plenty of ways to improve infrastructure that don't involve destroying our forests to cater to the one percent!"

"The resort isn't for the one percent," Cynthia said coolly. "I plan to become a member, and the Cunningtons are only three percenters."

"Guess she found someone to lift your spell," Ozroth muttered. "I liked her better with her mouth glued shut."

Mariel looked murderous as she glared at Cynthia. "Think I should cast it again?"

"Absolutely."

Mariel huffed, then shook her head. "That would violate the free speech rules of the town hall. Even conniving bitches get a say." She looked at Calladia apologetically. "Sorry."

Calladia shrugged. "If it quacks like a bitch . . ."

Rani spoke again. "You really think bragging about your wealth will make the town look more favorably on the spa? It isn't going to be a community resource."

"Not this government's fault you're poor," Cynthia said.

"I'm not poor. I just have empathy."

The exchange set off a wave of commentary from the assembly. A jet of green flame announced someone's displeasure, and the chandelier vibrated, sending shivering chimes through the air.

"This isn't about favoring the rich," Cynthia said. "The proceeds we gain will go directly to the community."

Calladia shot to her feet. "After you line your pockets, right? Don't think we don't know who's an investor in the company, *Mom*."

"Sit down, Calladia," Cynthia snapped.

Calladia's cheeks were pink. "We've talked about this countless times. You know why the resort is a terrible idea—"

"I know you're selfish and don't want to let anyone else enjoy nice things."

Calladia recoiled as an uncomfortable silence fell over the room. It was the first time Ozroth had seen the blond witch look hurt, and he felt a strange urge to protect her. What was wrong with these mortals who treated their children so cruelly?

"That's it," Mariel muttered. She stood up. "Calladia isn't selfish. The only selfish thing is supporting the destruction of our woods just so you can enjoy a facial once a week." Her voice was strong, but her hands gripped her skirt tightly. Ozroth nudged her clenched fist and was gratified when she grabbed his hand instead.

A bare-chested centaur stomped his hoof, and sparks flew from the stone floor. "Hear, hear."

An elderly man in head-to-toe sequins spoke up. "This town is mired in the past. We're so focused on our magical legacy that we're neglecting to think about building a future for Glimmer Falls."

"You can't build a future by tearing apart the ecosystem," Mariel said.

Cynthia glared daggers at Mariel. "We're working closely with environmental consultants, and they're positive there will be no ill effects."

"Bullshit," Themmie called from her position near the ceiling. Her wings were an agitated rainbow blur. "What's the name of the environmental consultancy you're working with?"

Cynthia cleared her throat. "Everwell."

Themmie's thumbs danced over her phone. "A quick search says the CEO is the son of the owner of the construction company you've hired."

"Corruption!" Rani cried. Similar calls echoed from half the assembly, while members of the other half shouted back, defending the project. The room erupted into a deafening din, and fireworks burst above the crowd as centaurs stomped their hooves.

"Order," Cynthia called. "Order!" When that didn't suffice, she raised her pearl necklace to her lips and started murmuring. Ozroth winced, flashing back to when she'd launched him into a shelf. He'd told Mariel he was fine, but frankly, that still stung.

A massive gong appeared on the dais. Cynthia grabbed the mallet and struck it.

GONGGGGGGG

She must have amplified the sound with magic, because it rattled Ozroth down to his bones. He winced, head throbbing.

The ache added to the pain of his bruised shoulder and battered horn. Demons healed quickly, so it was odd how much it still hurt.

As the sound reverberated, the attendees fell into shocked silence. Cynthia took center stage. She looked like a frost queen in her white attire, hair shining like gold while icy diamonds glittered at her wrists and throat. "When my ancestor Casper Cunnington founded this city, he knew it would grow and change. He hoped for that growth—that we would become a major landmark on the global magical map." Cynthia's gaze swept over the audience, and Ozroth understood how she had become such an influential figure. Besides her money, legacy, and power, she carried herself with regal authority.

"Right now," she continued, "we have an opportunity to add a little luxury to our daily lives while increasing tourism. The spa will welcome magical folk of all types, and residents will get a discount on the entry fee."

"How generous," Calladia snapped. "Destroy our forest, then give us a ten percent discount."

"Oh, please. Any effects on the forest will be minimal."

Mariel stiffened. She pulled her hand out of Oz's, then planted her fists on her hips. "I've already seen those effects firsthand, and they're far from minimal."

"Wait," Themmie said from overhead. "Firsthand? The project isn't slated to start until next week."

Mariel glared at Cynthia. "They're already digging."

Cynthia cleared her throat. "Just some preliminary site investigation."

Mariel turned to Calladia. "Can you project some images?" When Calladia nodded, Mariel pulled out her phone, swiped a few times, then handed it to her friend.

Calladia balanced the phone in her lap, then pulled a hank of thread from her pocket and began tying knots, lips moving soundlessly. The air above the phone blurred, and an image formed, growing as Calladia worked. With a final flick of her fingers, it sped towards the wall, colors and angles solidifying until it looked as real as a framed piece of art.

Gasps sounded around the room. The picture showed a cratered patch of earth covered in construction equipment. Trees lay fallen in the background, and Ozroth felt a pang at the thought of Mariel having to witness that destruction.

Calladia swiped through more photos. The fourth was a close-up of an animal lying dead in the churned earth, its body half crushed, with blood pooling beneath it. Ozroth recognized it as a wolpertinger, a rare creature from Bavaria with the head of a rabbit, the body of a squirrel, the wings of a pheasant, and a small rack of antlers.

The centaur made a distressed sound and flicked his tail. "Murderers!"

"A few casualties are to be expected." Cynthia looked unbothered by the gruesome image. "But the life of one wolpertinger is inconsequential compared to the benefits we'll reap from the spa."

Calladia moved to the next photo: a bush near a hole that had been carved into the soil. Its emerald-green leaves were shriveled and brown closest to the construction.

"We're at a confluence of ley lines, and the plants feed off the magic in the soil," Mariel said. "The digging is disrupting that magic."

"Any effects will be localized. Let's move on."

"What's the point of a town hall if you won't listen to your constituents?" Mariel's voice was filled with frustration. "The web of magic is already unraveling—I can feel it!"

"With what magical ability?" Cynthia asked scornfully. "You're a failure of a witch."

"Mom!" Calladia exclaimed. "Don't treat her like that."

Ozroth was at risk of breaking his fingers if he clenched his fists any harder. Furious words stuck in his throat, but Mariel had told him not to defend her, and he had to obey her wish. "Don't listen to her," he murmured. "You're brilliant."

"For once, the demon and I agree." Calladia's expression was stormy. "And I'm sorry about my mom. She's being her worst self today."

"She's right though," Mariel whispered. Her eyes were watery. "No one is going to believe what I feel with my magic."

A vein at Ozroth's temple pulsed. He was so mad he wanted to throw his folding chair across the room.

"If the melodramatics are over, can we wrap up this discussion?" Cynthia asked. "The contracts are signed; the project will go forward."

"Why were they signed before the town got a chance to vote?" Themmie demanded. "Be specific, because I'm livestreaming this."

For once, Cynthia looked uncomfortable. "Town halls are the community's opportunity to express their views. They're not a formal vote. I appreciate your honesty, and I understand your concerns. The construction will be carried out with as minimal damage as possible."

Mariel breathed in deeply. However vulnerable she felt, she wasn't done speaking. "There's already too much damage. It has to stop."

Cynthia scoffed. "Why should we listen to the village idiot?"

Ozroth saw red. He jumped to his feet as anger finally burst through his tenuous restraint. "Mariel is a brilliant witch," he said fiercely. A pulse of sharp energy tingled beneath his skin, and the hairs on his arms lifted. "And she's more powerful than you by far."

A number of people broke into laughter, and mocking words

filtered through the noise: "More powerful than Cynthia Cunnington?" "What a joke." "Everyone knows the Spark girl is a disaster." "She's making this up for attention." "It's a wonder the Sparks haven't disowned her yet."

"Quiet!" Ozroth boomed. A bolt of blue lightning cracked from ceiling to floor, singeing a black spot in front of Cynthia's feet. She shrieked and jumped back.

Ozroth stared in shock as chaos filled the room. That had been a coincidence, right? Some warlock had decided to fry Cynthia's conniving ass right when Ozroth was speaking. But his skin prickled with strange energy, and when he raised his hand, blue sparks danced between his fingers. "What in Lucifer's name?"

"He attacked me," Cynthia shrieked. "Get him out!"

Ozroth was too stunned to protest as a burly security guard led him away. Mariel, too, looked flabbergasted. She moved to follow, but Ozroth shook his head. "I'll wait for you outside." That was, assuming the mortals didn't arrest him. He didn't think what he'd—apparently—done was worthy of incarceration, but America was overly fond of its prison system.

Thankfully, the security guard left him outside. "Not the weirdest thing that's happened at a town hall," the man said with a shrug. "And besides, she had it coming." He winked before going back inside.

Ozroth examined his hand in the bloody light of sunset. The blue sparks had disappeared, and it looked the same as always.

Something had happened though. He'd felt electricity building inside his body before it had released so spectacularly. It wasn't the first time he'd felt that pricking, shivering energy either.

Bargainers had magic, but not like *that*. What was going on?

City Hall's doors opened, and people spilled out, still arguing. Ozroth leaned against the stone wall, watching as streetlights flickered on and people walked, flew, or galloped home.

Mariel and Calladia were some of the last out. Mariel's expression relaxed when she saw Ozroth lurking in the shadows. "Thank Hecate," she said, hurrying over. "I thought they'd arrest you."

"Why would they arrest him?" Calladia asked. "He missed." She crossed her arms, tapping her foot agitatedly. "Not that I necessarily endorse electrocuting my mother, but she was awful in there."

"I didn't . . . or I didn't mean to . . ." Ozroth trailed off, unsure how to explain what he'd done when he had no clue himself.

"Was that demon magic?" Mariel asked.

Ozroth shook his head. "I don't know what it was."

Both witches studied him—Mariel with contemplative concern, Calladia with narrow-eyed suspicion. "What do you mean?" Calladia asked.

"I have no idea what happened. I got angry, and then there was a lightning bolt."

"Witches and warlocks often have magical outbursts when they're learning where their skill set lies," Calladia said. "But you're not a warlock."

Ozroth's stomach chose that moment to growl loudly. He hadn't eaten lunch, he realized. Damn this strange new physiology he was suffering with: eating, sleeping, emoting, and now lightning bolts?

Mariel touched his forearm. "Let's get you dinner, and then we'll figure this out."

"Hold on," Calladia said. "Didn't you feed him spaghetti a few nights ago?"

Ozroth felt burgeoning dread. Calladia apparently knew more about demons than Mariel did—which meant she was starting to realize something was off.

Mariel's brow furrowed. "So?"

"Demons eat, what, every two weeks? So why does he need to eat now?"

Mariel shook her head. "He eats three meals a day. I read about demons at the library, and you would not believe some of the nonsense in those books."

"Right." Calladia faced Ozroth with a determined look. "Oz, I want you to be completely honest right now. Can you do that?"

Ozroth's throat was dry. He swallowed a few times, flipping through his options. He knew what Astaroth would say—*If it isn't related to a bargain, always lie to the mortals, and if you can't lie, make the truth seem like a joke*—but lying to Mariel didn't feel right, and Calladia seemed like she could sniff out bullshit a mile away. But if he confessed his abnormalities, it might undermine his mission. Not that he hadn't undermined it already . . .

Mariel turned beseeching eyes on him, and that quickly, the decision was made. He couldn't deny her anything when she looked at him like that. "I'll be honest."

"Demons as a species lie frequently to humans," Calladia said. "True or false?"

Ozroth hesitated before answering. He didn't need to give Mariel reasons to distrust him, but he had promised to be honest. "True."

"That's exactly it," Calladia said, pointing at him. "Either you're playing 3D chess, or you're a weird fucking demon."

"He's weird," Mariel confirmed before Ozroth could defend himself. When he scowled at her, she shrugged. "You can't deny facts."

"True or false?" Calladia said. "Demons only eat every few weeks."

"Not all demons," Ozroth said in a halfhearted attempt at misdirection.

Calladia wasn't fooled. "Do demons, as a species, eat every few weeks, outliers named Ozroth the Ruthless aside?"

She would have excelled as an interrogator in the high demon courts. Ozroth sighed. "True."

Mariel was looking back and forth between them, and he wondered what she was thinking. Would she judge him for failing to tell her about his issues earlier?

"True or false? Demons not named Ozroth sleep less frequently than humans."

Ozroth glanced over his shoulder, wondering if he could make an escape. The lawn in front of City Hall was lined with concrete paths that spread out like rays of the sun, and gawkers lingered among the foliage, probably waiting for more electromagnetic anomalies. "True," he gritted out.

"True or false? You, Ozroth the Ruthless, eat and sleep every day, even though that is not how any other demons live."

"Your questions are redundant," Ozroth snapped.

Calladia didn't flinch. "Say it."

The evening air closed in around him, smelling like cinnamon and sulfur. He tugged at the collar of his shirt. "True."

"True or false?" Calladia's brown eyes bored into him like a drill. "Something is wrong with you."

Ozroth barely heard Mariel's protest about how rude the inquiry was. His ears were buzzing. This was the issue he'd been skirting since the warlock's soul had anchored in his chest rather than moving peacefully to the demon plane. *Am I broken?* he'd asked himself countless times. *Is this the end of my usefulness?*

Am I wrong?

Sweat trailed down his temple. He closed his eyes and sucked in a breath, wondering why oxygen had never seemed like a rare resource before. "True."

Silence stretched out. Then Calladia spoke again. "Well? What is it?"

Small fingers laced into his. "Do you want to talk about this when we're alone?" Mariel asked.

He opened his eyes with a rush of gratitude and nodded.

"We're going home," Mariel told Calladia.

"Aw, come on. We were about to get answers."

"He has feelings, you know. I bet you wouldn't want to talk about your issues in public either."

Calladia tossed her ponytail over her shoulder. "What issues? I'm perfectly normal."

Mariel snorted. "Sure. You're a totally balanced individual who definitely doesn't need therapy."

Calladia stuck her tongue out. "Bitch."

"Cow."

The two women embraced, and Ozroth wondered if he'd ever understand humans. They were mercurial in their moods yet constant in their loves. Their lives were short, but they shone so brightly.

"Come on." Mariel squeezed his fingers. "Let's go home."

TWENTY-TWO

MARIEL SAT OZ DOWN AT HER KITCHEN TABLE WITH A MUG of chamomile tea. Tea was a balm for many ills, and Oz looked like he could use it. He gripped the mug so tightly it was in danger of shattering.

Mariel grabbed a tube of her break-in-case-of-emergency store-bought cookie dough, sliced it into circles, and popped them in the oven. She sat opposite Oz, her own tea at her elbow. "Well?"

Oz blinked, and she admired the sweep of his dark lashes. He was so hard in some ways, but the peeks of softness intrigued her. It was obvious he was vulnerable and out of his depth.

"It's okay," Mariel encouraged when he didn't say anything. "Whatever's going on, I won't judge."

His chest expanded on a deep breath. When he let it out, some of the tension in his shoulders loosened. "Something happened six months ago."

Mariel sipped her tea, giving him time to find the words.

"I was summoned for a bargain. Normally people summon

demons generically, but this one used my name." He inclined his head. "Like you did."

Ozroth din convosen. The words that had set them on this complicated path.

"The old warlock was dying of cancer. It was painful, he told me, and he still had months of dying left. He wanted to make a bargain: in exchange for his soul, I would grant him an immediate and painless death."

"That must have been hard," Mariel said.

Oz shook his head. "As bargains go, that's as easy as it gets. No drawn-out negotiations, no impossible tasks. I asked why he'd chosen me when any demon would do. He said his grandfather had summoned me long ago to salvage the crops when their community was starving. Afterward, the grandfather had never been the same."

"Why not?"

Oz hesitated. "It's a big thing, giving up your soul. It changes you in ways you don't anticipate. At any rate, the warlock developed an obsession with demons after seeing the change in his grandfather. He grew up to become a respected scholar, but he never forgot about Ozroth the Ruthless and the bargain that gave his community life but took something away, too." He pressed his lips together, staring into his tea.

"So he wanted to meet you?" Mariel asked.

"He wanted to know what his grandfather went through." Oz's mouth twisted. "Not that he knew for long."

"And you made a bargain to help him pass." Mariel ran her thumb over the handle of her mug. "That seems kind."

"It wasn't kind. It was my duty."

Oz was so quick to disagree, Mariel wondered if this was a sore spot. Astaroth had probably trained him to despise kindness as weakness.

The timer went off, and Mariel hurried to the oven. The cookies were golden brown, and the kitchen filled with their delicious scent. "We'll need to let them cool," Mariel said. Then she looked at Oz and reconsidered. "Actually, you'll probably like molten-hot chocolate chips."

She set a plate of steaming cookies in front of him. Oz eyed them, seeming to hold an internal debate, then grabbed one and stuffed it into his mouth. "So good," he moaned through a mouthful. "Thank you."

"You're welcome." Mariel felt the flush of pride that came with caring for another person. "So what happened next?"

Oz swallowed. "He wasn't making sense towards the end: mixing past and present, babbling about prices and gifts. He said he wanted me to understand, but he didn't say what." Oz grimaced. "In retrospect, I should have asked for clarification, but I wanted to get the bargain over with and return to my den."

"You live in a den?" Mariel asked, curiosity snared. "Like . . . a badger den? Or do badgers have burrows?"

Oz's lips twitched. "You and your questions."

"Sorry." Mariel refocused. "Tell me about the den later."

"I asked him to phrase his half of the bargain," Oz said around another mouthful of cookie, "but I wasn't paying as much attention to the particulars as I should have. He was still rambling, and I thought they were just the disjointed words of an old, confused man. *My soul for a painless passing*, he said, *and may it pass then to where there is pain*."

Mariel wrinkled her nose. "What does that mean?"

"I don't know. He recited a spell after that. I could tell general intent—he wanted his soul to go somewhere it would do good—so I didn't question it. The souls all go to the demon plane, after all."

The shape of whatever had happened to Oz was too hazy for Mariel to make out, but by the way he was breathing rapidly, they were close to the revelation. She placed her hand on the table palm up, and after a moment, Ozroth covered it with his own.

It baffled Mariel that she'd once found his hot skin revolting. She loved it now. It was like curling up under a blanket on a cold night, the tension in her muscles unraveling as he touched her. "Tell me," she urged. And then, since bribery never went amiss, she added in a cajoling tone, "I'll make more cookies."

His mouth tipped up on one side. "They are good cookies."

"And these are store-bought. I'll bake you cookies from scratch using my secret recipe."

"You drive a hard bargain." He winced. "Not that kind of bargain. That's not what I meant."

"It's okay." Mariel ran her thumb along his pinky finger. "I know what you meant."

Poor Oz. He couldn't have been more different from the demon described in those library books. He was sweating, and his eyes darted like he was charting exit routes from her cozy kitchen. Whatever he was about to confess must be truly awful.

"When the soul floats out of a body, I open a portal to the demon realm, where the soul joins thousands of others drifting through the air." His voice grew reminiscent. "It's a beautiful sight. The sky is darker there, anywhere from gray to purple to black, and the souls glow golden as they float past."

"Like fireflies," Mariel said. As terrifying as the thought of losing her soul was, the visual was beautiful.

"Have you been to China?" Oz asked. Mariel shook her head. She'd never even traveled out of Washington State. "I've been a few times, and the closest I've seen to what it looks like is the Lantern Festival. Every spring, they create lanterns out of paper and attach a candle. When they release them, the hot air makes the lanterns fly. The night sky fills with them, burning yellow and orange."

"That sounds beautiful."

He nodded. "The souls give off light, but they also give off energy. We feel more alert, healthier, more at peace with each new soul." He rubbed a hand over his heart. "It fulfills something we're fundamentally missing."

Mariel wondered how many other people had been given this intimate a look at the demon plane. "I'd love to see it," she said honestly.

"Maybe I could take you someday." Oz's expression was longing.

The word *someday* made her heart thump. It implied a future between them. She squeezed his hand. "So you opened the portal, and the soul floated through, and—" She broke off when Oz shook his head.

"It didn't." He closed his eyes. "It floated into me instead."

The tick of the hallway clock seemed loud in the ensuing silence. This was it, apparently. The revelation she'd been waiting for. "I don't understand. It went inside you? Like . . . you swallowed it?" That led to questions about how to pass a swallowed soul, but Mariel was determined to stay on track, so she waited for him to make sense of it.

When Oz opened his eyes, he looked weary. "No, it sank into my chest and disappeared." He grimaced. "Then I started feeling things. Fear, at first."

Mariel tried to wrap her head around what he was saying. "Do you not normally feel fear?"

"Not like that. It was so strong, I fell to my knees. Then I felt angry at that corpse on the bed for whatever he'd done to me."

Mariel remembered a line from a book she'd skimmed:

> *Demons are more cerebral than humans. While demons do feel a full range of emotions, those emotions are muted compared to the human experience, and they lack our species' most intense emotional reactions to stimuli.*

Oz was such a moody drama queen, she'd dismissed that as nonsense, but maybe it wasn't.

"Over the next few days, things got worse," Oz said. "I could feel the soul in my chest, shining and warm and *awful*. One moment, I'd be on the verge of tears for no reason, and then I'd see something beautiful and feel happy instead. It was a seesaw of emotions." He ran a hand through his hair. "Then came the physical changes. I started needing to eat and sleep every day. Sounds were louder, colors sharper, tastes more intense." He shivered. "It was—it *is*—overwhelming."

Mariel's lips parted. She stared at him, putting together the pieces of the puzzle that was Oz. No wonder he'd never seemed particularly ruthless. No wonder he had mood swings. He'd never felt emotions that intensely before. "I can't imagine how confusing that would be," she said. "After more than two hundred years, to feel like a completely different person. To have to change how you live."

He nodded. "I almost starved before I realized what was wrong. I'd locked myself in my den, reading books to try to figure out what had happened, and I grew weaker and weaker over the next few days. By the time I was reduced to crawling, I realized it was hunger, but I was too feeble to do anything about it." He shivered. "So I called Astaroth."

"How did he react?"

"He was horrified," Oz said flatly. "Absolutely appalled that I'd developed this weakness."

Mariel frowned. "Feeling things isn't a weakness."

"For a bargainer? It's the worst weakness imaginable. How can I do my duty if I give in to anger or . . . or guilt?"

It was a fair question. Mariel couldn't imagine taking another being's magic, even if the net gain was good. "That sounds hard."

He scrubbed a hand over his face. "It is."

And now he was trapped in another soul bargain. Mariel's own guilt intensified. "Is this the first bargain you've had to make since gaining a soul?"

He stared into his mug as if it held the answers to the mysteries of the universe. "There were two others. One woman wanted to be a supermodel. That was fine. But one man wanted revenge on his father." He closed his eyes tightly. "I had to use my magic to ruin a man's life, from his bank account to his health."

Mariel gasped. "That's awful."

"I've made countless vengeance bargains over the years and never lost sleep," Oz said. "But when I returned to the demon plane after that one . . . I cried." His face crumpled with shame. "And Astaroth saw."

There was a heaviness to his words that sent a chill down Mariel's spine. "Did he hurt you?"

He shook his head. "Not the way you mean—he's never punished me physically. But he ripped into me, told me what a failure I was, that I was an embarrassment to demonkind. He said if I couldn't pull myself together, the council would have to strip me of my position."

If Mariel ever got the chance, she'd sic Calladia on Astaroth to rearrange the demon's testicles. She worried her lower lip. "Would leaving your position be so bad?" If bargaining brought Oz grief, surely it would be better for him to find another job?

"It would be a disaster," he said harshly. "Without my duty, I have no purpose, no reason to be alive."

"Oh, baby." The endearment slipped out of Mariel without conscious thought. She circled the table towards Oz. He looked broken, staring up at her like she might condemn him. For lack of any better ideas, Mariel plopped down in his lap and twined her arms around his neck, playing with the soft ends of his hair.

His eyes widened, and he inhaled sharply. "What are you doing?"

"Comforting you." Mariel pressed her ear to his chest, listening to the steady thump of his heart. He smelled good—like her body wash, but with a smoky, spicy note beneath. Like dessert eaten in front of a roaring fire. "You have plenty of reasons to be alive," she said. "And you shouldn't be ashamed of crying."

His hand settled on her waist, holding her close. "Demons don't cry," he said, breath brushing her hair. "Soul bargainers don't, at any rate."

She nudged his chest with her nose. "I don't think it matters what demons do. I think it matters what *you* do."

"That's the point. I'm doing something abnormal. I'm a joke of a demon, hardly worthy of the title of soul bargainer."

She sat upright and pressed her finger to his lips. "Hush." His mouth worked around unspoken words, and goosebumps pebbled Mariel's arms as his lips brushed her skin. "My turn to talk."

He narrowed his eyes but didn't protest. His other hand abandoned a cookie to rest on her waist, too. Mariel liked the feeling of being held by him, his hands firm, his thighs solid beneath her. Despite all odds, he made her feel safe.

"So you have a soul," she started. Realization hit, and her eyes widened. "Ooh, that must be what caused the lightning! You told me a soul is the spark inside, right? The magic?" When he nodded, she grinned, satisfied at having solved a mystery. "So you have the warlock's magic now. That's why it manifested." Now that she thought about it, there had been a few other odd incidents with Oz: lights flickering, bulbs bursting, zaps of static electricity the same shade of blue as his lightning.

He licked his lips, and the tip of his tongue brushed her finger. "You're brilliant. That must be it."

She basked in the compliment. "So you have a soul," she said, "and it's made you a bit more human. The feelings, the magic . . . you're not just a demon anymore."

She could tell he was going to argue, so she clapped her palm over his mouth. "*Mmph mmph,*" he said, eyes narrowing in a threat so tepid she didn't pay it any mind.

"You can keep hating yourself," she said, "but I see nothing remotely worthy of that hate. You're different from other demons now—so what? You're unique. To me, that makes you more beautiful."

His expression softened. He nipped gently at her palm, and she finally lifted it to let him speak. "You think I'm beautiful?"

The need and doubt in his voice made Mariel's heart ache. She knew exactly how he felt. How many times had she been so desperate for kind words that she'd hardly dared believe them when they came?

Mariel kissed the tip of his nose. "Oz, I think you're more than beautiful. You're tough and intelligent. You're supposed to be harvesting my soul, but instead, you keep buoying me up and protecting me." Another kiss to his eyebrow, which earned a shaky exhalation. "You're unique in all the worlds, and I feel lucky to know you."

He clutched her close, burying his head in the space where her neck met her shoulder. "I don't want to make the bargain," he said, the words muffled by her skin. "I don't, Mariel. I can't bear to hurt you."

The precious, unbearable ache in her chest was spreading. Her eyes burned as tears welled. "I know," she murmured into his hair. "I don't want to make it either. In fact, I—" She licked her lips, wondering if she could—if she *should*—confess this precious, dangerous thing. But Mariel wasn't one for half measures when it came to the people she cared about. She owed him this honesty.

"I want you to stay," she said through a thick throat. "I want to date you—to court you." Maybe it was impossible, but she was falling anyway, her heart deaf to logic.

"Mariel," Oz breathed. He hauled her closer, making her straddle his lap. Her legs dangled awkwardly on either side of his thighs, but before she could move or speak or even *think*, his mouth pressed against hers.

He kissed her with open-mouthed, desperate passion, the pressure nearly bruising. Mariel shivered, opening her lips to welcome him. Her tongue flicked over his, and he met her lick with one of his own.

His mouth was hot. Hot like the air above a candle, like steaming water, like standing at the edge of a volcano and wondering what it would be like to fall in. Mariel wasn't a virgin, but she would gladly sacrifice herself for more of this burning need. She rocked over his lap, grinding against the hardness beneath his jeans.

"Oz," she breathed when he broke away to kiss down her throat. "Take me to bed."

He stilled with his lips over her pulse. "Are you sure?"

Mariel was on fire, her entire body sensitive and yearning for his. Wetness pooled between her thighs, and as she shifted in his lap, a spark of pleasure zinged through her. Feeling daring, she traced his horn with her forefinger. He shuddered, making a rough, hungry sound.

This had been inevitable from the moment he'd appeared in her kitchen. And, impossible and wrong as it might be, Mariel wasn't going to resist any longer.

"I'm sure."

TWENTY-THREE

MARIEL WASN'T SURE WHAT SHE'D EXPECTED AFTER HER proclamation. For Oz to fling her over his shoulder like a caveman before ravishing her, maybe. Something fierce, fiery, and aggressive.

What she hadn't expected was his soft sigh and the gentle brush of his lips. He cradled her cheeks, kissing her like she was delicate and precious. No ravishing in the works, apparently.

"I want you to know this is very special to me," he murmured against her mouth.

"Oh, Oz." She inexplicably felt like tearing up at his gruff sweetness. "It's special to me, too." Oz sometimes infuriated and alarmed her, but she'd fallen for him anyway.

He rested his forehead against hers, and their breaths mingled, humid and hurried. "I'm going to bring you so much pleasure," he vowed, and a shiver worked down Mariel's spine. He kissed her once more, then stood, hands anchored under her ass. Mariel squawked at the sudden movement and scrambled to wrap her legs around his waist. Maybe there would be ravishing, after all?

Oz strode down the hall, navigating with admirable accuracy for someone sucking on her tongue. He kneaded her bottom, and she couldn't wait to feel those large, capable hands all over her.

Ozroth entered the darkened bedroom. "Ow." His steps stuttered as he kicked something.

"Sorry. I forgot I was trying on shoes this morning." She'd compared a few pairs while he'd been hiding in the bathroom after their aborted dry-humping session, although in the end she'd gone with her trusty hiking boots.

Now Mariel was looking forward to some decidedly wet humping. Okay, maybe that wasn't the sexiest way to put it, but her capacity for rational thought was dwindling by the second.

"How you live in this chaos is beyond me," Oz muttered as he strode towards the bed.

She tweaked his ear. "Would you like to keep chastising me about tidiness, or would you prefer to fuck me into the mattress?"

"Good point." He tossed her onto the bed, and Mariel giggled. He followed her down, kneeling between her bent legs. Her dress was rucked up, and she squirmed at the feel of his jeans against her sensitive inner thighs.

He leaned over, and there was a click as he pulled the chain on her bedside lamp. Soft golden light suffused the bedroom.

Oz's eyes went heavy-lidded as he stared at her. When he licked his lips, Mariel shivered. "I want to see every inch of you," he said. "I want to watch you fall apart."

Wow. The library books hadn't mentioned anything about demon dirty talk. Emboldened by his obvious desire, Mariel rested her hands on the pillow beside her head and arched her back, pressing her breasts against the scooped neckline of her sunflower-patterned dress.

Oz groaned, and his hands covered her breasts. "Gorgeous,"

he rasped as he caressed them. His fingers traced the edge of the fabric. "I can't wait to get my mouth on you."

Mariel felt like the sexiest woman in the world. "What are you waiting for?" she asked breathlessly.

Oz growled, then flipped her onto her stomach. Mariel gripped the pillow as he undid the bow at her waist, loosening the sash. He tugged the zipper down slowly, the rasping sound overly loud in the still room. Mariel helped him pull the fabric off, leaving her in bra and panties, both lime green.

"If I'd known this was happening, I would have worn lace," she said.

His hands traced her waist, then her full hips. "This is perfect." He dragged a finger up her spine, then started working on the clasp of her bra. He swore as he fumbled with it, and Mariel bit back a laugh. Some things were universal across all planes, apparently.

He finally got the bra off and flung it across the room like a slingshot. Before Mariel could protest the cavalier handling of her lingerie, he'd turned her onto her back again, and then she couldn't think about anything but the fact that she was lying nearly naked in front of him.

His golden eyes seemed darker, the pupils dilated with desire. He rubbed a shaking hand over his mouth. "Beautiful," he said, staring at her bare tits. "Lucifer, how are you real?"

Mariel squirmed under his admiring look. He was over two hundred years old, yet her breasts had managed to stun him. She reached up to cup them, flicking her thumbs over her pink nipples.

Oz nudged her hands aside and took over. And oh, his hands were so much better than hers. His fingers were calloused and warm, and the gentle rasp over her skin made goosebumps pebble all over. He massaged her breasts, staring at her chest with something akin to awe.

When he pinched her nipple, Mariel gasped and tipped her head back. "Good?" he asked, plucking at the other nipple and sending a zing of pleasure through her body. She nodded frantically, clenching the sheets in her fists. "Good," he confirmed. Mariel caught a glimpse of his smug smirk before he lowered his head and fastened his lips around one nipple.

If his fingers had been good, his mouth was downright magical. He laved her with his tongue, then sucked, and the heat of his mouth intensified the sensation. Mariel ran her hands through his hair, then rubbed his horns in encouragement. They were warm and smooth, and touching them made him growl and suck harder, so she kept doing it.

He spent long minutes kissing, stroking, and nibbling her neck and breasts, leaving red marks that Mariel hoped would last. She wanted to see them in the mirror tomorrow: proof that someone wanted her beyond reason.

Oz kissed his way down her sternum to her stomach, and Mariel giggled when he traced his tongue around her belly button. When he dipped it inside, she tried to squirm away. He smiled against her skin, and Mariel caught her breath. Had she ever seen him look so happy and excited? Every inch of her he explored seemed to bring him endless joy.

It didn't seem fair that he got to kiss her all over, but she hadn't gotten a chance to touch him in return. "Take off your shirt," Mariel said.

He knelt up and stripped off his shirt, and Mariel sighed in appreciation. His chest was smooth, the skin stretched tautly over muscle. She followed the ridges of his abdomen with her eyes, licking her lips at the trace of happy trail above his waistband. Demons didn't seem as hairy as humans, which was nice in some ways—no beard burn—but that hint of pubic hair made her mouth water. She wanted to follow it with her tongue.

She tried to sit up and put the plan in motion, but Oz held her down. "It's still my turn."

She rubbed her thighs together, very aware of the wetness in her underwear. She was shockingly aroused, and he hadn't even touched her below the waist. "Hurry, then."

He smiled, slow and sensual, then licked his lower lip. "You humans don't know how to savor an experience."

Hecate, what if he made her wait for hours? What if this was a courtship thing, and third base was years away? Mariel wouldn't be able to bear that kind of delayed gratification. "I'm savoring it," she argued. "I just savor faster than you."

He chuckled and squeezed her hips. "Impatient."

"Horny," she corrected him. A stray thought assailed her, and she smothered a laugh in her palm.

"What?" he asked, fingers tracing circles over her skin.

"I was thinking that you're the horny one. You know, because of the—" She gestured at her head.

He snorted. "Are you done making jokes? If so, I'd like to lick you."

"Oh." Mariel flushed hot. "Um, yeah. Do that."

He slid her another one of those sly smiles before scooting down the bed. He tugged her underwear off, then hooked her legs over his shoulders. Mariel covered her face with her hands, titillated and mortified all at once.

"No," Oz said. His breath puffed hot against her labia. "Look at me while I taste you."

Mariel groaned. She wasn't going to survive the night. But she lifted her hands and peered down at Oz's face between her thighs. He looked wicked, with those gilded eyes and thick horns. Like every fantasy she'd never known was possible.

He blew a hot stream of air over her clit, and Mariel jerked. The air was followed by a leisurely lick. He tasted her thoroughly, tongue swirling over her contours as if mapping her out. Stuttered sounds climbed Mariel's throat as he circled her clit. She gripped the pillow as if that might stop her from levitating. It hadn't been in her magical skill set before, but if anything could send her to the stratosphere, it was Oz's mouth.

He wasn't going fast, but he wasn't being gentle either. That had been Mariel's issue with oral before—men tended to dab their tongues ineffectually, not providing nearly enough pressure while also clearly hoping the act could be done with as quickly as possible. But Oz ate her out with intense dedication, sucking on her labia, then nipping her inner thighs. When he dragged his teeth lightly over her clit, a lightning bolt of sensation made Mariel's back arch off the bed.

Oz pushed a finger inside her and Mariel moaned at the slight stretch. "Hecate, you're good at this. The best, the absolute—oh!" Oz took that moment to intensify his efforts, and the words flew out of Mariel's head as he devoured her like a starving man presented with a banquet.

The first finger was joined by a second, and he scissored them before curling them to stroke her inner wall. "Tight," he grunted between licks. "Need to get you ready to take me."

Mariel made a strangled sound in response. Her chest heaved, and tension built in her lower belly. She'd never come from oral before, but she was definitely climbing that slope. Her hips rocked without conscious thought, restless with need.

He pumped his fingers as he sucked her clit, and Mariel cried out. An orgasm washed over her in a hot, pulsing wave of pleasure. She reached down blindly, grabbing his horns and pulling him hard against her as she bucked, chasing the shivering bliss.

Finally, the throbbing eased, and Mariel came back down to earth. Oz was still going, growling between hungry licks, and

Mariel peeled her hands away from his horns to press on his forehead.

"Holy shit," she breathed, staring dazedly at Oz as he knelt between her legs and wiped his forearm over his mouth. His cheeks and chin were shiny with her wetness, and Mariel's thighs trembled as she looked at him. "That was . . . whew."

He grinned, showing even white teeth and those slightly long incisors that had felt incredible digging into her inner thighs. "You're delectable." The word sounded deliciously sinful in his accent.

She pushed herself into a sitting position, remembering how she'd manhandled his horns. "Did I hurt your horns? I didn't mean to grab so hard."

He groaned and tipped his head back. "You can grab my horns anytime you want. It felt so fucking good."

There had definitely not been any chapters on demon cunnilingus in the library, but Mariel was ready to write a whole damn book on the subject. "I'm keeping you," she blurted. Then her eyes widened. Shit, had she really said that out loud?

His expression softened. "Mariel . . ."

Desperate to change the subject away from their uncertain future, Mariel reached for the waistband of his pants. "Off."

"Bossy and impatient," he said with a grin. Her fingers scrabbled at the button of his jeans, popping it open before yanking down his fly. She was too impatient to wait for him to strip the jeans off, so she shoved her hand inside the loosened fabric and wrapped her hand around his dick.

Big.

Even though her touch was constrained by the jeans and the awkward angle, it was obvious Oz was packing. "The internet was right," Mariel breathed as she tugged gently up and down, feeling the steely column of his dick through the fabric of his underwear.

It was still unclear whether or not he had penis barbs or anything weird like that, but she couldn't wait to find out.

"The internet?" he gasped as she squeezed him.

"Never mind." Oz didn't need to know about Mariel's deep dive into demon porn. "Take off your pants."

His chuckle was breathless as he shifted out of her grip and stripped off his jeans.

"Now lie down and let me look at you."

"You're giving a lot of orders," he said as he stretched out over the comforter.

"It's my turn," Mariel said, scooting closer so she could trail her hands down his chest. He was gorgeous, with massive pecs and a six-pack. The sacred V led into black boxer briefs, which were tented with an erection.

Mariel needed to get her eyes, hands, and mouth on that cock, in that order. She bent over and gripped the waistband of his underwear in her teeth, tugging it down. He made a surprised sound, and Mariel felt a flush of pride. He might have over two hundred years of experience, but she had a few tricks up her sleeve.

She eventually had to use her hands to get the underwear fully off. At that point, Mariel sat back on her heels, eyes glued to what was already her favorite dick in the world. There weren't any barbs or anything alien-looking, but it was thick and long, the skin ruddier and darker than his naturally golden skin tone. Mariel's mouth watered as she eyed the veins twining up the side. Maybe her eyes were bigger than her metaphorical stomach, but she was going to suck the demon plane out of that dick.

"It's not as big as that dildo you summoned," Oz said, and wait, did he actually sound self-conscious?

Mariel's eyes snapped up to his. "Oz," she said very seriously, "this is the most perfect penis I have seen in my life. Truly, the Platonic ideal of penis."

His eyes crinkled as he chuckled. "You have a way with words."

"I have a way with more than just words." Mariel had panic-read a lot of articles about blow jobs before giving her first one in college, and she liked to think she was good at them. And if she wasn't good, at least she was enthusiastic, which counted for something, right?

There was only one way to tell if Oz agreed. Mariel dove into Plato's theory of forms mouth-first, opening her lips to suckle the head of his cock.

"Fuck!" He barked out the curse, torso coming off the bed. Mariel shifted until she was straddling his thigh, then took his cock deeper into her mouth. He tasted good, a musky mixture of salt, smoke, and spice. She wrapped a fist around the base, pumping in time with the bob of her head—she was ambitious, but not ambitious enough to try to swallow that whole dick without a lot of practice.

Oz was going wild. He cursed and shifted, making sexy, desperate noises as she sucked him. His hand hovered over her hair, so she grabbed it and pressed it to her head, winking to let him know he could pull her hair if he wanted. When he squeezed at the roots, Mariel moaned and ground harder against him.

"Unreal," Oz gritted out. The tendons in his neck were stark as he clenched his jaw, baring his teeth. "Fuck, so good."

Mariel twined her tongue around him like she was sucking a lollipop. Her jaw was starting to ache, but she was no quitter. If she could make this demon fall apart, she would.

Abruptly, he tugged on her hair to pull her away. His cock slipped out of her mouth with a soft *pop* as the suction broke, and Mariel pouted at having it taken away from her. "I want you to come in my mouth," she complained.

Oz shuddered all over. "Next time, *velina*."

She wasn't familiar with the word. "*Vel*-what?"

He rubbed a palm down his face. "It's Old Demonish," he muttered, seeming embarrassed that it had slipped out. "A term of endearment."

Mariel liked the sound of that. "Are you my *velina*, too?"

"*Velina* is the feminine version. I could be your *velino* though. The gender-neutral version is *veline*."

"My *velino*." She tried the word out. "In that case, my *velino*, why can't I suck you off?"

His chest rose and fell with ragged breaths, and sweat sheened his skin. "Because I want to fuck you now."

The breath wheezed out of her. Okay, Mariel could get on board with that plan. "Roger that," she said, then internally cringed. She didn't have the demon affinity for dirty talk.

Oz didn't seem to mind—or even notice—her awkwardness. He looked at her like she was the center of his universe, eyes filled with dark promises.

Mariel didn't have the capacity or patience to research the potential for interspecies issues, so she yanked open her nightstand and grabbed a condom. She'd always been an optimist, so there were a few Magnums scattered in with normal-sized condoms. The demon was definitely Magnum-worthy.

She nibbled her lip, looking at the long, gorgeous stretch of his body. "What position do you want?" She'd love to have him laboring above her, ramming her into the mattress, but she also liked the idea of getting to look at all his muscles. And she wouldn't say no to getting railed from behind . . .

"I want you to ride me," he said immediately. "At least at first. Until you get used to my cock."

Mariel shivered. "And then what?"

"Then," he said, licking his lips, "I do whatever I want to you."

It was a high-handed sentiment, but Oz was a high-handed

demon, and Mariel was too turned on to protest. She'd never considered herself kinky before, but if Oz wanted to fling her around a bit while growling filth into her ear, she was more than willing. She straddled him, fingers shaking as she tore open the condom packet. It had been years, and she'd never wanted anyone as much as she wanted him. She smoothed the condom over his shaft, then shifted until the tip of his cock was pressed against her.

"You don't knot, do you?" she blurted.

His forehead furrowed. "What's a knot?" he asked, clearly struggling to contain himself. His fingers flexed on her hips.

She'd never had to explain it to anyone before, since it was a common concept in the freaky corners of online fan fiction—corners she had visited many, many times. Horny didn't vanish when you were single, after all; it just required other outlets. "It's a thing in fan fiction involving inflating dicks, and since you're another species—"

"Inflating dicks?" He sounded horrified.

"Not the whole dick. Just the base, so the woman can't—" Mariel broke off at seeing his alarm intensify. "You know what? Let's pretend I never said that."

He nodded frantically. "Yes, please."

Trust Mariel to make things weird mere millimeters from penetration. She took a deep breath, then put on her best sultry smile. "Are you ready?"

"Yes!" Oz barked.

Mariel gripped his dick to position him. "I haven't done this in a few years."

"I haven't done this since the mid-twentieth century." He looked on the verge of a meltdown. "Please, do it now."

Mariel felt powerful as she dragged his cock back and forth over her apparently once-in-a-century pussy. "What about delayed gratification?" she taunted. "You should savor the experience."

"Fuck!" He squeezed his eyes shut. "Forget everything I've ever said."

"Gladly." Mariel started sinking down, and *oh*, the stretch was exquisite. He was hot, hard, and thick, and every inch threatened to knock the breath out of her. When she was fully seated, Mariel exhaled forcefully. She tried to speak, but only a groan came out.

Oz didn't seem to be doing any better. "Give me a moment," he choked out.

Mariel could use a moment herself. She was stretched so tight, she swore she could feel his pulse inside her. She shifted her hips experimentally, and Oz's groan spurred her on. After a courtesy pause to let him collect himself, Mariel braced her hands on his chest and started riding, savoring the heavy drag of his cock.

Oz's fingers dug into her hips, and his muscles flexed as he matched her rhythm. Yes, Mariel liked this vantage point very much.

He muttered things under his breath, praises and curse words. Mariel caught references to her breasts, her hips, her lips, her . . . hiking boots? There was a lot Oz appreciated about her, apparently, but he wasn't coherent enough for Mariel to get the particulars.

She grabbed the headboard for leverage and rode him harder. When he thumbed at her clit, she gasped. "Yes!"

He hit a perfect spot inside her with each thrust, and his look of steely determination told her this wouldn't be over until she'd been fully satisfied. Mariel relaxed into the knowledge, closing her eyes as she moved like a rolling ocean wave. She already felt the telltale tightening of an impending orgasm.

Oz lifted her off him, and Mariel's head spun. "Wha—?" The question was answered when he positioned her on hands and knees. "Yes," she panted as he knelt behind her. She'd gotten used to his cock, and now he was going to do whatever he wanted to her.

"You're mine," he growled, reentering her on a swift thrust.

Mariel cried out at the deepened penetration. Oz looped one arm beneath her, squeezing her breast as he hunched over her, sweat-slick abs pressing against her back. His other hand dropped to work her clit, and Mariel let out a high-pitched, mewling sound she'd never made before in her life.

"Yes, yes, yes," she chanted. Her breasts swung with each heavy thrust, and the pressure on her clit was going to send her through the roof. Then he pinched her clit between two calloused fingers, and the pleasure swelled into something uncontainable.

Her orgasm exploded in a wave of clenching heat. As her pussy fluttered around him, Mariel cried out, arms giving way until his forearm between her breasts was the only thing holding her up.

Oz kept thrusting, muttering filth and praise into her hair. "Tight and wet." "Perfect witch." "*Velina*, want to fuck you forever." But even demons were prey to their biology, and he came after a few more thrusts, shouting so loudly Mariel's ears rang.

He collapsed onto his side, taking Mariel with him. She panted, sucking in air like she'd run a marathon. Her head spun with giddy hormones and pheromones and neurotransmitters and Hecate knew what else, like a magical firework had gone off in her brain. Her fingers and toes tingled.

"Fuck," Oz said.

"Wow," she said in response.

"That was—"

"Yup."

It felt like she'd mainlined sunshine. Mariel smiled so hard her cheeks hurt. She'd finally had sex with her demon, and the only thing she wanted to know was how soon they could do it again.

TWENTY-FOUR

THERE WERE SOME EXPERIENCES SO PROFOUND, SO PERfect, they couldn't be put into words. Ozroth breathed in the scent of Mariel's hair, feeling blissful.

Had he ever been this relaxed? He could have melted into the pillows.

"Do demons have refractory periods?"

Mariel's question roused him out of his stupor. "Hmm?" How was she capable of stringing words together?

She wriggled against him. Lucifer, was there a sexier woman in all the planes? Her curves had been tantalizing under clothes; fully naked, she was a goddess. "I was wondering how soon you can go again," she said.

Ozroth groaned. She made him feel capable of impossible feats, but that was a bit beyond his power. "You can either wait twenty minutes or make a bargain for an instant erection."

Mariel laughed, and an answering smile tugged at his lips. The soul bargain was still a sensitive topic, aching like a bruise when pressed too hard, but being able to joke made it easier to bear.

Mariel nestled closer to him. "Is there a timeline for when we need to make a deal?"

Ozroth was still brain-dead from coming so hard he saw spots. He inhaled deeply, hoping oxygen would help. "Um," he said. Not a great start.

Mariel squirmed to face him. "I was thinking."

That made one of them. "About what?" He was captivated by the spray of freckles on her nose and the rosy, postcoital glow of her cheeks. Maybe twenty minutes was an overestimation.

"Earth to Oz." She poked his chest. "About the deal, of course."

"Right." How had he never noticed how many shades of green and gold were in her hazel eyes? They were a kaleidoscope of earthy colors, like the woods she loved so much.

"Demons live forever, right?"

Where was she going with this? "Yes."

"So your timelines are longer than ours, right? Like, you said courtship takes years."

He nodded. His hand moved to her ass, where he gripped a handful of soft, sexy flesh. Yes, he could definitely beat that twenty-minute estimate. How should he take her next? Against a wall?

"Soooo . . ." She drew the word out. "What if you stay here for a while? So we can research how to get out of the deal. And if we can't find a way out, then maybe you could hang out longer. Like . . . seventy years or so."

That snapped his focus back into place. "What?"

She looked embarrassed, nibbling her lip while her cheeks turned even redder. "I know this is a lot to propose, but you don't want to take my soul, and I don't want to give it up either. So, what if we keep the bargain in place until I'm ready to die?"

The thought of Mariel dying was like ice water dumped over his head. He clutched her tighter, until her nose was pressed between his pectorals. "I don't want to think about you dying," he said fiercely.

"Me neither," she said, voice muffled. He relaxed his desperate grip, giving her room to breathe. "But it's inevitable. So, what if you stay on Earth with me, then take my soul when I'm ready to give it up? We wouldn't be ignoring the bargain, just postponing it."

He turned her proposal over in his head. Astaroth would be extremely displeased. But Mariel was right: demon timelines were long.

Outrage stirred in Ozroth's chest at the thought of Astaroth's bet. Why should he sacrifice this beautiful woman—and his own heart—just so Astaroth could win points in the eternal pissing competition the elder demons engaged in? Their endless scrapping for power meant nothing to him, after all, and Mariel meant a great deal.

He imagined it: staying in Glimmer Falls, maybe moving into a house near Mariel (he had plenty of human money after centuries of saving and investing). He could see her every day, if she wanted. He could learn how to cook, make her breakfast, clean her house. He could make sure she always slept on sheets with hospital corners.

Seventy years wasn't that long for a demon, although watching her age would be agonizing. Ozroth had spent longer than that largely in stasis, his life unchanging except for each new deal. It was, however, a very long time for humans.

"You'd get tired of me," he said.

"No, I wouldn't."

"I would have to stay near you. Not within eyesight, but close enough that you'd see me all the time."

She squirmed to get more room to look up at him. "Would you hate that?" The vulnerability in her eyes threatened to break him.

"Lucifer, no. I love being near you. But you deserve more from life than to be saddled with a grumpy demon when you could be with someone normal." When the word *love* came out of his mouth, his heart skipped a beat, and he suddenly understood why humans placed such importance on the smallest words. He hadn't confessed to loving her, but it was close enough, and those words were inevitable if he stayed near her.

It was insanity. How could he have fallen this far, this fast?

Mariel wrinkled her nose. "I don't want someone normal."

"But you deserve someone normal," he argued. "Someone who can do spellcraft with you, who will give you children and grow old by your side."

"You can do spellcraft. Did you forget?"

In the postorgasmic haze, he had indeed forgotten his bizarre new magical talent. "It's not the same."

She'd been drawing a pattern on his chest with her fingertip, but her hand stilled. "It's okay to say you don't want to be stuck with me," she said quietly. "You don't have to make excuses."

That was the last thing he wanted her to take away from this. "No! That's not it."

"Then what is it? Please, be honest with me."

He took a deep breath, trying to think how best to phrase everything in his head. There was a reason no one asked men to perform complex tasks immediately after orgasm. His blood had pooled in his dick, not his brain.

He knew one fundamental truth though. "I'm not good enough for you."

Mariel sat up, looking outraged. "Bullshit," she said, jabbing him in the arm. "You're amazing."

He shook his head. "All I've done my entire life is take people's souls away. I have no real friends, no family, few hobbies. I've been miserable for so long, and you . . . you're like the sun breaking out from behind a cloud. You make everything bright and warm." The few days he'd known her had been some of the best of his life, even with their arguments and the existential threat of the bargain hanging over them.

"That's really sweet." Her lips trembled on her smile. "But you make me feel bright and warm, too."

He snorted. "I find that hard to believe." She'd get bored of him quickly.

"Are you questioning my judgment?" Mariel's tone sharpened.

Ozroth's eyes widened. He sat up to face her. "No, that's not—"

"Because I don't need you to speak for me." She crossed her arms.

Lucifer, he was messing everything up. "I wasn't—or I didn't mean—"

"If you don't want to be with me, say it," she said, speaking over his stuttering, half-formed protest. "If you would rather keep trying to take my soul, tell me. We need to be on the same page."

"I could hide." The words burst out of him. "Once you get tired of me. Maybe I can build tunnels underground so you wouldn't have to see me." Seventy years underground wouldn't be too bad. He could bring his books here, re-create his den. Close enough to make sure she was all right but far enough away that she wouldn't have to tolerate seeing him all the time.

Sharp pain on his arm made him jump. "Ow! Did you pinch me?"

She didn't look the least bit remorseful. "You were spiraling. Why do you think I would want you to hide underground?"

"I told you." His voice was getting louder. "You deserve better than me."

She waved her hand. "Ignore that outrageous sentiment for a

moment. Focus on *your* feelings. If you could stay here on Earth with me instead of taking my soul right away . . . would you want to?"

The question fell heavy between them, a line of demarcation between what was and what could be.

"Yes." The confession was so quiet it was less than a whisper.

Mariel heard it though. Her face transformed with a joy so bright, it took his breath away. "Then take a chance," she said, clambering onto his lap and wrapping her arms around his neck. "Stay with me. Maybe we'll find a way to get out of the bargain, but whatever happens . . . I want to give this a shot."

Stay on Earth. Defy Astaroth's order to deliver Mariel's soul by the end of the month. It would be a scandal in the demon plane, and it would ruin whatever remained of his reputation—what sort of bargainer abandoned his position out of love for a mortal?—but his reputation had been cold comfort during the centuries he'd spent alone. Reputation was delicate anyway, easily lost for any number of reasons. When he'd gained a soul, the same bargainers who had praised him had been quick to deem him a failure. Why should their judgment shape his actions?

The thought of risking his people's safety was harder to accept, but there were other soul bargainers left to carry on the work. Ozroth would rejoin their ranks in a few decades, once Mariel had passed. Without her, he would have nothing to live for but duty.

"So?" Mariel asked, cheeks dimpling and eyes sparkling. Whatever happened in seventy years, right now she was vibrant and smiling in his lap, and that was all he needed. "What do you say?"

For once, Ozroth didn't feel the heavy weight of duty or honor pressing down on him. Seventy years would pass far too quickly, and maybe she would ask him to move underground and out of sight in a few years, but Ozroth would take whatever time he could get. With Mariel in his life, the days, months, and years would be richer than he'd ever imagined. "Yes." His mouth stretched into a grin that matched hers. "I say yes."

Mariel squealed, then planted a loud, smacking kiss on his lips. He laughed and kissed her back, exhaling his tentative hopes into her mouth. His heart raced, and the butterflies were back, filling his chest with the flutter of a thousand brilliant possibilities.

Ozroth the Ruthless had existed for over two hundred years.

Tonight, he would finally start to live.

"So," Mariel said against his lips after their kisses had grown desperate. "How about that demon refractory period?"

In answer, Ozroth tipped her over, chasing her bright laughter down to the bed.

TWENTY-FIVE

"WHAT DO YOU THINK OF THIS?"

Ozroth accepted the ice cream Mariel was shoving at his lips. He licked the pink plastic spoon, then grimaced. "What flavor is that?"

"Espresso. What, don't you like it?"

They stood near an ice-cream truck at the south end of the city square. The street was closed to through traffic, and colorful tents bloomed like flowers everywhere he looked. The Glimmer Falls Autumn Festival was well underway, and Mariel had been overjoyed to show Ozroth a variety of food, handicrafts, and bizarre magical competitions over the past week.

She was a vision today, her brown curls bound up with a gold clip, her curves packaged in a low-cut burgundy wrap dress. Every time he looked at that belt, he imagined pulling it loose with his teeth.

He dragged his attention back to the topic at hand. "It tastes like sweet dirt," he said honestly.

She rolled her eyes. "Someday I'll get you to like coffee."

She said things like that easily now. *Someday.* Every time she mentioned the future so casually, Ozroth felt a flush of happiness. This entire week had been like walking on clouds. With that airiness, though, came the creeping fear that it couldn't last, that eventually he would plummet to earth.

She tipped her chin at his cup. "How's yours?"

He raised the spoon to her lips, feeling a familiar tightening below the belt as she wound her tongue around it lasciviously before winking at him. They hadn't been able to keep their hands off each other since that first night. Now that the issue of the bargain had been sidelined, Ozroth had dedicated himself to learning exactly how she liked to be kissed and touched, and Mariel had reciprocated eagerly.

Mariel hummed around the mouthful of ice cream. "Pumpkin spice? An unusual choice for a big, bad demon."

"I like the taste." He liked the taste of all sorts of sweet things, he was discovering: cookies, cake, honey, tea, pie, and, yes, anything pumpkin spice–flavored. He leaned in, brushing his lips over her ear. "But I like your taste even more."

She slapped his chest lightly. "Flirt."

Ozroth's cheeks hurt from smiling. Was that a thing? Joy so potent it invaded skin and muscle?

"Anyway," she said, turning to look at a performance on the green, "you may be a basic bitch, but you're my basic bitch."

"I'm your . . . what?"

"Don't worry about it. Let's watch the jugglers!"

She dragged him towards the green, where a troupe of jugglers performed in front of the fountain. Ozroth eyed the water suspiciously, wondering if anyone was swimming naked.

One of the jugglers was throwing flaming bowling pins high in the air. Ozroth reached out with his demon senses and was surprised to realize the man was an ordinary human. How was he doing that without casting a spell? Truly, humans could be bafflingly wonderful.

The other jugglers were magically inclined. They threw crackling orbs of light at each other, mixed with knives, chairs, soccer balls, and—was that a *cat*? The audience applauded as the items swirled overhead, sometimes changing trajectory midair. When a soccer ball flew off course towards the fountain, someone burst out of the water. "Header!" the topless naiad—Rani, he remembered—screamed as she headbutted the ball back into play.

Well, that answered the question of whether or not anyone was bathing nude. A mottled blue tentacle lifted out of the water next, and Rani high-fived it. No one in the crowd batted an eye.

"What is that?" Ozroth asked in alarm.

Mariel looked over at the now-thrashing tentacle. "Oh, that's just Jenny," she said. "Friendly local tentacle monster."

Ozroth looked askance at the rows of suckers. "If you say so."

Glimmer Falls was full of similar oddities, and Mariel had dragged him to a variety of unusual events and performances over the last few days. There had been a tightrope walker, a prognosticator, a troupe of air-dancing pixies, a pantomime play put on by shape-shifters, and more. Between events, they'd sampled muffins, mulled wine, spiced cider, and treats from numerous baking competitions. When he'd asked why Mariel didn't compete, she'd told him she baked for pleasure, not to win anything. "And besides," she'd said, winking at him, "the Pacific Northwest Floral Championships is my main event."

The flower competition would happen on October 31, the last day of the festival. Mariel was preparing for it feverishly, visiting her greenhouse multiple times a day to whisper to the plants, water them, and feed them magic. She was working on her display now—a bright, colorful mixture of flowers in hand-painted pots that rested on a table covered in shimmering gold cloth.

He'd been startled by her skill in painting the pots. Realistic scenes of plants and animals seemed to leap from the ceramic, the pigments infused with a shimmer of pixie dust. Themmie had provided the dust, shaking her wings over a bowl while complaining loudly about the indignity. The dust made the pigments extra vibrant and added dimension, making the images seem to move.

Mariel had endless patience and attention to detail for baking, gardening, and painting—so why did she struggle to bring that same attention to bear on her magic? Even though she practiced every day, her spellwork was unpredictable, and Ozroth had needed to corral more than one startled animal that had appeared in her kitchen.

Eating cookies, laughing, and rounding up alarmed geese wasn't how he'd ever imagined spending his days, but now he didn't want to do anything else.

"Want to visit the forest?" Ozroth asked, eyeing the lowering sun. Mariel had been going every day with her friends to protest the ongoing construction, splitting off to look for dead patches. She'd found several, unfortunately; the black rot seemed to be spreading, oozing out of tree stumps and turning green vines into blackened tangles. While she'd been able to heal all of the spots with her magic—one area in which she never struggled—the effort was taking a toll on her.

It was the one downside of the past week, other than Ozroth's growing paranoia that this happiness couldn't last. But Mariel ignored his arguments that she needed to rest. "The forest is like my family," she'd told him when he'd urged her to take a break, alarmed by the exhausted circles beneath her eyes. "Until we figure out what's causing this, I need to do everything I can to help."

Mariel worked in the mornings, so Ozroth dedicated those

hours to library research. Mariel had informed him he was being a snob about human books, so he'd agreed to look into possible causes of the black rot—as well as continue her search for a way to terminate the bargain.

"It's not that I want you to leave," Mariel had explained. "It's that I want you here of your own free will. I want it to be a true choice."

It was already a choice. He was choosing to go against everything he'd been taught about his life's purpose. But he knew what she meant. If the question of the bargain was resolved, there would be nothing hanging over them. Well, nothing but the inherent problems of an immortal courting a mortal, but Ozroth refused to think about that. Life was complicated enough.

Now Mariel looked at the tall clock. "Oof, yeah. I think Themmie's already there."

They headed east on foot, winding through the crowds of revelers. When a familiar voice cut through the chatter, Ozroth winced.

"Yoo-hoo! Mariel, dear! Oz! Hellooooo!"

Mariel groaned. "I was hoping we wouldn't have to see her until family dinner."

"We have to go to that again?" Ozroth asked with growing dread. It was Saturday, which meant only one more day of freedom from Spark family madness.

"It happens every week. Not optional." She walked faster.

"It's optional if you make it optional," he argued, lengthening his strides to keep up. She was nearly jogging now. "You just need to say no."

"Is that so?" Mariel came to an abrupt stop on the sidewalk. "Then you tell her."

"Wait—"

It was too late. Diantha Spark was upon them, a small yet terrifying figure in a pale blue pantsuit and purple stilettos. "I thought you hadn't heard me!" she exclaimed. Sapphires the size of robin eggs hung from her earlobes, and a purple beret topped with a miniature dragon anchored her brown curls. She snapped her fingers next to it, and the dragon opened its mouth and ejected a small spurt of flame. "Do you like my hat? Wally sent it to me."

"What was the occasion?" Mariel asked.

"He felt terrible about missing this year's Autumn Festival, so he sent this as an apology gift. They keep him so busy with those theme parks, but I'm sure he'll make it next year."

Mariel and Ozroth exchanged a knowing glance. It sounded like Mariel's uncle had delivered less of a gift and more of a bribe to keep Diantha off his back.

"Now." Diantha planted her hands on her hips and leveled a stern glare on Mariel. "I hear you caused a scene at the town hall."

Mariel groaned. "Mom, leave it."

"I will not," she said indignantly. "Cynthia told me you were rude to her in front of everyone."

"Oh, you care about Cynthia's feelings now? Didn't she win the pie competition again?"

Diantha gasped and pressed a hand to her chest. "That's a low blow. I caught her grinding up Viagra to put in her 'all magical' libido-enhancing pie, you know. Typical of her to bend the rules so she can win." She gave Mariel a knowing look. "Alzapraz says she's a toxic overachiever with no sense of boundaries."

"Are you sure he said that about Cynthia?" Ozroth muttered.

"Dear Oz." Diantha beamed as she lunged and wrapped her arms around his neck. He staggered back, alarmed. "I hear you nearly electrocuted Cynthia." She released him, then pinched his cheek. "And you said you weren't powerful."

"I'm not," Ozroth said, rubbing his cheek to wipe away the residual sensation. "I just got angry." He hadn't been able to manage another display of that magnitude since the town hall, despite Mariel's attempts to teach him a few words of the language of magic.

"So it's fine for him to shoot lightning at Cynthia, but if I talk back to her, it's rude?" Mariel crossed her arms. "That's a heck of a double standard."

Diantha shrugged. "Etiquette rules don't apply to demonstrations of power. And Cynthia could use a good electrocution, although I agree with her about the spa. I can't wait for a proper massage." She rolled her shoulders, then eyed Ozroth up and down lasciviously. "You have big hands. Maybe I can recruit you to rub me down while we're waiting for it to open?"

The last thing Ozroth wanted was prolonged contact with Diantha, especially contact that involved rubbing. Lucifer, he despised the self-centered woman. "Do you know why I was angry at Cynthia?" he asked. "She called Mariel a failure."

Mariel made a soft noise and rested her hand on Ozroth's forearm. He covered her hand with his, squeezing gently.

Diantha picked an invisible speck of lint off her sleeve. "Mariel, darling, people wouldn't say things like that if you worked harder."

"That's it?" Ozroth was appalled. "You don't think it was 'rude' for her to insult your daughter?"

"People insult me all the time," Diantha said. "Normally out of jealousy, but still. Being a Spark means drawing a lot of attention, both good and bad." She patted Mariel's shoulder. "The best way to silence your haters is to use magic to intimidate them until they feel like the inferior worms they are."

Mariel was giving Ozroth a look that he could interpret as a request to stop defending her. It was hard not to snap at Diantha about the exacting, hypocritical standards she applied to her daughter, but he bit his tongue. Nothing would change in Mariel's family dynamic until she truly stood up for herself.

"This has been lovely," Mariel said, "but we need to be going."

Diantha pouted. "Aren't you going to watch the battle royale? We're competing in an hour outside Mothman's Mushroom Mart. All the combatants are going to get naked and take magic mushrooms."

"That sounds like a recipe for disaster."

"It's going to be a riot. I've been taking hallucinogens all week to practice, and I learned a new spell for transforming my enemies into asthmatic lizards." Diantha fluffed her hair, and the reflections off her wedding ring threatened to blind Ozroth. "Roland is going to film it for GhoulTube, so I'll be sure to send you both the link. Oz, what's your email address?"

He was still struggling with the mental image of a bunch of naked, hallucinating witches turning each other into lizards. "I don't have one."

"Nonsense. What's your staff email for that magic college you teach at? The Antipodean something-or-other."

"The College of Antipodean Witchery," Mariel said, jumping in when it became apparent Ozroth wasn't going to muster up a lie fast enough. "They don't use traditional email. Messages are sent by, uh, ravens."

Ravens? Ozroth mouthed at Mariel while Diantha launched into an explanation of why cockatrices and other magical creatures were much more reliable messengers.

Mariel gave a half shrug. "I just finished binge-watching *Game of Thrones*." Her sly smile was intoxicating, and Ozroth stared at her mouth, wondering how soon he could taste it again.

"—be happy to teleport an oozlefinch from the nearest army base so you can write to me," Diantha was saying. "They're very fast, and their missile capacity is helpful for deterring porch pirates."

Ozroth snapped back to awareness just in time to realize Diantha was trying to set up some sort of horrific pen pal scenario with him. "No, thank you," he said, scrambling for a way to deter her. "Letters are so, uh, impersonal." His eyes darted, searching for an escape route. Should he dive under the caramel apple stand? Maybe he could take cover behind one of the stilt walkers . . .

"You are such a sweetheart, Oz," Diantha said. "Yes, we simply must spend more time together."

That wasn't what Ozroth had meant to propose. "Wait—"

Diantha steamrolled right over him. "Dinner tomorrow is going to be lovely. I'm importing paella from Valencia and mojitos from the most exclusive bar in New York City. Do say you'll be there early so we can chat more." She gripped Ozroth's forearm as she fluttered her eyelashes. Her manicured nails reminded him of claws.

"Early isn't possible," Ozroth said, panic rising.

"Then normal time it is." Diantha popped up on her toes— even stilettos didn't put her near Ozroth's height—and made loud, smacking kiss sounds near his cheeks. "See you tomorrow night, darlings! I'll be sure to tell you all about the battle."

She strode away, heels clicking on the cobblestones.

Ozroth blinked after her, feeling like he'd been run over by a truck. How was such a small woman capable of so much destruction?

Mariel folded her arms. "Great job saying no to family dinner."

He groaned and pinched the bridge of his nose. "She walked right over me."

"She sure did." Mariel nudged him with her toe. "Chin up, it happens to all of us. How about a pumpkin spice cupcake on the way to the woods?"

"Are you bribing me to join your protest?"

She winked. "No, I know you'll join the protest. I just like seeing you get excited about food."

Ozroth was so far gone for Mariel, he'd do absolutely anything she told him to. He wrapped his arm around her waist and tugged her in for a quick kiss. "Then let's grab a cupcake, *velina*."

TWENTY-SIX

T WO, FOUR, SIX, EIGHT, FUCK YOU, SHADY REPROBATE!"
Mariel smothered a laugh at Themmie's latest protest
chant. The pixie stood with other protestors in front of a bulldozer, shouting at the operator, who looked like he wanted to teleport far away. She wore a bedazzled *Save the Salamanders!* shirt
and was sporting a new undercut in her pink-and-green hair.

"Running out of rhymes?" Mariel asked.

Themmie's wings sped up, lifting her off the ground. "Just
getting more creative." She cupped her hands to her mouth and
shouted. "Two, four, six, eight, Mayor C should abdicate!"

The ranks of protestors had swelled since the town hall, and
dozens of witches, pixies, centaurs, and ordinary humans shouted
and waved signs decrying the construction. MAYOR CUNNINGTON
IS A DIRTY LIAR read one sign. STOP THE SPA! read another.

Mariel felt a warm glow in her chest at seeing the townsfolk
stepping up. With powerful figures like Diantha Spark and Cynthia Cunnington backing the construction, it had been hard to
find anyone willing to protest. Apparently the images of the de-

struction in the woods—and the revelation that construction had started before the town hall to discuss it—had made an impact. Construction had come to a standstill, with nocturnal creatures taking up the protest as soon as the day shift ended. Cynthia had promised construction would go ahead on Halloween no matter what, but if they could keep up this passion, the mayor and her goons didn't stand a chance.

Calladia jogged up, high ponytail swinging. "What did I miss?"

"Themmie's getting inventive," Mariel said.

On cue, the pixie belted out another chant. "What do we want? Fire salamanders! When do we want them? Always!"

The words reminded Mariel of the sick fire salamander, and her stomach dropped. When she looked at Oz, she could tell he was thinking along the same lines. His eyes roved over the forest, and his face was drawn in a tense frown.

Mariel still hadn't told anyone but Calladia and Themmie about the dead patches in the woods. She didn't know anyone else who excelled at nature-based magic, and while she trusted her two friends completely, she was afraid if the news got out, Cynthia would use it as an excuse to bulldoze more of the forest. Right now she was containing the issue, checking daily for new spots, but this wasn't sustainable. At some point, she'd need to bring in other people to figure out what was happening.

"I'll be right back," she told Calladia.

"Where are you going?" Calladia looked between Mariel and Oz, then groaned. "Don't tell me you're going to get frisky against a tree."

She'd kept Calladia and Themmie updated about the—*ahem*—developments in her relationship with Oz. Themmie had been delighted, pushing for a level of detail that Mariel had declined to give, and even Calladia seemed to have begrudgingly accepted this as the new state of things. Mariel smiled at Oz, who looked adorably embarrassed. "I can neither confirm nor deny."

Calladia shook her head, then made a shooing motion. "Off you go. Go affirm life or play genital tag or whatever."

Mariel dragged Oz into the trees. She wasn't actually planning on debauching him—or she hadn't been planning on it until just now—but she enjoyed his charmingly flustered expression. When she glanced at his crotch, she was delighted to see a bulge. "Ready to go already?" she teased, her worries about the forest lifting for the moment.

Oz looked over his shoulder to make sure they were out of sight of the protestors, then scooped her up and flung her over his shoulder. Mariel cackled as he carried her deeper into the woods, his hand planted firmly on her ass.

"Guess that's a yes," she said breathlessly as blood rushed to her head.

"With you? Always."

Oz lowered her to stand on a rock, and Mariel enjoyed the boost in height it gave her. Given the way he was staring avidly at her breasts, now at eye level, he enjoyed it, too. He abruptly buried his face in her cleavage, rubbing his nose back and forth and pressing kisses to her skin while she giggled.

"Gorgeous tits," he said, voice muffled.

"Just the tits?" Mariel asked playfully. She'd never felt as beautiful in her life as she had this past week, her ego fed with an endless stream of compliments and orgasms.

He squeezed her ass. "Gorgeous everything." He looked up, gold eyes lively with mischief. "So are we really going to get frisky against a tree?"

Mariel bit her lip. She'd planned to look for areas of rot first, but Oz was so big and handsome, and her stomach swooped whenever he looked at her.

"A quickie," Mariel decided. "And then I need to check on the woods."

"A *quickie?*" He shook his head. "You humans and your impatience. You deserve a long, slow seduction."

"Or," Mariel said, dragging a finger down between his pecs, "I need to be taken so hard and fast I feel you for a week." She leaned in, lips brushing against his ear. "We'll have to be quiet, of course. Can't have everyone hear you making me scream."

He shuddered. "You're a menace." But his fingers were flexing on her hips, and Mariel already knew she'd won.

She nipped his ear. "Come on. I dare you."

Two minutes later, Mariel found herself pinned against a tree while Ozroth thrust into her with deep, hard strokes. Her back scraped over the bark, but her dress provided some protection, and she didn't mind the slight sting anyway. She felt brilliantly alive, nerves singing with pleasure as Oz filled and overwhelmed her.

Her magic thrummed in concert with nature, passion feeding her power. Dormant seeds found new life in the soil, and flowers burst into bloom until Oz stood on a carpet of pink and red. A climbing vine reached a tendril down from a branch overhead, whisking off his hat before patting his head affectionately.

He grunted. "Don't let the plants molest me."

"They're just—ah!—excited for me." Mariel dug her fingers into Oz's shoulders, clinging to him as tightly as the vine wanted to. Wetness slicked her thighs—he'd barely needed to touch her before she'd been ready, her body attuned to his.

He squeezed her ass hard, his massive hands providing support as he bent his knees and thrust up into her. "Clit," he said gruffly.

Mariel kept one arm wrapped around his neck while she slid her hand between them. It was hard to be precise, given how hard he was fucking her, but with her fingers sandwiched between them, each thrust provided delicious pressure against her clit. She dug her heels into his ass, encouraging him to go harder. She was definitely going to feel this later, but she loved his feral groans and the overwhelming intensity of his passion.

"Come for me," he said savagely. "Let me hear it."

Mariel barely had time to remember there was a group of people a short walk away. She clapped a hand over her mouth, groaning into her palm as her body spasmed. Oz swore, gripping her even tighter as he pumped into her wildly.

He grunted, then sagged forward, panting. Mariel traced his horns, smiling when he shivered.

Oz gently lowered her to her feet. "Maybe the quickie has some merits," he said breathlessly. A goofy smile tilted his lips, and it astounded Mariel how much he'd changed from the surly demon she'd first met. He looked like a completely different person.

He tied the condom off, and then, for lack of other options, put it in his pocket with a grimace before tucking himself back into his pants. Hormonal birth control made Mariel break out and gain weight, and while she was looking into contraceptive spells, she didn't want to accidentally explode her ovaries. Demon-human pairings were rare, from what Oz had told her, but there were some half-demon children out there.

Mariel had been curious about those hybrid children. Not because she was contemplating having Oz's baby—babies were *way* down the line for her, thank you very much—but because she'd wanted to know which traits they adopted from each species. Oz had told her it was a randomized gamble—some hybrid children had full horns, some no horns, some in-between. Some were immortal and lived in the demon plane, but others, for unknown reasons, took on the human parent's mortality and lived relatively normal lives on Earth.

"Where do humans even meet demons?" she'd asked. "Hagslist?"

"It's common for demons to vacation on Earth," Oz had explained. "Things happen—especially when alcohol is involved."

Things certainly did happen. Mariel smoothed her skirt, reveling in the afterglow of some of those *things*. She felt vibrant and alive, as connected to her womanhood as she was to the natural world.

She laced her fingers through Oz's. "Come on. Let's survey the woods."

They hiked farther from the construction site. While the plants nearest the construction were struggling, it was a relief to see healthy trees and bushes thriving deeper in the forest. A hot spring steamed into the crisp late-afternoon air, and birds chattered from the branches.

Mariel felt the blackness before she saw it. Her magic had been skipping over root and stone, mingling with the natural power of the earth, but the sparkling magic of nature abruptly gave way to something dark and insidious. She felt nauseated brushing against that malevolent energy.

"That way," she said, releasing Oz's hand and hurrying towards a thicket of brambles.

Oz was there before she could shove her way through the thorny bush. He carefully parted the branches, holding them aside to clear a path. Mariel ducked through.

What she saw on the other side made her gasp.

What had once been a turquoise hot spring now looked like a bubbling vat of tar. Tendrils of rot spread around it like an infection, stretching into the distance. It looked like a forest fire had swept through the woods, blackening the ground and trees.

"I've never seen a patch this big," Mariel said, heart sinking.

Oz joined her, brushing leaves and thorns off his shirt. "Can you fix it?"

"I don't know." Mariel looked at the dying forest with despair. Fixing the spots as they cropped up was like a horrible game of Whac-A-Mole. Each time she felt drained to the point of near collapse.

She had to try though. She knelt at the edge of the rot and planted her hands in the soil. "*Cicararek en arboreum*," she said, calling on the earth to join her effort. Magic swelled, bright and beautiful, and the edge of corruption receded. "*Cicararek en arboreum*."

After five minutes, Mariel was sweaty and dizzy. Her vision blurred as she fed more magic into the earth. The forest was adding its own power, but she could feel the depletion in its energy. Between the construction and the strange, magical rot, the web of magic woven into the ley lines below the soil was fraying.

Mariel sat back on her knees, wiping her forehead with the back of her hand, then groaned to realize she'd only cleared half the infection. "I can't do it, Oz," she said, a swell of despair threatening to drown her. "I'm not strong enough."

He crouched beside her, rubbing her back in circles. "Don't push yourself too hard."

"I have to push myself." Exhaustion made her tone sharp. "No one else can do this."

"There has to be another solution. Something that doesn't require you to burn yourself out."

"Until I figure out what this magic is, I don't know what more I can do." She felt sick to her stomach, and not just from the effort of casting the healing spell over and over. She'd always been in touch with what the forest was feeling, and the corruption in the soil was bleeding over into her body.

She closed her eyes, struggling to regulate her breathing. This was the one area of magic in which she was supposed to excel. The only thing she had to offer the world, and it still wasn't enough. "I'm a failure," she whispered. "I'll always be a failure."

"Nonsense." Oz stroked her hair. "You're anything but a failure."

Her eyes burned. "You don't know what it feels like. I've been trying to live up to the prophecy for years, but I'll never be good enough."

He was quiet for a moment. "When I gained my soul," he said eventually, "Astaroth told me I was a joke of a demon. A disappointment. I felt so ashamed."

Mariel should be a good person and empathize with Oz, but a spike of irritation went through her nonetheless. It was petty, and Oz was trying to help, so she tamped down her frustration. "Astaroth is a jackass, and he shouldn't have said those things to you." She paused to form her words into the shape she needed him to understand. "But Oz . . . you were only judged for, what, six months after hundreds of years of being an amazing success?"

His silence was answer enough.

Tears slipped from beneath Mariel's closed eyelids. "I've been a failure my entire life. And now the one thing I can do isn't good enough, and the place I love most in the world will die because of it."

"It isn't your fault."

"I didn't cause it, but if I can't fix it, then I'm responsible, too. I'm the forest's protector."

"Says who?" Oz asked. "You're a witch with an incredible talent for nature magic, but just because you're good at something doesn't mean it's your responsibility."

Mariel's throat was tight, and her chest ached. How could she tell Oz that she *wanted* it to be her responsibility? "If I don't have this, I don't have anything."

"That's not true," Oz said, oblivious to the way she'd bared her heart. "You have Calladia and Themmie and me and your garden, and—"

"Stop!" Mariel's shout cut him off. "Just . . . stop," she said more quietly. "Don't tell me how to feel."

"I'm not telling you how to feel," he said stubbornly. "But you have more power than you realize, and it isn't only magical. You have people who love and respect you. Friends who would do anything for you. It isn't your responsibility to stand as the sole magical guardian of the forest."

Pigheaded demon. He looked nearly as frustrated as she felt. "It is though. And I'm failing at this, like I fail at everything." Mariel's entire life had been defined by the prophecy and her subsequent failure to live up to it. Now, confronted with a grave responsibility, she'd fucked up yet again.

Oz pinched his nose and sat back on his heels. "I'm going to say something, and you probably won't like it."

Mariel laughed, though there was no mirth in the sound. "Might as well kick me when I'm down." In the distance, she could see the black magic creeping closer again, tainting previously healed soil. Eventually, it would eat these woods entirely.

Oz took a deep breath. "Have you ever thought that maybe your self-doubt has become a self-fulfilling prophecy?"

Mariel's jaw dropped. He was right: she hadn't liked that at all. "Excuse me?"

"You're as harsh on yourself as your mother is," he said, persevering like the stubborn, jackass demon he was. "When you can't save the entire world on your own, you see that as a personal failing. Maybe you struggle with magic because you're putting unreasonable pressure on yourself."

She felt like she'd been slapped. "So it's my fault I suck?"

He winced. "That's not what I'm saying. I'm saying . . . you're amazing just the way you are, and when you can't fix something, maybe there's merit in asking for help . . . taking off some of the pressure you place on yourself."

"I refuse to ask my mother for help." The idea was abhorrent.

Oz grimaced. "Not her. But Mariel . . . I can see how strong your magic is, and I see the incredible things you're capable of. But you've convinced yourself you're never going to succeed, and even when you do amazing things, you tell yourself it's never enough. What if you let go of those expectations? Stop trying to perform to impossible standards?"

Mariel blinked rapidly as her entire being rejected the idea of forgetting expectations. "The standards aren't impossible. The Spark legacy—"

"Fuck the Spark legacy," Oz said vehemently. "You aren't your mother or anyone else you're comparing yourself to."

Mariel felt out of her depth. Whatever they'd been talking about at first, it wasn't what they were talking about now. "So I should give up and let the woods die? Is that what you're saying?"

He drove his hands through his hair. "I'm not saying this right."

"Is there a right way to say it?" Her stung pride demanded a rebuttal. He'd told her she was amazing, but the rest of his words felt like an accusation.

Oz was clearly struggling for patience. "I'm saying that no matter how good you are at nature magic, maybe this problem is too big for you to solve on your own. Maybe no one could do it alone, and you're torturing yourself with guilt rather than asking for help or finding alternate solutions."

Her temper still had ahold of her tongue. "A demon offering an alternate solution. How shocking."

He clenched his jaw, and a muscle flexed in his cheek. "That's unfair."

And yes, it was. He hadn't offered her a deal; he'd just said something that put her on the defensive. Mariel breathed deeply, struggling for calm. "I'm sorry. I need a few minutes to think."

He nodded. "Whatever you need."

"I get defensive," she said, feeling the need to explain herself. "I don't know why."

"You've spent your entire life being told there's something wrong with you," he said with his trademark bluntness. "Of course you get defensive."

"You're probably just trying to help." Oz gave her a *look*, so Mariel amended her statement. "Okay, you're definitely trying to help. You don't deserve me snapping at you because I don't like being told uncomfortable things about myself."

"Mariel," he said, tugging on one of her curls, "I also said good things about you. Do you remember any of those?"

Her mind blanked. He'd said she was self-sabotaging, that she was trying to meet impossible standards, that she should ask for help . . . "No?" she said in a small voice.

"That's what I thought." Oz kissed her temple, and some of the tightness in Mariel's chest eased. "You're seeing the worst, not the best. So you're going to take a few minutes to think, but before you do, I want you to listen. Really, truly listen."

Mariel looked at him, captivated by his fierce expression.

"Mariel," he said seriously, "you are beautiful, intelligent, and funny. You bring so much joy to the world. On top of that, you're an extremely powerful witch who can do incredible things. Needing help sometimes or not being perfect doesn't change any of that, and I wish you would be as kind to yourself as you are to your friends."

Her cheeks flushed. Oz had apparently mastered words of affirmation as a love language. A tender emotion swelled behind her breastbone, something that felt overwhelming and delicate all at once. Mariel didn't know how to express it other than by flinging her arms around Oz's neck.

"Thank you," she whispered into the crook between his neck and shoulder. He smelled like spice and smoke, and the warmth of his body soaked into her. He was like her own personal hot spring— something to sink into when she felt battered by the world.

He rubbed her back and kissed her hair. They knelt together in silence, just holding each other and breathing.

Finally, Oz stirred. "I'm going to walk the perimeter of this dark patch. I'll be back soon."

He was giving her time to gather her thoughts. Mariel watched his broad back as he walked away, head tipped down as he studied the ground. She appreciated that about him—his diligence, his willingness to be of service. The facade of the big, bad demon had been fully stripped away, and Mariel liked what she saw under-neath.

She sighed and focused on the issue at hand: the escalating corruption in the forest.

She'd liked the idea of fixing everything on her own. It had been a fantasy: standing up at family dinner and informing everyone that there had been a grave magical threat to Glimmer Falls, but Mariel had been able to stop it. She would have been the protagonist of a story, for once, rather than the sidekick or comic relief.

Oz was right though. If the issue was too big for Mariel to solve on her own, it wasn't an indictment of her magic. It meant she needed to ask for help. Themmie and Calladia couldn't do anything, but there was one person who had lived long enough that he might know what the issue was—and how to solve it.

"I'm bringing in Alzapraz," Mariel said when Oz arrived back at her side ten minutes later.

Oz nodded. "Want me to find him?"

"No need. He's coming to my house tomorrow morning for a lesson in the language of magic."

Normally spellcraft lessons made Mariel feel worse about herself, but Oz's intervention had shaken something loose in her. She loved her magic. She loved being able to feed part of herself to the natural world. She was *proud* of that magic, and she was tired of letting her family make her feel bad because she didn't fit the mold of the perfect Spark heir.

Maybe the problem wasn't that Mariel was bad at magic . . . it was that she'd never stood up for herself and what she was good at.

Oz held out his hand, helping Mariel to her feet. "Come on, *velina*. We've got a protest to attend." His smile grew wicked. "And then I have some ideas for how to spend the night . . ."

TWENTY-SEVEN

"AYORVA EN TIGASIUM," ALZAPRAZ SAID IN A QUAVERING voice, rapping his cane on the kitchen floor. "The *-um* ending on *tigasium* indicates that it's your skillet, not someone else's. If you wanted to heat Oz's skillet instead, you'd need to end with *-il*. Or *-sen*, if you're addressing the skillet directly. Except sometimes it's *-sun*. Or *-sinez*, for multiple objects." He tapped his bulbous nose, eyes sparkling under bushy white brows. "There are other variants, of course. If the skillet is yours but once belonged to Oz, you can end with *-silum*."

Ozroth watched as Mariel smacked her forehead with her palm. "Why do the suffixes change so much?"

It was ten a.m. on a drizzly Sunday morning, and the tiny warlock—bedecked in a purple velvet robe and plastic tiara—was delivering a refresher on the language of magic. Oz sat at the table, listening in, while Alzapraz and Mariel stood near a counter covered in an array of magical objects. Ozroth was taking notes—Mariel's notes were haphazard, if she took any at all—but the complicated words were already confusing him. How was he supposed to spell this nonsense?

"They aren't always suffixes," the ancient warlock said cheerfully. "Sometimes they go at the beginning, or you can add them to the verb instead. *Rotkva en iyiltransformen* is an acceptable way to say 'I transform the group of you into radishes,' but you can also say *transforma a rotkviyil*. And *tigasi a ayorvum* is another way to heat your skillet." He shrugged stooped shoulders, then winced when his back cracked loudly. "Whatever's easiest to remember."

"None of it's easy to remember," Mariel said. "That's the problem."

Ozroth sipped his pumpkin spice tea, fascinated by the discussion. The language of magic was famously complicated, its grammar changing in arbitrary and illogical ways that combined the structures of multiple languages. Very few people other than witches or warlocks bothered learning it, other than linguistics professors or masochists—a redundant distinction, he supposed.

Its incomprehensibility was part of why powerful magic users were so rare. Most low-level spellcasters learned what they needed in order to make their lives easier—spells to clean house or un-spoil milk, for instance—while only the most eccentric and dedicated bothered with more arcane spells. And since part of magic was intention and focus, even being fluent in the language of magic couldn't ensure a successful casting.

"Try the chalk," Alzapraz said, holding a white nub out to her.

"I thought that was only for big workings. Summonings and the like."

"Well, yes. But attaching a ritual activity to a spell helps while you're learning. Eventually, you won't need the chalk or any other physical focus for small spells."

Mariel grumbled, then drew lines on the counter. Some glyph

that must indicate skillet, with wavy lines emanating from it. "*Tigasi—*"

"Wait!" Alzapraz lunged forward, wiping the glyph clean with his sleeve. "Wrong glyph, unless you want to melt the skillet."

Mariel let out a frustrated shriek and threw the chalk. It shattered against the refrigerator, sending white fragments flying. One landed in Ozroth's tea, and hot liquid spattered his face and hat.

Mariel's face fell. "Sorry," she said, rushing over to dab at the droplets on his face. "I shouldn't have lost my temper."

"I would be mad, too," Ozroth said. "And besides, it feels nice. Like warm rain."

He would have told her about the hot thunderstorms that swept across the demon plane—although those smelled vaguely of sulfur, not pumpkin spice—but Alzapraz didn't know Ozroth was a demon, and Ozroth didn't particularly want that fact coming up at family dinner.

Alzapraz sighed and murmured a spell under his breath, waving a hand. The chalk reassembled itself, then floated back onto the counter. "No chalk, then." He stroked his long white beard, looking at Mariel pensively. "I don't understand why this is so difficult for you."

"You're not exactly making it easy," Ozroth said, bristling at the implication it was Mariel's fault. "You just told her a bunch of confusing ways to say the same thing."

"I don't think it's the language." Alzapraz squinted up at Mariel. "There is some sloppiness of technique with the chalk, yes, but I think it's an intention problem. You don't want to do this."

Ozroth stood, ready to defend Mariel further, but Mariel's hand on his arm stopped him. "You're right," she said. "I don't want to do this." Her tone was wondering, like she'd surprised even herself with the admission. She blew out a breath, shoulders relaxing like a burden had been lifted from them. "I don't care about using a spell to heat my skillet because I actually enjoy cooking and don't need shortcuts." Her voice grew stronger. "I don't like magic lessons in general. In fact, I hate them."

Alzapraz looked scandalized, as much as a person who was ninety percent dramatic robe and ten percent uncomfortably long eyebrows could look scandalized, but Ozroth felt a swell of pride. His witch was finally standing up for herself. "Tell him more," he encouraged her.

Mariel lifted her chin. "I hate always being told I'm not good enough. I hate that everyone sees me as a failure because they don't respect earth magic. I hate how no one is even remotely interested in what I am good at." She laughed breathlessly. "You probably don't even know what I'm good at, because you've never asked!"

The warlock fidgeted, picking at the gold fringe on his sleeves. "The Sparks have always been good at major magic. Summoning, teleportation, transmogrification—"

Mariel pointed at him. "That's exactly what I'm talking about. Only Mom's style of magic is 'major' in this family. My nature magic is considered 'minor,' even though I can heal entire sections of forest and keep plants blooming year-round."

The spider plant in her window rustled, and a potted fern hanging from the ceiling reached a curling frond towards Alzapraz. The warlock jumped when the fern brushed his tiara. He stepped away, eyeing it suspiciously. Ozroth didn't blame him. If plants could be menacing, that fern was doing its best, bristling like an angry cat.

"You have to admit, making flowers bloom isn't as dramatic as conjuring a sprite to do your bidding," Alzapraz said.

"You want dramatic?" Mariel asked. "I'll give you dramatic."

She stalked towards Alzapraz, and the warlock retreated until his back hit the counter. "Do you know what I could do right now?" Through the window, Ozroth saw autumn leaves spiraling into miniature cyclones on her back lawn, responding to her mood. Mariel's cheeks were flushed, and her chest rose and fell rapidly. She was captivating, utterly beautiful in her anger. "I could call on those trees out there to lift their roots out of the soil. I could ask them to wrap around your ankles and drag you underground to suffocate, and I wouldn't need chalk to do it."

"I'm immortal," Alzapraz squeaked.

"So? They'd keep you there forever if I wanted it." Mariel bared her teeth. "I could ask the roots to grow into you, one millimeter at a time. You'd spend eternity in agony, breathing dirt as roots wormed through your skin."

Ozroth probably shouldn't have found her viciousness arousing, but he hadn't been deemed "the Ruthless" for nothing. Soul or no soul, he could appreciate a display of power, and his jeans grew tighter. The moment Alzapraz left, Ozroth was going to drag Mariel to bed.

Still, he knew her. If she lashed out in anger, she would regret it. Ozroth took a step towards her. "*Velina . . .*"

She held up a hand to stop him. "But you know what, Alzapraz?" she asked, gaze fixed on the old man. "I'm not going to do that." Alzapraz sagged against the counter, relief written on his wrinkled face. "I'm not going to do it because I'm not like Mom or our glorious ancestors. I celebrate life and kindness. I like making things grow, and I don't want to cause anyone pain." The fern clutched at Alzapraz's sleeve, and he jumped. Mariel smirked. "But you should know that I could."

Alzapraz's wheezy breathing was loud in the silence that followed. Then the fear on his face transformed into giddiness. "So you're a Spark, after all," he said, grinning. "I haven't heard a speech that good since Malevola Spark told her husband she was going to turn his dick into a newt the next time he stuck it somewhere it didn't belong."

Ozroth cleared his throat. "Are you actually going to respond to what she said?"

Alzapraz nodded. "I confess, Mariel, I never really thought about your nature magic. You're right; we've all dismissed it as boring compared to everything the Sparks have historically excelled at." He shuddered. "But that dramatic threat has convinced me you're quite the force to be reckoned with."

"Magic can be appreciated for more than its dramatic potential," Mariel said. "Did you know the forest has been dying? Some kind of magical rot is killing the trees and poisoning the animals."

Alzapraz's beetle brows drew together. "That doesn't sound good."

"It isn't. Magic is woven into the ecosystem. What do you think will happen if the trees and flowers and animals all die?"

"Nature walks will certainly be less interesting." At Mariel's outraged look, Alzapraz raised a withered hand. "No, I take your meaning. Unlike your mother, I've been alarmed at the direction this town is taking. When you live as long as I have, you recognize how small pieces fit into the whole."

"Unless the small piece is named Mariel," she snapped.

"You aren't a small piece," Ozroth said. "You're a queen." When she turned an adoring look on him, warmth spread in his chest.

Alzapraz squinted at Ozroth. "Odd," he muttered. Then he focused on Mariel again. "I know the ley lines are sensitive. They need living creatures as much as we need them. I was hoping construction would be delayed after that disastrous town hall." He frowned. "Do you suppose the construction company is seeding this rot?"

"Maybe," Mariel said. "Or someone else who benefits from destroying the forest. So far, my magic is the only thing capable of stopping it, but yesterday I found a patch too big to fix by myself. I was hoping you could help me. *Without* involving my mother."

"I don't know if you've noticed," Alzapraz said dryly, "but I try to avoid your mother if at all possible." He tapped his cane on the floor, and the crystal on top sparked. "I'll consult my tomes. Will you text me the location of the rot?" At Ozroth's disbelieving look, Alzapraz let out a wheezy cackle. "I may be older than dirt, but I can figure out a touch screen."

As Alzapraz shuffled towards the front door, he reached up to pat Mariel's cheek. "You're a good girl who deserves far better than we've given," he said. "And I'm sorry for not doing more to defend you."

She sighed. "Thank you, Alzapraz. Do you suppose you can convince my mother to apologize, too?"

Alzapraz grimaced. "I'll work on it. But you know how she is."

"Yeah, I do." Mariel looked sideways at Oz, lips tilting in a smile that made her dimples pop out. "But I know how I am, too."

Ozroth was desperate to snatch her up and shower her with kisses. He wanted to strip her nude and bury his head between her thighs, licking orgasm after orgasm out of her. Mariel deserved only good things, and he was so proud of her for finally drawing a boundary.

Alzapraz turned at the front door, looking back at where Ozroth and Mariel stood in the entrance to the kitchen. "I'm watching you," he said, directing two fingers towards his eyes, then pointing at Ozroth.

Ozroth felt a spike of paranoia. Did Alzapraz suspect what he was, or was that a generic threat aimed at the new boyfriend? But then the door closed behind the warlock, and Ozroth forgot all about him. He finally had Mariel to himself, and he planned to make good use of the time.

He hoisted her into his arms, carrying her back into the kitchen as she giggled, then deposited her on a countertop. "That was so fucking sexy," he said as he dragged up her skirt. He mouthed down her neck, sucking on her smooth skin. The taste of her was intoxicating, with hints of vanilla and sweet blossoms, and he was quickly becoming an addict.

Mariel tipped her head back, giving him more access. "I can't believe I stood up to him," she said breathlessly. "It felt good."

"Watching you threaten him made me hard," Ozroth admitted, nibbling at the neckline of her cherry-red dress.

Mariel laughed. "Kinky."

Ozroth gripped her thighs under her skirt, kneading the soft flesh. He loved how she was built—soft and strong all at once, her curves enough to make his head spin. She was made for passion. "Everything about you makes me hard." He traced his thumbs over the crease between her belly and thighs, and she shivered.

"I'm wet," she told him.

That was all the teasing Ozroth could take. He shoved the hem of her dress to her waist. "Hold it there." When she complied, he dropped to his knees, then buried his head between her thighs.

"Oh!" Mariel dug her heels into his back as he licked over the fabric of her underwear. He could smell her, musky and feminine, and the scent made him even harder. She hadn't lied; she was wet, her tart arousal already dampening the fabric.

When he slid his tongue under the edge of her panties, Mariel moaned. The taste of her was like a drug. Wanting more, Ozroth tugged the crotch of her underwear aside, then dove in, licking and sucking with enthusiasm.

Lucifer, he loved this. Loved the way she moaned when he circled her clit, loved how slick she was, loved her sudden inhale when he pressed his tongue inside her. He used his entire face to pleasure her, nudging her clit with his nose and getting her arousal all over his cheeks and chin. He could do this forever, he decided.

Mariel rocked against his face, using her heels against his back as leverage. He could barely breathe, but breathing was overrated. He did pull away slightly at last, but only so he could slide a finger inside her while flicking her clit with his tongue.

Mariel cried out, and her pussy pulsed around his finger. Already coming? He kept going, fingering and licking her through the spasms. At some point, she'd dropped the hem of her dress in favor of gripping his hair. When she wrapped her hands around his horns instead, Ozroth nearly came in his jeans. He groaned as molten-hot pleasure spiked through him.

Ozroth surged to his feet and captured Mariel's mouth in a hard, desperate kiss. She kissed him back fervently as she fumbled with the button and zipper of his jeans. He fished a condom out of his back pocket and ripped the packet open as his jeans and boxer briefs puddled around his feet. Ozroth didn't waste time stepping out of the discarded clothing. He rolled the condom on, then tugged her underwear to the side, fitted the tip of his cock against her, and thrust inside.

They let out matching groans. "You feel so fucking good," Ozroth said. He was too riled up to go slow, but Mariel didn't seem to need time to adjust. She grabbed his ass, urging him on.

Ozroth fucked her with deep, hard strokes. Mariel braced her arms on the counter, leaning back so she could look at where he penetrated her. Ozroth looked, too, and the sight of his cock thrusting in and out of her wet pussy was nearly enough to end him. "You're taking me so well," he groaned.

"Harder," she ordered, squeezing his hips with her thighs.

Ozroth obliged, setting a brutal rhythm. He grabbed her ass with one hand, anchoring her, and slapped the other against a cabinet. The large spoons she kept in a jar rattled, and when a particularly hard thrust made Mariel gasp and reposition her hands, she knocked over a metal canister. Sugar spilled from it, sparkling bright in the sunlight coming through the window.

The pressure in Ozroth's cock was building, but he needed her to come again. Thankfully, Mariel seemed to be on the same page. She slid a hand between them, rubbing her clit in rough circles. He kept up the furious pace, fingertips digging into her ass.

"Come, *velina*," he said. "I can't—I'm going to—"

The pressure reached the point of no return. Ozroth's vision blurred, and he shouted as the tension released all at once. The light bulb overhead shattered. Mariel cried out, orgasming with him.

Ozroth felt like he'd transcended to a higher plane where perfect moments blossomed like flowers. "I love you," he panted against her neck.

Mariel stiffened. It took Ozroth's pleasure-fuzzed brain a few seconds to catch up and realize what he'd said.

Shit.

He knew he loved Mariel—what else could this aching, thrilling, giddy, wonderfully awful feeling be?—but maybe humans didn't make love confessions right away. Ozroth straightened, looking worriedly at Mariel. Her hazel eyes were wide, and her teeth were plugged into her lower lip. Hard to tell what she was thinking.

"Sorry," he said. "Maybe that was inappropriate according to human customs."

To his surprise, she laughed. "Oz, I don't think human customs apply to us. I've just never had a partner say that before."

"Never?" he asked incredulously. The notion that anyone she'd dated in the past wouldn't have fallen horns over heels for her was incomprehensible. "How can anyone know you and not love you?"

Her eyes grew watery, and she flung her arms around his neck. "Maybe it's too soon," she said, the words muffled against his chest, "but Oz . . . I love you, too."

"Really?" Fizzing happiness settled in his gut like the most exquisite champagne. He felt like he could fight a hundred night-beasts with his bare hands. He'd always thought of love as a weakness, but with Mariel's love settling over him, it felt more like armor.

Mariel nodded, cheek rubbing over his chest. "I didn't expect it. When you appeared in my kitchen, it felt like my life was over. How could I possibly deal with a demon who would be around all the time until he manipulated a soul out of me?" She placed a kiss directly over his heart. "Now I'm excited to have you around all the time."

Ozroth was, too. There was still guilt under the joy, a twinge of regret that this situation had been forced on Mariel, but if she'd never summoned him, he never would have gotten to know her. He wouldn't have learned how to love.

"I hated my soul," Ozroth said. "Feeling things was uncomfortable, and I thought it made me weaker. But now I can't imagine life without those emotions." He squeezed her tighter. "Without you."

Their path would be far from easy. Ozroth would have to explain his decision to postpone the deal to Astaroth, and who knew what the fallout from that would be? Beyond that, there were other issues. How they'd handle the need for constant proximity, for one. And, ultimately, what to do about the fact that Mariel was mortal and Ozroth was not.

His love for her wouldn't fade, he was sure of that. And he didn't care if she got wrinkles or her hair went gray. Her soul would be just as bright, her heart just as big. But the reality of seeing her age when he didn't . . . he didn't want to think about it.

"This will be hard," he told her.

"I know." She looked up at him, eyes blazing with passion and purpose. "But I want to see where it goes."

"Me, too."

She chuckled and shook her head. "You know, Calladia was worried you were lying to me, but you're almost painfully honest."

"I would never lie to you," he said.

Her smile was soft and sweet. "Promise?"

"Promise."

TWENTY-EIGHT

"D ARLINGS!" DIANTHA EXCLAIMED, HOLDING THE FRONT door wide. "You made it!"

Mariel's smile was more like a grimace as she hugged her mother. "We literally couldn't miss it."

Her mother was dressed in a yellow gown with an intricately folded neck ruff. Amethysts dotted her hair and glittered at her fingers, matching her purple manicure. About the only thing Mariel had inherited from Diantha—a debilitating complex didn't count—was her love of colorful clothing.

Mariel was still wearing the cherry-red scoop-neck dress she'd worn while Oz had his wicked way with her. She was deliciously sore between her thighs, and she savored that reminder of what they'd done . . . what they'd been doing almost nonstop since deciding to give their relationship a try.

Mariel felt electrified from head to toe, and not because of Oz's newly discovered magic. She'd never experienced a passion this intense, and it wasn't all lust. Oz was smart, supportive, and funny in his own dry way. She craved being near him, and he seemed to feel the same. He was obsessed with watching her prepare her floral display for the championships, commenting on her talent as an artist and the beauty of the blossoms.

Mariel felt like one of those blossoms herself, opening her petals to the sun. Or the clouds, really, since they were heading into the rainy Pacific Northwest winter, but Mariel knew better than anyone that there were no rules when it came to blooming.

She watched as Oz accepted Diantha's hug with clear discomfort. He still wore his battered black cowboy hat, but the blue shirt and black jeans were new. They were slowly building his wardrobe, and he'd even opened a small portal to the demon realm to grab clothes from his den. She'd gotten a peek at his bedroom and was unsurprised to see it was sparse and utilitarian. Oz had confessed that he'd never cared about art or decorations until recently. Astaroth had raised him to believe that attachments to anything, whether people or objects, made him weak.

If Mariel ever met Astaroth, she was going to give the demon a piece of her mind—starting with a taste of her knuckles. She'd never punched anyone before, but she was pretty sure she'd do an adequate job of it. Or maybe she'd ask Calladia to do it, since that would hurt more.

"Come in, come in." Diantha beckoned them into the portrait hallway. As always, Mariel avoided the beady-eyed glare of Great-Great-Uncle Trenton. Entering the Spark family home felt like walking the gauntlet, surrounded on all sides by relatives who were more talented than she was.

Mariel *was* talented though, she reminded herself. She just wasn't talented in the way Diantha Spark wanted her to be. But for the first time, Mariel felt tempted to ask her mother, *Who cares?* She was finally feeling comfortable in her skin.

The table was set, but only her dad and cousin Lancelot were seated beneath the looming heads of Wally's automatons. "I thought you got to be sick this week?" Mariel asked Lancelot as she sat across from him.

Lancelot tossed his head to get a hank of dramatically swooping black hair out of his eyes. "Mom and Dad promised me a new console if they get to be sick for the whole month."

"Is that worth it?" Mariel asked doubtfully.

"They also doubled my allowance." He shrugged. "Plus, the food's way better than Dad's cooking." He tipped his phone to show Mariel the screen, which was full of animated ghouls. "And I'm making major progress in *Poltergeist Go*."

"No whispering at the dinner table," Diantha said, taking a seat. She worked her usual spell to shorten the table, and Oz twitched as Diantha zoomed towards them. "Now all we need is Alzapraz. Where is the old codger? Roland, have you heard from him?"

Roland shook his head, not bothering to lower his newspaper.

Diantha murmured a spell, and mojitos appeared in front of the adults. Mariel took a sip. It was perfect, citrus and mint softening the burn of alcohol.

She watched Oz sample the cocktail. His eyebrows shot up, and he stared at the drink like it was ambrosia. "Incredible." He tipped it to his lips and chugged.

Mariel winced. "It's stronger than wine, you know."

Oz's golden eyes went wide over the rim of his now empty glass. "How much stronger?"

"Like . . . three or four times?"

"Oh." He looked at the empty glass mournfully. "I should have saved it."

"Don't worry, I'll summon another," Diantha said cheerfully.

A second mojito appeared in front of Oz. He looked at it with clear longing, and Mariel smiled. "It's okay to get tipsy," she told him. "We walked here, after all." Frankly, she would love to see drunk Oz. He'd seen her after margaritas, so it would only be fair.

"It tastes so good," Oz said. "Like colors exploding in my mouth."

That kind of sentence would normally make Mariel question how high a person was, but Oz had confided more in her since they'd made their relationship official. Sounds, scents, and tastes could send him into overstimulation. "Sip slowly," she advised. "Savor it."

His lips quirked. "Oh, now you appreciate going slow and savoring things?"

"Hush, you." Her cheeks burned; she could remember every single time he'd insisted on savoring her.

"I'm just saying, you should be consistent in your views."

Mariel leaned over and planted a smacking kiss on his mouth. "And I'm just saying, you should consider the consequences of teasing me."

"There are consequences?" He brought his mouth to her ear. "Do tell."

Mariel felt the familiar flush of arousal, and she would have outlined some of those consequences, but this was not the venue for it. Diantha was already watching them like a praying mantis on the hunt, and they didn't need to give the family more of a show.

"You lovebirds are adorable," Diantha said. "Any updates on procreating?"

"Mom!" Mariel said as Oz choked on his drink. "That's not appropriate."

Diantha waved her hand. "You don't need to be so precious about your sex life. And don't you want to give me grandbabies?" She batted her eyes, but if there was one thing she wasn't good at, it was playing the naïf.

Mariel normally would have deflected or agreed to make the awkward moment end, but an ember of outrage had settled behind her breastbone. She squared her shoulders. "If I have children," she told her mother, "it will be when I choose to. And it will have nothing to do with you, so I don't want to hear you mention procreation again."

Silence fell—even Lancelot's finger paused over his smartphone screen.

Diantha blinked. "We're family. We share everything."

"No, we don't." Mariel's voice grew more confident. "My relationship is my business. My uterus is my business. So please stop acting as if you own me."

"Oh, shit," Lancelot said under his breath, brown eyes widening.

The newspaper sagged from Roland's hands. Mariel met her father's shocked stare with her chin held high. He let Diantha walk all over him, but Mariel was tired of feeding into that dynamic.

Diantha stood, sending her chair scraping over the floor. Mariel braced herself, wondering what horrible thing her mother was going to summon to punish her.

"You," Diantha said, pointing at Mariel, "are an ungrateful brat."

Oz made a noise of protest, but Mariel met his gaze and shook her head. "My fight," she whispered.

His jaw clenched, and a muscle flickered in his cheek. Then he nodded.

Mariel squeezed his arm in silent thanks, then stood. "I'm not ungrateful," she told Diantha. "I'm setting boundaries."

"After all I've done for you?" Diantha demanded. "Years of paying for the best schools, the best training, the best of everything, and you repay me with baseless accusations? I don't act like I own you."

"You do." Mariel's heart raced, pumping adrenaline through her veins. She'd never confronted her mother this way, and it was as terrifying as it was thrilling. "You waltz into my house uninvited. You go through my things. You keep tabs on my magic."

"Someone has to." Diantha's fingers rippled agitatedly on the surface of the table, nails tapping a rhythm like a rattlesnake's warning. "Despite all the money and time spent on you, you're lazy. Your spellcraft is terrible. I've poured years of effort into making you a proper Spark, and yet you fail every time."

A familiar mix of rage and shame roiled in Mariel's gut, and her chest felt tight. Everyone was looking at her—Oz with concern, Lancelot with alarm, and her father with an expression of resigned disappointment. This was the part where she was supposed to wilt and apologize.

A few weeks ago, Mariel would have.

She took a deep breath and planted her feet, imagining soil between her toes. Below the foundation, the earth lay rich and dark. Worms twined through the dirt, while roots reached out slender fingers, anchoring themselves deep. *You will not move me*, those roots said. *I belong here.*

Mariel would not be moved either. Not this time. "I'm not a failure," she said. "I'm incredible at nature magic—you just don't respect it."

Diantha scoffed. "Playing with flowers isn't as important as other magical skills."

"What practical use does teleportation have?" Mariel asked. "I can fight disease in plants, make them bloom in winter, keep the natural world alive. You get to show off at parties."

"Watch your tone," her father said. "Your mother is trying to help."

"Watch my tone?" Mariel let out an unhinged laugh. "No, I don't think I will."

Diantha looked aghast. "What's gotten into you tonight? I know we didn't drop thousands of dollars on etiquette classes for you to end up like this." She gestured in Mariel's direction, and the dragon automaton overhead let out a puff of steam.

"I didn't ask for etiquette classes," Mariel shot back. "You insisted, like you've insisted on controlling every other aspect of my life. I'm tired of it."

"*Cockatrice din convosen!*" Diantha shouted.

Mariel flinched as a small dragon the size of a Great Dane appeared in the center of the table. It had two legs, a serpent-like tail, and the head of a rooster. It cawed shrilly, a horrible, metallic noise that left everyone covering their ears.

Cockatrices were rumored to kill with a glance, but that was a misunderstanding originating in medieval times, when they were used to torture prisoners. What they *did* do was let out such unbearable sounds, no one could stand to be around them. Eventually, a listener's ears would start bleeding. Diantha was trying to shut Mariel up by any means necessary.

As Mariel saw the pained looks from Oz and Lancelot, who were covering their ears to little avail, fury washed over her. Diantha was hurting more than just Mariel's self-esteem. She traced a pentagram on the tabletop with her finger. "*Aufrasen di cockatrice!*" she shouted over the unrelenting cawing.

The cockatrice vanished.

Mariel gaped at the spot where it had stood. Her ears were ringing, and it took a moment to catch up to what Diantha was saying. Her mother, against all odds, was suddenly beaming. "I knew you'd catch on eventually," she crowed. "You just needed a little push."

Mariel met Oz's eyes. "I did it," she said wonderingly. "I banished it."

"You did." His expression was proud.

"You just needed to be shouted at," Diantha was saying, and Mariel instantly snapped back to the conversation. "I can be rougher on you, if it yields results like this."

"No!" Mariel slapped a hand on the table. The griffin head roared. "That spell had nothing to do with you."

Diantha sniffed. "Obviously I was part of it. You've never successfully summoned or banished anything before."

"If I succeeded, it wasn't thanks to you," Mariel snapped. "That magic came from me."

A bolt of realization hit, and Mariel's jaw dropped. For the first time, she realized why her magic worked perfectly sometimes and failed other times.

It was clear no one else had experienced a similar epiphany. Her mother was still jabbering away about how to "shape" Mariel's talent, while Oz was grinding his teeth and clenching his fists, clearly trying not to intervene. Lancelot had snagged a spare mojito somehow and was sucking it down, looking furtively at the exit.

Testing her theory, Mariel traced another invisible pentagram on the table. "*Aufrasen en mojitoil,*" she murmured.

The mojito vanished, leaving her underage cousin sucking noisily through an empty straw. He yelped and jerked back in his chair.

Mariel wagged her finger at him. "Four more years before you can drink that."

He scowled. "You're not my mom." Then his mouth tugged into a smile. "Nice banishment though."

"Thanks." Mariel grinned. She was still angry, but the wonder of her realization was exhilarating. She straightened her posture and faced her mother.

"It'll be a shame if I have to summon a cockatrice every time you do a spell," Diantha said, "but if that's what it takes—"

"It's my turn to talk," Mariel said loudly.

Diantha paused midsentence. "About what? We've discovered the key to your magic. We need to practice."

Mariel shook her head. "No, *I* discovered the key to my magic. Do you know why my spellcraft fails around you? Because you're ordering me to do it. The impulse doesn't come from me."

"So?" Diantha's brow creased. "That's how everyone learns."

"Not when you've browbeaten me into having a complex about it!" Mariel was feeling more confident with every moment. "Part of magic is intent, right? The intent wasn't coming from me. I was so scared of messing up that it became a self-fulfilling prophecy."

Oz twined his fingers through hers, and she looked down at him. He was smiling, his craggy face transformed by delight. Laugh lines fanned out from his eyes, and Mariel wanted to bring out those lines as often as possible.

"I banished the cockatrice because I was tired of being told to shut up," she said. "I banished the mojito because it was my idea. And sometimes my magic has worked around Oz because it was my desire shaping the spell—not yours."

"I've only ever tried to push you to be the best witch you can be." Diantha pressed a hand to her chest, and her bracelet caught the light. The amethysts were bright and hard, like her. "You can't blame me because you're a slow learner."

Now that Mariel had begun this messy confrontation, she couldn't stop. Words poured out of her, the unstoppering of decades of resentment and grief. "Do you even hear yourself?" she asked. "You always try to knock me down. My whole life you've belittled me, telling me I'm slow or untalented, that I'm a disappointment and an embarrassment to the Spark legacy. Maybe you thought that would inspire me to work harder, but no matter how hard I've worked, it's never been enough for you. And I'm not a slow learner at all—my nature magic has been powerful from the start."

"There's more to magic than plants," Diantha argued, per usual ignoring any criticism aimed at her. "You need to be good at all of it. The stars and the wind and the earth all agreed—"

"I don't give a fuck about the stars and the wind and the earth!" Mariel shouted. "I don't care what you heard or thought you heard. I don't want to be like you. I want to be me."

"Language!" Roland said after a few seconds of appalled silence.

"And you," she said, turning on her father. "You've let her walk all over you and me for years. Whenever she's insulted me, you've supported her." In some ways, that had hurt more. Mariel knew what her mother was like: dramatic, narcissistic, and blind to her own failings. But her father was a relatively normal person, and he'd never defended Mariel from Diantha's harsher critiques.

He sighed and nudged his glasses up to pinch the bridge of his nose. "Mariel, you know we love you."

"Do I?" she asked, feeling the sting of a deep, unacknowledged wound. Oz had surfaced that pain when she'd first met him. *Do you think she loves you?* he'd asked, back when he was still trying to find leverage over her. He'd hit devastatingly close to home. "Love is supporting someone," she said. "Lifting them up, not tearing them down. Loving them as they are, not how you want them to be." Oz was a scowling, emotionally unstable demon with a checkered past, and she liked him just the way he was. "Oz has shown me more love in a few weeks than I've felt in years from my own parents."

"Why are you attacking us like this?" Diantha's eyes were dry, but her lower lip quivered theatrically. "After all we've done for you. The expense alone . . ."

"Money isn't love," Mariel said. "If we'd been poor and you'd treated me with patience and kindness, I would have ended up much happier."

Diantha burst into sobs. In an instant, Roland was on his feet and hurrying over to wrap her in his arms. "Look what you've done," he told Mariel as he stroked his wife's hair. "You made your own mother cry."

"Questionable," Mariel said. "But even if I did, the two of you have made me cry countless times. I'm tired of shutting up and taking it."

Lancelot did a subtle fist pump, and she smiled at her cousin. She wasn't alone in this family—she had Lancelot, Alzapraz, Lupe, and Quincy, not to mention Hector and Wally, the relatives Diantha had already chased away.

Mariel was finally ready to join them. "I won't be coming to Sunday dinners anymore," she said.

Diantha sobbed harder. "Then you can forget about me paying for graduate school."

The dream of an SoD in Magical Herbology hung before Mariel, fragile and fervently wanted. Without the Spark family trust, she'd need to scrap, save, and scramble to cover tuition.

The threat was oddly freeing. As manager of the trust, Diantha had always wielded money like a weapon against her family. Was a life free from student loans worth being treated terribly?

No, it wasn't. Mariel was an adult; she'd figure it out.

"That's fine," she said. "I'll work my way through school, take out loans. I am not going to let you hold my future hostage." Oz squeezed her hand, and Mariel welcomed the comforting gesture. She took a deep breath. "In fact, I won't see you at all until you change your behavior. Stop controlling me. Stop insulting me. Stop belittling nature magic. I am an adult and your daughter, and I deserve respect."

"I just wanted you to be powerful." Diantha's voice was watery enough that Mariel could finally believe she was crying. "Your future looked so bright; I thought you'd be happy if you could fulfill the prophecy."

Mariel tugged on Oz's hand. He stood, and Mariel leaned against him. "My future *is* bright. And I am happy." She smiled at Oz. "Want to get out of here?"

"Absolutely," he growled, and she could tell by the look in his eyes that he was going to take her against the nearest horizontal or vertical surface the moment he could. It was thrilling how aroused he got when she asserted herself.

The dining room door blew open with a bang and a cloud of purple smoke. Mariel jumped and turned to see what new abomination her mother had summoned.

It wasn't an abomination. It was Alzapraz, his robe smeared with mud, his beard full of twigs. He was sweating and furious-looking as he pointed at Oz. "You!"

Oz looked puzzled. "What?"

"Get away from her, demon." Alzapraz muttered a spell and gestured violently, and Oz was flung across the room. Mariel cried out as he hit the wall and was pinned there by Alzapraz's magic.

"Leave him alone," she said, moving towards Oz. Her body froze though, Alzapraz's magic extending to keep her in place.

The old warlock rarely flaunted his skill, but he'd been practicing magic for centuries. Though Mariel strained, she couldn't move an inch, and she didn't know a spell for getting out of mystical entrapment.

"What do you mean—demon?" Diantha asked, looking up from where her face had been smashed into her husband's chest.

Alzapraz chuckled darkly. "You never figured it out? I knew the second I saw him." He performed another spell, and Oz's hat flew off, revealing his horns. Diantha gasped, and Lancelot pushed back from the table so fast his chair fell over.

"You're dating a *demon*?" Diantha screeched.

"Please," Mariel said through a clenched jaw. "He's not like other demons. He's kind and good, and he loves me—"

"Bullshit," Alzapraz interjected. "I was in the woods, investigating the rot."

"Rot?" Mariel's father asked.

"It's bad," Alzapraz said, ignoring the question. "Getting worse, too. I could only clear small patches, and the dark magic ate them up again immediately."

"What does this have to do with Oz?" Mariel asked, straining to get towards her lover. He was trying, too—she could see the bulge of his muscles as he pushed against the spell. Blue lightning crackled above his head like a halo.

"I've seen that rot before." Alzapraz's bushy brows drew together as he glowered at Oz. "Centuries ago, when a demon was trying to force a wood witch into a deal."

Mariel's stomach tightened with burgeoning dread. "What are you saying?"

"The woods are being poisoned, but not by human magic." Alzapraz pointed a quivering finger at Oz. "By demon magic."

Mariel stared at Oz, unable to believe it. "He wouldn't do that to me." But Alzapraz had no reason to lie.

Calladia's previous warnings rang in her head.

Demons are notorious liars.

If I were trying to trick you into giving up your soul, the first thing I'd do would be to threaten the thing you love most.

What if Oz did it?

Mariel's heart cracked open. Tears flooded her eyes and trailed down her cheeks, and she was unable to wipe them away. "You lied to me," she sobbed.

Oz looked tormented. Lightning struck all around him, singeing the parquet floor. He didn't know how to control his magic yet.

Or was that a lie, too? Had he been manipulating her all along, lying about gaining a soul to get closer to her? Had he constructed an entire identity to appeal to everything Mariel wanted—validation, love, a protector she could protect in return?

"It wasn't me." The tendons in Oz's neck stood out as he strained to escape. "Please, Mariel, you have to believe me."

Alzapraz's hold on her loosened. Mariel wiped her eyes and nose, leaving a trail of snot on the back of her hand. She felt hollow, her gut aching with loss. "I don't have to do anything," she said. "Not for my parents, not for you."

She turned on her heel and ran.

She was all the way down the hill when she heard Oz's shouts behind her. Alzapraz had apparently released the demon. "Mariel, wait!"

Like hell she would. What was it doctors said? If you hear hoofbeats, don't expect a unicorn? Well, Mariel had looked at Oz, listened to his story, and decided he was a unicorn: the one demon in the entire universe with a soul, one who had conveniently fallen head over heels in love with the witch who wouldn't trade her soul. Over the past weeks, he'd fed into her loneliness and lack of self-esteem, building her trust while destroying something she loved.

How would it have ended? With the forest dying and Oz promising he could bring it all back and stop the construction if only she would make a deal? He'd probably tell her he loved her with or without her magic, and she would have believed him.

While Mariel had been falling in love . . . Oz had been plotting against her.

She fished her phone out of her pocket. She could hardly see the screen through her tears, but she navigated to recent calls. It rang three times before Calladia picked up.

"Hey, babe!"

"You were right." Mariel's voice was garbled by snot and tears.

"Whoa, what's going on?"

"Oz." Mariel couldn't get out any more of the story: her throat was choked up, and she was breathing hard from running.

"Oh, shit. Are you home?"

"Will be soon."

"I'll be there. We'll set a warding circle so powerful, his nuts will get blown to Mars if he tries to get in."

After they hung up, Mariel pushed her legs and lungs to their limits. She was an avid hiker, but long-distance running had never been her forte. She should have ridden her bike and let Oz walk to the dinner party, but like a besotted fool, she hadn't wanted to be separated from him. From *the demon trying to steal her soul.*

How could she have been so naive? Life wasn't a fairy tale full of true love and redeemed villains. The villains were called that for a reason.

Mariel had just never expected her heart to be the weapon wielded against her.

TWENTY-NINE

"MARIEL!" OZROTH'S VOICE BROKE AS HE PURSUED HER. She'd gotten a decent head start, but his legs were longer, and he was determined to catch up before she locked herself inside her house. "Please, listen to me."

He was reeling from what Alzapraz had said. The blight was demon-caused? Demons couldn't sense their own magic the way they sensed human magic, and as far as he knew, he was the only demon on assignment in the Pacific Northwest, so he hadn't even considered the possibility.

Now Mariel thought he was a monster.

His tattoo started to tingle, and he growled in frustration. "Not now . . ."

The summoning was insistent though, and the tingle turned into burning and then a pain like being stabbed with hot knives. He stumbled to a stop next to a house with an array of flickering jack-o'-lanterns out front. The carved faces grimaced at him, the magic flames inside making the faces seem to move.

He held his shaking hands out, palm up. "I await you, Master." *And you'd better talk quickly.*

Astaroth appeared, wearing a white suit and carrying his cane sword. "Where is the witch's soul?" he demanded.

"I need more time," Ozroth said. "A lot more time, actually."

"I gave you until the end of the month."

"Which isn't until tomorrow. Regardless, I'm not going to finish in time for you to win the bet."

Astaroth stiffened, and the menace in his expression sent cold sweat trickling down Ozroth's back. "Excuse me?"

Ozroth needed to fix things with Mariel, which meant his plan to remain on Earth was unchanged. "I'm staying here until she's ready to give up her soul. Probably another seventy or eighty years." Too little time to spend with the person he loved, but he would take anything he could get. Even another minute in her presence would be a gift, considering what she thought him guilty of.

"Absolutely not." Astaroth slammed his cane into the ground. "The bet—"

"Isn't mine." It was the sharpest tone he'd ever taken with his mentor, but if Mariel could stand up to her abusive mother, he could damn well set a boundary with Astaroth. "You made it; therefore you can deal with the consequences."

Wind lashed the treetops, rattling dead leaves loose. Astaroth's eyes bored into Ozroth. "You fell for the mortal," he said in a tone of disgust.

"There's no shame in that. You'll get the soul—just on my timeline."

"There is shame when you put your species at risk because a mortal spread her legs."

"Don't talk about her like that." Ozroth stepped closer. Astaroth was a projection, but he wished he could punch the disdain off the demon's face. "The realm can wait a few more decades for her soul."

"No, it can't," Astaroth snapped.

Ozroth recoiled. "What?"

"There's a . . . situation."

"What's happening?" Had another bargainer died in the line of action? Was something wrong in the demon plane? Ozroth was tired of being a soul bargainer, but he still cared about his home.

"I haven't been totally honest with you," Astaroth said. *Tap tap* went the cane against his boot. *Tap tap.* "You've done a tremendous job over the years—recent failures aside—but fewer and fewer demons are being born with the level of power and control it takes to be bargainers. We haven't been replacing losses in the ranks quickly enough."

Dread crawled down Ozroth's spine. "What do you mean?"

"The demon plane is dying," Astaroth said bluntly. "Bit by bit, the lights are going out. The high council has been covering it up, but there will come a time very soon when everyone will realize what's happening. After that . . . it won't take long to lose everything."

A heavy, horrible feeling settled in Ozroth's stomach, like he'd swallowed a stone. He could envision his home now—the elegant stone buildings, the walkways over steaming rivers, the golden orbs that drifted like massive fireflies, lighting the perpetual twilight.

Bargainers needed to be stoic and unfeeling, but the rest of the species had more freedom to form connections. If he was in the plane right now, he'd see evidence of those bonds. Couples would walk alongside the river, arm in arm. Children would play in the fire fountains, laughing as the flames tickled their feet and rained down on their heads. As twilight deepened into the black hues of night, demons would gather in their dens for supper, then sing songs older than the memory of the oldest demons.

Demons might not feel emotions with the same chaotic, over-whelming intensity as humans did, but they still felt them. They still lived and loved. They still valued their neighbors.

As the magic died, all those demons would, too. The plane was an ecosystem of intertwined life; none of it could survive without all of it.

Like Mariel's forest.

His heart felt like it was ripping in two. "You need more souls."

Astaroth nodded. "Not just more souls—more powerful souls. And we need them now."

The message was clear. Mariel's soul was very powerful. It would be enough to stave off disaster while the demons bar-gained for whatever they could get. "I understand," Ozroth said, feeling chilled. There had to be a way out of this, but he needed time to think.

"Chin up." Astaroth's smile was as sharp as the rest of him. "When you come back with the witch's soul, you'll be a hero."

Astaroth vanished, and Ozroth sank to his knees. He buried his head in his hands and screamed into his palms. How was he supposed to choose between his people and his love? No matter what he did, he would be a monster. To trade so many immortal lives for one mortal would amount to genocide . . . but how could he betray Mariel by forcing her into a deal?

It was an impossible situation, but so were many other things. It was impossible for a demon to have a soul. Impossible for a witch to summon a demon by mistake. Impossible for a soul bar-gainer and a witch to fall in love.

He staggered back to his feet, determined to find a path for-ward. Step one: finding Mariel . . . and convincing her he hadn't damaged the forest.

Who had though?

THIRTY

MARIEL HAD NO IDEA HOW OZ HADN'T CAUGHT UP TO HER by the time she got home. She was breathing hard, her lungs on fire from running. Calladia hadn't arrived yet, but she'd be there any minute, so Mariel hurried through the house and out back, needing the comfort of her plants. She was too shaky and unfocused to attempt a warding spell, but Calladia would be able to boot Oz out easily if he arrived first.

Oz . . .

Mariel collapsed in front of her greenhouse and started weeping. The dying grass curled over her fingers, and the apple tree dipped a bare branch to touch her hair. Plants gave of themselves so freely, so selflessly, even though people trampled them or plucked them or chopped them down to make way for buildings.

Mariel had wanted to give herself that freely, too. To present her beating heart to someone and, for once, have them honor and guard it. She'd bared herself to Oz literally and figuratively, sharing her body, her thoughts, her insecurities—everything. She'd thought he'd bared himself in return.

Too bad it had all been a lie.

"Mariel."

The low voice definitely wasn't Calladia's. Mariel scrambled to her feet and spun on Oz, who stood silhouetted in the kitchen doorway. "Go away," she said in a trembling voice.

He looked like he was in agony. "Please, just listen. I didn't do anything to the forest."

She scoffed. "Sure, it must have been another demon trapped in a soul bargain with a woman who loves the forest."

"It sounds ludicrous, but it's the truth." He took a step forward, then froze as a rosebush wrapped a thorny stem around his neck, threatening harm if he continued. "Are you making the bush do that?"

"Yes." Mariel crossed her arms. "And I'm not afraid to rip your throat out." That last part wasn't true, but Mariel was too devastated to think past the hurt. "You told me you had a soul. That you were the only demon to feel emotions so intensely. You told me you loved me." Her voice cracked on the last sentence.

"I do," he vowed. "I love you so much, Mariel."

"Liar." The accusation was as vicious as the ones she had lobbed at her parents. "That's what everyone does, isn't it? They see me and think it'll be easy to lie to me, to hurt me, to manipulate me however they want."

"Mariel—"

"*I'm not finished.*"

His mouth snapped shut.

"Tell me the truth," Mariel said. "If I asked you to . . . would you be able to fix the blight in the woods in exchange for my soul?"

His mouth opened and closed. Finally, he nodded.

Mariel laughed bitterly. "You were counting on me letting my guard down. Getting so desperate that I'd ask you to save the forest. Let me guess, you'd still love me without my magic?"

Oz's mouth twisted. "I would, but I didn't do this. I swear."

"Then who did?"

He started to shrug, then stopped when the vine tightened around his neck, pressing the points of thorns into his skin. "Another demon. I need to do some research, ask around . . ."

She scoffed. "What, you couldn't tell it was demon magic from the start?"

"It doesn't work like that. We feel human magic because we harvest it. I can't sense another demon's workings."

"How convenient," Mariel said. "You have an answer for everything."

Something rattled in the alleyway beyond her yard, like a foot striking a soda can. Mariel looked over her shoulder, but no one appeared. Calladia was still en route, apparently.

"I don't have all the answers," Oz said, and Mariel's gaze snapped back to him. "I don't know who's doing this or why. But I know one thing." He took a deep breath. "You are the best person in all the worlds, and I want to be with you. It's just . . . complicated. I need to figure some things out."

"Like what?" she asked nastily. "What else you can threaten? Is my greenhouse next?"

"That's not what I'm doing. But something bad is happening on the demon plane." His throat bobbed. "The plane is dying. They need more souls."

Mariel scoffed. If she'd needed more proof he was manipulating her, there it was. "Trying guilt as a tactic? All those poor, innocent demons who will die without my one measly soul?"

"It isn't measly," Oz said, "and I'm going to find a way to help them. But I want to look for a solution *with* you." He grimaced. "I have no idea what's going on in the forest. I don't know how to fix this. But I need you to believe me when I say I love you, and I haven't been plotting to steal your soul. Not after the first few days, at least."

"Mariel?" Calladia's voice came from inside the house. "Where are you?"

"In the back," she called. "With the demon."

"Mother*fucker*." Calladia stormed out, then positioned herself between Oz and Mariel. "I don't know what you've done, but you need to get out now."

"I haven't done anything." Oz raised his hands defensively. "There's been a misunderstanding."

Calladia pointed at the house. "Get out."

"I can't." He looked over Calladia's shoulder at Mariel. "Please, Mariel. Give me a chance. We can figure this out."

"No," Mariel said. "And no to ever giving you my soul. I don't care how long I have to search for enough nature witches to fix the blight—I'll find them. Even if it takes decades, even if the construction nearly kills the forest, I'll find a way to bring it back." She stood as tall as she could, putting her shoulders back. "You can't hurt me, Ozroth the Ruthless."

He flinched.

A millisecond later, a bolt of white-hot lightning shot down from the heavens. The earth trembled, and the sound of glass shattering followed a deafening thunderclap. Mariel was momentarily blinded. She blinked, trying to recover her vision . . . and saw a telltale orange flicker.

"No," she said, horror striking as hard and fast as the lightning bolt. "No!"

Her precious greenhouse was on fire. The glass walls were shattered, the metal frame blackened and bent, and the plants inside were wailing as they burned and died.

"Put it out," she screamed, running towards the flames. "Put it out!" The skin on her arms stung, and blood marked where small spears of glass had hit her.

"Mariel, stop!" Oz shouted. "You'll burn."

"Get away from her, asshole." Calladia punched Oz, who staggered back, hand cupped to his eye. The blond witch started weaving thread between her fingers, and a black cloud blotted out the moon. Torrential rain started pounding down, stinging Mariel's skin. She cried and shook, arms wrapped around herself as she watched smoke spiral up where rain met fire.

Soon the flames were out, though the ashes continued to smolder. Calladia advanced on Oz, her hair swirling in an unnatural wind as she knotted thread and muttered a spell. Oz was plucked off the ground as if by an invisible hand, then flung far into the distance, his yell fading to nothing.

"I'll set the wards," Calladia said.

Mariel nodded, then stumbled into the remains of her greenhouse. Glass crunched under her boots. She touched every plant she passed, pulsing magic into them and trying to find the flicker of life hidden deep inside. Some responded, sooty fronds stirring. Most didn't.

At the back of the greenhouse, Mariel found her display for the Pacific Northwest Floral Championships. The table was cracked down the middle, and black marks spiraled out over the cement floor around it. This was where the bolt had hit—right in her pride and joy.

There was nothing left but ash.

Mariel collapsed, ignoring the sharp pain when a shard of glass dug into her knee. The pain didn't come close to what she felt inside. In the course of thirty minutes, she'd lost her boyfriend, her illusions . . . and now the beloved plants she'd nurtured for so long.

The ones that remained were badly hurt, and Mariel felt their pain. What had once been her retreat from the world now lay in ruins.

Like her heart.

The sound of footsteps over glass came from behind her, and then Calladia's cool hand came to rest on Mariel's head. "I'm so sorry," she said. "So, so sorry."

"He killed them." Mariel's throat felt so swollen, it was hard to push the words out.

"Fucking bastard. I hope he lands on something sharp." Calladia crouched beside Mariel. "Let's get you cleaned up. Do you need to do anything else here?"

Mariel wiped her eyes, not that it did much to stop the tears. "Some are still alive. But they're hurting."

Calladia's mouth was a grim line. "Do what you can. I'll get the first aid kit and make us some stiff drinks."

The silence after Calladia left seemed eerie after an evening of shouting. All Mariel heard was the quiet drip of water.

"I'm so sorry," she whispered. "I shouldn't have trusted him."

But she had, and now her plants had paid the price. Her knees burned and her insides were knotted up, but Mariel forced herself to stand and start tending to the injured plants. She poured her magic and love into them, willing the blackened stems and charred leaves to turn green again. It would take time for them to heal to anywhere near where they had been before the lightning strike, but Mariel vowed to do everything she could to save them.

Ozroth the Ruthless had targeted her where it hurt most, but Mariel wouldn't give him the satisfaction of begging him to save what he had destroyed. She would build again—starting with the walls around her heart.

◆ ◆ ◆

MARIEL WOKE TO FIND CALLADIA SLEEPING NEXT TO HER. IT
was late morning; Calladia must have expended a lot of energy
summoning the storm and "launching the demon into the next
county," as she'd put it.

The whiskey could be at fault, too. Mariel's head throbbed,
but she couldn't tell if it was a hangover or the aftereffects of a
night of seemingly endless crying. Calladia had made them both
old fashioneds while Mariel poured her heart out, and by the
time they'd gone to bed well after midnight, Mariel had been
seeing double.

She sat up slowly. Everything hurt. Her legs and ass from running, her knee and arms from glass shards. Calladia had bandaged Mariel up, but the cuts still stung.

Calladia's eyes fluttered open. "What time is it?" she asked
blearily.

"Eleven."

Calladia groaned. "Damn you, whiskey."

Mariel got up and padded to the window. A few families were
on their daily strolls, and she almost managed a smile as a girl in
a princess costume pranced past, waving her plastic wand.

Then she remembered. "It's Halloween."

Calladia was slowly easing out of bed. "Themmie invited us to
some kind of pixie rave tonight." She grimaced. "Or we can nurse
a hair of the dog at Le Chapeau Magique instead."

"Halloween is when your mom said the construction would
start up again."

Calladia's eyes widened. "You're right."

Mariel worried her lip between her teeth. If this had been a
normal Halloween, she would already be at the central plaza, setting up her display for the Pacific Northwest Floral Champion-

ships. Her heart ached at the memory of her burned plants. She needed to sweep up the glass and get to work building a new greenhouse, but she didn't think she could face that blackened room yet.

Anger was quick to light. Oz had taken too much from her; she refused to let Cynthia's greed take any more. "I'm going to the construction site."

Calladia's face was tight with worry. "I don't think Mom was bluffing. They're not going to let the protests continue."

"What are they going to do, bulldoze me?"

"I mean, we are talking about my mother here."

"Good point. Still, they're more likely to arrest me." At the moment, Mariel gave zero shits about that possibility. She'd already lost so much; why not keep going?

Calladia sighed. "How did we end up with two greedy mothers who can't think past their bank accounts and their trophies?"

"More like how did they end up with us?"

"Teenage rebellion?" Calladia suggested. "We stuck it to them by trying to be good people."

Mariel wrapped her arms around her waist and leaned against the wall. "Being good sucks."

Calladia nodded. "You have no idea how many times I've contemplated launching those bulldozers over the mountains, but that wouldn't be fair to the construction workers."

Mariel huffed. "Definitely not fair. More like murder." Unlike Oz, the construction workers were mortal. He'd end up banged and bruised from Calladia's magic—Mariel had no illusions she was rid of the demon forever—but the humans would end up flat as a pancake.

Calladia's words sent a thought tumbling through Mariel's head, and she suddenly knew exactly what she would do today. She pushed off the wall. "I'm tired of being good. I'd rather do what's right."

Calladia eyed her warily. "I recognize that look. You're plotting something."

Mariel's heart beat with purpose again. She refused to give in to yet another form of evil. "I'm going to stop the construction."

"Cool," Calladia said. "But . . . how?"

"I'm still figuring that out." Mariel started grabbing clothes from the dresser. "Want to come?"

"More than anything, but I'm meeting my little witch for lunch. I can come after?"

Calladia was a mentor for Big Warlocks, Big Witches, an organization that paired young spellcrafters with older ones, who provided guidance and advice. It was an obligation she took very seriously.

"Yeah, swing by after," Mariel said. "I need to get the lay of the land anyway."

Calladia stretched. "Got it. Just don't do anything reckless before I get there, okay?"

"Sure," Mariel said, not meaning it in the slightest. She was out of fucks to give, and the demon plane hath no fury like a scorned witch.

◆ ◆ ◆

MARIEL SPIED ON THE CONSTRUCTION THROUGH THE TREES. Rani and a few other protestors stood in the path of the machinery, looking uneasy. Mounted police officers ringed the clearing, their pegasi stomping angrily at the ground.

"This gathering is illegal," a police officer said, his voice magically amplified. "Anyone who stays is trespassing on private property and will be arrested."

Warlocks and witches scattered at the threat. Soon all that remained were Rani and the centaur from the town hall. "We're not going down without a fight," Rani said. She wore kneepads, a Little Mermaid backpack, and a bike helmet—apparently her riot gear.

The centaur stomped a hoof. "This construction is illegal. It was decided at the whim of our corrupt mayor, and—"

"Last warning," the officer said.

"Bite me," Rani sneered.

The officer smiled, revealing fangs. "Gladly." He motioned, and the police moved in, batons and cuffs at the ready.

Mariel knelt and dug her hands into the soil, reaching for her magic. "*Gabbisinez en machina.*" She'd looked up a variety of spells on her smartphone while spying, and this one had appealed to her most. "*Gabbisinez en machina.*"

The plants ringing the clearing stirred. Brambles crawled over the grass, reaching thorny arms towards the construction equipment. Roots undulated in the soil and sent tendrils shooting towards the surface. A police pegasus reared when a climbing vine sprawled across its path.

"Who's doing that?" the officer demanded when vines snaked over the bulldozer's claw.

Rani looked around. When she saw Mariel in the bushes, she beamed.

Run, Mariel mouthed.

Rani poked the centaur's flank, then stood on tiptoe to say something to him. He looked at the bush Mariel was in, then nodded. "Mount up," he said, bending his front legs to bring his back closer to the ground.

Rani scrambled onto the centaur's back, and they galloped away. The police tried to pursue them, but the undergrowth was rising quickly, and roots and vines hindered their progress.

The bulldozer was now almost covered in a latticework of green. "*Gabbisinez en machina*," Mariel said again, feeding more power into the soil. She was growing light-headed, but she refused to give up. This forest was *hers*.

The woods responded to her call eagerly. The plants, too,

were angry at the intrusion into the landscape. Their blind rage reverberated in Mariel's chest, mingling with her own, until she felt nothing but hot fury.

"Fuck you, Cynthia Cunnington," she said, digging her fingernails into the dirt. "Fuck you, too, Mom. And most of all, a big, hearty *fuck you* to Ozroth the Ruthless."

The memory of her flowers burning tipped the scales. Mariel screamed as a dam gave way in her chest. Every pain she'd experienced over the course of her life mingled together, and the rush of emotion powered a surge of magic so strong, the trees swayed in the shock wave. Brambles wove together, trapping wheels and shovels, and construction workers fled as the forest took over the site.

Mariel stood, hair whipping in a magical wind. She stepped into the clearing, laughing when the nearest police officer backed his mount away from her. "You don't belong here," she said. Her voice sounded different—echoes of tumbling rocks and snapping branches lay beneath the words, and each breath she released tasted of evergreen.

The forest pulsed in her veins, its magic mingling with hers until she felt like an extension of the roots below.

"Stop this," the officer said, leveling a Taser at her.

Mariel tipped her head back and laughed. She'd never felt this kind of power before. The more she gave the woods, the more they gave back, an endless loop of furious magic.

It was intoxicating.

A vine snagged the Taser from the officer's hand. He dismounted and stormed towards her, fangs bared and baton raised. "I'm taking you to jail."

Mariel was done bending for anyone. She braced her feet and spread her arms wide. "I'd like to see you try."

THIRTY-ONE

OZROTH STAGGERED INTO GLIMMER FALLS AROUND NOON on Halloween. He was battered and bruised from being launched what he estimated to be thirty miles away. Thankfully, he'd landed in a lake, not on a rock, but it had still stung. Despite his best efforts, he hadn't been able to hitchhike back to town—something about a large, dripping-wet demon hadn't appealed to passersby—so here he was, feet swollen and aching as he dragged himself past an ice-cream parlor on the way to Mariel's house.

She would be horrified to see him again, but the tug in his chest drew him towards her. It was excruciating being that far out of town, the pain only lessening with each mile he walked.

Guilt was a throbbing pain in his chest, too. He hadn't willingly caused the lightning strike—hadn't even felt the prickling that normally alerted him to a magical outburst—but whether or not he'd meant to, he'd destroyed Mariel's greenhouse. He'd never forget her scream.

How could he have done that? There certainly hadn't been intent; it was the last thing he'd ever want to do. Yet he'd seen it with his own eyes, the white jag of lightning blinding as it blew the greenhouse apart. Overcome by a swell of self-hatred, he paused to ram his horns into the brick facade of the ice-cream shop.

"Yo," a female voice said. "What crawled up your ass?"

He turned to find Themmie holding a cup of strawberry ice cream. Her eyes widened as she took in his appearance. "Holy shit, what happened to you?"

He looked down at himself and grimaced. While he'd dried off, his clothes were wrinkled and dusty, and he was pretty sure he had a black eye. He felt ill from exhaustion. "Got on the wrong side of a witch."

"What did you do?" Themmie asked. "And where's your hat?"

He rubbed a self-conscious hand over his right horn. "The hat also got on the wrong side of a witch." Across the street, a couple openly stared, mouths agape. A father heading their way on the sidewalk took one look at him, then scooped up his child and crossed the street.

"We don't see a lot of horned folks around here," Themmie explained. "And when we do, they're normally trouble."

Ozroth's laugh was hollow. "You can add me to that list."

To his surprise, Themmie gripped his elbow and tugged him to a café table. "Sit down and tell me exactly what happened."

Ten minutes later, when Ozroth had wrapped up his distressed, rambling story, Themmie's mouth was agape. Her ice cream had melted, but she didn't seem to notice. "You're saying there's another demon in town?"

Ozroth grimaced. "It looks that way."

"No offense," she said, leaning back in her chair, "but I don't blame Calladia for launching you. You have to admit you look awfully guilty."

"I know." He jammed his hands into his hair. "And it doesn't help that I accidentally blew up Mariel's greenhouse."

She whistled. "That's fucked up. And you said you didn't feel it coming?"

He shook his head. "Not a clue. It came out of nowhere." His eyes grew blurry from more than just exhaustion, and he ground his knuckles into them. "I would do anything to undo it. Anything."

"It's weird that it happened to begin with," Themmie said. "Mariel blows stuff up all the time, but only when she's actually trying spells. You shot lightning at Cynthia during the town hall, but that was because you were angry at her. You weren't angry with Mariel."

"Of course not. I would never hurt her."

"Look, I'd be tempted to call bullshit and kick you in the nads," Themmie said, "but I lack Calladia's impulse control issues." She reached into her bag. "Besides, I have ethnography homework. So let's consider this a subject interview."

He groaned. "It isn't a joke, Themmie. I hurt Mariel without meaning to, and now she'll never believe I'm not poisoning the woods."

"It's definitely not a good look," she said, whipping out a glittery lime-green notebook and pen. She scribbled *Interview: Oz the Lovestruck (or Lying?) Demon* at the top of the page. "Run me through this again. When you have a magical outburst, what do you feel ahead of time?"

He wasn't sure why Themmie wanted this information, but she was his only link to Mariel, and he needed help. "Prickling all over my skin. The lights flicker, and the air feels . . . I don't know. Different."

"Got any synonyms for *different*?"

"Heavy? Or like it's waiting." He shook his head. "That doesn't make sense."

She waved the pen. "Magic inherently doesn't make sense. Sounds like you can feel the electricity before you summon it. So why wouldn't you feel it with a lightning strike that big? You said nearly frying Cynthia was as big a working as you'd managed, and this was a lot bigger than that."

Ozroth frowned, searching his memories. He'd been standing with Calladia in his face and a rosebush about to slit his throat, and Mariel had just called him Ozroth the Ruthless. That had hurt more than he'd have guessed. Had the air seemed heavy? Had his skin prickled?

"There was nothing," he said. "No hint. I wasn't even thinking about magic. And then there was this white flash—"

"Hold up." Themmie's head popped up from her notebook. "A white flash?"

"Yes. The lightning."

Themmie tapped the pen against the table. "Oz . . . isn't your lightning blue?"

The question brought his thoughts to a screeching halt. He stared dumbly at his hands, running through memories of his magic. Every static shock or lightning bolt had been electric blue. "Lucifer," he breathed. "It is."

Themmie closed the notebook and sat back in her chair. "I think I know what's going on."

"You do?" He sure fucking hoped someone did.

"Another demon is targeting Mariel and trying to frame you."

Ozroth's forehead furrowed. "Why? Demons don't interfere in the bargains of others. It's a point of honor."

Unless a demon had something important to lose . . .

He gasped as the answer burst into his fatigued mind. "It's Astaroth. He's trying to force Mariel into a bargain."

He should have realized it sooner. Ozroth had even told his mentor how much Mariel loved the forest and her plants. And while the demon had declared that boring . . . what if Astaroth had decided to focus his efforts there while Ozroth worked on her insecurity and longing for affection? He'd been playing them both—threatening and guilting Ozroth into offering a bargain while tormenting Mariel so she would take it.

"Cool." Themmie scooped up some melted ice cream. "Who's Astaroth?"

Ozroth stood so abruptly, he almost knocked the table over. "We need to find her before Astaroth does something even worse." Was the demon plane even in danger, or was this all about Astaroth's bet with the high council?

"She's probably protesting." Themmie checked her phone. "Shoot, I was supposed to meet everyone at noon."

"At the construction site?"

Themmie nodded. "Today's the day Cynthia Cunnington makes good on her threat. Either she runs us over, or we win."

The thought of Mariel facing down a bulldozer was almost as terrifying as the idea of her facing down Astaroth. "Can you carry me while you fly?" he asked. Pixies were stronger than most people expected.

Themmie made a face. "What, like a fireman's carry? You're way too big—I won't be able to see where I'm going." She eyed him up and down. "But if we could put you in a bag or something . . ."

That was how Ozroth found himself bundled into a sling fashioned from stolen potato sacks, dangling below a technicolor pixie as they flew towards the forest and the woman Ozroth loved more than anything.

THIRTY-TWO

MARIEL COULD BARELY SEE THROUGH THE HAZE OF magic. She was going beyond her previous displays of power, but her magic was stuck in a feedback loop with the woods, amplifying with every passing second.

A wall of brambles surrounded her. The police officer was whacking it with his baton, but the bushes grew thicker. The construction equipment was completely buried now, and a carpet of brilliant flowers spread out in every direction.

With Mariel's help, the forest was taking back the land that had been stolen.

Her magic brushed against patches of rot in the distance. They melted slowly, fresh shoots pushing back the decay. But the farther her magic traveled, the more patches of darkness she found, and even this overflow of magic might not be enough.

The police officer was shouting. "Trespassing, vandalism, assaulting an officer, and that's just the beginning!"

"Interesting," a British voice said.

Mariel jumped and nearly fell over, but the brambles gently

righted her. With her concentration disrupted, the flow of magic lessened, and the haze cleared from her vision.

A vaguely familiar blond man wearing a black fedora stood inside her fortress of brambles, examining the lattice of greenery.

"Who are you?" Mariel asked.

Then she remembered—she'd met him in the library. James Higgins, the journalist. The hat was the same, though he no longer wore his glasses, and his tweed had been replaced by a pristine white suit. He'd seemed like an absentminded professor before, but his smile now made her think of a shark.

He swept his hat off, revealing black horns. "Astaroth of the Nine," he said, bowing. "Pleased to officially meet you."

She gaped. This was Oz's evil mentor? She'd expected someone . . . bigger. Not a British dandy with questionable taste in hats. "Fuck you," she spat.

He straightened, looking unperturbed. She saw now that he carried a cane topped with a crystal skull, which he tapped rhythmically against his shiny white shoe. "Now what have I done to make you despise me so?"

"Brainwashed and tormented a helpless child, for one." She belatedly remembered that that part of Oz's story could be bullshit, too, but whatever had actually happened, this monster had helped twist Oz into his current form.

Astaroth chuckled. "I assume you mean Ozroth? Whatever he's told you, I assure you I offered him the best of everything. The best training, the best accommodations, the best position he could dream of in demon society."

The words rankled; they made her think of her parents. The best of everything, but none of what a child actually needed. "Why are you here?" she asked. "And why were you at the library?" On the other side of the brambles, the cop was still shouting, but she was far more concerned about the threat in front of her.

He was still tapping that cane. The crystal skull was way too much, and his tiepin was an upside-down cross; if she'd thought Oz was a cliché at first, this was a whole different level. "It's come to my attention that Ozroth hasn't been performing up to par," Astaroth said. "And I know a way to get out of a demonic bargain."

Mariel sucked in a shocked breath. "You do?"

His smile was sharp. "Making a bargain with a different demon."

The spark of hope fizzled out. The thought of making a deal with Astaroth was abhorrent. "No, thank you. One bargain is plenty."

"Are you sure? You've gotten yourself into trouble. I can make the police forget this incident."

"And steal my magic in exchange?" She shook her head. "No."

The demon scowled. "Ozroth told you that?"

"Yes, and he already tried to bully me into a bargain." She planted her hands on her hips. "If he didn't succeed, you won't either."

Astaroth studied her with eerie ice-blue eyes. The fedora and skull cane would have been laughable on anyone else, but there was something unsettling about the way the demon held himself. He was still except for the relentless tap of his cane, and there was something in his eyes that made Mariel uncomfortably aware that this was an ancient being in a youthful body.

"Ozroth hasn't been direct with the issue," Astaroth said. "He hasn't offered something you truly need."

She scowled. "He blew up my greenhouse."

Astaroth's eyelids flickered slightly. "I can fix it, you know. I can fix a lot of things."

Unease built in Mariel's gut with every passing second. The cop was screaming obscenities, but she didn't dare take her attention away from the demon. He'd been awfully quick to offer a fix for her greenhouse.

Had Oz offered to fix it? She tried to remember if he'd said anything after the lightning bolt. He'd shouted at her to stop, that she'd burn.

Her stomach sank. Demon magic in the woods, demon lightning in her backyard . . . It had all seemed so clear when there was only one demon in Glimmer Falls. Now she was facing a second demon—one who hadn't paused before offering her whatever she wanted. One who had already felt out what she might trade her soul for during their conversation at the library.

"No," Mariel said, trying to keep her voice from shaking. "I don't want your help."

"I think you're underestimating exactly how much you could get out of a bargain." Astaroth stepped closer, and Mariel braced herself, trying not to retreat into the embrace of the brambles. "You don't have to trade a soul for just one thing. I could keep you out of jail, fix your greenhouse and resurrect your plants, stop the construction permanently, and heal the blight in the woods. All that and more." He gestured around them. "Isn't sacrificing your magic worth saving all this?"

Astaroth was promising everything she wanted, but Mariel felt cold. "I didn't tell you about the blight," she said through numb lips.

Astaroth shrugged. "I've been checking in on Ozroth. Nasty fungus, isn't it? Yet so easily cured."

That was all Mariel needed to hear to fully understand that both she and Oz had been manipulated. It wasn't a fungus; she believed Alzapraz in that. It was demonic magic.

This, then, was the face of a true liar: calm and smiling, promising wonderful, impossible things. No scowls or surly responses, no rough charm. Just a bargain too good to be true.

"You know," Mariel said as anger knotted her stomach, "I've heard better pitches from used car salesmen."

His smile didn't drop, though his eyelashes fluttered. "What?"

"Your pitch. The best deal of my life, yada yada yada."

"It's not a pitch." A muscle under his eye twitched. "It's an offer to fix all your problems."

"I want my problems fixed," Mariel said, "but definitely not by you."

Astaroth's fingers flexed on the cane head. Mariel's skin prickled.

"So selfish," he said with a soft cruelty that made Mariel flinch. "Everything you love could die, but you don't care, so long as you have your magic."

Guilt wormed into Mariel's heart. The demon was an expert manipulator, she knew that. He was the reason the things she loved were dying. But if Mariel could save Glimmer Falls and the land around it, even if it meant losing something she loved . . . wouldn't a truly good person make that sacrifice?

"Mariel!" The cry came from overhead, startling her out of self-recrimination. A moment later, a large fabric sack plummeted to the ground, landing with a thump. "Ow!"

The sack thrashed, and Oz clawed his way out. "You could have flown lower," he called to someone overhead.

Mariel had never been happier to see someone. She knelt by his side, helping to remove the fabric. His clothes were rumpled, his horns dusty, but the sight of his familiar face—even with a black eye—was enough to make her heart skip a beat. "You really didn't hurt the forest, did you?" she asked. "Or my greenhouse."

He shook his head, eyes fervent. "I would never hurt anything you love."

Mariel wanted to cry. "I'm sorry I accused you. It was Astaroth all along."

"You have nothing to be sorry for." Oz glared at the other demon as he struggled to his feet. "This bastard though . . ."

"So my recalcitrant apprentice appears at last," Astaroth drawled. "Here to finally make a bargain worthy of your training?"

Oz clenched his fists. "Is the demon plane actually dying? Or was that another lie to force me into making a bargain?"

"Yes, it's dying," Astaroth said. But Mariel was watching the trickster closely, and she noticed another minute flicker of his eyelid.

"He's lying," Mariel said. "His eye twitched."

"Oh, please," Astaroth said with the withering disdain the Brits did so well. And wait, why was the demon British? "Been watching too many crime dramas, have you?"

"You had the same twitch when I mentioned Oz destroying my greenhouse. In poker, that's called a tell." That was admittedly the only thing Mariel knew about poker.

"You have big opinions for such a puny mortal."

"If I'm just a puny mortal, why are you so desperate to force this bargain?" Mariel asked. "Why infect the forest, why destroy my greenhouse, why come here to offer a new bargain?"

Oz's head whipped towards her. "He offered a new bargain?"

"Apparently it's the only way to break an existing bargain, though I wouldn't believe a word out of this jackass's mouth."

Astaroth was grinding his teeth. "Have mortals forgotten respect?"

"Yes," Oz said. "And honestly? Good for them."

"You didn't deny doing any of those things," Mariel told Astaroth. "You've been trying to force my hand, but you framed Oz to do it." The blackberry thorns bristled with her outrage, and a tendril reached towards Astaroth's shoe.

"If Ozroth had any sense," Astaroth said, sidestepping the creeping vine, "he would have done the same." His cane was tapping faster now. "You're a fool to summon a demon and refuse to treat with him. What did you expect, that he would be your subservient lapdog forever?"

"No," Mariel said at the same time Oz said, "I would be." She cast a fond glance at him, then grabbed his hand. "Not a lapdog," she told him. "A partner."

"Ew," Astaroth said.

Oz's eyes crinkled as he looked at Mariel. "So back to plan A? If the demon plane isn't dying, there's no urgency to making the bargain." He cast a withering glare at Astaroth. "His bet with the high council isn't my responsibility."

"Plan A," she agreed. It would be hard, but she wasn't willing to give up on a future with Oz.

When she looked at Astaroth, she was alarmed to see his eyes had flooded black. The next moment, Oz jerked forward, falling to his knees in front of Astaroth. Although his muscles strained, he didn't move.

"Let him go!" Mariel tried to lunge forward, but the demonic magic held her back like a force field.

Astaroth gripped the top of his cane—and pulled out a sword. Below the skull pommel, the hilt was pitch black, and streaks of iridescence wound through the silver blade. Mariel cried out when Astaroth leveled the blade at Oz's neck.

"Here's a test," Astaroth said, fixing those inky eyes on Mariel. "You're selfish enough to let the forest die to keep your magic. Are you selfish enough to let him die?"

"Don't do it," Oz said through gritted teeth. "It isn't just your magic, Mariel. It's your emotions."

She gasped. "What?"

Astaroth backhanded Oz. "Will you shut up?"

"The soul," Oz said, spitting blood. "Look what happened to me."

The warlock's soul had entered Oz's body, giving him

magic . . . and emotion. How had Mariel never realized the connection before? It had been right in front of her.

"What happens?" she asked.

"You'll become cold and rational." Astaroth said it like that was a good thing. "Unburdened by human frailties, your judgment unclouded by emotion. Some of the world's most influential figures traded their souls and went on to live full lives."

It wouldn't be a full life without laughter or tears. Being human was messy, but Mariel couldn't think of anything worse than losing that emotional core.

"You can't kill Oz," she said. "He's your best bargainer."

Astaroth scoffed. "Not anymore." He put pressure on the blade, and blood trickled down Oz's neck.

"Stop," Mariel said, panic squeezing her throat. She couldn't lose Oz. He held her heart, her hopes, her future.

"You know how to stop this," Astaroth said calmly. "Make a deal."

Mariel stood frozen, unable to think past the fear. There had to be a way out of this; she just needed time to think—

Astaroth sighed. "Very well." He pulled the sword back. "Off with his head."

"Wait!" Mariel cried as the silver blade sliced through the air. It froze a bare inch from Oz's neck. "I'll make a deal."

"Mariel, no!" Oz struggled against the magic holding him in place, muscles bulging as his body shook.

"Finally." Astaroth arched a sardonic brow as he looked down at Oz. "Looks like she wants something badly enough to trade, after all."

Oz looked at Mariel with desperate eyes. "Please, *velina*, don't do this. You'll lose everything."

Mariel swallowed hard. "I know." Her magic, her emotions . . . without her soul, Mariel would be a hollow shell. But if Oz died, she'd never be able to live with herself. By going through with a deal, she would save Oz, but she could also save the forest and all the living creatures in it.

A glimmer of an idea surfaced through the haze of panic. She didn't want to give Astaroth anything. And if she could get the wording right, Oz would always have a piece of her.

"I haven't got all day." Astaroth checked his pocket watch. "The high council meets in an hour to call in the bet."

Mariel glared at him. "Excuse me for taking a few seconds to contemplate the end of my life as I know it."

"Let me die," Oz begged. "Please, Mariel. I've lived long enough."

Her eyes welled with tears. "No," she said. "You were existing. You only just started to live."

He was crying, too. After a lifetime spent ensconced in numbness, he had little practice with grief, but she knew he would grieve the loss of who she'd been. Mariel didn't want to give him that pain, but there was no other option.

"I'll trade my soul," Mariel said, "but I have conditions."

Astaroth waved his hand. "Go on."

"You'll release me from the deal with Oz. Then you'll stop the construction on the resort and spa, and the land around Glimmer Falls will never be destroyed or used for a construction project ever again."

"Easy enough." He closed his eyes. "Hmm," he said, lips turning up in a smirk. "Looks like the identity of the original owner of the land has finally been discovered, and she left a will stipulating that the land remain a nature reserve in perpetuity. The mayor's office is in an uproar, and they're about to ring the foreman to halt digging." He chuckled. "Although you halted it quite successfully yourself. I'll add in cleaning up the scene and making the police forget all about it, just for you." His eyes opened, and he pinned Mariel with that eerie black stare. "Now for the exchange—"

"I said conditions, plural," Mariel snapped. "You might try listening more closely."

"Cheeky." Astaroth flourished the sword. "But I'm in a generous mood."

Mariel ignored him and looked at Oz, willing him to see everything she felt for him in her eyes. He'd given her courage and laughter and taught her to value herself for who she was, rather than the standards put upon her by others. He'd made her feel beautiful and strong.

She could be strong enough to do this.

"You'll clean up the magical rot and never do anything like that again. Plus, you'll fix my greenhouse and bring all the plants back to life. And fix my Autumn Festival display. And you'll free Oz immediately."

Astaroth grumbled. "Boring, but fine. Anything else?"

"One more thing." She held Oz's gaze. "May my soul pass to where there is love."

Oz's eyes widened. "Mariel . . ."

She smiled with trembling lips, then took a deep breath and concentrated, forming the words of the most important spell of her life. "*Almaum en vayrenamora.*" My soul goes to my beloved. She bowed her head. "I'm ready."

Astaroth scoffed. "What was that nonsense?"

She glared at him. "Do you want the trade or not?"

"Where there is love," he muttered to himself. "Bloody nonsense. Humans are ridiculous."

Oz was trembling. His cheeks were wet, and more tears began to fall. "*Velina,*" he whispered, and she wondered if he knew what she was doing.

Of course he did. He was Oz, and he knew her better than she knew herself.

Astaroth raised his hand, and Mariel braced herself. There was a tug in her chest, then a sharp, tearing sensation. She screamed in pain.

Mariel couldn't see the moment her soul left her body, but she felt it. Her chest turned cold, and the familiar tingle of magic disappeared. As she sank to her knees, the flowers turned their faces away from her.

Then Mariel felt nothing.

THIRTY-THREE

O ZROTH CRIED OUT AS MARIEL DROPPED TO THE GROUND. Her face went calm and still, the spark snuffed out.

Ozroth had felt many emotions since meeting her, but never something like this. Grief was a maelstrom in his chest, the storm so powerful he thought he might die from it.

He wanted to die from it. Mariel was right—he'd only been existing before meeting her. But what she didn't understand was that she was the source and the meaning of everything. A life without her wasn't worth living.

Her soul hovered in the air, a golden orb so bright it hurt to look at. Astaroth reached for it. "My, my," he said. "What a pretty one this is." The soul drifted towards Astaroth's outstretched hand . . . then passed him. Astaroth's brow furrowed. "What the—"

Ozroth braced himself as the soul sank into his chest. It was a thousand times more intense than when the warlock's soul had filled him. White heat seared his insides, and the rush of magic made his skin prickle with electricity. He could feel the pulse of the world, the spark inside each flower and tree, the hungry sprawl of roots below the ground. As the flowers turned to look at him, he realized Mariel was right—the plants loved her.

Now that she was inside him, they loved him, too.

Ozroth struggled to breathe past the inundation of magic. No wonder she saw the world with so much hope. Her soul was bright and beautiful, full of glittering emotions that tumbled over each other like gemstones. He was full to bursting with her essence.

Ozroth didn't think he could live like this. He didn't *want* to live like this.

"Odd." Astaroth sheathed his sword. "I suppose it went to the creator of the original bargain. You sent it to the demon realm, right?"

Apparently Astaroth had only noticed the soul disappearing, not where it had gone. Ozroth nodded numbly, not wanting to risk putting the lie to words when he was so distraught. He stared at Mariel through tear-blurred eyes. She looked different—still and solemn, when before emotions had danced over her face in lively succession. She might as well have been a statue.

Astaroth helped her to her feet. "How do you feel, my dear?"

Ozroth wanted to rip out his mentor's innards for daring to speak to her, much less touch her. The moment he got free, Astaroth was as good as dead.

Mariel looked down at her hands. "Empty."

Ozroth ached for her. He'd been numb before, but never completely without feeling. Most of the people he'd made deals with were sociopaths eager to do anything for power or revenge. Most of the rest had been dying anyway, and figured they had little to lose. Mariel though . . . she was the kindest, most vibrant person he'd ever met. She ought to have decades of love and laughter ahead of her. Now even the grass at her feet leaned away from her.

Astaroth smirked at Ozroth. "I know how your paramour is

feeling. He looks ready to rip my head off with his bare hands. He won't get the chance to, of course."

Ozroth knew Astaroth would kill him. Mariel had asked the demon to free him, but she hadn't specified what would happen afterward. He wouldn't have minded dying, but with Mariel's soul inside him, he needed time to figure out what to do. If they both died, their twin souls would end up drifting aimlessly in the demon plane, and he wasn't ready to give up on Mariel yet.

A vine brushed his cheek, comforting him in its limited way. He focused on Mariel's magic, letting his consciousness sink into the web of life. She had sacrificed so much for him and the woods she loved—he wouldn't let it be for nothing.

There had to be a way to bring her back. Maybe he could steal another soul for her. She wouldn't have her nature magic anymore, but since he was unable to make a trade to return her soul . . .

Ozroth sucked in a breath, remembering a time immediately after he'd gained the soul. He'd asked Astaroth if he could bargain it away, and the demon had shaken his head. "Only mortals can trade souls. And besides, it wouldn't be an equal exchange. You're too eager to get rid of the soul. It wouldn't be a sacrifice."

Ozroth had believed him. Of course demons couldn't make deals from the other side—they didn't have human magic.

But Ozroth did have magic. It had once belonged to the warlock, but it was his now, which meant maybe he could make a bargain, after all. And this time, it would be an equal exchange.

A leaf fluttered to his shoulder, perching there like a small red bird. Even with the forest sinking into the death and decay of autumn, the promise of rebirth lay deep within the soil.

"I want to make a deal," Ozroth said.

Astaroth blinked at him. "You can't. We've talked about this."

"That was before I wanted something equal to a soul." Conviction filled him. Even if the attempt failed and he ended up dead or numb, at least he would have tried.

"You're not a warlock," Astaroth said in a patient tone, as if explaining basic facts to a child. "Demons can only make deals with mortals. It's the way the magic works."

Ozroth wasn't so sure he *wasn't* a warlock now. "I want to try. You're honor-bound to negotiate when a deal is requested."

Astaroth cast his eyes to the leaden sky, pinching the bridge of his nose as if staving off a headache. "Let me guess. You want to reverse her deal? Give her back her soul and pretend this never happened? Because that won't work when I've already granted her wishes." He gestured, and the bramble wall receded. The police officers were gone, and the ground was whole and unbroken once more. The magic bonds keeping Ozroth in place loosened.

"No," Ozroth said, gaining confidence with every second. He might be kneeling in front of his former master, but power filled him, connecting him to the web of life. He had a strength Astaroth could only dream of. "I want to trade *my* soul."

It was a trick of semantics, the kind Astaroth had trained him to employ. Since Mariel had given him her soul, it belonged to him now, which meant he had *two* souls. Both souls burning in his chest were his to do with as he wished . . . and he hadn't specified which one he was trading.

Astaroth was a very old, very powerful demon, but he'd never dealt with a situation like this before. He didn't know the rules any better than Ozroth did—and probably knew them worse, since he didn't know Ozroth could perform magic.

"It isn't going to work." Astaroth sighed. "But if you insist . . ."

"I do."

The last of the magic holding Ozroth in place let up, and he staggered to his feet. He reached for Mariel, but she looked at him blankly, standing frozen in the drooping grass. Her love for him was gone, too.

Not gone, he told himself. Left with him for safekeeping.

"I want to trade my soul in exchange for mine and Mariel's safety," he said. "No murder, no torture, no harassment, nothing. You and your minions leave us alone to be together, and you sever the bond that lets you summon me."

"Sure," Astaroth said sarcastically. "Be together with your empty shell of a girlfriend." He tapped his cane against his boot. "And when this deal fails, I will remove your head from your shoulders."

"So be it." Ozroth took a deep breath. "I wish for my soul to go where there is love," he said, repeating Mariel's words.

"Seriously?" Astaroth's brows arched.

Ozroth ignored Astaroth, focusing on his intentions for the spell. In his mind he repeated the words Mariel had said, knowing this could go very wrong if he made a mistake. What had Alzapraz said about the language of magic? -*Um* was the ending for "mine," so when Mariel had said *almaum*, she must have said "my soul." But there was a variant for something that was his but had once belonged to her. He racked his brain, trying to remember the notes he'd jotted down during Alzapraz's linguistics lesson in Mariel's kitchen.

If the skillet is yours but once belonged to Oz, you can end with -silum.

With the spell words settled and his intentions clear, Ozroth closed his eyes and took a deep breath. "*Almasilum en vayren-amora.*" He had no idea what it meant but had a fervent hope that *almasilum* meant "the soul that is mine but once was hers."

Astaroth guffawed. "Have you lost your mind? Are you trying to perform a spell?"

"It's a tribute to her." Ozroth met his mentor's disbelieving stare stoically. Let the demon think him a besotted fool. If he'd calculated right, this would be the greatest trick carried out in the history of bargaining.

Astaroth shook his head. "Then die a sentimental fool."

Looking between Mariel's blank face and Astaroth's smug sneer, Ozroth wondered why he'd let this vain, cruel demon shape so much of his life. He'd lost the core of who he was, the little boy who had held his mother's hand while watching the fire lilies bloom on the darkest night of the year. He'd become numb, with nothing to live for but duty and pride.

Now he had so much more to live for.

"The bargain is struck." Astaroth's eyes flooded black, and Ozroth braced himself, wondering if he'd made the biggest mistake of his life.

THIRTY-FOUR

M ARIEL DISPASSIONATELY WATCHED THE SCENE PLAYING out in front of her. Ozroth was bargaining with Astaroth. His gold eyes sparkled with tears, and he kept looking at Mariel like he was desperate for something.

Mariel knew she'd once had feelings for him. Intellectually, she knew she'd had feelings about a lot of things, but she couldn't remember what that was like. She'd evidently cared about something enough to make a demonic bargain, but looking between Ozroth and the autumn trees, she couldn't fathom what had been so special about them.

Regardless, it was done. The bargain was complete.

She shivered. Her body felt cold, but the chill didn't come from outside; it emanated from a hollow place inside her chest. Something had been there once, but she could only guess at the shape of it from its absence.

Ozroth was saying something now—a spell. He'd never tried any spells before. Idly, Mariel wondered if he would train as a warlock over the coming centuries.

Astaroth laughed. The demon stood out starkly in the autumn landscape, a slash of white amid bark and flame-colored
leaves. She thought of ice and snow and a cold so deep it never
melted.

"The bargain is struck."

Ozroth shouted and clutched his chest. She couldn't see anything happening, but presumably Astaroth was sending the soul
on its way. Then Ozroth would be just like her.

It was easier being like this. She felt no torment, no conflict,
just calmness.

"Wait—" Astaroth turned to face Mariel, looking shocked.

Suddenly, it felt like a small sun was sinking into her chest.
She shrieked as the heat burned down to her bones. It was alive,
prickling with energy, and as Mariel collapsed to her knees, the
warmth spread until it filled the hollow space in her chest.

Emotions burst like fireworks, a rush of *fear-grief-hope-hate-
love* as everything that had been missing flooded back. Her eyes
blurred with tears, and when she blinked them away, the world
looked brighter. Colors were more vivid, and best of all, she could
feel the pulsing, beating heart of the world. The trees rustled, and
the autumn flowers that had wilted by her feet burst back into
bloom.

"Oh," she gasped, clutching her chest.

"What have you done?" Astaroth screeched.

Oz ignored him, striding towards Mariel and crouching beside her. "How do you feel?" he asked, eyes bright with concern.

An overwhelming wave of love flooded her. "You saved me,"
she sobbed, flinging her arms around his neck. "You're so clever,
velino."

Almasilum en vayrenamora. My soul that once belonged to her
goes to my beloved. Oz had manipulated the language of magic
to keep his original soul while returning hers.

She peppered his cheeks and forehead with kisses, then drew back to study him. "How do you feel? Are you all right?"

He nodded, grinning so widely it carved deep lines into his cheeks. "Back to normal."

"What did you do?" Astaroth demanded, storming over. He slammed the tip of his cane into the ground next to Mariel, but she didn't flinch. The demon had agreed never to harm either of them again. "You cheated somehow."

"No," Oz said, helping Mariel stand with him. He faced his mentor with his chin up and shoulders back, pride written over his handsome face. "I made a bargain, fair and square."

"Only mortals can make bargains," Astaroth sputtered. "You don't even have magic."

Oz looked at Mariel, and she knew what he wanted. She racked her brain, then stood on tiptoes and whispered a few words into his ear.

He nodded and focused on Astaroth. "*Spalitisin di canna*," he said, pointing at Astaroth's cane sword.

A bolt of blue lightning shot from his hand and cracked the crystal skull. Astaroth swore and leapt back, falling into a pile of decaying leaves. "What in Lucifer's name?"

Someone buzzed by overhead, and then a hammock containing a person fell to the ground. "Ow!" Calladia said as she crawled out.

Themmie landed nearby. "Are you hurt?" she asked, fluttering over to Mariel. "Oz told me another demon is responsible for everything that's been happening."

Mariel grinned and pointed at the cursing pile of leaves. "Meet Astaroth of the Nine, who just lost a bet with the demonic high council."

The demon popped to his feet, brushing leaves off his now dirt-streaked suit. "There's still time to make a better deal," he said frantically. "Do you want a mansion? A billion dollars? Your own private island?"

Mariel beamed at Oz. "There's nothing you can give me that I want more than what I have."

"This motherfucker is Astaroth of the Nine?" Calladia asked. "Where'd you get the fedora—a pickup artist convention?"

"I don't take sartorial critiques from people wearing spandex," Astaroth sneered back.

"Oooh, shit," Themmie said, backing away.

Calladia cracked her knuckles and walked towards Astaroth. She wore daisy-patterned leggings, yellow tennis shoes, and a blue tank top that said *Sweat Like a Girl*. "So you're the demon who's been destroying the forest?" Calladia asked, grabbing a tie from her wrist and starting to put her hair up.

"She's busting out the bar brawl ponytail," Themmie said. "He's in for it now."

"Is she really going to fight him?" Oz asked Mariel in a disbelieving tone.

"Just watch," Mariel said gleefully.

"The demon who destroyed my best friend's greenhouse," Calladia continued. "The one trying to force Oz and Mariel to make a bargain."

Astaroth stood his ground, apparently not realizing the danger he was in. "What a nice, bright soul," he said, looking Calladia up and down. "Do you want to become a princess? Own a diamond mine?" He leveled that sharp smile on her. "Say it, and it's yours."

Calladia stopped in front of him. "I do want something, but I can't get it through a deal."

He waved his hand. "Nonsense. I can give you anything."

"Mmm, no thanks." Calladia smiled at him sweetly. "I take what I want."

She punched him in the throat.

Themmie crowed as Oz gasped. Mariel laughed, feeling lighter than she had in a long time. She was free from a bargain and about to watch Astaroth get his ass kicked.

"Bloody hell," Astaroth wheezed, cupping his throat.

Calladia wasn't done. While he was still staggering from the hit, she did a roundhouse kick to his side, then grabbed his shoulders for leverage and kneed him in the groin.

Oz winced and made the universal male noise of involuntary sympathy, but Themmie cackled and clapped as Astaroth bent over with a pained sound.

"Who the fuck are you?" Astaroth asked in a higher-pitched voice than normal.

"The witch kicking your ass." Calladia tossed her ponytail over her shoulder. "Did you know I launched Oz into the next county when I thought he was behind everything? That should have been you." She pulled thread out of her pocket and started tying knots.

Astaroth's eyes widened. "Wait—"

Calladia muttered a few words under her breath, then punched the demon square in the nose.

The last Mariel saw of Astaroth, he was a screaming speck vanishing over the mountaintop.

Calladia brushed off her hands, then joined the others. "That was satisfying."

Oz gaped at her. "I can't believe you did that. Do you know how many enemies Astaroth has vanquished over the centuries?"

Calladia mimed dusting off her shoulders. "Never underestimate a witch with a mean right hook and anger-management issues."

Themmie high-fived Calladia. "Nice work. He won't forget that anytime soon."

"He sure won't." Calladia's expression softened as she looked towards Oz. "Sorry about throwing you halfway to Oregon."

He shrugged. "You defended your friend and the love of my life. I'm glad you did it." He winced and prodded his blackened eye. "Mostly glad."

Calladia wrapped Mariel in a hard hug. "I'm so glad you're safe."

Mariel sniffled against Calladia's shoulder. "Me, too."

"So," Themmie said when they separated. "Is it just me, or does it look totally different around here? Why are the bulldozers driving away?"

Mariel laughed. "It's a long story." Then her eyes widened. "Wait, what time is it?"

Themmie consulted her phone. "Two p.m."

Mariel's heart raced. She'd asked for her greenhouse to be restored, but had Astaroth delivered? "The Pacific Northwest Floral Championships are at three," she told Oz. "And if he fulfilled the bargain . . ."

He grinned and grabbed her hand. "Let's go get your display."

THIRTY-FIVE

O ZROTH STOOD NEXT TO MARIEL'S DISPLAY TABLE, GIDDY with excitement. They were positioned on the northern side of the green, opposite the end with the clock, and the judges had almost made their way around the line of floral displays.

Mariel fussed with the green velvet wrap dress she'd put on for the occasion. "Do I look okay?"

"You look perfect," Ozroth told her. Themmie had done Mariel's makeup and hair, and she looked ready for the catwalk. Her cheeks were pink, and her curls shone glossy brown in the afternoon sunlight that periodically broke through the clouds. The crimson curve of her mouth was tempting.

Mariel caught him looking at her lips. "You can ruin my lipstick after the judges leave."

"They'd better get here quickly," he growled, grabbing her waist and hauling her close so he could nose at her hair. She smelled like spring meadows and autumn woods.

She wriggled free, giggling. "Let me double-check everything."

He watched as she double- and triple-checked her display. Astaroth had fulfilled all terms of the bargain, and the blossoms were as radiant as ever. When Mariel had seen her resurrected greenhouse, her cry of delight had made joy bloom in Ozroth's heart.

How was it possible they'd gotten here after so much heartbreak? Two hours ago, Ozroth had been convinced he'd lost the love of his life. But here she was: whole, healthy, and still in possession of a soul.

Astaroth was *not* here, and that thought turned Ozroth's smile wicked. He hoped the demon had landed on something hard. He didn't know what the price would be for losing the bet, but frankly, he didn't care. Next on his agenda was visiting a tattoo removal specialist. Ozroth was done with his mentor.

He might be done with soul collecting altogether, in fact. "Does it spark joy?" Themmie had asked him while they'd been setting up the display, and though that was a weird way to phrase it, the question had made perfect sense. Joy sparkled in his heart like champagne bubbles whenever he looked at Mariel. When he thought about returning to bargaining, his heart felt cold and heavy.

"It doesn't," he'd told her.

Themmie had shrugged. "Then Marie Kondo that shit."

He'd blinked at her, bemused. "What?"

"Throw it out. Figure out what sparks actual joy for you and keep that."

He'd grinned as he'd watched Mariel complimenting a small blossom, praising it until it opened its petals wider. "How about a literal Spark?"

Themmie had cupped her hands around her mouth and made a siren noise. "*Weeeooooo weeeoooo*, dad joke alert!"

Ozroth still wasn't sure what a dad joke was, but he was sure about one thing: Mariel made him happy. And he, against all odds, made her happy, too.

"They're coming," Mariel said excitedly, clutching his sleeve.

Ozroth reached into his pocket and grabbed the needle he'd taken from Mariel's sewing supplies. He poked it into the pad of his index finger, then held his hand over the fire lily. Flame started flickering inside the blossom.

"Your hand!" Mariel grabbed it. "I don't want you hurting yourself."

He shrugged. "Demon. It'll heal in a few minutes."

The judges walked up, although a few stutter-stepped at the sight of his horns. He smiled pleasantly, knowing it would take time for people to get used to the sight of a demon in Glimmer Falls. One judge was Mariel's werewolf boss, who winked at her before eyeing Ozroth suspiciously. Ozroth nodded at him in acknowledgment. This one friend of Mariel's would take time to win over, but Ozroth had nothing but time.

That was the only thing dimming his happiness: the knowledge that he would live on long after Mariel died. Still, he was determined to seize joy from every moment he had with her.

"Exquisite!" one of the judges raved as she leaned over the vibrant display to look at the fire lily's pyrotechnics. "What spell did you use?"

"No spell." Mariel sounded confident, but her fingers were clenched in her skirt. "There's a secret gardening technique to get them to burn."

"Love a good secret technique," the judge said. "Tell me about the rest of the blossoms."

Mariel launched into a passionate speech about the varietals she'd cultivated. Ozroth listened, a smile curving his lips. Mariel's display was by far the most beautiful—he'd done the rounds, wondering if there were any competitors he needed to take out—

and her enthusiasm was contagious. He had no doubts who would win.

The judges moved on to the next table, and Mariel's shoulders sagged as she blew out a breath. "Whew. Glad that's over." She turned to Ozroth. "Do you—"

Ozroth cut off her question with a hard, passionate kiss. He bent her backward, forearm pressed into the base of her spine, and as Mariel wrapped her arms around his neck and kissed him back, cheers and hoots erupted around them.

When he finally tipped her back up, her lipstick was smudged over her chin. He must have looked similar, because Mariel cackled, then wiped the edge of his mouth with her thumb. "Red's a good color on you."

"Mariel, dear, we're here!" Diantha Spark's voice was unmistakable, and Ozroth and Mariel shared a look of alarm before facing the oncoming tornado.

Diantha looked more subdued than normal though. With her arm tucked into Roland's and Alzapraz trailing behind—Mariel had called the old warlock earlier to let him know Ozroth was innocent—Diantha approached hesitantly.

"You've never looked at my displays before," Mariel said. Her jaw was stiff.

"I know," Diantha said. "And I'm sorry."

Ozroth was taken aback. Mariel must have been, too, because her jaw dropped. "You're what?"

Diantha winced. "Sorry," she repeated. "For all of it. Ignoring your gardening and pushing you too hard. You're right, I didn't pay attention to the things you loved or were good at."

"Wow," Mariel said, blinking rapidly. "That's . . . unexpected."

"We had a family meeting," Roland said. "Alzapraz told us you had a similar conversation with him, and that we've been too harsh on you." He sighed. "I'm sorry, too. We do love you."

"And these . . . things . . . are delightful!" Diantha exclaimed, pointing at a flower. "What is that, a daisy?"

"A bird-of-paradise," Mariel said.

"And this." She leaned over the fire lily. "Did you set it on fire?"

"Sort of."

As Diantha cooed over the flowers, Alzapraz hobbled over to Ozroth. "Sorry," the warlock said. "In my defense, you were the only demon in town that I was aware of." He held out a hand. "Truce?"

Ozroth shook gently, not wanting to break any fragile bones. "You should always defend the people you love." He tipped his head towards Mariel. "I'd do the same for her."

"So you do love her." Alzapraz studied Ozroth with dark, ancient eyes. "A demon and a human in love. Rare, but not impossible." He shook his head, making the golden tassel on his hat wiggle. "Weird though."

The word *Sunday* caught Ozroth's attention, and he focused on what Diantha was telling Mariel.

"—maybe we can have dinner like old times—"

"No," Mariel said gently but firmly. "I'm not comfortable going back to family dinner yet. And when or if I am comfortable again, I don't want it to be like old times."

Diantha started to argue, but a gentle nudge from Roland's elbow—and a less subtle poke from Alzapraz—made her snap her mouth shut. She pressed her lips together, then nodded.

"Boundaries," Alzapraz said approvingly. "Haven't seen many of those in this family."

After a few more awkward exchanges, the Sparks moved on to look at other flowers. Mariel puffed out her cheeks and exhaled. "That went easier than expected."

Ozroth wrapped his arms around her. "I'm proud of you."

Mariel smiled. "I'm proud of me, too. And I want what my mom says to be true . . . but I'll be careful. And even if it isn't true, I feel powerful on my own." She leaned her head against his shoulder. "Thank you. For supporting me, and for helping me see my own worth."

"I could say the same thing," he said. "You're a miracle, Mariel. My miracle."

"Do they have miracles in Hell?" she mused. When he swatted her ass lightly, she laughed.

A trumpet blast halted conversation. The judges had congregated at the center of the park, where a trumpet-wielding faun presided over a table full of ribbons and trophies.

"We have our winners!" the werewolf announced.

Mariel squealed and grabbed Ozroth's hand, tugging him over to join the growing crowd.

"We'll start with Best in Show, then move on to category awards. In third place of the Pacific Northwest Floral Championships—Supernatural Division: Miras Muratov!"

As a middle-aged warlock wearing bright red sneakers danced up to the podium, Mariel leaned into Ozroth's side, nibbling her nails. "He had really good dahlias. And did you see his moon-flowers?"

"Still not as good as your display," he reassured her.

"In second place: Rani Bhaduri!"

Mariel squealed and clapped as her coworker—the unfortunate nude bather—collected her trophy. "I know everyone will accuse Ben of being biased, but honestly, she's an incredible gardener."

When the clapping died away, Ben cleared his throat. "And now, for Best in Show—Supernatural Division, the trophy goes to . . . Mariel Spark!"

Mariel shrieked and jumped up and down, while Ozroth

clapped and cheered as loudly as he could. He beamed as Mariel headed up to accept her award, a glass trophy shaped like a lotus blossom.

When she returned to Ozroth's side, he couldn't help himself. He picked her up and spun her around, then dipped her into another kiss. When he was done, there wasn't a scrap of lipstick left on her face.

"What should we do after the ceremony?" Mariel asked.

"I have a few ideas," he growled in her ear. "They involve my tongue and—"

"Celebratory milkshakes!" The exclamation broke them apart, and Ozroth turned to see Themmie and Calladia grinning at Mariel. "*Obviously* milkshakes," Themmie said.

Mariel looked at Ozroth's put-out expression, then giggled. "Milkshakes first," she said. "Tongue later."

◆ ◆ ◆

AN HOUR LATER, THE FOUR OF THEM SAT CRAMMED INTO A booth at the Centaur Cafe. Ozroth sipped his chocolate milkshake— which was indecently good—and listened to the women gossip about the festival. An array of trophies sat in front of Mariel: Best in Show, of course, but also Best in Class: Exotic Bloom for the fire lily, Best in Class: Dianthus, Best in Class: Bird-of-Paradise, and the confusingly named category Best in Class: Looks Tasty.

"The centaurs vote on that one," Mariel had told him. "I gave them a few pansies to graze on afterward."

"What a day," Calladia said, leaning back in the booth and cradling a vanilla milkshake. "Oz did magic, Mariel gave up her soul, and I punched a demon."

"Don't forget the important role of transportation," Themmie said. She was on her third strawberry milkshake and seemed to be vibrating.

"We need to talk about your method of dropping people off."

Themmie snorted. "Look, if I have to suffer the indignity of flying your ass all over town, you can suffer the indignity of being carried in a bag."

"It's less the carrying that's the issue," Ozroth chimed in. "More the dropping."

Themmie pointed a highlighter-yellow nail at him. "Not a peep out of you. Who do you think convinced Calladia not to sauté your balls?"

He winced. "Point taken."

"I wasn't going to sauté them," Calladia said, stealing one of Mariel's fries. "I was going to liquefy them."

"Not better," Ozroth wheezed, cupping himself reflexively. As he did, his finger brushed the button of his jeans, and a small spike of pain went through him. He studied his finger, which still held a small red pinprick from feeding the fire lily. "Huh," he said.

"Are you okay?" Mariel asked.

"It still hurts," he said, staring at the red spot. His face still hurt, too.

Mariel grabbed his wrist, then kissed his fingertip. "All better."

"No, but really. This is weird."

"What's weird?" Calladia asked.

He turned his hand to show the women the small injury. "I pricked my finger earlier. Normally an injury like that would heal in a few minutes."

"Ooh." Themmie whipped out her phone to take a photo. "The mystery of the demonic finger," she said in a sepulchral voice.

"Don't put that on social media," he warned her.

She rolled her eyes. "Fine. But you owe me a selfie."

"We already took a million selfies," Mariel pointed out.

"There's always time for one more! But really, why is your finger still jacked up?" Themmie asked Ozroth.

"I have no idea." He gently prodded the skin around his eye. "Does the black eye look any better?"

Calladia winced. "Worse, actually."

Many things had changed in his life recently, but this was new. "Could it be the soul? It's caused all sorts of other symptoms."

Mariel's eyes widened, and she gasped. "Oz, wait." She licked her lips, looking nervous. "Remember what Astaroth said? That demons can only make deals with mortals?"

"Astaroth had no idea what he was talking about," Ozroth said. "Since no demon had done it before, he assumed it couldn't be done."

"Oh, shit," Calladia said, apparently catching on to whatever Mariel's train of thought was. "You think . . ."

Mariel started combing through Ozroth's hair like a monkey looking for lice.

"What are you doing?" he asked, baffled.

She gasped again when she reached his temple. "Look," she told the women, tugging on a hair.

Ozroth sat still while Calladia and Themmie leaned over to look at whatever Mariel was showing them. "Do I have something in my hair?"

Themmie snapped a picture. "Not in your hair. Actually your hair."

"That makes no sense . . ." He trailed off when she turned her phone to face him, showing the image she'd captured. Mariel's fingers were pale against his jet-black hair, and she was pinching . . .

"No," he said disbelievingly. But there it was, plain as day: a white hair.

"Was that there before?" Mariel asked.

Ozroth shook his head. His hair had always been stark black.

"I have a theory," Mariel said, letting go of his hair and shifting on the bench to face him, "and I can't tell if you'll like it or not."

"What is it?" he asked, though he had a suspicion himself.

"I think gaining a mortal soul . . . made you mortal."

His heart was racing too fast. Mortal? He'd always known he was going to live forever, or at least until he got tired of existing and had someone chop his head off. But if he was mortal . . .

"Think about it," Mariel said. "You got a soul and human magic. Didn't you also start eating and sleeping more frequently, like a human would? And if your wounds are healing slowly and your hair is going gray . . ."

"I'm aging," he said, hardly able to believe it. The prospect was terrifying, but as it unfolded in his mind's eye, it opened up a new world of possibilities. "I can age with you," he said, heart in his throat as he looked at Mariel.

She looked close to tears. "Do you want that? Growing old is scary, and no one wants to die."

He imagined a human life for them: traveling the world, getting married, maybe having children one day. Her hair would gray along with his, their bodies growing frail. And yes, they would both die.

But Mariel was always going to die, and Ozroth wasn't sure he'd want to continue on without her anyway. Now, instead of watching her age while he stayed healthy and strong, he would get to go on the journey of life with her.

He tipped his head back and laughed, giddy at the prospect.

"Is that a good response?" Calladia asked.

"I can't tell," Themmie said.

Mariel still looked anxious, so Ozroth leaned in and kissed her. "I can't wait to grow old with you," he said against her lips.

At that, Mariel did start crying, but he knew they were happy tears, so he just held her, feeling like his heart would burst from joy. No more bargaining; no more cold, unfeeling, unending existence. Instead, a messy human life, lived fully from top to bottom. Lived alongside the person who meant the most to him.

"We'll get matching canes when it's hard to walk," he told her.

"No swords in them." Mariel's lips curved against his shirt. "Or wait, maybe I do want a sword."

"Definitely a sword." Themmie nodded. "Terrorize the old folks' home."

Mariel wiped her eyes and sat up straight. "It'll be an adventure," she said. "And I can't wait."

"Me neither." He raised his milkshake in a toast. "To us."

Mariel smiled and clinked her own chocolate milkshake against his. "To us . . . and to whatever life brings."

ACKNOWLEDGMENTS

I can't believe the day of publication is finally here! This book wouldn't be possible without the help of a lot of very lovely people, whom I will attempt to thank in their entirety below (this is way harder than writing the book, FYI).

First off, thank you so much to Jessica Watterson for being the best agent an author could wish for. Thank you times infinity to my incredible editor, Cindy Hwang, for reaching out and taking a chance on this whimsical and literally very horny (DAD JOKE ALERT) romance—you truly changed my life. Thank you to the whole Berkley team, including Kristin Cipolla and Stephanie Felty in publicity, Catherine Barra and Jessica Mangicaro in marketing, Angela Kim in general supreme helpfulness, Stacy Edwards in production editorial, Shana Jones for copyedits (thanks to you, Oz is now wearing/removing an appropriate number of shirts), Katie Anderson for art direction, and Jess Miller for the phenomenal cover. For the UK edition, endless gratitude to Rachel Winterbottom, Áine Feeney, and the entire Gollancz team for championing the book, as well as Jessica Hart for designing the UK cover and Dawn Cooper for the fabulous illustration.

This book wouldn't be where it is now without the generous efforts of beta readers: Celia Rostow (who also designed my website and various graphics, you ANGEL), Blake Vulpe, Kate Goldbeck, Sarah Tarkoff, and Angela Serranzana. Thanks as well to early enthusiasts Vivien Jackson, Jessica Clare, and Jacqueline Sewell, who helped me believe in the book when I was a nervous newbie to publishing (I am still a nervous newbie, but one with external validation now, which helps a lot).

No author is an island, and I've had the great fortune to be part of many supportive writer/reader/fanfic groups: the Wicked Wallflowers Coven and the larger community of incredible podcast listeners, the Berkletes, the Words Are Hard crew (Ali, Rebecca, Julie, Victoria, Celia, Jenna, Claire, and Kate), the PL (who pitched in to help me buy a new laptop when I was in desperate need, the same laptop I used to write this book—THANK YOU), the Fancy Drunk Lady Book Club (Julie, Meredith, Angela, and Rachel), and the SDLA Sisters who may or may not be being digested by a Sarlacc at this very moment (Ali, Thea, Kirsten, and Katie, and may more join our ranks in the future).

Thank you to my family, who lift me up and cheer me on, even when I'm writing some truly alarming stuff (especially my amazing parents, who in no way resemble Diantha Spark or Cynthia Cunnington), and to the friends who do the same, with a special shout-out to Sarah Tarkoff for being the absolute greatest, Amy Prindle for being my forever friend, Jenny Nordbak for introducing me to romance in the first place, Gabriel F. Salmerón for being my fish father, and Brittany Hoirup for the flowers and cheerleading.

Fan fiction gave me a creative outlet and a community when I was struggling to break into this career, and I'll forever be grateful to the people I met in the Star Wars and other fandoms. The Reylos introduced me to everything from knotting (!) to how to do my makeup, and I'm delighted to see other fic authors pursuing this career as well (special shout-out to Kirsten Bohling for being my fic sister since our first day in Flydam, Ali Humphrey for the heartfelt chats, MrsMancuspia for the amazing art, Jenna Levine and Katie Shepard for all the support and publishing panic DMs, and Ali Hazelwood for being the rising tide lifting all boats and the funniest, kindest person you can imagine).

If I've missed anyone in this list, please forgive me!

Lastly, thank YOU, dear reader, for picking up this book in the first place. I hope it brought you joy.

Keep reading for an excerpt from
Sarah Hawley's next novel . . .

A DEMON'S GUIDE TO WOOING A WITCH

ONE

CALLADIA CUNNINGTON WAS GOING TO WRECK THIS DE-mon's shit.

Astaroth of the Nine, immortal soul bargainer and agent of evil, flailed and cursed from a pile of leaves. All Calladia caught was a flash of white fabric and pale blond hair, but she didn't need to see the details to know she hated him.

They were at the edge of a clearing in the forest outside the small town of Glimmer Falls, where Astaroth had just tried—and thankfully failed—to steal Calladia's best friend's soul.

Mariel Spark, said best friend, grinned as the demon thrashed. The witch's freckled cheeks were rosy, and her curly brown hair was dotted with leaves and flowers, as it often was when she'd been doing magic—which she obviously had, since the clearing was covered in a wild tangle of vines. Mariel's nature magic abilities were unparalleled, even if the rest of her spellwork was unpredictable.

"Meet Astaroth of the Nine," Mariel announced, gesturing at the demon, "who just lost a bet with the demonic high council."

Her bright smile was a relief to see after weeks of stress. It had all started when Mariel accidentally summoned a demon named Ozroth the Ruthless for an unbreakable bargain: her soul (aka magic and emotion) in exchange for any boon he could offer. Being attached to her soul, Mariel had refused to complete the bargain and, in true chaotic good fashion, had promptly fallen in love with Oz.

This had obviously complicated matters. Nevertheless, Oz had shown every sign of returning Mariel's feelings, and Mariel had hoped there might be a way to break the soul bargain.

Calladia hadn't trusted Oz, though. What witch would, when her best friend was in danger? When the plants around Glimmer Falls had begun dying of a magical plague, she'd suspected Oz was poisoning the woods to gain leverage to force the nature-loving Mariel to make a bargain to save the ecosystem. When Mariel's beloved greenhouse had burned to the ground, Calladia had been convinced Oz was the culprit, so much so that she'd punched him in the face and cast a spell to launch him into the next county.

Then the third member of their friendship trio, a pixie named Themmaline—Themmie—Tibayan, had gotten word that Oz wasn't the demon sabotaging the woods at all. It was actually the work of his mentor, a demon named Astaroth of the Nine, who had placed some kind of bet with his fellow demonic high council members around Oz's success. Astaroth had then done everything possible to terrorize and manipulate Oz and Mariel into making a bargain.

So yeah. It had been a weird month.

Here they all were though, with the true villain identified and the gang back together. Themmie stood next to Calladia, shaking out her rainbow-hued wings and looking bright as a spring flower with her green-and-pink hair. The pixie had air-dropped Calladia into this clearing for the final showdown, but apparently they'd missed it, because Oz and Mariel stood hand in hand, looking healthy and happy, while Astaroth was currently cursing from a pile of dead leaves.

Calladia would get the details of what had happened later. Just because she'd missed the showdown didn't mean she couldn't write the epilogue, and right now, there was some major punching to do.

Astaroth staggered to his feet, and Calladia was momentarily taken aback. The black horns pointing back from the sides of his head matched Oz's, but any resemblance ended there. While Oz was burly and rough featured, with dark hair, gold-tinged skin, and a fondness for wearing basic black, Astaroth was lean, pale, and cultured looking. If his jawline was sharp, his cheekbones could slit throats. His white suit was streaked with dirt but looked expensive.

Astaroth grabbed a black fedora off the ground and jammed it onto his head, breaking the illusion of extreme hotness. It might not be as bad as Oz's battered cowboy hat, but demons clearly needed to up their hat game. And wait, had he just picked up a cane with a *crystal skull* on it?

"There's still time to make a better deal," Astaroth told Mariel, pointing the skull at her. "Do you want a mansion? A billion dollars? Your own private island?"

His accent was British, which was weird. Oz had what was apparently a normal accent for people who lived on the demon plane, which was sort of Australian but with something archaic-sounding mixed in.

Mariel smiled up at Oz. "There's nothing you can give me that I want more than what I have," she told Astaroth. Oz returned her smile, his craggy features softening into a besotted expression.

That was disgustingly cute, but there was still an evil demon issue to take care of, and if Calladia excelled at anything, it was finding violent solutions to everyday problems. Not that a demon manipulating your friend into giving up her magic and emotions was an everyday problem, but that just meant the violence would be even more justified.

She advanced on the demon. "This motherfucker is Astaroth of the Nine?" she called out. "Where'd you get the fedora—a pickup artist convention?"

Astaroth's eyes snapped to hers, and a chill went down her spine. They were the lightest blue, and combined with his white-blond hair and pale skin, he looked like he'd been carved from ice. His lip curled in disdain. "I don't take sartorial critiques from people wearing spandex."

Wow. Jerk. Calladia's workout top and leggings were practical and comfortable, which was more than she could say for his ridiculous getup. She looked him up and down, debating which part she wanted to smack first. Should she shatter his kneecaps? Punch him in the throat? Turn his nuts into pulp?

She cracked her knuckles and walked closer. "So you're the demon who's been destroying the forest?" she asked as she tied her blond hair up in a ponytail. "The demon who destroyed my best friend's greenhouse. The one trying to force Oz and Mariel to make a bargain."

Astaroth didn't retreat. "What a nice, bright soul," he said. "Do you want to become a princess? Own a diamond mine? Say it, and it's yours."

The demon had the kind of wicked smile some might call mind scrambling, but Calladia's mind remained definitively un-scrambled. Revulsion washed over her. Pretty men were always trouble, and this one was more trouble than most.

She stopped within hand-to-hand combat range. More fool

him for letting her get that close. They were the same height—five foot ten—which surprised her. After all the hype about what a big, bad, horrible demon Astaroth was, she'd expected him to be enormous.

"I do want something," Calladia said, "but I can't get it through a deal."

His eyes lit up; no doubt the wheels were turning in that diabolical mind as he tried to turn the situation to his advantage. Fail to get Mariel's soul? He'd apparently settle for Calladia's and call it good enough. "Nonsense," Astaroth said smugly. "I can give you anything."

"Mmm, no thanks. I take what I want." She gave him her sweetest smile, then punched him in the throat.

Astaroth wheezed. "Bloody hell," he choked out.

Calladia settled into a fight stance, then pivoted her hips and planted a roundhouse kick to his side. He staggered, and she followed up by grabbing his shoulders and kneeing him in the groin. Contact.

Astaroth made a gratifying bleating sound and bent over. "Who the fuck are you?" he demanded in a much-higher-pitched voice.

Was there anything more satisfying than victory, especially at the expense of someone who had underestimated her? Calladia grinned and got ready for the coup de grâce, one of her favorite spells for taking an enemy out. "The witch kicking your ass. Did you know I launched Oz into the next county when I thought he was behind everything? That should have been you."

Magic needed to be grounded in words and action. While some witches preferred chalking runes or performing elaborate ritual dances, Calladia liked the intricacy and portability of thread for casting. She pulled a coil of string out of a pocket in the waistband of her leggings and started tying knots. One to amplify force, one to provide propulsion, more to link her fist with the action of her spell.

"Wait," Astaroth said, looking alarmed.

Power swelled, a sizzling, sparking wash of heat that raced from her chest to her fingertips as she murmured the spell. She made a fist and punched Astaroth in the nose.

The spell added explosive force to her hit, and Astaroth was launched off the ground and sent hurtling over the treetops. Calladia shaded her eyes and watched as he dwindled to a speck over the nearest mountaintop, his scream fading to nothing.

"That was satisfying," she said, brushing her hands off and turning to her friends. Mariel was hopping up and down with glee, and even Oz, whose normal range of expressions fell firmly on the "grumpy" spectrum, looked impressed. Of course, he'd experienced that exact same spell earlier, so he ought to know. And shoot, Calladia should probably apologize for beating him up, but in her defense, she hadn't known Astaroth was manipulating events from the shadows.

Oz shoved a hand into his shaggy black hair, then shook his head. "I can't believe you did that. Do you know how many enemies Astaroth has vanquished over the centuries?"

Calladia mimed dusting off her shoulders. "Never underestimate a witch with a mean right hook and anger-management issues."

Themmie went up on her toes and gave Calladia a high five. "Nice work," the short pixie said. "He won't forget that anytime soon."

Calladia looked towards the distant mountains, a smile on her lips. "He sure won't."

TWO

ASTAROTH OF THE NINE—DEMONIC HIGH COUNCIL MEMBER, legendary soul bargainer, and renowned liar—was having a very bad day.

He limped down a firelit stone corridor within the high council's temple on the demon plane, leaning heavily on his cane sword—the crystal skull top now blackened and splintered from a spell—and cursing witches and traitor demons under his breath. His former protégé, Ozroth the Ruthless, had just handed him a neat and complete defeat, turning a soul bargain that ought to have been a coup for Astaroth into an embarrassment. And for what?

Love.

Astaroth scoffed at the absurdity. A demon soul bargainer falling in love with the witch whose soul he was supposed to take? Human-demon pairings were rare, but they did happen—Astaroth knew that all too well—but this was unprecedented.

It should have been a simple bargain. After Ozroth had shown signs of decreased performance as a soul bargainer, thanks to accidentally gaining a human soul during a bargain gone awry, Astaroth had been determined to help his protégé recover his edge. When Mariel Spark, a powerhouse of a witch, had accidentally summoned Ozroth for a bargain, it had seemed the perfect opportunity to resurrect Ozroth's ruthlessness and gain a beautiful, bright human soul for the demon plane.

Ozroth hadn't claimed the witch's soul though. No, he'd dawdled and brooded and pined for the witch like bloody Lord Byron himself (and Astaroth ought to know, since he'd shagged that dramatic bastard for a few months in the early nineteenth century). Unlike old Georgie though, Ozroth lacked the charisma and sartorial panache to pull off romantic brooding, so Astaroth had quickly stepped in to make the deal himself and save both of them embarrassment.

Then it had all gone wrong.

A few impossible spells later, Ozroth and Mariel remained in a disgustingly happy relationship, with both partners still in possession of their souls. And Astaroth had bargained away any leverage he might use to punish them.

He scowled at a torch sconce shaped like a hellhound's three gaping maws. The other members of the demonic high council would rip into him as viciously as a pack of hounds if they sensed an opportunity to reduce his influence and promote their allies. The scent of his blood was in the air, and there were no shortage of aspirants in the hunt for power.

The huge black doors leading to council chambers loomed ahead. Each was banded in silver and held half of the crest of the high council: a nonagon with nine spokes arrowing towards a stylized flame in the center.

Dread squeezed his insides with an iron fist. Astaroth rested with his back against the wall for a moment, closing his eyes and breathing through the surge of undemonlike fear. After six centuries, he knew how to force his secret weaknesses under control.

His aching leg welcomed the respite. It had been broken during his defeat, thanks to one of Mariel's allies, a violent blond witch wearing *spandex*, of all things. Humiliating enough to be punched in the throat, kneed in the groin, and nearly launched into the stratosphere by the witch; her naff attire had added insult to injury. The same accelerated healing that kept demons immortal meant he could walk on the damaged leg, but he hadn't had time to change out of his dirt-and-blood-stained white suit before being summoned to council quarters.

It's fine, he told himself, tapping his cane sword against one white, stack-heeled dress shoe as if that could knock off the grime ground into the leather. *So you lost this bet. Make another one, then win that.*

The high council was fond of bets and wagers, which were an excellent way to test rivals, since it was dishonorable to refuse a bet. Frustrated after centuries of deadlock with his main rival on the council, an aggressive demon fundamentalist named Moloch, and with the council muttering about Ozroth's fitness to continue as a soul bargainer, Astaroth had rolled the dice. If Ozroth succeeded in his next bargain within the allotted time, Astaroth would win whatever prize or punishment he wanted from Moloch. If Ozroth failed, Moloch could decide the prize or punishment.

A wager with open-ended terms was a risky move, but Ozroth had never failed to complete a bargain, even if he had felt some guilt about it recently. Astaroth had been sure Ozroth would seize the witch's soul promptly and win the bet.

Ah, to return to such an innocent time.

The door's silver sigil gleamed in the wavering glow of torchlight like a flame-pupiled eye, judging Astaroth with its stare.

Bets had been lost in the high council before. The results were never pretty.

But Astaroth had centuries of cunning and experience on his side, and he was determined not to go down without a fight. Besides, any legendary schemer had a backup plan. He'd been investigating Moloch for years, looking for a weak spot to target, and he'd finally discovered the evidence he needed to take out his greatest enemy on the council. Moloch might win this bet, but he would soon lose everything else.

Astaroth straightened, cracking his neck before shifting his weight onto both legs. Sharp pain shot through the injured leg, but he gritted his teeth and started walking without a limp.

The scent of his blood might be in the air, but Astaroth had fangs as sharp as any hellhound's.

Time to show them.

◆　◆　◆

THE EIGHT OTHER DEMONS OF THE HIGH COUNCIL SAT AROUND a table shaped like the council crest. The slab of basalt was carved with the sigil's design, and molten silver circulated through the grooves. Thanks to a spell commissioned from some long-ago warlock, the silver never cooled, nor did it damage the stone. It flowed endlessly, making the flame shape at the center seem to dance. Torches burned in sconces around the room, highlighting rich tapestries depicting famous demon victories, but the high ceiling was shrouded in shadow. Living stone gargoyles perched in the rafters, barely visible in the darkness.

Astaroth had always appreciated a bold aesthetic, and the council chambers delivered. Gothic drama practically dripped down the walls, and although most of the demons in this room, Astaroth included, had smartphones in their pockets, for the next hour, they would all pretend they were suspended out of time.

The council members stared as Astaroth strolled towards his chair with an air of lazy arrogance. He lowered himself onto the emerald-green velvet seat, biting back a sigh of relief. Appearances mattered more than substance in his world. Reality was crafted from lies on top of lies, and Astaroth had long been the best liar of all.

Baphomet, the eldest demon on the high council, raised one disdainful eyebrow. "About time you joined us."

The demon was massive, with a braided red beard and thick ivory horns that curved along the sides of his head before ending in wicked points. Astaroth was fairly sure Baphomet filed his horns to make the tips that sharp, and he shuddered at the thought of doing the same to his own sleek black horns. Baphomet dressed like he was straight out of the Viking era—which he was— in furs, metal, and leather. The attire smelled unpleasantly musty, but Astaroth couldn't deny the demon had cultivated a distinct brand.

Baphomet was the most important person in the room. He was the council's nominal head, having committed to a centrist position, and he served as tiebreaker whenever the four conservative and four liberal demons failed to come to an agreement. He also played dictator as needed.

It was his position both Moloch and Astaroth had their eyes on.

"I was held up," Astaroth said. Unlike the other demons, his accent was crisply British, thanks to centuries spent living mostly in London on the mortal plane, rather than here on the demon plane. *To better understand and manipulate mortals*, he'd told the council.

They didn't need to know that his reason for spending time with humans was more complicated than that.

"You look wretched," Sandranella, the demoness to Baphomet's right, said. Her dark skin and black horns contrasted sharply with her cloud of white hair, and she was dressed in her typical 'elegant but don't fuck with me' attire: a sapphire brocade gown with a metal breastplate. She was as close to a friend as Astaroth would allow himself to claim.

"I'm trying out a new aesthetic," Astaroth said, examining his nails.

"What, looking like you got your ass kicked and then rolled around in mud?"

That was exactly what had happened, but Astaroth wasn't about to admit it. An image of his assailant flashed through his mind: brown eyes, blond ponytail, an oval face with a determined chin. The woman had been tall and leanly muscled, but she was merely human, and nothing about her had screamed, *Your balls are in danger!* "It's called deliberately distressed clothing," he said, shoving thoughts of the witch away.

"It's certainly distressing me," Sandranella said, looking him up and down disapprovingly.

"Enough chatter," Baphomet boomed. Astaroth wondered if the demon practiced that voice alone in his den, calculating which volume level best qualified as "booming." "We are here to resolve the wager proposed by Moloch."

Astaroth maintained a laconic smile, despite the urge to grind his teeth and spit at Moloch. His longtime nemesis sat across from Astaroth, an oily smirk on his face. Moloch might look cherubic, with rosy cheeks, blue eyes, and curly brown hair, but he was the cruelest snake Astaroth had ever met. Admirable—except that his treachery was often aimed at Astaroth. They'd been born around the same time, and their fierce rivalry had intensified over the centuries as Moloch had become the preeminent demon warrior and Astaroth the preeminent soul bargainer.

When Astaroth had been named to the high council, he'd thought he'd finally surpassed Moloch in status . . . until Moloch had been raised to the council that same day. Now there was only one position left to fight over: Baphomet's.

Astaroth had been searching for dirt on Moloch for a long time. He would need to be careful in how he revealed his recent discoveries, considering the situation.

Moloch stood, smoothing a curl over one dun-colored horn. He wore a gray tunic over a blue shirt—an echo of his origin in the late 1300s, though his gray trousers were more modern. "Before we learn how Astaroth has fared, let us recap the terms of the bet," he said. His eyes glittered in the torchlight, and the satisfaction in them said he knew exactly how Astaroth had fared. "One month ago, we discussed Ozroth the Ruthless during a high council meeting. His failure to deliver a warlock's soul to the human realm, and the subsequent discovery that he accidentally absorbed that human soul, caused grave concern among the council. When it was recommended he be put down to avoid future failures, Astaroth interceded, promising that Ozroth would deliver a new soul within a month."

Astaroth's expression didn't change, though he was entertaining a fantasy of garroting Moloch. "Don't use such passive language, Moloch," he said lightly. "You were the sole member of the council to recommend my protégé be killed, rather than given a chance to prove himself."

Moloch shrugged. "A faulty weapon is more likely to harm the wielder. With the demon plane dependent on souls, it made sense to eliminate the problem as quickly as possible."

Without the human souls that drifted like enormous fireflies in the perpetual twilight of the demon plane, all life within the plane would gradually die. It was why demons and witches had formed a symbiotic relationship. The witch or warlock provided a soul—their magic—to keep the demon plane alive, and in exchange, a soul bargainer granted them a wish.

Moloch didn't care about the demon plane so much as he cared about spiting Astaroth though. "One would think after all these years you'd have learned patience," Astaroth said, "but you've never seemed to enjoy the long game."

A dimple appeared on Moloch's cheek. "I'm enjoying it right now."

Not as much as I'll enjoy spilling your dirty laundry at this table in a few minutes, Astaroth thought. Moloch had won the battle, but Astaroth would win the war.

"Enough posturing," Sandranella said. "Or at least whip your dicks out and measure them so we can get this over with. I have a happy hour on the elven plane to get to."

"No need," Astaroth said. "My dick is definitely bigger."

Moloch cleared his throat and puffed up his chest. "That's patently false, but let's move on. The wager dictated that if Ozroth succeeded in his next soul bargain before the end of the mortal month of October, Astaroth could decide the consequences dealt to me. If Ozroth failed, I would decide the consequences dealt to him."

Sandranella met Astaroth's eyes and shook her head. *Bad choice,* she mouthed.

Yes, he was well aware.

Moloch's grin was sharp. "So, Astaroth, did Ozroth succeed in claiming a soul within the allotted time frame?"

A muscle under Astaroth's eye started twitching. "No."

A murmur went around the high table. The conservative demons looked chuffed—they were undoubtedly hoping for Astaroth's removal from the high council so one of their allies could take his place.

"Would you care to tell us what went wrong?" Moloch asked, clearly hoping for an opportunity to humiliate Astaroth further.

"No," Astaroth said.

"Will Ozroth be returning to his duties as a soul bargainer?" Moloch pressed.

"Also no. Are you done with the pointless questions?" Because as soon as Astaroth claimed the floor, he would let the rest of the council know what kind of snake they held to their bosom.

"Not quite." Moloch sauntered around the table, looking like the cat that got the canary. "You've always been overly fascinated with humans, haven't you?"

Foreboding prickled down Astaroth's spine. "I would hardly call it a fascination," he said, striving for a bored tone. "I spend time among them to better learn how to manipulate them into bargains."

"So you've always said. The flat in London, the many, many mortals you've had carnal relations with—yes, I know all about that—the ridiculous fashion shows you attend . . . all of it is to better manipulate humans, hmm?"

Moloch knowing that Astaroth had shagged mortals was not good. While many demons appreciated humans, seeing them as symbiotic counterparts, the conservative members of the high council disdained them as lesser beings, and Astaroth had always been careful to keep the, ah, *extent* of his interactions with humans a secret. "What's your point?" he asked.

"I've wondered about you for centuries." Moloch stopped just out of range of the sword hidden in Astaroth's cane. Pity. "Something's always seemed . . . different about you."

The smile vanished as cold sweat beaded on Astaroth's forehead. Moloch couldn't know . . . could he? "It's probably the long track record of success," Astaroth said. "You haven't had a decent war to fight in decades."

"I did some research," Moloch said, ignoring the barb. "The records around your birth are surprisingly sparse. With a mother like Lilith, one would think she'd trumpet the immediate arrival of an heir, rather than waiting forty years to claim you as her son."

"Who can say why Lilith does anything?" Astaroth asked. "She's mad." Fear festered in his gut though, and his throat felt tight. There was a reason his wonderful, exasperating mother hadn't publicly claimed him right away, and if it was revealed, the high council would never see Astaroth the same way again. Which meant a death sentence for his ambitions.

Ambition—power—was everything. It was the *only* thing.

"I do agree she's insane," Moloch said. He reached into his pocket and pulled out a leather-bound book with gilt edges. "But Lilith's diary contains some very interesting information."

Bloody fucking fuck. Did his cursed mother have to document her entire life? She had a whole bookshelf of similar-looking diaries in her den, filled out over the centuries, but Astaroth had never dreamed she'd write down the secret the two of them alone shared.

"What part of 'Lilith is insane' are you missing?" Astaroth snapped to cover up his unseemly fear. "Just because she wrote something down doesn't mean it's true. She writes explicit War of the Roses tentacle fan fiction, too." Way, way too much War of the Roses tentacle fan fiction, which she posted to AO3 like a horny human teenager, rather than the millennias-old demoness she was.

"Wow," Sandranella drawled. "Are the tentacles aligned with Lancaster or York?"

"I wouldn't say 'aligned with' so much as 'inside of,'" Astaroth said, "but that's not the point. If she can confidently write Henry VI taking it up the arse from a Yorkist squid, she very well might have invented all sorts of falsehoods about me."

Moloch bared his teeth. "You're very defensive for someone who doesn't even know what I'm accusing you of. Unless you do?"

Astaroth struggled to shove down his rising panic. Proper demons—powerful demons—didn't panic. Moloch was speaking in vagaries in hopes of prompting a confession. "Whatever it is, I know it's nonsense."

"Maybe," Moloch said with a shrug. "We'll find out soon enough."

Baphomet tapped on the table. "Enough of these cryptic clues," he said in that rumbling bass voice. "Let's move on with the session."

Right. Because after whatever devastating punishment Astaroth was about to receive, the council would carry on as always, discussing everything from community resources to the growing unrest among the hybrids who chose to live in the demon plane, rather than the plane of origin of their nondemon parent.

Astaroth's stomach churned again. He was one of the few voices on the high council in favor of protecting the rights of the hybrids and nondemons who lived on-plane. It was a tricky balancing act, and without his input, more conservative voices would prevail. If Baphomet didn't intervene—and he wouldn't if the majority were in favor of Moloch's plans—the council would swerve in a fundamentalist direction it would take centuries to course correct.

"Very well," Moloch said. "Let's discuss the terms of my victory. Obviously, Astaroth will be removed from the high council."

Astaroth's blood raged at the demotion, though he had planned to do the same to Moloch. Still, the punishment could have been worse, and there was always scheming to be done. Once Moloch was discredited, Astaroth would be back on top. "If you insist, I will gracefully resign for the moment," he said, preparing to stand. "But first, I have some information to share with the council—"

"I'm not finished," Moloch said sharply. He snapped his fingers, and a gargoyle leapt down from the rafters to open the council room doors. "The second part of your punishment will take place now."

Astaroth stared, confused and alarmed, as a woman with long black hair, pointed ears, and glitter-spangled velvet robes entered. When he opened his demon senses, he saw the golden glow of a soul emanating from her chest. A human witch, then, one with fae ancestry. "Who is this?"

Moloch smirked. "You'll find out."

Another snap, and more gargoyles jumped down. These ones gripped Astaroth's arms with granite fingers, keeping him in his chair.

"Get your hands off me," Astaroth said, struggling to break free. There was a reason the gargoyles were used as demonic security though, and their stony strength was more than enough to subdue him. "Everyone needs to know something about Moloch—"

Moloch talked over him again. "Astaroth, formerly of the Nine, I hereby banish you to Earth."

Astaroth's head spun. "What? No!" He liked Earth, but he couldn't shape demon politics if he was stuck there full-time.

Sandranella stood, looking alarmed. "Moloch, that's an excessive punishment."

Moloch shrugged. "He accepted the wager."

Sandranella turned to Baphomet. "You must put a stop to this. It sets a dangerous precedent."

"Moloch is right," Baphomet said. "Astaroth accepted the wager. He can take the punishment."

Astaroth's boot heels scraped over the flagstones as he tried to escape, but it was no use. The pain in his still-healing leg was nothing compared to the riot of agonized emotion in his chest. He'd always felt more than a demon ought to, and the surge of anger and fear threatened to drown him. "You can't do this," Astaroth said. His mask of control had disintegrated. "You can't!"

"Watch me." Moloch motioned to the witch, who raised her hands. She moved them in an intricate, roiling dance, inscribing symbols in the air.

"What is she doing?" Sandranella asked, looking between Astaroth and Moloch. "We don't need her to banish him."

"Oh, she's not here to banish him," Moloch said. "She's here to do something else . . . and once she does, I'll finally have proof that Astaroth has been lying to us for centuries."

Magic built in the air, prickling like electricity. The witch spoke a spell in the language of magic, and a concussive wave of power slammed into Astaroth's chest. He shouted as fire writhed through his veins, and his vision whited out. His mind seemed to split into kaleidoscopic fragments.

"What did she do?" Sandranella asked, the words garbled as if he were hearing them from underwater.

Moloch's voice echoed distantly. "Once the witch confirms it worked, I will reveal all."

Astaroth felt sick and sluggish. He couldn't let it end like this. He needed to let the council know about Moloch's crimes.

He forced his thick tongue into motion. "Once the others find out what you've been doing—" he slurred, "they'll—"

"What I'm doing is taking out the trash," Moloch interrupted.

"Baphomet," Astaroth said, turning blurred eyes in the direction of the council head. "You must listen to me."

"Enough," Baphomet said. "End this, Moloch."

Moloch snapped his sharp canines at Astaroth. "Ready to go?"

The haze cleared from Astaroth's vision in time for him to see Moloch open a portal. The fiery-edged oval hovered in midair;

through it, he saw a darkened suburban street on the mortal plane. Iron lamps cast pools of gold over the pavement, and trees rustled in the wind.

The gargoyles muscled Astaroth out of the chair and shoved him towards the portal.

"No, wait—" Astaroth's head was spinning, his normally ordered thoughts a chaotic jumble. Terror wrapped around him like clinging vines.

Moloch was grinning like a fiend. "See you soon," he whispered.

Then Moloch kicked Astaroth in the backside, and Astaroth stumbled through the portal into the mortal realm. The pavement rushed towards him, and the world went black.

Photo by Mahina Hawley Photography

SARAH HAWLEY is a cohost of the *Wicked Wallflowers Club* podcast and the author of *A Witch's Guide to Fake Dating a Demon*. She has an MA in archaeology and has excavated at an Inca site in Chile, a Bronze Age palace in Turkey, and a medieval abbey in England. When not dreaming up whimsical love stories, she can be found reading, dancing, or cuddling her two cats.

Ready to find
your next great read?

Let us help.

Visit prh.com/nextread

Penguin
Random
House